Church
Street
Under

Church Street Under

A Casey Cavendish Mystery

Katherine Fast

LEVEL
BEST BOOKS

Dedicated to Jeffrey Fast

Praise for Church Street Under

"The deepest play is in private homes, as Katherine Fast proves with a page-turning tale of deceit, betrayal, and murder in the wainscoted viper's nest of Boston's leafiest (fictional) suburb. Fans of Fast's indomitable Casey Cavendish may find themselves wishing our heroine had never left the relatively warm embrace of the Ohio penal system."—Robert Carlock, executive producer and screenwriter of Emmy Award-winning TV sitcoms.

"Kat Fast writes with deft agility and a refreshing narrative style. *Church Street Under* plumbs the murky depths of a wealthy New England family's dark past with a well-paced, focused directness that engages the reader from page one and never lets go."—Gerald Elias, author of the award-winning Daniel Jacobus mystery series

"In *Church Street Under*, Casey Cavendish searches for the father she's never known and finds herself in a deadly battle for an inheritance she never knew existed. I couldn't turn the pages fast enough, rooting for Casey, the wily underdog to survive and find her family at last."—Barbara Ross, author of the Maine Clambake Mysteries

"Fans of traditional mystery will love *Church Street Under*. A colorful cast of characters, a fearless heroine, and a superbly plotted story. Katherine Fast has done it again!"—Bruce Robert Coffin, award-winning author of the Detective Byron mysteries

Chapter One

September 9, 1975

C asey downshifted as the MGB roadster twisted up the hill toward the address where she hoped to meet the man she believed to be her father.

Her palms slid on the steering wheel. Might not be her brightest move, appearing on his doorstep without any warning. She could write a letter. After all, he hadn't made any attempt to make contact with her in thirty-three years.

To calm herself, she focused on the scenery. After flat northern Ohio, she welcomed the rolling hills and stone walls of the northeast. Although stretches of the road looked like countryside, telltale driveways and mailboxes suggested houses tucked out of sight. Warning signs for burglar alarm services alerted potential thieves of something worth stealing within.

Casey dodged landscaping rigs parked along the road. Small armies of workers manicured lawns with powerful mowers. As the road curled and ascended, Casey slowed to gawk at the houses, impressed and shocked at the affluent display. She was used to small-town living with simple clapboard houses where neighbors called out to each other from front porches.

She'd come east because she'd burned her bridges in Ohio, the place she'd known as home, and needed a fresh start, and the only friend she had after ten years in prison was her former Black cellmate LouAnne who offered her a room in Somerville, Massachusetts. But most important of all, the last known place her suspected father lived was in Welton, Massachusetts.

She started at the rude blast of a horn. Mesmerized by the houses, she hadn't noticed the Mercedes riding her bumper. As Casey flicked on her turn signal, the woman driver gave her a second, longer honk. Casey slowed to a crawl before pulling over. As the woman passed, Casey threw her a kiss. The Mercedes swerved. Casey smiled and read the family's educational pedigree on the rear window: prep schools and Ivies with one deviant UMASS sticker for the black sheep.

When she crested the hill, the woods abruptly yielded to a long, barren vista dominated by a monolithic stone structure on the scale of Grand Central Station. No shrubs, trees, flowers—nary a bramble nor a dandelion decorated the parched landscape. The sign in front said Jesuit Retreat, Retirement and Health Center.

Confused, Casey pulled into a visitors' lot across the road. She checked the address, but she knew that she was in the right place. But Jesuit? Jesuits were an order of Catholic priests. There were two buildings: a residence hall replete with a chapel bigger than most churches and an infirmary.

She didn't have to go in. No one expected her. No one knew where she was. Turn around and chalk it up to a ride in the New England countryside. She shifted into reverse.

Chicken. What do you have to lose? She jammed the car into Park and switched it off. She slammed the car door with enough force to propel herself toward the forbidding six-story residence. She felt like Dorothy approaching OZ. Maybe that was the point.

She mounted the stairs between enormous concrete columns and pushed open the oversized wood entrance door. Inside, it smelled dank and musty and was at least ten degrees cooler. Casey paused to let her eyes adjust to a long, dimly lit corridor. Her steps echoed as she passed a gauntlet of severe-looking men in forbidding portraits.

"May I help you?" a disembodied voice called.

Casey cast about for the source and located a middle-aged woman behind a desk at the far end of the corridor. As Casey drew closer, she made out graying hair drawn into a tight bun and sharp eyes behind bifocals perched on a large, wedge-shaped nose. Her smile welcomed, but her voice challenged, and her eyes registered Casey's every move.

"Hello. I hope I've come to the right place," Casey stammered. *Of course, she'd come to the right place.* Casey corrected her diffident stance and offered the gatekeeper a false smile of her own. "I'm here to visit Joseph Dempsey."

The woman's smile faltered and then regrouped. "And who might you be?" The woman's stare was as rude as her words.

She could use that nose as a weapon. "My name is Cassandra Cavendish. Mr. Dempsey was a friend of my mother's when he attended Oberlin College."

"That would be some time ago," the woman muttered. She raised her chin and peered down her nose to examine Casey through the bottom lenses.

"Yes." Casey let the silence hang. She hadn't expected to be interrogated by a receptionist.

"Have a seat." The woman pointed to a pair of straight wooden chairs lined up against the wall. She swiveled about and spoke in undertones on the telephone. When she hung up, she shuffled paperwork on her desk without a glance in Casey's direction.

The silence mushroomed as minutes passed. Casey felt like a schoolgirl in detention. Who did the receptionist call? Was Joseph Dempsey on his way? *Sit. Stay.* Never long on obedience, she rose and studied the portraits that lined the corridor. Each picture led a few steps closer to the door and freedom.

"Miss Cavendish?"

"Oh!" Casey whirled and crouched in a fighting stance. A tall man standing behind her jumped back and raised his arms.

"Sorry, I didn't hear you." She straightened, willing her heart to slow, her breathing to calm. "Sorry," she repeated.

Everything about the man was gray: his eyes, hair, and even his skin. But the picture of Joseph Dempsey in the Oberlin College yearbook had wavy chestnut hair, deep-set brown eyes, a straight nose, and a mouth that bowed up at the sides—a fair description of Casey. Even factoring in the toll of years, the man before her couldn't be her father.

"I'm Father Gannet. Come in."

3

Casey followed the priest into a small, dark room. Father Gannet took a seat at a table in the center of the room and gestured for Casey to sit opposite him. He placed a thick manila folder on the table. Casey leaned forward and cocked her head to read the tab, but Gannet drew it to him and covered it with his hands.

"Agnes tells me that you are here to visit Father Dempsey. Would you mind telling me your relationship to him?"

"Father? *Father* Dempsey?"

Gannet steepled his long fingers under his chin and gazed at her with tired eyes.

For a split second, a voice in Casey's overloaded mind chanted, *"Here's the church. Here's the steeple. Open ..."* She shook her head and forced her eyes from his fingers. Years ago, her mother told her that her father had left before she was born and wasn't coming back. Now Casey realized he'd joined the Jesuits.

As Casey explained her family's connection to Father Dempsey, Gannet leafed through papers in the folder. "Emma Cavendish was your mother?" he asked, refocusing on Casey.

I already told you. Casey nodded, wondering what kind of information was in the file and why he asked so many questions. "My mother and father are both dead. My great aunt, Mae Cavendish, suggested I contact Joseph Dempsey and a few other people when I got to the East Coast."

"You're new here?"

Casey pushed back in her chair. "Is there a problem? Is Father Dempsey sick?"

"I apologize for the interrogation." He extracted an envelope from the file and pushed it toward her. "I'm afraid I have sad news. Father Dempsey died last year." Casey stopped breathing and shook her head.

"We tried to notify your family, but, as you can see, the letter was returned. I'm sorry." He watched her face while he nudged the envelope closer. Casey shied away from it. Written and underlined across her mother's name, she read "Deceased—Return to Sender."

"No," was all she could say before the lump in her throat choked off her voice, and a wave of sadness engulfed her. She stared at the letter. Inside her, a fragile bubble of hope burst. Over the years, she'd harbored a desire, a need to find her birth father. Now she'd never meet him.

Growing up, she'd known that Bill Cavendish wasn't her father. Her mother had answered her honestly when she'd asked, "What's a bastard?"

"An illegitimate child, one born out of wedlock. Why? Is someone calling you names?"

"Am I a bastard?" Casey persevered.

"Well, a bastard is an illegitimate male child. I don't know the word for an illegitimate female. It's true that your father and I never married."

"So, why is my name Cavendish?"

"I had to call you something, honey. Because I didn't marry your father, I couldn't use his name."

"Why didn't you marry him?"

"I was already married. To Bill Cavendish. It's a long story, sweetheart. Don't let anyone upset you by calling you a bastard. Your father was a wonderful man." The sadness and finality in her mother's voice ended the conversation. Although Casey had asked questions over the ensuing years, her mother had refused to identify her father.

"I seem to have lost you." Father Gannet re-steepled his fingers and interrupted Casey's reverie. His expression changed from inquisitive to compassionate.

She couldn't say Joseph Dempsey was her father. "My mother thought the world of him. I wanted to meet him and find out more about him." Casey glanced longingly at the file, but Father Gannet reinserted the returned letter and placed the file out of reach.

"He was a devoted priest, one of our most gifted teachers, and the finest pianist we've ever had. I'm sorry I can't help you more." He rose in dismissal, shook her hand, and left her stunned at his abrupt departure.

Alone in the room, Casey ran her fingers across the inscription on the gold locket she wore around her neck and fought off tears of disappointment. During her mother's last sickness, she'd given Casey the locket with "IOOF" etched on the front in elaborate letters. "IOOF stands for the International

Order of Odd Fellows," she explained. "Your father bought the locket for me at an antique fair." She laughed and then coughed deep into her chest. When she could breathe normally again, she continued. "He said it was a lovely locket for a lovely lady—and that I was certainly odd enough to wear it."

After her mother died, Casey placed her mother's picture inside the locket on the left side and left the right side blank. Now it would remain empty.

Em had caused a scandal as a student by marrying Cavendish, her philosophy professor. A year later, after Casey's brother was born, Cavendish left Em and moved in with another student lover, this one male.

When Cavendish had a stroke, Em shocked the Oberlin community again by taking him back and nursing him until he died. Casey was born ten months later. No one in the town or college thought for a second that Cavendish was her father. Casey believed that Joseph Dempsey and her mother were lovers during the last year of Cavendish's illness.

Casey sat in stunned silence for five minutes before retracing her steps to the entrance hall. Why wouldn't Father Gannet share the information in the file? What was in it that she shouldn't know? She should have at least asked to see Father Dempsey's picture. "Damn," she muttered.

"Miss Cavendish?"

"Sorry." Now, Agnes, the receptionist, had caught her blaspheming in a holy place.

Agnes beckoned to her with the crook of a bony finger. Casey had to lean forward to hear her whispered words. "While you were speaking with Father Gannet, I called Mary Waddington, Father Dempsey's sister. She recognized your name and asked me to get your phone number."

Casey wrote her name and number on a slip of paper.

Agnes fixed Casey with a stern look. "She lives right here in Welton, just off Church Street." She handed Casey a paper with a name and address on it. "Best if she calls you. Her health is very delicate."

Casey muttered a weak "Thank you" and walked quickly through the brooding hallway to the exit.

Chapter Two

Casey pounded her fists on the steering wheel and howled. Damn her father for dying! And damn her for caring about something she'd never had. But that wasn't strictly true. Until now, she'd owned a child's dream. Unrealistic, impossible, and all hers. Her howls yielded to sobs and a flood of pent-up tears.

When she was all cried out, she wiped her eyes and blew her nose. No home, no job, no lover, no mother—not even a father she'd never met. But she had this little roadster, a gift from a lover who'd betrayed her. He'd tried to buy his way back into her affections by giving her the car. She'd accepted the car...and taken off. It had become a symbol of her new life.

Except she didn't have a new life. *Come on, Casey. Quit dragging your toenails.*

You're healthy. You're young. Well, thirty-three. You have a place to stay. And your freedom. In the glove compartment, she had an official letter of apology for wrongful incarceration from the state of Ohio. But her exoneration didn't make up for ten lost years, and the very fact that she'd been in prison—innocence be damned—made her untouchable.

So, what next? No idea. She'd had such high hopes. Jump in her little car, head east, make a new life for herself where no one knew her past. And here she was. Alone. Except for LouAnne, she didn't know a soul. Out of work with no prospects and, so far, not even any nibbles. There must be a gazillion liberal arts graduates pounding the pavement looking for work in the greater Boston area. People here talked funny, and they sure didn't know how to drive. She couldn't afford to rent an apartment of her own. She uncurled her fist and looked at the wadded and wrinkled note the receptionist had given her. The woman had drawn her a crude map showing how to reach Mary Waddington's house.

Nothing to do and nothing more to lose. She threw the car into first and spit gravel out of the visitors' lot. As she cruised down the road with her window open, she hummed to allay the growing tightness in her chest. She should be on top of the world instead of teetering on the edge. She took long, regular breaths. Everything was just ducky, as her mother would say. Casey talked to herself, trying to brazen it out. She was a survivor, a Phoenix rising from the ashes. Literally. Images of a blazing hayloft flashed before her. Three people had died in the fire, but she'd lived to tell the tale. Except she didn't want to talk about it, to anyone, not even a shrink.

She drove into the center of Welton and, after a few false starts, located Church Street. Lost in her thoughts, she almost missed the turnoff onto a smaller lane. She slowed and drove to an unmarked Y in the road. A sign on the right side read, "President's Lane, Private Road, No Trespassing. Police take notice." She stared at the sign in disbelief. Really? Who owned a road? She shrugged and followed the left arm that dipped down a steep hill toward the first human-sized house Casey had seen in the town.

Except it wasn't a house. It was a derelict old train station. Once, it might have been charming, but now gray paint peeled from the sides, a few windows were broken, and the pedestrian approach was overgrown with weeds. Beyond a platform behind the building, rails were barely visible, disappearing through tall arches under the Church Street bridge.

Clearly, this wasn't Mrs. Waddington's house. Her place must be on the lane that had angled off to the right. Casey wasn't supposed to visit without calling first, anyway. That was a good enough excuse to take advantage of a glorious fall day and explore the quaint little station. She reached under the passenger seat and withdrew a sketchbook and pencils she always carried with her. She'd discovered in prison that sketching and painting was the best therapy for quieting her mind.

Grass grew up in the broken and pitted drive where there had once been parking spaces. On each side of the arches, steep stone steps led up to

Church Street. Perfect. She sat on the bottom step by the arch closest to the station to catch the late afternoon sunlight on the gray clapboards of the abandoned building.

Past the station, a pathway led up the far side of the hill. Intervening trees partially blocked the view, but what she saw suggested an enormous white mansion. Mary Waddington must be loaded. Instantly Casey had second thoughts about contacting Joseph Dempsey's sister. What would she say? "I think your brother, Father Dempsey, is my father." Not welcome news for a good Catholic. Mrs. Waddington would think that ex-con Casey was trying to shake her down.

The station was just her size. She liked the dimensions of the building and the gingerbread trim. Soon she was lost in concentration, sketching in the contours of the building. She could imagine living in a little place like this.

Something rustled in the bushes above her. Casey froze. She was alone. No one knew where she was. She held her breath. Her mind screamed for action, but her muscles wouldn't obey. LouAnne's voice whispered advice to her as she fought for control, "Go *toward* 'em, not away." Casey launched all of her one hundred pounds backwards. She fell hard and struck her elbow on the stone step. She rolled to the side and rubbed her elbow. Looking back, there was no one behind her.

You're imagining things.

She cradled her head in shaking hands. Maybe LouAnne was right. At breakfast, Casey had admitted to recurring nightmares and the pervasive feeling that someone was watching her.

LouAnne's words came back to her. "Girlfriend, you need a shrink. No one's watching over you, or after you. You're on your own. Even the heat don't care what you do. Get used to it, 'cause you sure enough driving yourself crazy."

Casey shook her head. Maybe your mind splits when things get too damn crowded inside. Too many voices talking at once, and hideous images torturing her sleep. Last night she dreamt her hair caught on fire while she crawled through an endless tunnel.

She glanced at the station and sighed. The fugitive light she'd hoped to catch had come and gone.

Another voice logged in. "If you can't go back, might as well go forward." Casey silently thanked and dismissed her Great Aunt Mae. Something sure was wrong. She'd had conversations in her head all her life, mostly with herself, but—

A dark form landed on the ground next to her. Casey lurched forward. With a startled cry, the form dove into the brush next to the station. Moments passed without a sound. Casey peered into the bushes. Two enormous orange orbs glared back at her. She sat back. Wouldn't want to frighten the kitty.

She rose very slowly and walked toward the bush. "Hi, puss," she said softly. She talked in her best cat voice for a few minutes. Out of the corner of her eye, she caught a slight movement. Moments later, a light pressure brushed against her leg. She looked down and met the golden eyes once more.

She offered her fingers for sniffing. "Goodness, you're going to be a momma cat soon." Casey stroked the cat's silvery gray fur and long tail. "Kind of young for motherhood, aren't you?" The kitty couldn't be but a year. She continued to talk while she and the kitty returned to the step where she'd been sitting. Her pencil lay beside her sketch.

All the voices in her head stopped at once. A new, dark line on the drawing separated the clapboards from the foliage. Amazing how one simple stroke made the foreground pop and the background recede. Was she screaming? No, the cat hadn't startled. Casey couldn't take her eyes off the line. No one would believe that she hadn't drawn it. But *she* knew.

The cat plumped down the step and waddled toward the closest arch under the bridge that spanned the railroad tracks. Casey tore her eyes from the line and forced herself to watch the cat's lazy progress. Such a distended belly above dainty, gray paws.

The cat's tail pointed straight up and then curled at the tip. Curious. That's a sign of interest, but the cat was walking *away* from attention. Mewing coyly, the cat flopped over, and rolled before a pair of men's work boots.

A modern-day Jesus look-alike emerged from the shadows under the bridge. The only visible parts of his face were a long straight nose and intense black eyes. He fixed Casey with an appraising, cold stare and thrust his gloved hands into his coat pockets.

Knife? Gun? Casey hit the ground and rolled to the side.

The man withdrew a baggie and a small bowl, fed the kitty, and then retreated into the shadows.

Casey scrambled to her feet and dashed up the crumbling stone steps leading to Church Street. Halfway up, a hand in a glove with ragged, cutout fingers clamped around her ankle. The hand was human but barely so, a paw with blackened, cracked nails.

"Stop!"

She turned. The man's eyes bored into her. She hadn't made him up. She wasn't crazy. And she wasn't going to let this bridge troll hurt her. She kicked her free foot with all her might.

Once again, the blow didn't connect, but the man released her and pointed his gloved finger at poison ivy covering the step just above her. Then he retraced his steps and faded into the shadows. Casey crouched on the step and watched him reappear and push a bicycle to a water spigot at the side of the station. A small cart stuffed with green leaf bags trailed behind the bike. He opened one of the bags, retrieved a few cans, turned on the water, and rinsed out the cans. He stuffed the cans back in the bag, mounted the bike and pedaled up the steep incline.

Casey watched him turn onto Church Street and disappear. He had to be mighty strong to get to the top of the hill without standing on the pedals. She shuddered at her puny defense. Who was she kidding? He had let her go.

Still shaking, she gathered her materials and walked to her car parked in front of the charming little station. Charming, except for the troll under the bridge. Advice from her mother came back to her. When you criticize in fear or anger, look quickly down to the right, and you'll see yourself. Troll? Think again. Homeless, maybe, but a strong young man, maybe an artist, who was kind to animals and had saved her from poison ivy.

Casey was young and strong, loved animals, and was just this side of homeless herself. There but for the grace, she thought as she fired up the roadster.

By the time she reached Route 128, rush hour was over. She wound the engine through the gears, then puttered along in the middle lane at a comfortable, passive-aggressive speed with cars whipping by on either side. A pick-up drew up beside her in the passing lane. A good ole boy leaned out the passenger window and puckered his lips.

Gag. Casey braked and glanced at the tailpipe. According to LouAnne, the bigger the tailpipe, the bigger the asshole. Once again, Lou's Laws proved true: the pick-up was specially outfitted with dual extra-wides.

Lou advised her to take things slow, saying she was "prison smart and life stupid." Casey'd grown up belonging to a community, feeling anchored in time and space, secure in the claustrophobia of a small college town. That was Before. During the prison years, she lived the American dream secondhand through TV ads, sitcoms, and late-night shows, the inescapable backdrop of prison life. Now, driving past office buildings, chain stores, and warehouses, she was homesick for a life that didn't exist anymore.

Focus, girl. No use rehashing the past. Time for new beginnings. Live in the moment. Go forth.

Shit, *exit!*

A red alarm blinked on the dash as Casey executed what LouAnne called a Massachusetts drift, veering across three lanes to the exit and braking at the last possible second to insinuate the roadster between two other cars. The driver behind her showed his appreciation with an international hand signal. A second red light came on.

As she began the merge onto Route 2, the whole dash glowed red, and the engine cut out. The roadster came to a halt on the overpass between two major highways. Traffic pinned her in the merge lane. Well, she was living in the moment. A crash test dummy. She watched cars race towards her in her rearview mirror, closing her eyes before certain impact, breathing again when the cars missed. Don't look. If you can't see it coming, you won't tense up, and the whiplash won't be as severe. She stared through the windshield and counted the cars which passed that hadn't hit her.

A siren wailed, and strobes flashed as a cop screamed up behind her. Casey's knees jellied, and her forehead beaded. Her worst nightmare, repeating.

"Put 'er in neutral. I'll push you past the exit," a disembodied voice boomed.

Get a grip! He didn't say, "Get off the bike. You're under arrest." He said, "Put 'er in neutral." With a shaky hand, Casey complied.

Two and a half hours later, the gas station attendant who had towed the roadster gave her a ride to the nearest subway station.

What the hell was she going to do without wheels? She'd felt so free driving that spirited little car—away from her past, from death and destruction, prison and an unfaithful lover—only to have it freeze up on her when she needed it most. Her freedom ride. She left the subway station and walked toward the rowhouse she shared with LouAnne.

She heard the party before she saw the house. Casey wasn't in the mood. She slipped through the door and up the stairs to her cubbyhole room, unobserved by the revelers in the living room. She stripped, jumped into bed, and covered her head with pillows. To keep her mind off her troubles, she thought about the homeless man who fed his cat beneath the Church Street underpass and could ride his bike uphill without standing on the pedals. She hadn't thought of the homeless as being strong or artistic. He'd had a life Before, just as she had.

"Count your blessings," Aunt Mae advised in Casey's ear. Casey still had a bed, her health, and her freedom. Someday, she promised herself, someday she'd have a home, maybe like the derelict little train station.

Chapter Three

Casey startled awake amidst a horrendous nightmare where she was singing at the top of her lungs in a hayloft imploding with fire. She cast her eyes around the tiny room, confused at first about where she was. As she shed the vestiges of the dream, she noticed familiar objects—shoes, backpack, and her clothes hanging on a hook in the corner and remembered that she was in the closet-like space that was her new home.

She dressed and went downstairs to the living room, where she surveyed the wreckage from the night before. LouAnne and friends were making up for lost time, or, in LouAnne's case, done time. Wine and beer bottles, glasses, pizza boxes full of crusts, and tomato-smeared paper napkins crowded the coffee table. On a side table next to the Barcalounger an ashtray threatened to overflow. The couch had been pushed back to make room for dancing.

Casey struggled to open a window fronting the street to let in a little fresh air, but it was painted shut. She tried a second window with the same result. Just as she was about to admit defeat, a figure grumbled to life from behind the couch, shedding an afghan as he stood. The muscular black body was naked except for his Speedo underscants that accentuated, rather than covered, his privates. With a quick upward jerk, he freed one window and then the other, grabbed the afghan, and sank back behind the couch.

"Thanks."

No answer.

Casey leaned out the window and took in deep breaths of fresh air. Their dilapidated rowhouse crowded the sidewalk. She spotted three free parking spaces that must have been vacated at the crack of dawn. There were no garages in this neighborhood, so parking spaces were at a premium. Her little roadster wasn't waiting for her this morning. She almost fell out the window when she spotted a black Civic parked across the street.

"Look like you seen a ghost."

Casey grabbed the windowsill to steady herself. She hadn't heard LouAnne come into the room. "George drove a car like that one across the street." She looked closer. Massachusetts license plates. Strange streaks on the side. Taped to the rear hatch window was a handmade For Sale sign.

Casey chided herself. She knew full well that her erstwhile love wouldn't have followed her to the East Coast. He was ensconced in Ohio with his six-year-old daughter, basking in the ever-hopeful female attentions awarded a handsome, recently widowed professor.

LouAnne joined her at the window. Easily six feet tall, LouAnne wore a deep-necked African caftan that emphasized her ebony skin. "Benny's car. He lives next door. Forever fussin' with that heap. Looks like hell, but it runs good." LouAnne snagged two empty beer bottles by their necks, scooped up an ashtray, and disappeared through a door that led into the kitchen.

Casey stared at the black car. She was the one who had decided to leave Ohio. George had made a half-hearted plea for her to stay, but then gave her his dead wife's little roadster to appease his sense of guilt for leading Casey on. He never had any intention of marrying an ex-con.

Last night after a brief look under the hood of her car, the garage mechanic had estimated a minimum of $2,000 in repairs. "Probably higher. You drive a classic car, ya gotta expect some hefty maintenance."

"The car was a gift, and I don't have two thousand dollars."

"I can help you sell it."

The mechanic must have noticed her quivering lower lip, because he backed down. "I know a guy has a big old barn full of antique cars. Maybe you can keep it there. You want to keep it, don't you?"

Casey nodded.

LouAnne returned to clear up the pizza remains. "Had a little party last night."

Casey raised her eyebrows and glanced toward the inert figure partially covered by the afghan.

LouAnne chuckled.

"Leftovers?" Casey suggested, looking at the well-muscled arms. Her bond with LouAnne was deep. In prison, her cellmate had been a loyal companion and a fierce protector.

"My bro, Rosie," Lou replied. "He'll be staying with us a bit."

"Roosevelt Washington," growled the figure. He raised his head and stretched his legs, fixing Casey with a slow, insolent look. "No more'n a snack." He broke into a grin. "I better git 'fore she has my ass." He dodged a cushion LouAnne winged at him.

LouAnne ducked as the cushion came flying back.

Casey moved out of the line of fire, enjoying their antics. Her laughter died in her throat as she passed the coffee table. The pizza box had covered a wooden cutting board with a single-edge razor blade and the remains of white powder that looked like confectioner's sugar. She backed away in disbelief.

LouAnne followed Casey's eyes. The easy banter died in the smoky air. Rosie unwound like a big cat and escaped to the kitchen.

"Don't worry. I told 'em not to bring that shit here again."

Casey's throat was so tight she could barely speak. "I can't be around that stuff, Lou." She backed to the door.

"C'mon. I'm making breakfast. Rosie's right, you're just skin 'n' bone."

Casey kept going. Much as she loved her, LouAnne was part of a nightmare Casey wanted to put behind her. Staying at Lou's was a mistake, but she'd needed a place to land. Now she wanted to crawl into a quiet hole, close her eyes, ease her soul, shed the last decade, and emerge as a butterfly, free to ride the wind. Even a moth.

Outside, something wiggled under the Civic. A shoe. She crossed the street for a closer look and realized she'd never mistake this car for George's Civic. The black paint job was mottled with ocher spots.

"How much will you pay me to drive this crate away?" she joked to a pair of legs that extended behind the car.

A skinny young man in sweats crawled out from under the car and wiped his hands on a rag. "You mustn't disparage this fine vehicular specimen. Only the aesthetics are affected. She has a young heart, low mileage, and a set of solid, uncompromised tires."

"Forward and reverse?" Casey circled the car noting the rakish magnetic lightning bolts streaking across the sides.

"You laugh, but she's a dream to drive. And you always command the right of way—a priceless advantage on rotaries and merges."

The front grill had whiskers painted on the bumper and black spots for pupils on the headlights. Across the rear hatch, someone had painted "Muttmobile."

"With all its advantages, how can you part with it?"

"My new friend has a car, and he's allergic to animals. I had to spend all my off hours walking dogs to pay for insurance. That's why the back seats are yanked out—for the dogs. And the name, of course. I will miss her, though."

Casey shifted uneasily, worried the guy would spill his whole life story. Luckily, he was young. "What are you asking?"

"$500 takes her away," he said, stroking the hood.

"$200 tops, and only if it runs." She paused, surprised at her offer.

He frowned, pursed his lips, and fixed the car with a mournful expression.

"Cash," she said.

He smiled and held out the keys. "Name's Benny."

"Casey." She rummaged in her bag and came up with five twenties.

"You said two hundred dollars," he said, retracting the keys.

"The title gets you the other hundred."

"Oh, yeah. Jeeze. I'll get it. It's upstairs. I used to keep all that kinda crap in the glove compartment until Hugo took offense at it one day."

"Hugo?"

"Rottweiler. Beautiful dog, but a mean streak."

Casey peered inside at deep ridges in the console and an empty space where the glove compartment should have been.

Benny dashed into the house and came back with a shoebox stuffed full of bills and a pen. He set it on the roof of the car and rifled through the papers until he found a ratty, but still official-looking, document. He stared at the paper, helpless.

Casey took the title and pen, filled in her name, and handed back the pen and the other hundred. "Sign here."

He did as he was told, gave her the keys and the title, and then, with a flourish, opened the driver's door for her. He ran around and hopped in the passenger seat. "Let's go. I want to show you some of her custom features."

Casey turned the key and was rewarded with a responsive purr. She stalled the car twice, getting used to the clutch. They lurched down Mullins Avenue, bucking each time she shifted. When she adjusted the rearview mirror, she was surprised to see a taxi riding her bumper. She downshifted, forcing the cab into a spastic dance behind her.

Benny called out to a friend walking by, leaned over, and hit the horn. Dogs barked and howled from under the hood.

Casey stomped on the brakes, certain she had hit a large dog. The taxi driver swerved alongside the Muttmobile with inches to spare. The driver cursed her in Portuguese. She drowned him out with another howl of the horn.

"Quick study," said Benny.

"Any other little surprises?"

Benny reached behind the passenger seat, grabbed a portable red police flasher, and slapped it on the dash. "Battery operated." He demonstrated by flipping a toggle switch. The light flashed and twirled just like the real thing, and when Benny touched a button on the rear of the contraption, a siren whooped and began to wail. He laughed and turned it off as the car bucked again.

Casey drove in silence for half a block while she regained her composure and control of the car's forward motion.

Benny produced a spray can from under his seat. "Any sign of rust, just sand her down and give her a blast of this."

That explained the Muttmobile's brindle coat. At the stop sign, she pressed down the directional signal. Nothing.

"Have to signal by hand."

Casey sighed and rolled down the window. "Is there anything else that doesn't work?"

"Oh, it works all right." Benny smiled and stared straight ahead.

Casey pushed the control for left and right directional signals with no result. She glared at Benny, but he continued to smile and look forward. She followed his gaze to the brass Great Dane head ornament mounted on the hood. When she pressed the directional signals, the head swiveled obediently to the left or right. Benny leaned over and held down the lever, causing the head to rotate 360 degrees.

"Let me guess. M.I.T. undergrad in engineering."

Benny scowled, insulted. "The silly tricks with the car? Any liberal arts major could rig those."

She shook her head and tapped an M.I.T. sticker on the window.

Benny chuckled but then grew serious. He touched his forehead and closed his eyes. Seconds later, he intoned, "You come from a flyover state in the Midwest. Say...Ohio."

Casey laughed. She was wearing an Oberlin College sweatshirt. She concentrated on weaving through the twisting streets. When she realized she had been down the street twice before, she asked Benny for help.

"Hang a left."

"It's one way."

"You're from Ohio, and you're only going one way."

Casey drove down the street, aware that parked cars on both sides were facing her.

"Right at the Stop sign."

But before they reached the corner, a Volvo pulled out of a parking space and headed directly toward them.

"Now what?" Casey had never been fond of playing chicken.

Benny shrugged, his eyes wide.

Casey slammed the flasher on the dash, pushed the controls for lights and siren, and stomped on the accelerator.

"Jesus!" Benny screamed, sliding low in his seat.

The Volvo screeched to a halt. With a transmission-grinding howl, the driver reversed and jackknifed into the parking space.

Casey slowed to pass, allowing the driver a better look at the Muttmobile.

"What the fuck do you think—" the driver hollered.

"He's having a baby," Casey gestured toward Benny who was doubled up in the passenger seat, groaning. Halfway down the block, she peeked in the rearview mirror. She could barely make out the taillights of the Volvo. She looked harder. "Snowing?"

Benny twisted around in his seat and guffawed. Bills from the shoebox flew in every direction. Casey braked.

"No, no. Let her rip. Anything important, they'll hit me again. If they can find me."

Casey didn't argue. She spotted a street sign on the next corner, the first such sign she'd encountered in Massachusetts. By some miracle, they had completed the circle to Mullins Avenue.

"Hey, you just ran—"

Casey had missed the Stop sign. "All the same," she muttered as she drove down the street. The car lurched to a stall in front of the rowhouse. Benny patted the nose of the car goodbye and escaped to his house.

LouAnne stood at the curb waving a slip of paper. With her nose high in the air, and a snooty falsetto voice, LouAnne announced, "A Mrs. Waddington of President's Lane in Welton requests your presence at tea."

The euphoria from the joy ride evaporated as Casey took the note and shoved it in her pocket. She hadn't filled LouAnne in on her visit to the Jesuit Center or the blowup of the roadster.

"What you doing drivin' Benny's heap? Where's your cute little car?"

A lump in Casey's throat kept her from answering.

LouAnne took one look at her and drew her into her arms. "What's the matter, hon'? What happened?"

Casey shook her head. She knew she was going to break. She tried to escape, but LouAnne held on, rocking her back and forth until the sobs and then the tears came.

When Casey was all cried out, LouAnne made her a cup of coffee.

Casey told Lou about the Jesuit Center and the priest, Joseph Dempsey, who had died a year earlier. "The receptionist asked for our number and said that Father Dempsey's sister might want to give me a call. She gave me Mrs. Waddington's address. I checked it out. It's a mansion that overlooks a little abandoned train station." Casey ended her recitation with her encounter with the man under the bridge and the fate of the roadster.

"I'm sorry about your father," said LouAnne.

"Not sure he was my father." But she knew in her heart that her mother had loved the man dearly and that he must have been a wonderful man.

"Maybe you can learn more about him from Mary."

"Mary? I didn't know her name was Mary. How do *you* know her?"

LouAnne shed her street patois and sat up straight. "Why *everyone* knows Mary Waddington." Her voice took on the intonation and diction of upper-crust New England.

The instant transformation had startled Casey the first few times she'd witnessed it in prison. LouAnne explained that she'd grown up rough on the streets with her mother who worked the theater district. During one court appearance, her mother caught the eye of the judge. They married a year later. LouAnne spent her high school years in posh suburbs and earned a degree from Wellesley College.

"My father golfed with Presley Elsworth Waddington. His nickname was Prez. They call the mansion the White House and the private road President's Lane. The house is a showplace where they entertained. High society was shocked when Prez left his social register wife, Beth, for his secretary, 'shanty Irish' Mary Dempsey."

LouAnne must have noticed Casey's confusion. "Shanty Irish? What my father would call poor, Irish immigrant white trash." LouAnne chuckled, and her voice changed back. "Tha's before daddy brought home a ho."

"Anyway," her voice changed again, "it was a big scandal followed by a nasty divorce. Beth took off with their son for California, Prez died a few years later, and now Mary knocks about in the White House with her disabled sister."

Casey was quiet for a moment, taking it all in. "So, she's a widow with an estranged stepson. The receptionist at the Jesuit Center said she had very delicate health. Didn't have many friends in town. Sounds kind of lonely. What's the chance she'd welcome a stranger—someone who appears after ten years in prison—claiming to be the daughter of her brother, the priest?"

"Well, think on it. Never know, she may open her arms." LouAnne watched her closely. "I don't believe it. You're nervous. All that time in prison, and you're afraid of a harmless little old lady serving you tea? What you got to lose?"

Casey nodded. Sure 'nough nothing more to lose. She didn't want to admit, even to herself, how devastated she felt when Father Gannet told her Joseph Dempsey had died. So much for discovering her roots and possible family.

She retrieved the phone number from her pocket and dialed. To her relief, she got an answering machine and left a message saying she would love to join Mrs. Waddington for tea the following week.

Chapter Four

Wednesday morning, Casey woke to the smell of bacon and the sound of Lou and Rosie laughing in the kitchen. Usually, they were still asleep when she got up. Once again, she'd had nightmares of fire, pitchforks, and never-ending tunnels. In the bathroom, she groaned at her pallid image in the mirror. She felt like two cents worth of dirty ice. She splashed water on her face and trudged downstairs to the kitchen.

"'Bout time you stirred your stumps," LouAnne chided, handing her a glass of orange juice.

"Why are you two up so early?"

"Turning over a new leaf. I got me a job at the Women's Center. Have to be there by seven-thirty. Rosie, he wakes up when there's food."

"Congratulations! What's the job?"

"Counselor for battered women. Something I know firsthand." Lou handed Casey a warm plate with bacon and a stack of three pancakes. "Looks like you could use a little nourishment." She eyed Casey critically. "Why you moping around like you lost your last friend? And what you doing with that ratty old backpack? Thirty-something and looking like you're s'posed to be in class. Talk to me."

"I still feel like a student," Casey objected. "That's when my life ended."

"Don't I know it. How do you think I feel? When I went 'In' I had me a little girl. Now she's all grown up, and don't want nothing to do with her mama. Says she got another mama, took care of her when I left."

"Sorry, Lou." Lou's ghetto patois grew stronger when her emotions were close to the bone. In prison, no one knew her story beyond the fact that she'd killed her husband, and that her baby girl lived with her grandmother in Massachusetts.

"Now listen up. You got lovely skin, teeth to die for, a sneaky little smile, and eyes that don't need makeup—and with just a little attention, that hair that's all knotted up behind will shine so bright it'll blind a guy across the room. Stop slouching around, look up, and wear something besides ash cloth."

"I got all fixed up for George, and look what good that did. He dumped me the second—"

"George, George, George. You just now discovering men can be shits? You giving up on half of the world 'cause of one toad?" Lou banged the skillet into the sink. "I don't want to hear no more whining. Use what the good Lord gave you. I'm here to tell you it's time. That's all we got, sister. Time."

Lou warmed to the topic. "Honey, let the sunshine in. Open the doors we closed up so tight Inside. No more sideline shit. Jump in, play the game. Catch the pass. Run like hell."

Without looking at her, Lou lobbed a glass she was drying in Casey's direction. Casey snagged it just before it hit the floor. "Got a few moves left. You don't shape up, I'll sic Rosie on you. I saw you watching him."

"You calling? I be ready to serve," Rosie hollered from the living room.

LouAnne laughed as heat flooded Casey's face. "You white folks a giveaway with that blushing. Now sit down here and listen to big Lou."

"Yes, Mama."

"I thought people were watching me 'cause I was wearing *eau de prison*—but it just ain't so. They watching 'cause I'm a big, beautiful, Black mother, and proud of it. Don't like me, step aside, I'm a-comin' through. Now you sit there and let Lou show you a few tricks. Close your eyes."

Casey hesitated, but then did as Lou ordered. Lou released Casey's hair from the band and stroked it down one side and then the other. Suddenly, she grabbed a pair of scissors and a hank of hair and lopped it off. Casey's

24

eyes popped open. She gawked at her hair on the floor. She lunged at Lou in protest, but Lou was ready for her and much bigger. Lou twisted Casey's arm until she sat back down in the chair. "Nothing to be done but even off the other side," she said, laughing at the fury in Casey's eyes.

An hour later and three inches of hair lighter, Lou applied makeup. She must have been planning the session for a while to have products on the ready that matched Casey's coloring. Despite her embarrassment, Casey had to admit that the results were startling. Her eyes, always her best feature, dominated her face. Blush highlighted her cheekbones, and her "sneaky little smile" was outlined with mauve lipstick. When Lou was finished with her, she called Rosie for an appraisal.

He uncurled his long frame from the couch and ambled to the doorway. "Uh huh! Where you been hiding, sister?" Rosie growled, appraising her with sultry eyes. Once again, Casey turned crimson, demonstrating that she didn't need blusher.

Rosie scooped her up under one arm and carried her kicking and screaming into the living room where James Brown was playing on an oldies station. When he put her down, Casey tried to slap him, but he caught her arm, folded it behind her, and drew her close to him. "There. Now you been touched by a man. Didn't kill you. Put some light in those eyes." Casey was surprised to find herself laughing.

He released her to dance. "In the knees, girl. Move from the knees." He placed her hands on his knees to show her. "Now you," he said, feeling her knees as she moved. "This one's got potential," he hollered to Lou. "A few lessons with the master, all she needs."

Casey slugged him in the stomach, catching him by surprise. Not that it had much effect, his midriff was rock solid, but he released her and grinned as she bolted for the door.

"Stand up straight," Lou hollered after her.

"Yes, Mama," Casey sassed. She took the Muttmobile for a spin, sure that everyone was watching, but for the first time in ages, enjoying it. Despite her objections, she felt like a new woman. Not a girl, not a student, not George's reject—a new woman.

Chapter Five

After a full week cooped up scouring the *Boston Globe* Help Wanted ads, Casey was both depressed and stir-crazy. Her newly minted history degree and questionable employment history that included a stint in the library at the Ohio Reformatory for Women in Marysville, Ohio, didn't qualify her for the technical positions available.

On Wednesday, the day of the dreaded tea with Mary Waddington, she considered calling in dead, but after a morning of disheartening phone calls, decided she needed to get out of the house. Besides, she couldn't face LouAnne calling her a chickenshit again for being afraid of a simple tea.

She still had her doubts. She didn't have time to go swanning about the posh suburbs to a rich old widow's house. Well, that wasn't a good excuse. She had too much time, but what was the point? The man she suspected was her father was dead. Mrs. Waddington would probably peg Casey for a gold digger the minute she discovered she'd done time. No way the specter of a priest's illegitimate child would be welcome news.

Just go. She dressed in a basic black dress that Lou had assured her was appropriate for going to the dump or a party, along with her only jewelry, her mother's aquamarine ring and locket.

She hopped into the trusty Muttmobile. The car ran like a top with its spinning dog head on the hood. As she drove west, she practiced a number of conversations before laughing aloud. After ten years in prison, was she really scared of a little tea? Funny, the answer was yes.

In no time, she took the exit to Welton. Although she dawdled down the streets under the speed limit, all too soon, she spotted the turn down to the

Church Street station. Branching off the drive to the right, a narrow road led up the hill toward the White House. The street sign read "President's Lane. Private Road."

Casey still found it hard to believe that the town had private roads. She nosed the hound up the road, but came to an abrupt halt and stalled out at an imposing wrought iron gate with high stone fence on both sides. Probably designed to block the view of riffraff who had ignored the Private Road warning. Although the gate had been left open, Casey decided to park down by the little station. She backed up and took the turn leading to the bottom of the hill. No reason to embarrass Mrs. Waddington by parking the Muttmobile in front of her mansion. As she got out of the car, she cast about but didn't see any sign of the man who lived under the Church Street bridge.

She walked back up to the branch in the road and took the lane leading to the gate. Beyond it on the left, a gingerbread bungalow painted in teal with white trim guarded the formal drive to the main house. A hundred feet farther up, another lane led off to the right. Finally, she caught sight of the mansion that stood on the crest of the hill overlooking the station. It really did resemble the White House, with its east and west wings and monumental size.

A circular drive led to the front entrance. Behind the house a long lawn led to open fields ending in a stand of tall trees. Clearly, all the land went with the house. She knew from the conversations with Lou that Mrs. W was loaded, but the extent of her wealth was mind-boggling.

As she raised her hand to ring the doorbell, two enormous gray dogs the size of small ponies bounded around the side of the house, barking furiously. Casey flattened herself against the door and prayed they weren't hungry. The biggest dog skidded to a stop in front of her and barked inches from her face. "Nice puppy," whispered Casey. To her surprise, the wolf nuzzled her with its hairy muzzle, leaving a wet trail of dog nose across her midriff.

"Guinness! IRA! Come!" a woman's voice hollered from the side of the house. "Don't worry, Casey, they're pussycats."

"Nice kitty, kitty," soothed Casey, hoping the disembodied voice would materialize before the second hound bowled her over in joyful greeting.

"Here!" demanded the woman rounding the east wing. The dogs abandoned their new toy and obediently loped to her side. "I'm sorry if they scared you. Hello, I'm Mary Waddington." A short, rather plump, middle-aged woman approached, holding out both hands in greeting.

There was nothing Casey could do but extend her own hands in response. She was surprised when the woman grasped her hands and laughed. "Call me, Mary, dear. I'm afraid the lurchers have frightened you. Come inside."

"Lurchers?" was all Casey could say as they left the dogs behind. The entrance opened to a gracious marble foyer dominated by a staircase that rose to a landing, and then branched off to the left and the right.

"Lurchers are half-breed Irish dogs. These two are a mix of greyhound and Irish wolfhound. They came here from Dublin courtesy of Aer Lingus and Greyhound Rescue."

Mary led her through a formal living room to the right of the foyer that featured a fireplace decorated with Delft tiles. The scent of lilies wafted from a flower arrangement atop a mahogany sideboard. Through a doorway, Casey saw a cherry-paneled library packed floor to ceiling with books.

"Like a museum, isn't it?" chuckled Mary as she led Casey back to the foyer. On the left side of the house, Casey followed her through a conservatory with a grand piano. She tried not to gawk at the original artwork on the walls. French doors led to a porch and patio. They walked through a dining room with a breakfront full of delicate china. Throughout, Oriental rugs quieted their footsteps.

"Come on back to my digs where living takes place on a human scale." She led Casey to the kitchen at the back of the house. "I prefer the servants' quarters, myself. I'm always worried that I'll bust something out there. Make yourself at home."

Casey breathed freely for the first time, relieved to be in a homey, eat-in kitchen with a large fieldstone fireplace and windows that captured the view across the meadows. She sat at a small circular table while Mary bustled about, gathering mugs and silverware and a plate of scones. "What do you take in your tea? Milk? Cream? Sugar?" Without waiting for an answer, she rattled on. "I'm so glad you decided to come. I was afraid you'd cancel and I wouldn't get a chance to meet you."

"Sugar, please." Casey didn't drink tea and never used sugar, but responded out of guilt because she had seriously considered "bagging" the tea. She smiled to herself at her lousy, unspoken pun. As Mary chattered on, Casey realized that the woman was as nervous as she was.

"Joseph would have loved to meet you, I'm sure. He always spoke so kindly of your mother. Em, or is it Emma? As you know, he died just this last year, God rest his soul." Mary crossed herself dutifully.

"Her name was Emma,' but everyone called her Em.' She died years ago."

"I'm so sorry. That must be why the letter I wrote her about Joseph's death was returned. I remember Em also had a boy. How is your brother? How old would he be now?" Mary asked solicitously.

"Thirty-five. He's recovering from a very difficult year. He was injured, and his wife died in a fire last summer. He's now living with our great aunt."

"Oh, my heavens! You've had your share of tragedy."

A fiery image flashed through Casey's mind of her brother's wife Martha in the hayloft when the barn imploded, and she disappeared into the inferno. Casey shuddered and forced her attention back to Mary who was watching her with a look of concern.

"Are you okay?"

Casey could only nod. She still couldn't talk about the last days in Oberlin when so many had been hurt or killed. Mary let a moment pass before changing the subject again. "And Mr. Cavendish?"

For a second, Casey didn't understand Mary's question. "Oh, sorry. You mean Em's husband. He died before I was born."

Mary's head tilted to the side with a quizzical expression.

"I never knew him," Casey added quickly.

"Well, let's let the family rest for a bit. Tell me all about you," Mary suggested, pulling up her chair.

"There's not much to tell." Casey groaned inwardly. *I should've known the woman would ask me questions! What to say?* Casey remembered one of Lou's Laws: "Lie real close to the truth. It's easier to remember."

"I grew up in Oberlin and graduated from the college. I worked in a library in central Ohio. Last year I moved back to Oberlin to live with my great Aunt Mae and work in the library, and now, well, now I'm here. I'm staying with friends in Somerville and looking for work."

"Such a pretty young thing, you must have a boyfriend ...?" Mary let the question hang.

"Not now. I had a fellow back home, but that's over with. It's one of the reasons I came East." Casey hoped that her admission would stem the tide of Mary's questions. "And you?" she asked boldly, redirecting attention to her hostess.

"Do I have a boyfriend?" laughed Mary.

"No, no!" Casey blushed. "I didn't mean—"

"Turnabout is fair play." Mary refilled their cups. "Els—my husband—died years ago, and I've been rattling about in this mausoleum ever since. I should move down to the gatehouse. It's much cozier, but ..." Her voice drifted off. She looked as if she were going to say more, but then thought better of it. "Please forgive my nosiness. I get lonely here sometimes, and when there's a new face, I ask too many questions." She seemed to cast around for something to say. "You're wearing a lovely locket."

Casey smiled and fingered the locket. "The initials stand for International Order of the Odd Fellows. My mother and a friend found it in an antiques fair. Mother gave it to me shortly before she died. She laughed and said I was odd enough to wear it. It's my favorite." Casey unfastened the chain and handed the locket to Mary, thankful for the change of topic.

Mary donned a pair of glasses with bottle-thick lenses that hung around her neck on a cord. Opening the locket, she gazed at the tiny picture of Em. "Beautiful. Must be your mother." She closed the locket, turned it over, and ran her fingers over the etched letters on the back. Her expression changed from pleasant smile to momentary surprise and then to one of sorrow as she handed the locket back to Casey. Before she could say more, the telephone rang.

"Sorry, but I have to take this," Mary said as she lifted the receiver off the wall phone next to the table. "Hello?"

Casey heard a woman's voice on the other end of the line, but couldn't make out the words. She toyed with the locket and read the familiar inscription that had affected Mary, "Em, love, Jed." There was no question in Casey's mind that Jed was Mary's brother, but what good did that do now? She'd never meet him. There was nothing for her here. Her tea was cold. She glanced at the door, wondering if she could make it back through the maze without a guide.

"I'm so glad you called. How is Worthy doing?" Mary listened to the woman's response, interjecting a few "Oh's" and "I see's."

Casey rose to clear the cups, but Mary quickly waved her down, mouthing, "Wait." Reluctantly, Casey obeyed.

"Well, I'd be delighted to see you both. I was just talking with my niece. I would love to have you all for dinner on Friday."

Casey sank into her chair.

Mary hung up and pushed the scones toward Casey. "That was my stepson Worthy's wife, Cherie. She and Worthy are coming for a visit. I haven't seen him in …" She looked up to calculate. "Thirty-some years." She smiled at Casey. "I hope you'll come to dinner Friday."

Stunned, Casey could only nod. *Her niece.*

Chapter Six

Dumbstruck by Mary's casual statement about their kinship, Casey muttered, "Excuse me," and escaped to a bathroom they'd passed on the way to the servant's quarters. She hadn't expected Mary to know about, much less acknowledge, her paternity. Thinking back, she realized that there weren't enough clues for Mary to have reached her conclusion. Unless Mary knew more than she let on, the soft-spoken, kindly lady was playing her. Casey splashed water on her face and returned to the kitchen, determined to find out what Mary did and didn't know.

Mary stood by the counter with her back to Casey, concentrating upon an apparatus she held close to her eyes. Curious, Casey approached quietly. Mary reached for a fat pen on the counter and removed the cap revealing a needle. She plunged the needle into the muscle of her upper arm, recapped the pen, and placed all of the paraphernalia into a cookie jar at the corner of the counter.

"Hope you're not squeamish."

Casey jumped at Mary's voice. Mary knew she was watching her. She turned as Casey shook her head.

"I just gave myself three units of insulin to control my blood sugar level. After eating, it goes up. I'm a type 1, early-onset diabetic. You must have noticed my thick glasses earlier. I've lost most of the sight in my right eye and have less than thirty percent in the left. Truth is, I'm blind in the dark. In light, I can make things out when there is contrast. I can also read some with magnifiers, but it's a trial."

"How often do you have to do the test?"

"It depends— at regular intervals, morning and night. If I have anything going on, like an infection, I'm particularly vulnerable. Then I check more frequently because things can go haywire fast. You needn't worry. I take insulin with food."

"When did you decide I was your brother's daughter?" Casey asked abruptly.

Mary smiled. "The moment I set eyes on you. You have his eyes, mouth—his coloring. Not a question in my mind. He also had pictures of you growing up that I found after he died. He'd saved them along with a picture of your mother."

Casey swallowed quickly to control the growing lump in her throat.

"I wish you could have met him. It would have meant a great deal to him. You must have suspected that Jed was your father. Why didn't you say anything to me?"

"Jed," Casey whispered. *The initials on the locket.*

"Joseph E. Dempsey. 'E' for Enniskillen, where he was born."

"I would have come earlier, but I was in prison," Casey blurted, and then, mortified at her admission, she looked down and studied her nails. Short, clipped neatly. LouAnne had encouraged her to grow them.

"You have very graceful hands." Mary's eyes followed hers.

Mary hadn't reacted to her statement about prison. "You knew?"

"Yes, dear. I always do my homework." Mary toyed with her cup. When she spoke again, a vein of iron crept into her voice. "I knew about prison, and I also know you were completely exonerated from the charges. You must be very bitter. Ten years is a huge chunk out of a young life."

Casey struggled to breathe normally and waved her hand in front of her face. "Where does all this come from? I never even met the man!" she objected when she could speak again.

"Disappointment. Frustration. Everyone wants to know who their parents were," soothed Mary.

"How did—"

"Jed subscribed to the *Oberlin News Tribune*. I got his mail after he died. At first, I thought he got the paper because he went to college there, but then I found a scrapbook full of clippings from the paper about you and your mother. I was curious and renewed the subscription and followed town events during the past year.

"I was surprised when you appeared at the Jesuit home. I didn't expect you. I made a few discreet inquiries." Mary's voice was flat.

Casey's lump evaporated. "Like the FBI," she muttered. *The woman had spied on her!*

"I don't blame you for being angry, Casey, but there's something you must understand. I'm viewed as a filthy rich widow, sick, legally blind, and childless—in other words, a perfect target." Mary paused and stared at Casey. "I've learned to be very, very careful. Money is a magnet, attracting rich and poor alike—anyone who could benefit, which is everyone. I've become a recluse."

Casey glared at her. "I don't want your damn money. I didn't even know my father had a sister. I just wanted to meet him." Her voice cracked. She rose and headed for the door, determined not to break down in front of Mary.

"I'm sorry, Casey. Don't listen to my words; listen to my heart. I'm just a paranoid, silly old Irish woman! You'll forgive me and come to dinner Friday, won't you? I'd love to show you Jed's scrapbook."

Mary's voice had melted to kindly again, with a touch of a plea in the invitation.

Although she knew Mary was manipulating her, Casey was sorely tempted by the mention of a scrapbook. She hesitated. "Yes. Time for me to go. You must be tired. I'll let myself out."

"Thank you, dear."

Casey retraced her earlier steps to the front door, wondering how Mary could keep it so clean. Halfway through the conservatory, she heard a high keening wail from the back of the house. *Mary!* She spun about and ran as fast as she could back to the kitchen.

No Mary.

"It's alright, Vera. Relax. I'm sorry I couldn't get to you sooner. It's not your fault."

Casey inched forward, following Mary's voice down the hallway leading toward the bathroom. Mary was bending over a woman on the floor in front of a wheelchair, stroking her hair. Mary stiffened. "Is that you, Casey?" The hallway was dark except for the spillover light from the kitchen.

"I'm right behind you. Is everything okay? Can I help?"

"I hoped you didn't hear. The switch is behind you, but before you turn on the light, I need to warn you that my sister had an awful accident and is very badly disfigured."

"Ohhhh. Ohhhh." An agitated cry interrupted Mary's speech.

"It's okay, Vera. Casey is Jed's daughter."

Casey switched on the light and gasped at the severely deformed woman on the floor. Vera stared back at her with moist eyes. She raised a club-like hand to her mouth to cover a wide scar that bisected her lips and cheek. The fingers were twisted and curled as if every one of them had been broken. From the smell of urine and the overturned chair, Casey figured that she'd fallen trying to get to the toilet.

"Hello, Vera." She approached slowly, knelt, and took the trembling and deformed hand in hers. "Or should I call you Aunt Vera? I've just learned that I have a whole family that I'd never known about before."

At first Vera pulled back, but then, listening to Casey's voice, she relaxed. Her face took on a rictus that was meant to be a smile. "Orry," she said.

"Sorry," translated Mary. "Vera lost most of her tongue in the … accident. We'll be fine, Casey, don't worry. You can go."

"You'll be fine a lot faster if you let me help her up."

Mary looked at her long and hard before turning to her sister. "What do you say, Vera?"

Vera nodded, a tear running down her face.

Chapter Seven

Friday evening Casey poked along Church Street in the Muttmobile. She was early for the dinner at Mary's. When she reached the turn-off to the train station, she hesitated. Instead of taking President's Lane and parking in the circular drive as Mary had suggested, she drove down the hill to the train station. She killed the engine and looked around. There was no sign of the guy who lived under the bridge, the man that she'd mentally nicknamed Can Man.

Casey looked at her watch for the umpteenth time. Quarter to six. She couldn't arrive early. She got out and walked to the station. The pale gray clapboards were in dire need of paint, and a few of the roof tiles were askew. She mounted the steps to the door and tried the handle, but the door was locked and the windows were boarded over. She sat on the bottom step, taking care not to snag her new stockings. She'd come dressed in a champagne-colored shift with a matching jacket that she and LouAnne had found in the Goodwill outlet that afternoon. Her only adornment was her locket and her mother's aquamarine ring.

LouAnne must have realized how nervous Casey was when she'd helped Casey with her hair and put the last touches on her makeup. "Quit stewing and enjoy your dinner with Mary."

"Her stepson and his wife are coming."

"You're not wearing prison stripes, and as you say, you 'haven't done anything wrong.' Think of it this way. You're helping Mary. She probably invited you as a buffer for a very awkward situation."

Casey was rehashing this last thought when she felt soft fur rubbing

36

against her stocking. "Hello, Little Mother." The pregnant little gray cat that she'd met on her first visit to the station had come to greet her, mewing silently and offering her head for scratching. Casey petted her gently. The kitty looked as if she'd swallowed a football. When she had all the attention she wanted, she found a spot on the drive with the last of the evening's sun. She lay down gingerly, protecting her swollen belly.

Last night she'd asked LouAnne for advice about the dinner.

"Put your napkin in your lap and chew with your mouth closed."

"Seriously, Lou."

"Well, for god's sake, don't arrive on time. Be fashionably late. And take a small gift for the hostess."

"More clues, please. How late is fashionable, and what can I take to a woman who has everything?"

"Fifteen minutes to a half hour, unless your hosts are German, Scandinavian, or Asian, then arrive on the dot. Bring a bottle of wine, flowers, or a box of candy." Casey guessed she was as ready as she ever would be for the dinner. She didn't know squat about wine and had seen plenty of flowers in the White House, so she'd opted for a fancy box of chocolates.

Casey whipped about at motion in her peripheral vision. Can Man emerged from the shadows of the arch under the Church Street bridge toting a large garbage bag over one shoulder. She held her breath as he walked toward her. He veered off before he reached her and headed to the side of the station.

He must have seen her. Muscles tensed, poised to dash to the car, Casey watched him empty the bag of cans and bottles on the ground. He twisted a spigot, and a stream of water gushed forth from a hose. He squirted each piece of trash with the hose and then put it back into the bag. When he was done, he removed a glove with the cutout fingers he'd been wearing on his left hand and sprayed it with the hose.

Casey tried not to stare at the burn scars and skin grafts on the hand. As he pulled on the glove, he looked directly at Casey. "Amazing what a little water can do." He twisted the spigot back. "Mary turned it on," he explained.

"You know Mary?" blurted Casey.

"*Everyone* knows Mary." *Even me*, was implied by his defiant tone.

"Sorry, I didn't..." She stopped, at a loss for words.

Can Man gave her an appraising look. When he spoke again, his tone changed from sardonic to appreciative. "All decked out tonight."

Casey nodded toward the White House. "Dinner."

"Ah yes, meeting the prodigal." Can Man pointed to threatening, fast-moving clouds racing to crowd out the last of the sun. "Better hurry." He slung the bag over his shoulder and walked back to the underpass with Little Mother trotting behind.

She glanced at her watch and realized that she had pushed "fashionably" to the limit. She got in and fired up the Muttmobile, wondering what had happened to the strange man, how he knew about the guests who were coming to dinner, and why he lived under the bridge. Actually, she'd be homeless soon if she didn't find a new place to live and a job. And she had a scar of her own.

Gusts of wind buffeted the sides of the Muttmobile. Individual splats of rain quickly grew into torrents pounding on the hood. As Casey drove through the gate on President's Lane, she noted that all approaches to the mansion looked upward. Spotlights illuminated the White House on the top of the hill, offset against the darkened sky. With windshield wipers on full, the White House appeared and disappeared in waves of rain.

Casey pulled over on the far side of the circular drive and sat in the car waiting for a pause in the downpour. She cracked the window to enjoy the freshening smell of rain cleansing the air. She imagined scenes of yesteryear when luxury cars swept into the circle under moonlit skies, and valets opened doors and greeted elegant guests. Instead of lightning, flashbulbs of *Town and Country* photographers would have captured the horsey, old moneyed set for the society pictures in the next issue.

At a momentary lull in the storm, Casey jumped from the car and dashed to the front door. As she pushed the doorbell, she heard laughter within. Out of breath and drenched, she bent over to brush a leaf off her stockings just as the door opened. *Damn!* So much for making a graceful, fashionably late entrance.

Chapter Eight

C asey looked up into the smiling face of a maid who greeted her with a towel and led her to a powder room off the foyer. She dried off as best she could, careful not to smear the makeup that LouAnne had so carefully applied. No reason to appear like a drowned raccoon.

The maid introduced herself as Gilma and led her to the dining room.

"I'm so glad you made it, Casey," Mary exclaimed. "I have to admit to being a tad nervous. I haven't entertained in ages."

Casey surveyed the formal setting. The anemones were perfect amidst crystal wine and water glasses that sparkled on a lace tablecloth.

"My grandmother tatted the tablecloth. Els' first wife left behind the china plates and silver." Mary adjusted a crystal knife holder. "I've been worrying about this dinner for the past week. I hope I haven't gone overboard." She gasped. "Oh god, I shouldn't even think that word!"

Casey gave her a quizzical look.

"Last June, Cherie and Worthy were thrown overboard when their speedboat crashed into his partner's boat in a race. Worthy's partner and his wife were killed. Worthy and Cherie have been recuperating in Maine this summer. Evidently, he had a severe concussion."

"Taxi's coming, ma'am," the maid called from the foyer.

Mary led Casey into the living room where they joined Vera in her chair by the front window. Mary drew a curtain aside so that they could watch the arrival. The rain had abated as quickly as it had arrived, although gusts of wind continued to lash the trees. The taxi pulled into the circle. The driver retrieved their bags and carried them to the door, returning to stand next to the man who must be Worthy.

Mary squinted. "Tell me what's happening. What does he look like?" Vera looked to Casey to answer.

"He's tall and lanky. Dark hair. I think the cabbie's waiting for him to pay, but he's looking all around at the house and the grounds."

"Dark like his father. Bet he makes Cherie pay. Els didn't like the feel of money on his hands."

"He's gripping a bouquet of flowers."

"Thoughtful like Els."

Casey continued. "The woman's tall and stylish. Blonde. She's juggling a paper bag and trying to open her purse. She handed bills to the driver who was counting them. Now he's scowling. She's turning away and walking to the house."

"Beth was a tall blonde beauty, and she was also cheap. Maybe he married his mother," Mary said, releasing the curtain.

Vera crossed herself and rolled her eyes.

Mary laughed. "I hope not, too. Are you sure you don't want to come to dinner and meet them?"

Vera nodded emphatically and turned her chair toward the servants' quarters, propelling the wheels forward with her club-like hands.

Just as the doorbell chimed, Gilma appeared. "I'll get that, ma'am," she offered.

"No, but thank you, dear. I'll be greeting them meself. Myself," she corrected, looking a little sheepish at her slip.

Casey watched her straighten, take a deep breath and walk through the foyer. With a big smile, Mary threw open the door. "Welcome home, Worthy. Hello, Cherie." She shook hands with each of her guests to personalize her greeting.

"Oh!" Mary drew back with a frown. "Worthy?" she said, clearly startled.

Worthy offered her the bouquet with a smile. As she took it, Mary glanced down at his hand and nodded as if in recognition. "How sweet of you! You shouldn't have." Mary relieved Cherie of the paper bag. "Wine and flowers," she fussed. She turned and handed both to Gilma beside her. "As you've probably guessed, I'm Mary, and this is my niece, Casey Cavendish. Casey, meet my stepson and his wife, Worthy and Cherie Waddington."

Stunned by Cherie's picture-perfect looks, all Casey could mutter was a weak "Hello." Cherie rewarded her feeble efforts with a pearl-white smile. "Looks like you got caught in the rain," she commented, giving Casey's wet clothing an appraising once-over with her long-lashed azure eyes.

Casey noted Cherie's cream complexion, patrician nose, and shoulder-length haircut that accentuated her long neck. Her light blue silk blouse was open at the neck and tucked in at the waist, emphasizing a surprisingly full bosom. Black crepe slacks draped over long, graceful legs, completing the classic hourglass figure. *Don't stare.* She extended her hand in greeting. Cherie's cold hands gave her a start.

"Cold hands, warm heart," quipped Cherie.

Worthy grunted at her remark. Husband and wife exchanged a sharp look. When he took Casey's hand, she winced at the feel of the scarred stub of his index finger. "Sorry ... uh, Hello." Casey stammered before she realized that he'd anticipated her reaction with a sardonic smile.

"Come in. Just leave your bags by the door," Mary said. She led her guests into the living room. "Please make yourselves at home." Cherie settled herself into a deep leather couch, and Mary sat in a matching leather chair. Casey took a place on the loveseat that completed the arrangement before the fireplace. Worthy ignored Mary's implicit offer of a seat next to Cherie and walked around the room exploring.

"I'm so glad you came," Mary prattled to Cherie. "It must be so very strange for you." Casey listened to Mary and Cherie talk, but she was hyper-aware of Worthy as he circled about.

"And even stranger for him," responded Cherie, looking over her shoulder at her husband. She lowered her voice. "He took a big hit on the head during the accident. Severe concussion. It's taken him months to get back to normal." She lowered her voice even more so that Casey and Mary had to lean forward to hear. "He's still struggling with occasional memory lapses, although he hates to admit it. His best friend and partner in the firm died in the accident. They were like brothers."

"How awful for you both." Mary sat back, folding her hands in her lap.

Casey squirmed, surprised that Cherie would bring up such personal information so soon after arriving. She glanced sideways at Worthy who moved from one piece of furniture to another, caressing surfaces as if they were old friends. He sat in a chair before a large rolltop desk and twirled around once with a small smile on his face. How odd it must seem, meeting Mary so many years after the childhood trauma that changed his life, seeing his old home through estranged adult eyes and a debilitating concussion.

Cherie must have sensed their silence. "I'm sorry, Mary. I shouldn't burden you with our troubles. It's just that I feel so comfortable talking with you. It was the same on the telephone. I feel that I've known you forever."

"Thank you, dear," Mary acknowledged, but Casey noticed that she didn't reciprocate, but rather chose to change the subject. "Were you close to Drew's wife as well?"

"Not really. Nan and I got along and liked one another well enough, but nothing like the bond between Drew and Worthy."

Mary pressed a button on the side of a small table next to her chair to summon Gilma. Casey marveled at Mary's transformation from the down-to-earth woman who'd served her tea just days ago into a sophisticated matron directing a formal evening with practiced control.

Worthy came into view, attracted to a picture on the side wall.

"That's one of my favorites," Mary commented, drawing him into the conversation. He continued to study the picture. "The colors are so vibrant, they seem to sing," she added.

"I always loved it."

"Actually..." Mary paused. "I can't remember what hung there when I first moved in, but it must have been colorful for you to remember it. That picture is one that my nephew painted for his mother. Els and I kept the antiques, but he encouraged me to add my own personal touches. I'm glad you like it."

Worthy nodded but didn't reply and continued his tour of the room.

"Where are you staying, Cherie?" Mary asked to re-seed the conversation.

"A hotel," grunted Worthy, wandering into the library.

"Oh no, that's unnecessary. You'll stay in the guest house. It's empty."

"That's so kind of you." Once again, Cherie lowered her voice. "He needs more rest. He's doing better now, but he was so profoundly depressed I had to quit my job—I'm a nurse—to take care of him. For months, he barely spoke, and I had to force him to eat. He'd get so confused and then frustrated. He tried to cover his lapses at work, but that just made matters worse. He finally had to take a leave of absence from the firm."

Ah, there's the rub. Casey recognized the deeper message in Cherie's confession and wondered if Mary had picked up on it. They were income free. That's why they were visiting their estranged stepmother. Casey gave Cherie an empathetic nod, relieved to know the playing field.

Gilma reappeared and placed a tray of grapes, and cheese and crackers next to a bowl of nuts on the coffee table. She waited expectantly beside Mary.

"What would you like to drink, Cherie? We have just about everything you can imagine," Mary added in encouragement.

"In that case..." Cherie winked and gave Mary a conspiratorial smile, "I'd like a vodka martini with as many olives as you can spare. Light on the vermouth. Worthy will take—"

"Club soda with lemon."

Mary practically levitated from her seat. She'd lost track of Worthy and hadn't realized he was directly behind her. "Scare me to death. Come sit, Worthy, and talk a moment." She caught her breath and smiled to cover her outburst. "Just like your father; he wasn't a drinker either."

Cherie smiled and patted the couch beside her in invitation. Instead, Worthy sank into the loveseat beside Casey.

"What would you like to drink?" Gilma asked, appearing suddenly at Casey's elbow.

"White wine?" She kicked herself mentally for sounding as if she were asking permission rather than giving her order. Time for her to contribute to the conversation. "I was early, so I drove down to the train station where

I was distracted by a little gray cat that I'd like to paint someday." Casey cut herself off. She was babbling and just realized she'd forgotten the specially wrapped German chocolates that were in the back seat of the Muttmobile.

"I didn't realize you were an artist. Will you show me your paintings sometime?" Mary asked.

Casey dodged the question. "And I didn't realize that you owned the station. Can Man washed off the bottles and cans he'd collected using the water spigot at the side of the station. He said you'd turned it on." Casey accepted a lovely crystal wine glass from Gilma. The wine was smooth and sweet, but she hadn't a clue what kind it was.

"Can Man?" Mary looked confused.

"The fellow who lives under the bridge and rides around on his bicycle collecting cans."

"Oh, you mean Jackson."

"I didn't know his name." Casey instantly regretted the crude nickname she'd given the homeless man. "What's his story?"

Mary hesitated before answering. "Everyone has a story, dear, but Jackson's isn't mine to tell. By the way, I only own the building. The railroad owns the land. And Jackson doesn't live under the bridge. He has rooms over the garages and is in charge of maintaining the grounds and taking care of the dogs."

Feeling scolded, Casey considered crawling under the oriental carpet. She pushed back in her seat and twisted her wine glass in her fingers, admiring the reflections caused by the delicate facets in the glass. She couldn't help but feel the seductiveness of the fine things surrounding her. The towel the maid had handed her was some fancy Egyptian cotton thread, much different from the towel she'd clipped from the Holiday Inn on her journey north. The artwork looked original, the glasses crystal, and the antiques expensive.

She felt a flicker of resentment at the opulent display of privilege, worlds apart from her life with LouAnne and Rosie in Somerville or anything she'd known growing up in small-town Ohio. Mary must have known she'd be out of her element when she invited her. Maybe that was the point.

She changed her focus to Worthy who stood and crossed the room to look at another picture. It looked like a Picasso she'd studied in Art History. Worthy made a good match for the glamorous Cherie, tall and austere with a lithe frame and the graceful elegance and superior mien of an aristocrat—or at least how Casey thought an aristocrat would appear.

Worthy picked up a statue of a stalking cat from a table. He tapped it with a fingernail from his good hand, as if to test the material.

"Resin," said Mary, watching him. "Aren't they amazing? It's called the 'Cubist Collection' done by a Scottish sculptor whose name, of course, escapes me right now."

Worthy looked at Mary and nodded and then included Casey in his range. He flashed her a lopsided smile that transformed his face into a boyish, yet still intense, expression. His gaze lowered to the glass in her hand.

"Beth's crystal?" he asked.

"Beth?" Casey asked.

"Mother dearest," said Worthy, but offered no further explanation.

"Worthy always called his mother and father by their given names," broke in Cherie. "Beth never acknowledged her age. So, a growing child with obvious birthdays who called her 'Mother' was out of the question." Cherie paused to hand Gilma her glass for a refill. "How times change. Now, all she wants is grandchildren. But I bet no child will ever call her 'Grandma' and live to tell the tale."

"How is Beth?" Mary asked.

"Alive and kicking," Worthy interjected. "Mostly kicking."

"As I may have mentioned on the telephone, Worthy and Beth have had another falling out, so we haven't seen her or spoken with her recently," Cherie explained in a confidential tone.

Casey found the way Worthy tuned in and out of the conversation unnerving and was embarrassed when Cherie talked about him as if he weren't in the room.

"Right." Evidently, Mary felt the same way. She rose abruptly. "Time for dinner." She led them across the foyer into the dining room for the first course.

Casey trailed behind. So much unspoken in the air, much of it attesting to dysfunctional relationships, past and present. The White House itself was enough to take her breath away, but combined with this strange cast of sophisticated yet damaged characters, it was almost overwhelming. *You're Casey Cavendish. You haven't done anything wrong, and you're hungry. Chew with your mouth closed, and don't jump up to clear the plates.* She'd chalk up the evening to a fascinating and outrageous experience and then escape to the Muttmobile and her common digs.

Chapter Nine

Casey entered a wonderland of crystal and light. Tiny prisms danced magically across the ceiling and walls as lights reflected off the crystals in the chandelier and glass goblets. The sumptuous array of fine china, silver, and lace took her breath away. The air was perfumed with the scent of lilies from a large floral bouquet on a sideboard behind her. She didn't know whether to be awestruck at the beauty around her or horrified at the display of wealth. She'd need a tour guide to explain all of the treasures. Casey found herself seated across from Mary, between Cherie on her right and Worthy on her left.

"Els said that you always dressed for dinner," Mary commented to Worthy as they took their seats.

"Not me. They did. I was fed in the kitchen during cocktail hour and then trundled off to bed."

"That must have been lonely for you," said Mary.

"Not at all. The servants were much more fun than Beth's stuffy friends. My mother was then, and continues to be, a very beautiful, vain, and foolish woman who attracts more of the same to her table."

"If I'd known, we'd have eaten in the back the way we normally do."

"Oh no, this is lovely," commented Cherie to no one in particular. She lifted a fork and examined the silver pattern and seemed to weigh it in her hand.

Outside, the wind slammed shutters against the house as the storm regained its strength. A bolt of lightning branched across the dark sky, followed by a clap of thunder that rattled the windows. The lurchers howled in protest from their pen.

"Please excuse me for a moment. I love the storms, but they upset the dogs." Mary rose and left the room.

Gilma entered and filled water and wine glasses.

Moments later, Casey heard Mary talking to IRA and Guinness, and then, to her surprise, she returned to the dining room with the two dogs in tow. "Els told me how much you loved dogs, so I know you won't mind me bringing them in. My big babies. They're terrified of the thunder."

Mary gestured downward with her hand. Guinness and IRA sank into the plush Oriental rug without protest. "Not too shabby for two strays from Dublin town, eh me lovelies?" Mary soothed in a voice that betrayed a slight Irish lilt.

As she spoke, the lights dimmed for a second. IRA took advantage of the distraction to inch forward and check out the company, sniffing at Worthy. Worthy shrank instinctively when the dog rested his enormous head in his lap.

"IRA, you're a *down dog!*" Mary commanded imperiously. IRA lay down beside Worthy with a disgruntled huff. Mary snapped her fingers twice. "Crawl like soldiers," she whispered. Both dogs inched toward her like Marines in basic training elbowing through the mud. When they were behind her chair, Mary told them to stay. "I'm so sorry. I should have left them outside—"

"I loved dogs when I was a boy. Until two neighborhood dogs tried to dismember me," Worthy said, eyeing IRA warily. "You seem to have them under control."

After Gilma poured more wine for Cherie, Mary extended her hands to Worthy and Cherie and beckoned for Casey to do the same, so that the foursome was holding hands. "This is a tradition in *my* family," she said. "Don't worry, I won't pray over you," she comforted. "It's very simple. We just join hands, and all say, 'Glad to be together.'"

"Glad to be together," they said in unison.

As Casey released Cherie's hand, she noticed a blazing display of diamonds on her manicured ring finger.

Cherie nodded, answering the unspoken question in Casey's eyes, and then flicked a curl backwards to reveal a matching earring.

Gilma appeared and ladled soup into bowls.

Casey shifted her attention to Mary and found herself staring yet again. She'd been so focused on Worthy and Cherie when she first came that she hadn't paid attention to Mary's appearance. Now she noticed how light makeup enhanced Mary's naturally dramatic features. Her hair was swept up atop her head. A few escapee tendrils curled about her ears. In the low light, she was positively stunning.

When Casey had come to tea, Mary had worn baggy clothes that covered her waist, making her short figure look plump. Now she wore a fitted suit of deep teal Ultrasuede. Casey mentally caressed the soft material. Custom tailored because of Mary's diminutive stature. Mary looked ten years younger than she had upon the first meeting. Now Casey figured that Mary was about fifty-four or five.

Mary's small hands, always in motion while she talked, were also bejeweled: emerald-studded wedding rings on her left hand and a large diamond in an antique setting on the right.

Mary gave Casey a conspiratorial smile. Jauntily, she flicked a stray curl aside to reveal a matching emerald earring.

"As for full disclosure," Worthy said, "my bride's sparklers are paste. We're waiting for Beth's diamonds to be resized to fit Cherie's larger fingers."

After a moment's stunned silence, Mary jumped to the rescue. "You look lovely tonight, Casey. Forgive us our show of jewels—it goes with the territory. You sparkle all on your own."

Casey murmured, "Thank you, Mary." Not knowing where to look, she studied a curiously shaped crystal object above and to the right of her place setting.

Mary followed her gaze. "When Els invited me here for one of his dinner parties, I asked if that was a baby's barbell." She laughed. "His snooty guests were mortified, but he loved it. He explained that it was a knife rest, so you won't soil the fancy tablecloth."

"You worked for him at his company before you were married, didn't you?" asked Worthy, tuning into the conversation.

"I was his secretary. When I first met him, I thought he was a monster. He was so focused on making the business work, I thought all he cared about was money, money, and more money. He did care about it, but only as a way to prove himself. But no matter how much he made, it was never enough …" Her voice trailed off. "How I do prattle on. I'm sure you are not here to relive my romantic beginnings with your father."

"On the contrary," Worthy countered. "I'm very interested in what happened. After all, your romance had quite an impact on my life."

"Let's be clear. My involvement with your father didn't begin until *after* your mother took off with El's' partner," Mary replied, meeting Worthy's stare with a challenge of her own.

"Worthy, this is not the time—" Cherie interrupted. She held out her glass for another refill.

"It's good to clear the air," Mary continued. "Your mother, as you said yourself a moment ago, was a beautiful, vain, and foolish woman, but I never doubted that she loved Els. She had the affair with Clive to get Els' attention. When that ploy didn't work, she took the only thing he cared about—you. It pretty near broke him."

"That's not the story I heard over the years. Beth told me that—"

"Stop!" Cherie demanded. "I'm so sorry, Mary. He's not himself. Please excuse us." Cherie pushed back her chair to leave, signaling Worthy to do the same.

"Sit down," Mary ordered, steel in her voice. "We need to understand one another." Cherie and Worthy exchanged a glance and obeyed. Casey was torn between decking Worthy and crawling under the table, but she was also curious.

"As Els' assistant, I couldn't help but see what everyone in town knew. Beth took out a restraining order against Els, claiming that he had slammed your fingers in a car door and had left you untreated for hours. But," Mary turned to Worthy, "as you know, your mother slammed the car door on you in one of her drunken rages."

Mary paused. She stared straight ahead and spoke as if no one else were in the room. "Beth got custody. Even though she was rolling in money of her own, Els had to pay child support and tuition fees for your private schools," she spat with a bitterness that shocked Casey. "I wrote the checks. Beth tried to reconcile, using you as a pawn, but by then Els and I were together. When she found out about me, she swore Els would never see his son again. He never did."

Mary took a sip of water and continued her monologue. "When Els was dying, he begged me to find you, Worthy. I swore I would. I tried for years to open a dialogue with Beth, but all she wanted was money."

She turned to Cherie, her voice now a whisper. "That's why I was so surprised when you called." She looked over at Worthy, "And why I was so horrified to hear about your accident. I could have lost you without ever having met you."

The silence in the room was shattered by lightning, followed by an enormous clap of thunder. "The gods are bowling," Mary joked to ease the tension as the lights faded out and then back in. "I also worried that I had lost you," she said to Casey. "Imagine my delight when you appeared looking for your father."

Gilma entered with a tray of parfait glasses filled with lemon sherbet. Worthy bent toward Casey and whispered, "It's not dessert. It's to clean your palate for the next course." Casey imagined smearing the "not dessert" across his smug countenance. She didn't bother to conceal the dislike on her face.

Once again, Mary changed course while Gilma refilled the water glasses. "Gilma is studying to be a chef. Describe the entree for us, would you, dear?"

"It's called '*Filet de Boeuf en Croute*,' Beef Wellington," Gilma answered, hesitant at first, her voice gaining confidence as she spoke. "The pre-roasted tenderloin is sliced and filled with mushroom and *foie gras* stuffing and baked in a *brioche* dough."

"We've been languishing in the aroma of the *sauce ragout* that has been simmering in the kitchen for two days," Mary added.

"The recipe suggests red Bordeaux-Medoc to accompany the meal,'" Gilma continued, reaching to a sideboard for a bottle. "May I?"

51

Mary nodded, and Gilma poured wine into her glass for tasting. "Excellent," Mary said, indicating that Gilma pour wine for the other guests.

"You don't drink?" queried Worthy.

"No."

"May I ask why?" Worthy pressed.

"No." Mary let the word drop with finality and set about serving the meal.

They all ate in silence, the only sounds the storm raging outside and the click of cutlery inside.

Chapter Ten

C asey reminded herself to chew. Luckily, she had no dog in this fight, and she could sit back and watch the drama unfold.

"Well, we've pretty much tortured the subject of our relationship to Mary," Cherie said to Casey. "How about you?"

"She's the daughter of my brother Joseph," Mary interceded. "We called him Jed."

"Do you have other family?" Cherie asked Mary.

"Yes. Two sisters and a nephew."

Casey had met one sister, Vera, but was surprised to learn that she had yet another aunt and a first cousin. "Do I have any other relatives I don't know about?"

"No. I'm sorry for all the surprises, Casey. My two older brothers died in Ireland, and my parents are both gone. There were no other children." An expression of sadness and loss washed over Mary's face as she spoke of her family. All four of the diners were silent for a moment.

"Right," Mary said decisively, forcing a mood change. "Gilma wanted to make a baked Alaska for dessert, but I decided upon something much more plebian: tapioca pudding and a biscuit."

"Fish eyes and glue," Casey blurted before she could catch herself. "Sorry, that's what my brother always called it," she said, but Mary was herself again, laughing.

"You have a brother? Now I'm confused. I thought you and the sisters and a nephew were the only family." Cherie was counting noses.

"I have a half-brother on my mother's side. He has no blood relation to

Mary." Cherie's fingers relaxed on the stem of her wine glass. The level of interest in her family surprised Casey.

Mary rose and disappeared into the kitchen.

Cherie and Worthy exchanged yet another heavy look. "I think you've done just about enough for tonight," Cherie hissed.

Worthy shrugged and nodded at Cherie's empty glass. "So have you."

Cherie offered a false smile and signaled for a refill.

Casey felt invisible. In prison, invisible meant safe. Here, it was plain rude. *Too many mind games.*

Mary's voice preceded her into the room. "This is a picture I found in your father's things." Worthy intercepted the picture Mary handed toward Casey. "Amy," he muttered.

"No, Worthy. That's not your Amy. That's my brother Jed and his dog Max. I found it when I was looking for pictures to show Casey."

Casey took the picture from Worthy and found herself smiling at a laughing boy fending off an enormous German shepherd who was intent on kissing his face.

"I'm afraid that all the pictures we have of Jed were taken before he took Orders, so only his early years are represented."

"Took Orders? Your father was a *priest?*" Cherie swiveled in her chair to study Casey. "How did that make your mother feel? Preferring abstinence to her," Cherie continued, slurring slightly.

"Poverty, chastity, and obedience," corrected Mary with an edge.

"My mother couldn't marry him. She was already married."

A flash of blinding light was followed by a thunderclap that shook the window panes. The lights went out. Footsteps ran from the room.

"Shit, I spilled my wine," Cherie swore.

Casey felt liquid running down her arm.

"You've had too much anyway," Worthy responded.

"We've all had quite a night of it," Mary said in a soothing voice. "Gilma will be back with candles momentarily, and the lights will be on soon. It never lasts long, but every time we have a big storm, we lose power. All the trees, you know. I rather enjoy a good storm. It puts us all on equal footing.

I can't see much in the light, but *none* of us can see in the dark."

Casey found the disembodied conversation eerie, but she, like Mary, was a friend of the dark, and she also loved the drama of the big storms. Footsteps returned, followed by a creaking sound she couldn't place. Seconds later, Gilma lit a candle and placed it in the center of the table.

"You hit the target," said Worthy, looking at the splash of red wine soaking into Casey's jacket.

"Oh, dear. Take it off so we can soak it," said Mary gesturing for Gilma to help.

"No, it's okay. Really." Casey balked, but Gilma was already tugging off her jacket. Gilma stopped and gasped, staring down at the scar that curved up Casey's arm.

"Jesus, Mary, and Joseph," whispered Mary.

Cherie and Worthy's heads rotated toward Casey like a matched pair of cats at the scratchings of a mouse. "That's a mean cut," Cherie commented. "Looks like a knife wound," she said, eyeing Casey's arm.

Casey put her hands in her lap, ignoring Cherie's implied question. This was her worst nightmare. *Where was that damn invisibility?*

Worthy eyed her scar with interest. "Did you win?" he asked simply.

Casey glowered at him. "Nobody wins a knife fight."

Gilma draped an afghan over Casey's shoulders.

Cherie let out a blood-curdling scream and pushed back from the table.

IRA and Guinness scrambled to red alert beside Mary. Next to her, Vera sat in her wheelchair, her eyes locked onto Cherie like a hawk measuring its prey. A smile twisted her ruined mouth.

"At ease," Mary said to the lurchers. She placed her hands on their heads, releasing them from their vigil. Both lowered to their haunches slowly, but their ears remained at full alert, tracking the tension in the air. "Meet my sister, Vera Dempsey. Unfortunately, she cannot speak, or she would greet you herself. I'm sorry if she startled you."

Vera's eyes were riveted on Cherie.

"Why is she staring at me?" Cherie blurted, speaking as if Vera were also deaf.

Mary placed her hand on Vera's arm to distract her. Casey noted that she didn't disabuse Cherie of the notion that Vera was deaf. Vera shifted her attention to Worthy until Mary patted her arm a second time. Vera's gaze softened as she nodded to Casey.

"I asked Vera to join us after dinner in hopes that we could take a little tour of the grounds and discuss our plans for the White House, but the weather just didn't cooperate."

"Plans?" Worthy asked.

"Yes. But they will have to wait for another day. We've had a full and somewhat emotional evening. You must be tuckered out after your trip." Mary reached into her pocket and produced two sets of keys, handing them to Gilma who appeared as if summoned. "Gilma will drive you to the guest house and get you sorted out there. It's just around the bend, but the weather is foul, and there are the suitcases as well. The car will be yours to use while you're here."

As Casey watched Mary efficiently close down the evening with a controlled and practiced hand, she doubted if Mary had had any intention of giving them an after-dinner tour. Certainly, she would have known the weather forecast as she waited for the couple to arrive. Just as she knew Worthy would latch onto her mention of "plans" for the White House. Maybe the whole evening had been artfully choreographed.

"Perhaps you will join me Sunday afternoon after you've had a day to recover? The weather is supposed to improve by then. We'll have an informal bite in the alcove where you used to eat or a picnic outside if it's warm enough." Mary pushed back in her chair in a clear signal.

"Yes, of course. We'd like that." Worthy rose and helped Mary with her chair before turning to his wife. *He has some manners*, Casey admitted.

"Thank you for the spectacular dinner. I'm sorry for the mess I made." Cherie nodded to the maroon stain on the lace tablecloth. Despite her apology, Casey didn't feel as generous toward her as she did toward her husband. *Double standard?* She chided herself. Did it help that Worthy was a handsome man with a rakish smile?

"Not to worry."

Cherie nodded stiffly to Vera and then leaned forward and gave Mary an airbrush kiss on the cheek. Gilma led the couple out of the dining room and through the living room.

"Good night," said Casey as the parade reached the front door.

"Oh dear! Pardon my manners. I forgot that you—" Cherie's intonation was perfect and totally insincere. She retraced her steps and awarded Casey with her very own airbrush treatment.

"Are you quite through, love?" Worthy took Cherie's arm and guided her to the door.

"Shut up!" Cherie hissed under her breath, but not out of earshot, as the door closed.

Chapter Eleven

Vera released an ugly cackle and smiled her twisted mouth toward Mary. Mary smiled back. Vera touched her nose twice with her hand and cackled again. "I know, I know," Mary replied as if they were having a conversation. Vera pushed her head forward and bared her broken teeth. "Don't be catty, Vera," Mary scolded, but her eyes twinkled. When Vera mimed Cherie's hair flip, Mary gave up all pretenses and laughed aloud.

"Forgive us. Over the years, we've learned to communicate in our own peculiar shorthand. Sometimes I think we read each other's minds," Mary apologized.

"What was so funny?" Casey had a pretty good idea that Vera was making derogatory signals about Cherie, but wanted Mary to confirm it.

"Ohs aahb," giggled Vera, prompting Mary.

"Nose job," Mary translated. "And capped teeth," she said before Vera had a chance to continue.

Vera caught Casey's eye and lifted her hand to her mouth and sucked in.

"Yes, I noticed she was a smoker, too," Casey confirmed Vera's unspoken question. Vera beat her clubbed hands together in delight.

"Now, now, girls. Be charitable. Cherie is worried to death about her husband. He's clearly not himself, confused and deeply depressed. They're going through a bad patch, as is often the case when couples undergo severe trauma. Cherie has her hands full, just holding him together right now."

Vera rolled her eyes at Casey. Casey wrinkled her nose back.

"It must seem strange to meet Worthy for the first time as an adult. You're very generous to put them up and give them a car." Casey draped the afghan over her chair and gathered her damp jacket to leave.

"Promises haunt you sometimes," Mary said, but then abruptly changed the topic. "Casey, if you have a moment, we could look at a few pictures of Jed that Vera keeps with her. There are more pictures in our family home in West Boylston, but they will have to wait for another day. It's an hour or so away."

"Sure, I'd love that." Finally, Casey would learn about her father.

Mary pushed Vera's chair to the right of Casey's chair at the dining room table. "As I mentioned to you before, all the pictures we have are from the early years up through college." Mary retrieved a cigar box that Vera had tucked beside her in her chair. Inside were dog-eared snapshots, some smeared with fingerprints. Mary handed Casey the pictures one by one, describing the context and the people in each scene. Casey held the pictures so both she and Vera could see them, although she was confident that Vera had looked at them many times before.

"I've labeled them on the back as best I can. This one is Jed at Easter, the year we moved to America. That's the dog who 'followed him home from school,'" she said affectionately. "Mother pretended to believe him. Jed was the baby and was properly pampered by all of us."

Casey studied the young boy with black eyes and shaggy hair. He had a jaunty, cocky smile on his face. In the next picture, Jed posed in a baseball uniform, glove in one hand and bat in the other. The following photo was cut out of a glossy book, probably a school yearbook. Jed smiled angelically at the camera while making rabbit ears behind the boy's head on his right.

"Here's Jed in the boys' choir. He had a beautiful singing voice. Brought tears to our eyes with the old songs, wouldn't he now, Vera?" Casey heard a bit of Irish lilt return as Mary spoke to her sister. "Jed was the only one in the family who could make Mother smile. For years, he was the glue that held us together."

"When I look at these pictures, somehow...why did he become a priest?" Casey asked awkwardly.

"You mean, 'Why would such a normal, happy boy enter the church?'"

Mary asked, voicing Casey's unspoken question. "Don't worry; it's a natural reaction. When he was a boy, we would often find him in church. He said he loved the silence, mostly to tease us—he was the only male in a house full of women: a passel of aunts, a mother, and three sisters—but I think he gained strength from the sanctuary of the church.

"He chose the Jesuits because he was a natural scholar. Like a sponge he was. He tormented the priests with all his questions. He challenged everything. His years at Oberlin were his last struggle. He told me once that his mind raged with theological arguments, but the only place his soul felt at peace was in the church.

"It must be hard to understand. If I had to guess, I would say that leaving your mother was the hardest decision in his life. Entering the church was probably the easiest." Mary shuffled a few pictures. "The rest are class photos. The last one is the four of us children at Jed's high school graduation."

Casey examined each picture in turn, watching Jed grow up before the camera. In the graduation picture, Jed posed in his black robe with one arm around Mary and the other around another woman. Vera sat before them in her wheelchair wearing Jed's graduation cap, looking up at him with adoring eyes. Casey looked more closely. "Isn't she the receptionist from the Jesuit Center?"

"I'm afraid I haven't introduced you properly to your newly found relatives. Agnes is our elder sister. Soon, you must come to West Boylston. We have all of the proper family pictures there."

A tear ran down Vera's cheek as she studied the graduation picture.

"Vera loved Jed so. And he doted on her," Mary explained gently.

Casey reached in her jacket pocket and pulled out an envelope. She'd done some fancy scissor work of her own at the Oberlin College Library the week before she'd left Ohio. Now, she placed the picture she'd clipped in front of Vera. In it, the young man laughed as he walked up the steps to the Conservatory of Music on his hands. A mop of dark hair partially covered his face. Casey's mother, Em, stood to one side, giggling and clapping her hands at his antics. "I made this copy for you," Casey said, adding the picture to the collection in the cigar box.

"Ank. Ooo."

"Thank you," Mary translated automatically, but Casey understood.

Mary reached for a ratty old scrapbook on a side table and handed it to Casey. "Here's another thing I found among a collection of Jed's books."

Casey opened the cover and was stunned to see her own life documented year by year before her. She leafed through a book of school photos and occasional snapshots. "There aren't any pictures of Mom in here," she murmured, disappointed by the omission. "But that would have been against their unwritten rules. I found a collection of letters bound with twine in the attic after she died. One letter said, 'You don't include pictures of yourself, but I don't need them. Your image is forever etched in my heart.'"

The three of them were quiet for a moment before Casey asked her next question. "Did he know I went to prison?"

"I really don't know. When I cleaned out his room, I found the scrapbook and this last picture of him." Mary handed Casey a picture she had been withholding.

Em Cavendish looked deeply into Jed's eyes. He held her hands in his. They could be saying their wedding vows. "The love between them was so clear and deep. Like to break your heart. The picture was taken before the ceremony on the day of his ordination. After the ceremony, Jed belonged to God."

"It's all so sad," said Casey.

Vera put her club on Casey's arm. Casey covered Vera's club with her other hand. The silence between the three of them was heavy but strangely comforting.

"Was your mother unhappy?" Mary asked.

Casey thought for a moment. "No. No, she wasn't. She was always in the middle of some cause, stirring the pot. When I see her, she's usually laughing."

"See her?" Mary prompted.

"I see her face in the clouds. I often hear her laugh, and sometimes I get a whiff of her perfume. So many things bring her back."

"You're rich with memories." Sadness crept into Mary's voice.

"How about your parents?" Casey dared, curious, but worried that she might be overstepping her bounds. How should she regard Mary? As an aunt, a parental figure, an acquaintance, a new friend?

As if reading her mind, Mary reassured her. "Don't worry. Ask all the questions you want. If I don't choose to answer, I won't. Easy enough, eh?"

"Thank you," said Casey, her worries assuaged. But, as the seconds passed, she realized that Mary hadn't answered her question. The sound of a telephone ringing in another part of the house broke the silence. Mary and Vera both looked at the clock on the mantel and then exchanged a private glance. Mary rose and left the room to answer the phone.

Casey scooped up the pictures and leafed through them one more time before returning them to the cigar box, keeping her ears tuned to Mary's conversation in the next room. Actually, there wasn't that much to hear, just a few words from time to time uttered in a slow, measured cadence.

"Sounds like you've got a problem," Mary said with a bitter laugh.

Casey felt Vera watching her. Embarrassed by her own nosiness, she got up. "Time to leave."

Vera shook her head and held up her hand behind her ear. She had been eavesdropping as well.

"No. Not this time. I've got him now." Mary hung up.

As Mary reentered the room, Casey busied herself with the photo album.

Vera's eyebrows rose in a question. Mary nodded with a grim smile. "*Alia jacta est*," she murmured. Vera frowned a question.

"You always were poor at Latin," Mary responded.

But Casey wasn't. *Alia jacta est.* The die is cast.

* * *

After Casey closed the door, she shrugged and rolled her shoulders to relax the tightness in her neck caused by the tension in the house.

The skies had cleared as quickly as they had descended. In the absence of a moon, the blanket of stars seemed close enough to touch. She walked through the soft night quiet toward her car, reveling in the smell of the newly washed earth.

Alia jacta est. All evening, undercurrents and eddies had swirled just below the surface. At times, Casey had had the sensation of sinking into a morass of secrets and sorrow, sucked into the vortex against her will. Mary seemed intent on including Casey in her plans, but Casey thought not. Better to beg off Sunday.

They had all been playing roles, walking around on a fantastic set, watching each other, waiting for cues before delivering their lines. So different, and, she had to admit, exciting and intriguing. But nothing good would come of this convergence of characters.

She was so deep in thought she almost walked past the Muttmobile. She'd come to find her father, not this weird mismatch of people. You couldn't make this stuff up. A bearded artist with a ruined hand who collected cans, a diabetic, nearly blind Irish widow who rattled around in a mansion with her horribly disfigured sister in a wheelchair, a concussed prodigal stepson missing a finger, and his wife, too perfect to believe. For the first time in eleven years, Casey was the normal one.

Chapter Twelve

Although Casey had had two days to dream up a suitable excuse to avoid Mary's Sunday afternoon picnic, she found herself sitting cross-legged on the grass in the shade of the huge beech tree behind the White House, half listening to small talk. Mary and Vera sat on lawn chairs to the left of Casey, Cherie and Worthy to her right.

She wasn't sure she wanted any prolonged contact with Mary and her crazy family of misfits, but she harbored a sort of morbid curiosity about them, not unlike rubbernecking a bad accident. She was surprised at her attraction to the trappings and habits of the rich and the lure of outrageous wealth. Worthy and Cherie were members of the beautiful and privileged jet set she'd only read about. Mary and Vera, Jackson, and the late Jed were equally intriguing.

From the vantage point atop the hill, Casey could see all the way to Boston, thirteen miles away. That is if she could keep her eyes open. She hoped Mary would get to her plan soon. Sunday afternoon lethargy was winning over chitchat. Her eyes drooped and she struggled to keep her head from swan dives.

"Is that the new wholesome heartland look?" asked Cherie.

It took Casey a moment to realize Cherie was speaking to her. In jeans, t-shirt, and sneakers, Casey looked like she'd crashed the wrong party. She rewarded Cherie with an insincere all-American smile.

The couple before her had a different take on the word "informal" than she did. Cherie languished in a lounge chair, her well-toned midriff showing between a snug, knit top and low-slung hip huggers that accentuated long shapely legs. Delicate pink toenails peeked out from soft leather sandals.

Worthy sported a shirt with a preppy buttoned-down collar and slacks with creases intact. He'd rolled up the sleeves in the afternoon heat, revealing tan, sinewy arms. Little blonde tufts of hair on his fingers reminded her of George. *Don't go there.* She stared at Worthy's stump to force the issue. She refused to fall for another married man's hands again. She was trainable.

Worthy got up and stretched and walked behind her. Casey was instantly alert, muscles tensed, awareness heightened to a potential threat. *Relax, girl, you're not Inside anymore.* She resented him for making her self-conscious. She liked to see all of the players on the board. Shifting to the side, she glanced over her shoulder. Worthy lounged against the trunk of the beech tree, watching her.

Heat rose in her face. She turned back quickly and looked straight into Cherie's level gaze. Cherie leaned toward Casey and whispered. "Don't bother. He prefers blondes."

"He's safe. I prefer gentlemen," Casey shot back. If they were cats, she could clear the air with a single vicious swipe. Alas, she'd have to cloak her animosity in the veneer of civility. Worthy helped himself to a handful of nuts from a small table laden with finger sandwiches and crudités and sat next to Cherie.

Unaware of the undercurrents, Mary launched into her program. "Agnes, Vera, and I have come up with a plan to simplify our lives. For the past few years, I have been trying to scale down. This place is too much for me, especially when I'm sick, and at those times, Vera doesn't get the care she needs. In a nutshell, we've decided to form a non-profit corporation that is a self-sustaining venture. We're still in the planning phase, deciding..."

Vera touched Mary gently and then made a rolling motion with her clubs that suggested that she "back up."

"Sorry. I get ahead of myself." Mary sounded as if she were presenting a formal report at a board meeting.

Cherie lit a cigarette and leaned back in her lounge chair like an actress out of an old movie, releasing a slow plume of smoke into the air. Worthy shifted position to avoid the smoke wafting his way. Casey couldn't see the look he gave Cherie, but she responded with a defiant "up yours" look and flicked ashes on the grass, barely missing the cooler with ice and sodas next to her chair.

Both of their heads snapped forward at Mary's next statement.

"I've sold my interest in Els' company and am disposing of our other properties. We now have the wherewithal to fund a non-profit corporation. It's time to move forward."

"Other properties?" asked Worthy with a frown, taking notes like a good student.

"Oh, I can fill you in on all of that later. We had houses and properties in the United States and around the world. Whenever Els thought he might like to return to a location, he bought a place to stay. It's taken me seven years to liquidate."

Cherie sighed and took another long pull on her cigarette. Worthy leaned forward and nodded his appreciation for Mary's efforts.

"You've come at the perfect moment. Just last week, Vera and I made a list of what we needed to accomplish next, and at the top of the list we wrote 'lawyer' and 'nurse.' Obviously, I have access to legal counsel and medical services, but if you'd be willing to stay on for a bit and help us out, we could provide employment and a temporary place to live."

Worthy nodded thoughtfully. Cherie ground out her cigarette in the grass. She seemed to be trying to get her husband's attention, but he was focused on Mary.

Casey watched the dysfunctional quartet posture for one another's benefit. They were still at the sniffing dog stage, circling and testing each other, interested but wary. *I got no dog in this fight*, she reminded herself, remembering one of LouAnne's favorite sayings. Nevertheless, she felt a growing sense of exclusion as Mary continued. She was painfully aware of the gulf between herself and the couple before her.

"After Father died in Ireland, Mother brought us to America. We moved into a big old Victorian house in West Boylston with our grandmother and her four sisters. To make a long story short, the older generations died off, and Vera came to live here with me. Now, Vera, Agnes, and I have decided to sell our old family home in West Boylston.

Vera nodded her approval.

"Casey, I'm hoping I can convince you to help us prepare the house in West Boylston for sale. It would be a way for you to learn about your father's side of the family and also a way to make money while you're looking for work. I could hire someone to go in and gut the place, but there's so much history there that would be lost.

"The upstairs is in a sorry state. Every time one of the aunts would die, they'd just close the door. The old folks hadn't the energy to sort out the detritus of their siblings."

Oh goody. Casey could still conjure the parched old-woman smell that had permeated her great aunt's house before she had cleaned it up. Imagine the trash of five poor old maids. Her reaction must have been written all over her face, because Mary reassured her before she could refuse. "I know you will have lots of questions. There's no rush other than my own impatience to move forward. Think about it, and let's talk further in a few days."

Casey remembered finding curios and little treasures at the bottoms of drawers, in cabinets that hadn't been opened in years, and even in the freezer compartment of the refrigerator where she'd found a box of her Aunt Mae's jewelry. Six people had lived and died in the home in West Boylston. There was a good possibility that a few of their earthly treasures remained behind closed doors.

Worthy shifted in his chair. "How much of the estate do you intend to tie up in this project?" he asked, getting back to business.

"We haven't firmed up the plan yet, but we'll set aside enough for the sisters to live on. Certainly, we don't need all of the land. We could donate the lower forty to the Welton Land Trust and save a bundle on taxes.

"We want to simplify our lives and leave a legacy that's a tribute to Els as well as our family. Money ruins lives. We have become isolated because of it. My sisters are the only people I trust. We want to get out of here while we have some good years left. If I were to leave the estate to an individual, or individuals, it would be an act of hate, not love."

"Try me," quipped Worthy with a wolfish grin. They all laughed, but the sound was hollow.

"I know I'm preachy on the subject, but I feel very strongly about it. Money killed Els—he could never get enough of it. More, more, more. It consumed him." She paused. "And us."

"Well, I, for one, am intrigued by your project," Worthy assured her. "How is the property zoned?"

"Good question. The property is around forty acres total. The house and three or four acres around it are residential and would need to be rezoned. Much of the land beyond has some sort of environmental zoning. And, the old train station is commercial." She smiled at the last.

Worthy nodded. "So, people could live here and make or grow things and sell them in the station."

"You've got it."

"Who are these people?" asked Cherie.

"We haven't decided yet. We're leaning toward rehabilitation, a halfway house for mental patients, or a home for the disabled. We could serve at least one of these groups with our plan."

"What do you have for legal counsel?" Worthy asked.

"I've used Els' lawyer for my will and the odd legal bit, but I don't think the firm could handle this project."

"Are you qualified?" Casey asked Worthy.

"Of course." He gave her a withering look. He turned to Mary. "I can help in the planning stages, but you'll need a Massachusetts firm to finalize the project."

Casey sat back, angry with herself for the dumb question and at Worthy for his condescending response. She was the only one who didn't know Worthy's qualifications. Mary would have investigated them, the same way she had Casey. With a growing sense of isolation, Casey told herself that she wasn't interested in Mary's money or her plans. Nevertheless, she resented Worthy and Cherie's assumed place on the inside track.

"What do you need in the way of nursing?" Cherie asked.

"Well, not a lot at present, but it's important. I'm a type one diabetic. It's become obvious that I will need someone close by who can give me injections if I have a hypo, and of course, at those times, care for Vera."

"So, on call, but not full-time?"

"Yes. I could hire a local nurse to come in, but why add more staff if you're here and willing? Please, though, feel free to refuse. It wouldn't be a problem."

"No, no. It sounds like the perfect solution to me." Cherie smiled sweetly at Mary and managed to hold the expression long enough to include Vera.

Gag. Enough. "Mind if I let the dogs out?" Casey asked.

Chapter Thirteen

Casey had greeted the dogs upon arrival before they were penned for the party.

Mary smiled. "No. They'd love it. Take them for a romp in the field if you want. We have an invisible fence, so they won't run off."

Invisible fence? Around forty acres?

Casey walked to the garage, released the latch to the pen, and was instantly smothered with dog kisses. She giggled and pushed the dogs away, and ran down the steep slope to the open field. The dogs thundered past her, romping and wrestling, chasing one another in car-length strides across the meadow. Every so often, they gamboled back to check on her.

After a few seconds, she got her stride and loped along a narrow path winding through the tall grass. She breathed in the drying, ripe smells of fall. The sun warmed her hair and shoulders while a soft breeze cooled her face. The chirring of a cicada accompanied the soft padding of her shoes. Fat grasshoppers jumped off the path at the very last second. At the edge of the meadow, she came across a small stream. She shed her sneakers, rolled up her pantlegs, and waded into the icy cold water, picking her way on stones until she reached the far bank. A stand of willow trees beside the stream created a secret hollow beneath a drooping canopy. She ducked inside and leaned against a trunk to catch her breath.

Through weeping green branches, she watched people sipping cool drinks on the lawn of the magnificent white house on the hill. Imagine the reaction of the townsfolk when the White House became a halfway house or a shelter? Mary was taunting them. Altruism, yes, but payback as well.

Casey loved it and wished she had a part to play. She could do without Cherie, but ... *Slow down, girl.* This morning she didn't want anything to do with any of them. This afternoon she was feeling left out of the loop. Admit it. Mary's ideas excited her more than any of the jobs she'd applied for in the past week. Mary's plan was a daring, in-your-face, downright cool project.

Casey whistled for the dogs. Nothing. She whistled again and then caught sight of two specks in the distance that grew larger by the second. They sure could run. Moments later, they splashed through the stream and shook themselves next to her.

"Thanks, guys." She shook herself in imitation. "Get a drink." As she waded back through the stream, the dogs dashed past, wetting her a second time. On the far bank, Guinness pranced just out of reach with a mouthful of shoe, pleased with herself, teasing her new toy human. IRA settled a few yards away, chomping the heel of his prize.

"You come here!" she commanded, trying not to laugh. "Now!" Guinness made a few dodge-and-weave moves to let Casey know who was in control and then let her wrestle the shoe from her mouth. "IRA. Come!" IRA cocked his head to one side. He rose slowly and came to her side, sans sneaker.

"Devil dog," she muttered, claiming her shoe, but she tousled his head affectionately as she walked back to the house, flanked by panting dogs. Casey loved their company and the wide-open field and Little Mother. She'd miss them. She wouldn't be able to paint at the train station if they converted it for commercial use. She looked up at the White House and admitted that she'd even miss Mary and Vera, weird as they were. She wasn't at all sure she wanted anything to change.

Casey's laugh startled the dogs. She'd covered the full spectrum: from wanting to get far away as fast as possible, to feeling left out of the excitement, to wanting things to remain the same. "Maybe I'm the crazy one after all," she chided herself.

Guinness butted her hand for a pat. "C'mon, you lazy slugs. Let's go," Casey broke away from the dogs, running toward the house. They overtook her in seconds and ran circles around her until she let them into their pen.

71

She filled their bowls with water and dry food before rejoining Mary and Vera under the tree.

She dropped to the grass. "Solved the problems of the world yet?" she asked, trying to sound light and unconcerned.

"No, but we're making progress," responded Mary with a twinkle in her eye. "How about you?"

Casey thought she heard a bit of a challenge in Mary's voice. "Going to the dogs," Casey laughed. "Where is West Boylston? And where are your co-conspirators?" Cherie and Worthy were nowhere to be seen.

"Inside. Cherie asked for the bathroom, but I think they wanted a moment to settle an issue they didn't want to bother us about. They are both rather strong-willed individuals."

You are too kind. "You and Els were pretty strong-willed yourselves. How did you manage?"

Mary chuckled. She glanced over at Vera who snored softly, head resting on her chest. Mary wiped Vera's chin with a napkin. "Come. I'll show you." She led Casey inside to a china cabinet in the formal dining room. Inside was a large crystal punch bowl and three cups.

"Els and I were given a *really* ostentatious punch bowl with twenty cups for a wedding gift. Much gaudier than this set. When we argued—and we had horrendous arguments about the business, about Beth and Worthy, about how much salt to put in the potatoes—the offended party would grab a cup and take it out back."

Mary unhooked a cup and led Casey back outside. She walked to the garage where slate steps led down to a gazebo shielded by a protective circle of hemlocks. On the first step, she pretended to throw the cup onto the step.

"It took us fifteen years to get to the punch bowl." Mary shook her head and smiled. "That anniversary, he gave me a new set 'for the next fifteen.' As you can see, we were well into this new set when he died."

From inside the house they heard Cherie's voice. "What the hell are you up to? You don't do brunettes."

"They don't realize the windows are open," Mary said under her breath.

"I haven't had much experience, but I'm open-minded," Worthy countered. "She looks delicious. What the hell do you care?"

"I'm not sharing all this with anyone else."

"Then I suggest you keep your voice down and get your head on straight."

"You do your Ranger Rick, legal eagle thing, sweetie. I'll take care of the rest, and I'll find you another little blondie dessert. And you can tell Mary I have no intention of changing that freak's diapers. Tell her—"

Mary smashed the cup on the slate. "Dammit! Casey, can you help me? I've made a mess," she called out in a voice meant for all ears.

The back door slammed. In seconds, Worthy appeared with an abashed smile. "Let me get that." He took pieces of glass from Casey and knelt to pick up the rest. "I'm afraid we're feeling the strain of the times. And," he admitted, "my bride was a bit nervous about the meeting and consumed her weight in alcohol before we came this afternoon. I'm not sure that she'll be the most reliable candidate for a nurse right now."

Nicely done. His artful recovery let Cherie off the hook with Vera. Casey watched Worthy turn his charm on Mary. How endearing and vulnerable, sucking up to her maternal instincts. Would Mary recognize the lie? Cherie was stone sober.

Mary straightened her blouse and pushed a strand of hair from her face. Casey left her basking in Worthy's spotlight and picked up her backpack. Time to go. LouAnne and Rosie had agreed to help clean up the apartment before they packed up and left.

Cherie had resumed her position in the lounge chair. She and Vera studied one another in silence. Neither blinked. *More childish games.*

Without looking away, Cherie addressed Casey. "Are you going to muck out the stables for them?"

Casey ignored her.

Cherie lowered her voice to a whisper. "Kind of strange, a whole house full of Catholics and so few offspring. I thought mackerel snappers bred like rabbits."

"And I thought you were told to mind your manners."

"Manners would be wasted."

"Must you go?" Mary called across the lawn. Her voice held a note of surprise and disappointment. "I thought we could throw a few steaks on the grill later..." Mary and Worthy took their respective chairs. Mary let the suggestion ride the silence, giving Casey the clear signal that she was expected to stay.

"I'm sorry, but I have plans with my roommates."

"Roommates? Surely you see them often. If you give them a call, they'll understand."

When Casey didn't reply, Mary continued. "At least you can sit and chat for a little longer, can't you?"

Casey hesitated. "Sure." She'd appease Mary with fifteen minutes and then bow out. She settled into her place in the grass.

"Who are these people you live with?" Mary's petulant tone hinted of disapproval. She was used to getting her own way.

"LouAnne, an old friend from Ohio, and her, uh, brother, Rosie," Casey answered simply, wondering how much Mary already knew.

"Three of you live together? What is it, some hippie commune? Isn't that a little strange?" Cherie peppered her with questions, eager to fuel Mary's disapproval.

Casey cast her eyes about the assembled company with a naughty grin. "To tell the truth, my roommates are beginning to look positively normal."

Mary hooted her approval, signaling the return of her sense of humor.

Cherie persisted. "LouAnne sounds Ohio, like Stephanie Jo or Mary Sue."

Casey smiled sweetly at Cherie. "Yep," she agreed. "Not a lot of Stephanie Joe Peabodys, or Mary Sue Cabots hanging on the Welton town green."

Cherie leaned over and rummaged around in the cooler, taking her time to formulate a reply. Moments later she emerged with a can of ginger ale. "Open this for me, would you, Cassie? Pop tops are murder on a manicure." Cherie held out the can.

"Name's 'Casey.'" She extended her hand but didn't move to take the can that was just out of reach.

"Here, let me," Worthy jumped up, surprising everyone. He snatched the can from Cherie and held it at arm's length as if it were a bomb. He whirled, pointed it toward Cherie, and popped the top.

Liquid spewed forth like a fire hose. Cherie saw it coming but couldn't move fast enough. "Nooooo!" she howled. The spray flattened her hair, ran down her face, and drenched her blouse.

"Not nice to shake the can, my dear," Worthy scolded, handing her the overflowing can. She grabbed it and threw it back at him.

Wimpy throw. Worthy dodged easily. Casey seized the moment and sprang to her feet. "Gotta go. Thanks again, Mary, for a lovely afternoon."

"Come for lunch tomorrow," Mary ordered.

"Yasm." Casey grinned and gave Mary a mock salute. Vera winked at Casey, and Casey threw her a kiss. "Toodles," she said to Cherie and Worthy. "It's an Ohio expression," she explained, wrinkling her nose at Cherie as she bolted for the Muttmobile.

Chapter Fourteen

C asey, LouAnne, and Rosie sang along with tunes on the oldies' radio station as they prepared Sunday night dinner. When a favorite came on, Rosie cranked up the volume high enough that the bass reverberated on the linoleum floor. Casey fished two strands of spaghetti out of the boiling pot and flung them against the splash guard behind the burners.

"What you doin' girlfren?" LouAnne exclaimed.

"If they stick, the pasta is done," Casey explained.

The pasta wiggled and fell to the stove. LouAnne picked up a piece and chewed it. "Not done," she agreed.

Rosie danced around the large kitchen playing sous chef. He had prepared the garlic bread and chopped up vegetables for a salad, and now his only remaining duty was to top off their wine glasses and entertain Casey and LouAnne. No one was feeling any pain.

Next to Casey, LouAnne stirred her "World Famous Sauce." Earlier, Casey had caught her adding a teaspoon of ground coffee and a cinnamon stick to the pot.

As Elvis began crooning, Rosie thrust his hips forward, lowered his lids to sultry, and lip-synced "Love Me Tender" into a beer bottle. Casey swooned. Moments later, LouAnne stomped toward her brother, waving a wooden spoon, singing "These Boots Are Made for Walking" with Nancy Sinatra.

Casey hadn't laughed so hard in years. She grabbed an empty wine bottle for her microphone, but the next song was "A Bridge Over Troubled Waters." The melody transported her to a simpler time and hit her with a sudden, unexpected stab of loss. *I've had too much to drink.* Not wanting to spoil the mood, she rose and carried the wine bottle to the wastebasket in the corner of the kitchen. Just before she dropped the bottle into the bin, she spied two telltale empties of commercial spaghetti sauce.

"Test the pasta again for me, will you, Lou?" Casey called out over the music to distract Lou while she retrieved the empty bottles.

At the stove, Rosie dipped his finger into LouAnne's World Famous Sauce. LouAnne captured two strands of pasta and backed up a few strides. With great fanfare, she wound up like a major league pitcher, hesitating for the signal from the splashguard, shaking her head until she got the signal for the pitch she wanted. Just before she hurled the pasta, Casey raised the empty sauce bottles over her head. "Lookie what I found!"

Startled, LouAnne threw a wild pitch and hit Rosie squarely in the temple. The strands stuck.

"Done!" LouAnne exclaimed.

Rosie howled, picking pasta off his head. He winged the pieces at LouAnne. She ducked, and Casey caught the strands on the nose.

In instant retaliation, Casey pelted Rosie with a handful of black olives.

"Fast little honky!" Rosie dodged LouAnne, picked an olive off the floor, and hurled it back. Casey fended off the first olive with her hand. Rosie kept up the barrage, adding cherry tomatoes when the olives ran out. Casey grabbed the Italian bread and used it as a bat, splatting a juicy double over Rosie's shoulder. From behind, LouAnne dumped a bowl of Parmesan cheese into Rosie's hair and ruffed it in, turning it into a punk cream Afro.

The ensuing food fight was fast and furious, involving avocado, olive oil, more pasta, and eventually some of the World Famous Sauce. The battle ended when Rosie wrestled his sister to the floor and tickled her until she begged for mercy. Casey watched them tussle from across the room. She could escalate the battle by creeping up behind him with a few pats of butter, but her sides ached from laughing. Instead, she poured herself a glass of wine and gnawed on what was left of the bat.

"Uncle!" LouAnne surrendered, but Rosie didn't stop. "Uncle!" she gasped. "Stop!" she begged when he continued tickling. "Uncle Tom!"

"That's better, Sis." Rosie released her and helped her up.

Together they surveyed the carnage. A skinny worm of pasta dangled from the overhead light. Tomato seeds clung to the walls. The drab linoleum floor shone with a thin coat of oil.

"We'll have to paint. We've pretty much wrecked the place," Casey said. She tossed the end of the bat onto the floor and watched it co-mingle with sauce, squashed olives, and grated cheese.

"Already a wreck," said LouAnne.

"Doesn't matter. We be outta here soon, anyway," Rosie grumbled from the stove, shoveling sauce into his mouth.

Instant quiet. "Soon? How soon?" Casey repeated. She had known something was up when LouAnne had asked twice if she would make it for dinner, but she hadn't expected this. No one spoke. "Okay, who's going to explain?" she asked as the silence dragged on.

"We been meaning to talk to you," LouAnne began. "The shelter's moving to a big old Victorian home in Jamaica Plain. They need a couple to be housemother and handyman. Free room and board and a car."

When Casey didn't reply, LouAnne forged on. "We'd ask you to join us, but the apartment is just a big attic with a bath."

"Hold on. Rewind. Did you say a 'couple'?"

"Yeah. Bummer. Gotta get married," Rosie interjected.

"*Married?*"

"Shit, girl, don't get hinkty on me. Do what you gotta do."

"What's the big deal?" LouAnne fished a gold wedding band out of her jeans pocket and slipped it on. "What do you think?"

"But legally, he's your *brother*. How can you—"

"He look like me?" LouAnne challenged, rising to her full height, towering over Casey like a Valkyrie.

"You all look alike," Casey teased.

Lou tried to hold her fierce glare, but couldn't suppress her laugh. "Truth? We were raised under the same roof, but we're not blood brother and sister."

Casey stared at her friends, slack-jawed. And then hiccupped.

Rosie mimicked her dainty hiccup. In seconds the room sounded like a mad frog farm.

After the second wave of silliness passed, they scavenged what they could from the pots and sat at the round table in the kitchen corner. "When will you go?" Casey asked.

Rosie and LouAnne exchanged a quick glance. Apparently, LouAnne lost the mental coin toss. "Soon as we can pack up," she said in a soft, apologetic voice. "Be good to move in before they change their minds."

Casey nodded. She felt her friend's eyes on her, but couldn't meet them. She studied the blue flower pattern on her plate.

"Probably have to kiss the security deposit goodbye, but we can share another month's rent. Give you time to find a roommate or a place of your own. I know it's awful sudden and all, but we just couldn't pass it by. We'll help you with this mess," she added lamely.

Casey looked up at Lou and was surprised to see tears glistening on her cheeks. Stifling her own sob, Casey hugged her.

"Ah, shit," said Rosie, enveloping both of them in his arms.

Chapter Fifteen

M onday morning Casey read the *Boston Globe's* apartment
listings in search of an apartment she could afford without
taking a roommate or three. Other than LouAnne and Rosie,
she didn't know anyone in the area. She'd really love to live in a place all
her own where she could lounge in her jammies with a glass of wine in the
evening, reading a book and listening to music. A quiet place where she
could write and draw. Much as she would have enjoyed trying city living,
Boston's prices were outrageous. She'd circled three possible listings when
the phone rang. She picked it up hoping that one of the apartment owners
she'd called earlier was calling her back.

"Well, girlfrien', we got us an opportunity, and a bitty problem." LouAnne
jumped right in without announcing who she was. "'Member, I told you
Mr. No was going to take both a month's security and charge us an extra
month?"

"Uh huh," Casey nodded. Mr. No was their nickname for the landlord.

"Well, he called, all sunshine this morning with an offer we can't resist.
Now, it's not bad, but we'll hafta haul ass to take advantage. No has a live
one—a couple—married students who have some kind of big hound and
need a pre-wrecked place that allows pets. If we be out by October first,
No'll return our security deposit *and* let us out of the last month on the
lease."

Casey flipped her calendar. "October first is a week from Wednesday—"

"You stay with us until you find a spot. No problem, but it just can't be
permanent like we said. I can explain to the people at work. They want us

so bad, won't be a worry. I know it's quick, but, two months' rent's nothing to sneeze at. You take one month; we get the other."

"Did you mention the spaghetti and all? Like a few rug burns and stains, and a boarded over window in the back?"

"I said the place could do with a lick of paint. He said he was planning to do that anyway and was putting in new appliances, too. The old ones can be ours if we haul them away. He must be really gouging the new folks."

A glaze slid over Casey's eyes. She wanted to go home. She just didn't have one. She forced herself to tune into Lou's words.

"...You probably will need a toaster and an iron, and maybe a fridge, and we never used the vacuum. Could be a godsend, honey. Hell, we can even yank a couple phones."

The silence on Casey's end was growing, but she couldn't speak.

"Think about it, girl. No way you can stay in that dump. Got no protection there without big Lou and Rosie. You're better off with us for a bit. Besides, you ain't got much to move."

For the first time, LouAnne's end of the line was silent.

Casey drew a long breath. "Don't worry about me, Lou. Give me five minutes. I'll be ready for the new plan, I promise. You just surprised me. You're right about the apartment. I don't want to rattle around there without you guys. As long as you *really* don't mind me sleeping on the floor until I find a place...."

"Thanks, sugar. Hey, if a lady named Susan calls for a reference, you've known me since college. It's true. We met the year you were supposed to graduate."

Casey was confident that Lou could conjure a full-blown life story, one close to the truth for ease of memory, but without a few of the less appealing details. Like the fact that she had stabbed her husband to death.

"Oh, that's another thing. You know anywhere we can get us some pack up boxes?"

"Let me think on it and call you back, Lou." She didn't want to talk. She'd rather crawl into a dark hole, but seconds after she hung up, the phone rang again. She couldn't afford to ignore it.

"Casey Cavendish. How may I help you?"

"Casey, it's Mary. Is this a good time to talk?"

Casey sighed. "Fine." What could Mary want now? "Sorry to be so formal. I was waiting for a return call. Actually, you beat me to the punch. My next call was to thank you for the lovely dinner Friday night and the beautiful afternoon yesterday." Close to the truth. There was good food Friday, and Sunday was a perfect fall day.

"You are too kind. Personally, I thought Friday night was very strange and Sunday, even stranger. Listen, I was serious about having you out to the place in West Boylston next weekend, but I overstepped asking you to help pack it up. I can see why a young lady would be less than thrilled sorting through old people's remainders. But I thought you might be interested in seeing some of the family photos."

"I'd love to," Casey replied honestly.

"Agnes, Vera, and I are going out there this afternoon to tag a few things to include in the White House estate sale."

It took Casey a moment to remember that Agnes was Mary's sister, the receptionist she'd met at the Jesuit Center.

Mary prattled on. "Would you care to join us? I know it's last minute and all—" She let the invitation hang.

"I wish I could, Mary, but I just learned that my roommates and I have to move out of our apartment before the first of the month, so I'll be spending time on the telephone looking for a new apartment."

"Oh, my goodness. Why so sudden?"

Casey responded to the compassion in Mary's voice and told her all—well, most—of the details surrounding the move.

"Do you need anything? How can I help?"

"Do you know where I could get some cardboard boxes for packing?" Casey asked, remembering Lou's request.

"Sure. At the dump. I get everything there."

The dump? Mary? Casey's mind reeled at the idea of a rich Welton widow dump picking.

"I'll get you a sticker for the dog car. The dump has a little building where people leave books, bikes, computers, appliances—all manner of things they don't need. You'll probably need a few things. Might as well get them free. Stop by this afternoon, and I'll give you your new sticker. What's your license plate number?

"Mutt01."

"See you then, dear."

Casey was about to demur when she heard a dial tone. Mary sure had a way of insinuating herself into her life. Then again, Casey liked the idea of having a sticker. Free goodies in a town full of rich folks' discards could be a godsend. She had a few hours to make calls. She dialed the next number on her list of possible apartments.

Twelve calls later, Casey let out a long sigh. Five answering machines said to leave a message. Four apartments were spoken for, one was too big and out of her range, leaving two possibles, one on a main drag over a cigar store and the other with a bath shared with other renters. She'd had enough of gang showers.

It was a little early to go to Mary's, but she was going stir-crazy and needed a break. She decided to visit her favorite little station and sketch for a half hour. She hopped into the Muttmobile and drove to Welton with visions of sugarplums and free rockers dancing in her head. The dump sounded too good to be true, but there was serious money in Welton. She passed through town and out to Church Street. As she drove down the hill to the station, she slowed and frowned at a group of cars and pickup trucks in front of the building.

She parked off to the side but didn't get out. Workmen crawled over the station like ants. A radio blared country music loud enough to be heard above the hammering, sawing, and drilling and the playful banter of workmen shouting to each other. With an unexpected twinge of loss, Casey realized that Mary was giving the station a much-needed overhaul.

She looked under the Church Street bridge for Jackson but didn't spot him or his bicycle. She looked closer and spied a tarp and the kitty dish, a small pile of cans, and another of bottles.

She took out her sketchbook and turned to her earlier drawing of the station. It was no longer hers. Never had been. But she'd secretly owned the abandoned station in her mind, a tiny little house of her own, and now that dream was quashed along with many other silly dreams of the past.

Get over it, girlfriend, Lou's voice chided.

Go to hell, Lou. Too many bossy voices telling her what to do.

A burly man naked to the waist sauntered toward the car amid catcalls from the other workers. He draped his arms over the roof, exposing hairy armpits and a beefy gut that hung over low-slung cutoff jeans. "This here's a construction site, ma'am," he drawled down to her, speaking to her chest. The man's belly filled the driver's window. Multi-colored snakes, dragons and scorpions tattooed his arms, but he wasn't half as scary as some of the women in prison. She drew breath through her mouth to avoid choking on his manly odors.

"I need to check a few dimensions." Casey shoved open the door, catching the man off guard. She marched toward the station, flipping to a fresh page in her sketchbook.

Quickly he regained his swagger and strode after her. "Now, listen here, you can't—"

Casey turned quickly, causing him to stop short or barrel into her. Her nose reached the height of his offending armpits. He glared down at her, and then did what most any good old boy would do in an awkward moment. He scratched his lower belly and hitched his crotch to rearrange his privates.

Casey struggled to keep a straight face. She threw her head back and swiped her nose with the back of her hand. Then she scratched her belly and hitched her crotch.

Workers on the roof whistled and stomped. "Get 'em, tiger!" Armpit made an elaborate bow to cover the rising color in his neck and face and gestured toward the station, "After you."

As she reached the steps to the station, a taxi rolled up the drive to the White House. "There's my boss. Gotta go." She returned to her car, relieved that she didn't have to play out the charade. She drove up the hill and through the gate without looking back. She parked in front of the White House and regained her composure before approaching the house and ringing the bell.

"Hi, I was just checking out the work you're doing on the station," Casey explained moments later as Mary answered the door to the White House.

"Come on in for a sec. The inside of the building doesn't need much, but the outside was in bad shape. I hope you'll like the new buckskin color."

Casey nodded and changed the subject to avoid admitting her dismay at changes to the station. "I didn't see Can ... Jackson at the station today."

"He's busy helping me out with the cars and dogs and a few other things," Mary said as she led Casey to the servants' quarters. Casey was disappointed to see Cherie draped over a chair in Mary's kitchen. They glanced at each other but didn't speak.

"I got the sticker," said Mary. "Affix it on the inside of the driver's window, and you're good to go. One other thing you both need to know—and you can tell Worthy—" she said to Cherie, "is the code for the gate and the house alarms. You'll need it when Vera and I are in West Boylston. It's the same for all: "PREZ or 7739, whichever is easier for you to remember."

Mary rummaged around in a drawer beside the sink and came up with two keys with red yarn ties. "Once you turn the key, you have sixty seconds to punch in the code on the pad beside the door. When you leave, enter in the code and close the door within sixty seconds. If the alarm goes off, just punch in the code to disarm it. If you wait more than ten seconds, the police will come. There's a number pad beside the gate as well for cars we own that don't have remote entry buzzers. Same code: PREZ. Easy enough, eh?"

"How often do you change the code?" Cherie asked.

"I should change it every month, but the truth is, I never have. I'd have to read the manual, wherever that is. Besides, I like PREZ."

The doorbell rang. Mary kept talking while she walked out of the room. "That'll be Agnes with the van." She returned with two small overnight bags. "Cherie, help me load Vera and her chair into the van."

Cherie gave Vera a derisive smile and shrugged. Vera grimaced back.

No love lost there.

Casey stepped forward and took the bags from Mary and followed the procession to the front door. She instantly recognized the hatchet-like nose of the woman waiting impatiently as the receptionist at the Jesuit Center. Mary quickly introduced her as her sister Agnes. Using the automatic lift, Mary and Cherie loaded Vera inside the van.

"Cherie, we won't need your help again until we return mid-week."

Cherie gave Mary a mock salute and brushed by Casey without a word.

Mary got in the passenger seat, rolled down the window, and beckoned Casey closer for a word. "Come stay with us next weekend and help us sort things out. We'd love to have you. Basic work should be finished on the station by the time we return, and you can stay there if you'd like. It's small, but really charming inside. You'll like it." Before Casey could respond, she'd closed the window, and the van drove off.

Casey drove back to the apartment, deep in thought. She hadn't known Mary more than a week, but in that time, she'd been impressed at how easily Mary got around for a person who was sight-impaired. A person who didn't know of her disability might not notice anything at all unless it was dark, or Mary had to read something.

Casey recalled the smug look on Cherie's face as she stared at Vera. Casey could taste her dislike for Cherie. She rolled down her window, checked her mirrors to make sure there weren't any people or cars around, and spit. She felt better and a little naughty.

She drove on, thinking about the strange events of the past hour. For someone wallowing in money, Mary certainly wasn't living the high life. She had said that money was a curse, but surely she could have hired a nurse for Vera before Cherie appeared, and she didn't need Worthy for a lawyer. Yet she welcomed them with open arms and gave them a place to stay. And why have them live in the servant's quarters and frequent the dump for treasures?

And why was she so friendly and generous to someone she barely knew? Casey might be Jed's daughter, but Mary had her hands full just staying alive and caring for Vera. Casey didn't have the answers, but weird as the situation was, she was attracted and intrigued by Mary, although she wasn't sure how much she should trust her.

Chapter Sixteen

Late Monday afternoon, Jackson pedaled along Church Street onto the drive that led down to the station. Approaching the turnoff to the White House, he noticed that the gates hadn't closed completely. He dismounted and pulled the gates together and listened for the metallic clunk signaling that the bolts were secured in the ground. He'd have to remind Mary to make sure they closed properly.

He glanced up the drive to the White House and was surprised to see a nondescript white car parked off to the back of the circle with the trunk open. It wasn't one of the Waddington cars. Mary, Vera, and Agnes had left early in the morning in the van. Gilma only came when she cooked for them, and besides, he'd recognize her car.

A woman hurried out the door toward the car carrying something in both hands. Probably the estate auction person. Mary had said she'd be by this week to value items. Just like Mary to give her the key and the code. She was too trusting, but he couldn't worry about it. The woman returned to the house for another load. He thought about reopening the gates, but decided against it. If the woman got in, she knew the code and could get out. Better to leave them closed.

He remounted and cruised down the drive toward the station. The trailer behind his bicycle had two full bags of dirty cans and bottles. People were such pigs. The workmen painting the station were no better, tossing cigarette butts and wrappers and soda cans everywhere. He'd sort and clean the lot and cash out at the supermarket, then get a bagel and coffee next door. He'd sit outside at one of the tables with a paper and watch people watch him. As if he emitted a repelling magnetic field that caused mothers to steer their children wide, old ladies to pick up their pace, and the bullyboy landscaping jocks to slow down and sneer. A lot of attention for an invisible person.

Little Mother greeted him, winding between his legs while he unloaded the catch of the day. He stroked her and made a mental note to buy more cat chow. He hoped the new couple was all partied out. Their loud music and shouting matches at the guesthouse had kept him awake the past few nights and set the dogs to howling last night.

He hurried. He was hungry, and he wanted to finish before dark.

He took off his glove and massaged the tight, unnatural skin. He heard a sudden loud whoosh. Flames surrounded him. He gasped for air, choking on the dense smoke that engulfed him. Heat seared his eyes. He dropped to the ground and crawled to the side of the station, clawing his way along the wooden slats until his good hand felt the water spigot. He turned it and thrust his flaming hand into the water that gushed forth, dousing the pain. Slowly, his eyesight returned, and the vision subsided. He leaned against the station for support.

Give yourself time. You'll get over it. The doctor's voice reassured him. But when? When would the horror subside? The new meds seemed to be working, and he'd had fewer spells these last few months, but he still had the occasional vision powerful enough to bring him to his knees. He hadn't blacked out for over three months, but couldn't escape the flames and the guilt and the haunting eyes.

Move. Keep going. Action was the key. With his heart still pounding, he cleaned and sorted the cans and bottles into separate bags and threw the bags into the bike trailer. He mounted the bike and forced himself to feel real pain by pedaling slowly up the drive in high gear, punishing his legs to distract his mind.

As he ground up the hill, the white car pulled up to the closed gates. A woman got out, walked to the gates, and pushed. When they didn't open, she rattled them.

Maybe she didn't know the code. He shifted into a lower gear for more speed. The woman would be pissed off if she thought she was locked in. Wouldn't like a derelict to spring her, but tough toenails.

She lifted a metal plate embedded in the stone pedestal beside the gate. Seconds later, the bolts to the heavy gates released, and they swung open. As Jackson crested the hill, the car roared by, spitting gravel at him. He shook his fist at her. Stupid cow hadn't bothered to close the gate.

Sure was in a big hurry to leave. Alarm bells sounded in his brain. He didn't recognize the car.

He raced up the drive to the White House. The side door on the west end was ajar. With a sense of foreboding, he pushed it open.

Chapter Seventeen

On Monday morning, when Mary, Agnes, and Vera had arrived in West Boylston, they'd turned off onto a drive that branched after fifty feet. The left branch led to the old Victorian family home, the right to a small bungalow where Agnes lived. They had dropped Vera off in Agnes' house before driving to the main house where they spent the better part of Monday divvying up the family treasures. They'd concentrated on items on the first floor of the rambling, three-story house. The upper floors were crammed with earlier family members' belongings. As each of the elderly sisters had passed, no one had the will or the energy to clear out their belongings. Their mother, Rose was the last of the older generation to go. They'd buried her two years ago.

By evening, feeling tired and somewhat dispirited from the day's work, Mary and Agnes drove back to the little bungalow where they joined Vera at the kitchen table. Mary was knackered and thirsty, but although it was Agnes' house, Agnes hadn't offered any refreshment.

"Would you ladies care for a spot of tea?" Mary rose, filled the teakettle, and took three china cups from a tall antique cherry cabinet.

In her thirties, Agnes had run off with the first man that looked twice at her, only to return a year later in humiliation. Because, as she claimed, her "delicate nerves couldn't possibly suffer all the confusion of the big house with her mother, aunts, and sister," Mary and Prez had purchased the little bungalow next door for her. The real reason was that no one wanted to live in close quarters with Agnes.

Mary placed milk and sugar on the small round table. She gathered a pen and pad of paper and a set of different colored round stickers that they had used to identify who got what when the big house was sold. Items marked with yellow would be packed for Agnes; red to be moved to Welton for an estate sale; blue for the little station, and green to go to charity.

When Rose died, Agnes claimed she couldn't possibly care for Vera because of her own delicate health and job at the Jesuit Center, and so Vera had come to live with Mary in the White House. Mary hadn't been to West Boylston since their mother's wake. Now she looked around Agnes' house with interest, noting which treasures her sister had already claimed and moved from the big house—like the cherry cabinet and the china teacups that had been their mother's prized collection, a set of brass pots by the fireplace, and the familiar quilt that their mother had made out of scraps of old clothing.

In the past year, Agnes had come to the White House numerous times but had never returned the invitation. Now Mary wondered how much more plunder Agnes had salted away before she and Vera had arrived. Maybe she should have just surprised Agnes. No matter. The problem was disposing of stuff, not collecting more. Besides, many of the things Agnes had taken belonged to their mother, and Vera wouldn't want those reminders around her. Bad enough to be visiting the old house.

"You will keep the cabinet, won't you, Agnes?" asked Mary.

"I didn't think you'd mind me taking it. It didn't seem that you needed more furniture. I thought I'd take a few other small bits, but if you want anything I've moved or put a sticker on, just say the word. I don't need much."

Mary noted Agnes' aggrieved tone. Despite her apparent disdain for Mary's affluence and lifestyle, Agnes had a well-developed taste for the finer things in life, especially when they were free.

Vera bumped her chair up to the table next to Agnes. Mary suppressed a smile and placed a straw along with a tea bag and one teaspoon of sugar in Vera's cup. Agnes pushed back and stalked to a cabinet and retrieved three mugs. "If you don't mind, I'd prefer that you use these." She took a different seat across the table from Vera. Vera glared at her and leaned forward. Mary caught her club before she could brush the porcelain cup off the table. "Don't be naughty, now, Vera."

As Mary rose and replaced the china in the kitchen cabinet, she glanced out the window. "There's a new set of patio furniture in Chatham. Would you mind if I take your old set for the little station I'm fixing up?"

"Actually, I'd planned…."

"Never mind. Lawn furniture shows up all the time at the dump. Here, you do the stickers. I just thought you might like to make a little money at the estate sale, but you can move the whole house if you want." She handed the set of colored stickers to Agnes.

"You needn't take that tone with me, Mary. It's different for those of us who haven't had much. I've said it before, and I'll say it again. You and Vera should take the Chatham farmhouse. I can stay right here in the old family place. It doesn't have as many ghosts for me as it does for Vera."

Mary sighed. She was weary of the ongoing discussion about who should live where and why. "I thought we were agreed. I know the farmhouse in Chatham is beautiful and worth oodles of money, but you're retiring and can move. I *hate* the place, and I know you like it, Agnes. Why not just let it be?" Mary threw up her arms in exasperation. Agnes didn't know Mary intended to sell the old Victorian house.

"I wasn't so much thinking about your feelings as I was about…others." Agnes delivered her venom with the graceful self-denial of the nun that she had always wanted to be.

"Right. Vera wouldn't be happy here. So, why not take Vera to Chatham with you?" Mary turned off the whistling teakettle, aware of the sudden silence behind her. She poured the boiling water into the mugs slowly, giving her older sister time to contemplate a life of caring for Vera.

As she gave Vera her mug and straw, Mary briefly caught her eye and winked to reassure her.

Mary pushed a mug toward Agnes. Agnes stirred the teabag back and forth in her cup with an attitude. Mary let the silence drag, wondering what self-effacing ploy Agnes would devise to make it look like a sacrifice to accept one of the more valuable properties on Cape Cod. Agnes played the victim better than anyone Mary had ever met. Mary wished that Agnes had chosen one of the homes overseas before they had been sold off, but alas, she had settled on the Chatham place ostensibly so that she could be closer to Mary, should she need care. Mary knew that the real reason was that Agnes was afraid of traveling.

So much spoken, and unspoken, bullshit. Throughout the lifetime of Mary's illness, Agnes had never lifted a pinkie to help. She was the only one in the family who refused to give Mary an injection because she was terrified of needles.

Mary watched Agnes fiddle with her tea bag. Poor Agnes with her delicate sensibilities, her migraines, nerves, and mysterious ailments; Agnes who kept a pharmacy of ointments and tablets on her bed table. Agnes, the only healthy one of the lot. She'd turned into a gray old maid by thirty-five and would likely die of a severe expression.

Mary shifted her gaze to Vera and tried to remember how she looked that last summer in Ireland before the "accident." She was taller than Mary and looked a lot like Agnes, but nature had been kinder and given her a gentle nose, colored her in, and sculpted her with voluptuous curves. The only features of Vera's that remained unchanged were her light brown hair and her blue eyes with startling dark rims around the irises.

"Why are you in such an all-fire hurry?" Agnes demurred.

"I haven't been very well lately. I've decided to put my affairs in order while I can."

"Oh, come now, don't be melodramatic. It's tiring and unattractive. What's the real reason?" There had been numerous times in the past when Agnes had accused Mary of being a hypochondriac, staging convenient "fits" to get attention or to avoid onerous tasks.

"Actually, I'm not feeling that well right now. If you'll excuse me for a moment, I'll use the bathroom."

As she walked down the hallway, Mary noted several new pictures that had come from the family home. She resisted the temptation to peek into Agnes' bedroom as she passed. In the bathroom, she sat on the toilet seat and took out her equipment. She pricked her finger and read the blood level.

Not good. She retrieved a bottle of Glucozade from her bag and drank half of it before returning to the table. Enough of the stupid charade.

"Time for an executive decision. I will remain in Welton. Agnes will take the house in Chatham. The only remaining issue is where Vera wants to live. How about we let her make the decision?" Mary smiled brightly, pleased to note a slight tic developing in Agnes' left eye. Despite her endless sisterly advice, Agnes had yet to spend a day alone with Vera since the "accident." Mary had no intention of ever letting that happen, but she did enjoy watching Agnes squirm.

"I would be willing to move to Chatham. The house is very tastefully decorated but it doesn't have ramps for a chair, does it?" Agnes knew full well that Beth Waddington had been the one who had decorated the Chatham house and never missed the opportunity to mention it to Mary.

"Ramps are cheap." Mary cut off her older sister's further remarks. "Vera, dear, where would you like to live?"

Vera looked at Agnes, grimaced her best smile, and raised her eyebrows in a question. She made windmill-like motions with her clubs.

Agnes gulped and turned to Mary. "What's she saying?"

"She wants to know if there is swimming in Chatham." Agnes never addressed Vera directly, often speaking of her in the third person the same way their mother had. "Of course there's swimming," Mary said to Vera with a smile.

"I couldn't manage an invalid. My own health is too frail. I'm afraid that just isn't an option," Agnes declared.

Vera turned and placed her club on Mary's hand. Mary smiled at her. "Love you, too."

The phone rang, startling all of them. Agnes answered and handed the telephone to Mary. "For you."

"Vera *hates* the water," muttered Mary before walking into the living room with the telephone.

"Mary, someone's been in the White House. I thought it was the estate sale lady, but now I'm afraid that it was a burglary."

Mary recognized her nephew Jackson's deep voice. "Have you called the police?"

"Not yet. I decided to call you first."

"Good. Retrace your steps and wipe off everything you might have touched when you were in the house. Leave it just as you found it and come collect us. I'll phone the police later. If you're willing, I have a little research project for you to do for me."

"You feeling all right?"

She couldn't fool Jackson. "Dicey, but we'll be back in Welton tomorrow. Thanks, bye."

When Mary returned to the kitchen, Vera made a cradling motion with her clubs and raised her eyebrows.

"Yes. That was Jackson. Someone broke into the White House. Don't worry. He's okay."

Chapter Eighteen

After checking on Mary and Vera when they returned from West Boylston, Jackson retired to his rooms above the garage. They were perfect for him. He could keep watch over Mary and Vera, care for the dogs and be close to the equipment he used to maintain the grounds and cars.

Over tea, Mary told him that Casey called him Can Man, the homeless troll that lived under the bridge. Understandable. Jackson barely recognized the man that stared back at him in the mirror. Weathered and dirty with a black beard and nails, at least on the hand where he still had nails. Time to clean up his act.

He clipped the beard as close to the skin as he could and then lathered up. The last time he'd held a razor, he'd intended to use it on his wrists but had been too drunk to carry it off, passing out in a bathtub in a dive in Fitchburg. The owner of the flat had found him fast asleep in dirty, cold water and called the cops.

Mary had rescued him then, as she had so many times on his long road to recovery after the fire. She'd never given up on him, even though he'd let her down repeatedly. Mary's current request was strange, but there was no way he could refuse her.

So many mortifying memories. How many times had he bottomed out? With each stroke of the razor, he relived them all: drunk tanks, assault charges after he beat the crap out of two guys trying to roll him in a park in Waltham, the lockup ward in McLean mental hospital. Arrested for shoplifting cat food from the Hannaford Supermarket. Hospitalized after breaking into a cabin for a place to sleep and eating rancid food. Breaking a leg when a landscape rig sporting a large American flag and a bumper sticker, "Jesus Loves You," sideswiped his bicycle and ran him off the road into a culvert. He cut himself and swore. Pay attention.

He filled the old claw foot tub with hot water and eased into it carefully, resting his head against a bathtub pillow, soaking before lathering up. The unexpected scent of lilac brought an instant image of his wife Dorothy sitting on their front porch sipping a glass of white wine in the evening.

Only in unguarded moments would fleeting images invade Jackson's consciousness, reminding him of his wife in the early years who lit up a room with her breathtaking smile. He'd loved her way beyond her innocence, way longer than he should have, reluctant to release the memory of bygone sweetness, always hopeful for the small windows when she would lapse into her former self. They had had a few really good years.

It had taken a long time for him to lose the rage he'd felt after she had set the house ablaze with a careless cigarette. The fire engines were already at the house when he pulled into the driveway around three in the morning. Jackson rubbed his hand, remembering how he had flung himself into the flames to rescue the boys, and how two firemen had dragged him burned and crazed, from the house.

He still felt guilt for his part in the tragedy, but over the years, had realized that it was a shared guilt from a failed relationship that neither of them had been able to save.

He had never appreciated her bouts of depression and the depths of despair until he experienced them for himself. She'd led a picture book life, but somewhere along the way, she lost her compass. Once alcohol got its grip, she couldn't even remember conversations from the night before. It was amazing she'd functioned as well as she had for as long as she did.

Only after his own descent into alcohol, depression, and homelessness could he understand on a visceral level. Because, of course, he had had it all once himself and then squandered it on his way to the bottom.

Jackson shuddered. The water in the tub was tepid, and his thoughts were leading him to places he didn't want to go. He refilled the tub and scrubbed off layers of filth. Despite his efforts to think positive thoughts, his mind returned to his short bouts behind bars that had left an indelible mark on him: the deafening negativity, violence exploding at random, the selfishness and distrust of cellmates, and the lawless whims of sadistic guards. Hopes nurtured over the years seeped away with the loss of personal responsibility and pride.

How had Casey survived ten years of her prime behind bars without escaping into a bottle or giving into depression? In the time he'd watched her, she seemed scarred but unbroken. Jackson remembered one of the defiant quotations from *Samson Agonistes* that Jed had written on the attic ceiling: "My heels are fettered, but my fist is free."

God, he missed his Uncle Jed. What a wonderful contradiction that man had been! Both the first and the last person who should have become a Jesuit priest. When Jed took orders and left the house in West Boylston, Mary had moved Jackson into Jed's room in the attic. He'd lived in the room for a month before daring to change anything to make it his own. Mary had forced the co-mingling of belongings by dumping Jackson's books and sports equipment, and teenage paraphernalia into the middle of the room one day when she was cleaning.

He'd had to put stuff up and away, beginning the process of melding his world with Jed's. In the end, it had become their room, reflecting both of their personalities. Jackson always hoped he would absorb Jed's better qualities by living in close proximity, sleeping and breathing the same air.

When Jackson left for college, they just closed the door.

He refilled the tub once more and only got out when all but the taut scar tissue on his hand was wrinkled. He stared at it for a moment. Don't go there. Fix up the inside of the little station and then go on a research mission for Mary. Can't let her down.

Chapter Nineteen

Wednesday morning, Casey circled yet another Help Wanted ad and then threw her pencil across the room and crumpled the paper. At the job fair she'd attended earlier in the week, all of the positions were for tech or medical jobs. When one headhunter asked what languages she knew, she'd replied that she had four years of French and two of German. The woman had rolled her eyes. "No, no. Computer languages."

"*Life isn't fair, and nature isn't benign,*" she muttered, channeling her mother's voice. Her mother's life reflected the truism, marrying a gay man, falling in love with a priest, raising two children alone, and dying young. Now Casey was carrying on in the same tradition.

Not one nibble on the freshly prepared resume she'd sent out the past month. She wished she could talk with her mother. She looked out the window at the cloudless sky. No Em today. *Casey, girl, you are losing it, hearing voices and clouding.*

Hell, she didn't want any of the lousy jobs anyway. She wanted action. She wanted to hit something. She jumped up, grabbed her bookbag, and rushed outside. She threw her bag into the Muttmobile with too much force, knocking over a coffee cup balanced on the center console. Cold coffee drained through the hole in the floor. She slammed the car door hard enough to rattle the windows and fired up the beast.

She stared straight ahead and assumed a jaunty smile. Godammit! She hadn't done anything wrong. She'd visit the little station and check out the new paint job. As she passed a black Mercedes sedan on the highway, the man turned to stare at her. She swiped her face and nose on her sleeve in a most unbecoming manner and considered flipping him off. Better not. He might be a potential employer. She blew him a kiss, twirled Hugo's head, and released the barking dogs under the hood.

She pulled off at the drive leading down to the station and braked at the bottom of the hill, staring at the transformation. Brand new. Amazing what a few new windows and a lick of paint could do. She released the clutch before the engine cut off. The Muttmobile lurched forward and stalled. Casey leaned forward and rested her head on the steering wheel.

A soft knock on the car window startled her. A tall figure blocked the driver's window. With her luck, some cop would ticket her for stalling out in the Fire Lane of a defunct train station.

She craned her neck to identify the figure. No uniform. The man had short black hair, bushy eyebrows, and dark eyes. *Can Man.* Clean-shaven with a dark shadow, he was dressed in a plaid shirt and jeans. He still wore the glove, but it was clean. He studied her with a concerned expression.

"I'll be okay," Casey said to the closed window, turning her head away and fumbling with the key.

He tapped harder on the window.

Irritated, she rolled down the window.

"Come with me. I have something to show you," Jackson said before she could speak. He opened the car door for her and then walked to the front door of the station, turning and beckoning for her to follow before entering the building, leaving the door ajar.

Casey didn't budge. She wasn't about to follow a strange man into an abandoned train station, no matter how clean his fingernails were. She might be unemployed, but she wasn't stupid.

However, she was curious. What would he have to show her? She got out and peered through the window, but it was too dark inside. If she left the door open, she could beat a hasty retreat if need be.

It took a moment for her eyes to adjust to a single room with an overhead loft. A refrigerator and sink lined the side wall, and a door to what was probably a bathroom stood in the right corner. Jackson knelt on the floor against the left wall talking softly to a cardboard box. Casey crept up behind him.

Little Mother lay on a towel with three tiny balls of gray fluff attached to her side, purring. Forgetting her fears, Casey knelt beside Jackson and spoke softly to the kitty. Jackson beamed at Casey, looking for all the world like a proud papa. "Middle of the night," he whispered, answering Casey's unspoken question. "Isn't she beautiful?"

Outside, Casey and Jackson dangled their legs over the edge of the wooden train platform facing the overgrown train tracks at the back of the station. Casey was the first to speak. "You have ears."

"And you look like a train wreck," responded Jackson.

Casey laughed. The worm had turned. She was about to be homeless, and she already looked like hell. "I'm discovering that I'm unemployable."

Jackson listened but offered no comment.

"You don't seem surprised," she said, a bit miffed by his lack of response.

"Mary said it would probably be hard for you to find work," he said finally.

Casey waited for more.

"She filled me in on your background."

Casey hugged her knees to her chest and rocked back and forth, trying to make sense of events completely out of her control. Can Man, or Jackson, or whoever the hell he was, knew her name, her history, and probably her blood type.

"I'm Mary's nephew," Jackson offered, as if that would explain his transformation and access to information.

True? Casey studied his features but didn't see a family resemblance other than his dark coloring. She was amazed at what a pair of scissors, a razor, and a little soap could do. "You clean up ril good," she said in her best Ohio country voice. "What brought you out of your cocoon?" The question was nosey and rude, but right now, Casey didn't give a damn.

He paused and studied her as thoroughly as she had studied him. "Mary said she needed my help. No one has said that for a long time." His expression turned somber, but he offered no further explanation. He shifted the focus back to her. "What will you do now?"

"Eat worms."

Jackson laughed aloud. He was good looking when he laughed. Casey liked being able to see his ears and chin. She got up and walked across the platform to a pile of paint cans, drop cloths, and brushes stacked against the station wall. Although Jackson's jeans were clean, they had drops and smudges of paint on them that matched the overflow on the lip of one of the cans. "You're doing the inside work?"

He nodded.

"You staying here?"

"No. I have an apartment over the garage. I take care of the cars, dogs, and the property. And watch over Mary." He gestured toward the inside of the station. "It's small, but it will be a neat little place when I'm finished—one large living area and kitchenette, a sleeping loft, and, of course, a bath. You could do worse, if you're interested."

He knows I have to move? She slumped to the floor, dumbfounded and not a little pissed off. She jerked her hands, feet, and head. "I'm a puppet playing a role in someone else's drama."

"Take a number."

Casey glanced at him, wondering how Mary was manipulating his life. Something Jackson had said earlier bothered her. "If she's so much in control, why do you need to watch over her?"

"I'm not sure what she's up to, but with her dicey health, she may be playing a dangerous game."

"Play with fire, you'll get burned," Casey murmured.

Jackson's head snapped back as if she had slapped him. His black eyes fixed her in a fierce stare. Instinctively, Casey shrank from the wild man who had frightened her so badly a few weeks ago.

Jackson drew in a deep breath. He wrenched his crazed eyes from her, stood, and walked to the door. "Sorry," he said. "My problem. You didn't do anything wrong," as he left.

Casey hurried around the outside of the station to the Muttmobile, door still ajar, awaiting her escape. The image of her gravestone rose before her with the epitaph, "She didn't do anything wrong," etched in granite.

She sank into the Muttmobile with a sigh of relief. She reached for the keys in the ignition. Damn! Not there, and they weren't on the seat next to her. She scrounged around on the floor. No keys. Could she have left them in the station? Double damn. Reluctantly, she got out and took one last look around the car. There they were, wedged between the front seats. As she retrieved them, she heard a hollow, low moaning accompanied by rhythmic thumping. She listened carefully. The sound came from her left, not from the station.

She squinted into the dark recesses of the Church Street underpass, but the late afternoon sun's long shadows made it impossible to see anything. Why would Jackson be under the bridge? None of her business. Leave.

The slow thumping continued. Concerned, Casey walked toward the sound. Out of the sunlight, she paused to let her eyes adjust. Jackson sat against the stone arch, butting his head against the wall. Closer, she noticed that his eyes weren't focused. *He's crazy. Really crazy.*

She froze, tempted to help, but not knowing what to do. He dropped his head into his hands and sobbed. Casey stepped closer. "Hello," she called in a hesitant voice.

"Get away!" he howled, waving his arms. "Get out! Fire!" Tendons bulged in his neck, and his eyes looked as if they would leave their sockets.

Casey backed away. As she re-entered the sunlight, the rhythmic thumping began again. She turned toward her car, telling herself to move slowly, not to run. She spied a pile of rags next to the paint cans and brushes on the front step of the station. She couldn't just leave him pounding his head to mush, thinking he was on fire. She grabbed a clean rag and wet it under the water spigot on the side of the building.

She retraced her steps. Jackson's low moans echoed against the sides of the underpass. She approached slowly. One side of his head was bruised and bloodied. "Here. This will help," she said softly. He watched her with hollow eyes. She continued talking to him in low tones without any sense of what she was saying. When he seemed calm, she knelt beside him and placed the cool rag against the side of his head as gently as she could.

His hands flew to his head.

"I won't hurt you." She soothed him with the cloth and the murmur of her voice. She sat next to him and began humming. When he closed his eyes, she reached over and stroked his temple, tentatively at first, and then when he closed his eyes, with a monotonous circular motion. She felt the resistance gradually drain from him. His muscles relaxed, and he lowered his head to his chest.

Casey closed her eyes and hummed the slow melody of an old slave song she'd known since childhood, "Follow the Drinking Gourd." Jackson groaned as she stroked his brow and continued humming to calm herself and her strange companion.

Little Mother appeared and climbed into Jackson's lap, circling to make a bed against his flannel shirt. Casey petted the kitty into a rusty purr and then rose quietly and walked to the Muttmobile.

In the back she found an old blanket, once used to protect the car seat from the dogs, that now served as a cover for destroyed upholstery. She returned and carefully draped the blanket over cat and man. She stroked his forehead lightly and turned to leave.

Jackson grabbed her hand as she rose, his black eyes fixed on her. At his sudden move, Little Mother shot into the bushes. Casey stared at the hand gripping hers, shuddered, and stifled a cry. Jackson wasn't wearing his glove. Scar tissue pulled the skin taut over the bones of his left hand.

His eyes followed hers. He grimaced at his disfigured hand, drawing it away.

Instinctively, Casey held onto the retreating hand and pulled it to her cheek. They stared at each other for a few moments before Casey placed his hand on his chest and drew the blanket up to his chin.

She felt his silent eyes follow her as she retraced her steps to the car. It was nearly dark. She started the car, but didn't turn on the headlights until she drove up the hill toward Church Street. Her hands shook on the steering wheel. She might not know what her next move would be, but at least she wasn't homeless and crazy.

Well, she revised with a wry smile, she was soon-to-be homeless, and she was crazy enough to spend the afternoon under a bridge singing to a wild man and a cat.

Chapter Twenty

On Thursday, with less than a week before she and her roommates had to vacate the Somerville apartment, Casey took stock. She hadn't been able to locate an apartment that she could afford. She was almost out of money, and with none coming in, she didn't have enough to pay rent plus a month's security deposit, even if she could find something.

She screwed up her courage, swallowed her pride, and called Mary and asked if she could move into the little station on a temporary basis.

"I'd be absolutely delighted. Stay as long as you like, dear."

Casey waited until she hung up before dancing a jig around the living room. Yes! She called Lou and made arrangements to move.

Friday morning, Casey watched LouAnne toss a wooden chair onto the pile of rejected furniture on the curb in front of their row house. She studied the chair—a sturdy old workhorse whose supporting dowels had become unglued, probably because one of the giants, Rosie or Lou, had sat on it. It had been Casey's chair in the kitchen. She lifted the chair from the pile and hauled it to Rosie's pickup, handing it up to him with a sheepish grin, embarrassed by her sentimental gesture.

"Hey. Good eye, there. Perfectly good chair 'cept for sitting on." Rosie lashed the chair to the other things Casey had decided to take to the station: the solid round oak table and four chairs, a coat tree, a mirror, a box with cooking utensils and books, two Hefty bags of her clothing, and the church pew.

She took a last look as Lou locked the door. Although she wouldn't miss the peeling paint and grunge linoleum, it was the first place she'd lived that wasn't institutional or owned by family. She clicked a mental picture, leaving the familiar with a momentary sense of loss and a twinge of expectation and adventure. Her mind jumped from the rowhouse to the station, arranging and rearranging the furniture as they rumbled down the street.

"Just goin' down the road aways," murmured Lou to herself.

Casey had heard Lou say the same when inmates passed away in prison and when others left for the Outside. A death and a rebirth: loss followed by unknown opportunity, a soothing mantra of goodbye for now.

Rosie swerved back and forth down the street to avoid canyon potholes, cursing under his breath.

"Get those seat belts on in case I'm hauled over for crazy driving."

They bumped along in silence, each lost in private thoughts and plans. When they reached the highway, Rosie switched on the radio and pushed the oldies station. The familiar strain and thump of James Brown blared from the speakers behind the seats in the cab. He turned the volume down to ear bleeding. "Playin' our song, sugar," he said with a wolfish smile spreading across his face. He patted Casey on the knee to remind her where the dance action was.

LouAnne picked up the tune, Casey sang the alto harmony, and Rosie bubbled up and down in bass, singing along with the radio until they reached Route 128. Lou rolled down the window. "Air's different out here."

They had been ribbing Casey about living the high life with rich white bread, telling her she'd need to buy designer clothes and have her nails done in a salon. "Need facials, and a massage." This from Rosie set Casey to giggling. They left the highway and drove toward the center of Welton. "Big mother houses," said Rosie.

They picked up a cruiser from a sneaky lay by on Crescent Street. Luckily Rosie was ready for him, creeping along just under the speed limit. The cop followed them to the turnoff to the station and then continued on down Church Street, talking into his radio.

"Just a little friendly profiling," muttered Rosie.

At the base of the hill, they piled out of the cab.

"It's a toy house!" exclaimed Lou, her eyes alight with a child's wonder. Jackson had put the last licks of paint on the gingerbread under the eaves.

Rosie walked around the side, examining the little building. "Looks brand new. Did a nice job."

Lou Anne jumped back suddenly, nearly bowling Casey over. Little Mother popped through a newly installed cat flap in the front door.

"Relax, Lou. Just an itty bitty little kitty." Rosie squatted down and made soft cat-luring sounds, offering his hand. To Casey's surprise, Little Mother sniffed Rosie's hand and then rubbed against him, purring. She flopped over and offered Rosie her swollen tummy.

"Her name is Little Mother. She has three kittens inside."

"Like to scare me to death." Lou Anne knelt and offered the kitty her hand. Little Mother ignored her, rubbing her chin against Rosie's knee. "Little Tart, more like it."

Little Mother started upright at the sound of tires popping on gravel and darted back through the cat door.

"What are dirty pennies made of," whispered Lou, watching a beefy policeman unwind himself from the car.

"Dirty copper," replied Casey automatically. All three of them stood to face the policeman, who sauntered toward them with a gait designed to intimidate. Not big enough to play for the pros, thought Casey, watching the officer's muscle-bound movements, but still a roast of a man.

"Morning," the officer said, taking in the size of Rosie and Lou Anne, and eyeing the eclectic mound of possessions jammed into the bed of the pickup. "Need directions?" he suggested pointedly.

"No, sir," said Rosie. He rose and walked to the truck and lowered the rear gate.

When Rosie moved, the policeman automatically widened his stance, hands on hips with one close to his unsnapped leather holster. "This is private property."

"Yes, sir." Rosie unlashed the wobbly chair and handed it to Casey. "Don't' just stand there planted, sis. I ain't got all day." Rosie wasn't exactly ignoring the cop, but he wasn't giving him his full attention either, although his words were respectful.

"Sis?" the cop asked Casey, frowning. He looked from the tall Black man on the truck bed to the small white woman before him.

Casey put the chair down and withdrew her keys from her jeans pocket. She shrugged and awarded the cop a broad smile and unlocked the front door. "Different fathers."

"Mind gettin' the end of this thing, officer?" Rosie pushed the church pew toward the edge of the truck bed.

The cop was so startled by the request that he complied and helped Rosie jockey the pew through the front door. Inside, he looked around quickly. "Nice." He returned to his cruiser and was gone before Rosie could make a second request.

"Mind gettin' the end of this thing, officer?" mocked Lou Anne. Rosie jumped to the ground, whirled around, drawing imaginary pistols, twirling them, and jamming them back into their holsters.

"No suh. Yes, suh. Three bags full, suh." Rosie stopped in the middle of his self-mockery. "Uh hunh," he uttered, his eyes taking in another visitor posturing at the head of the stone steps leading down from the White House drive to the station.

Cherie waltzed down the stairs as if she were on a movie set, long legs poured into tight jeans accentuated by tooled leather boots. "Moving in already?" Cherie addressed Casey, ignoring Rosie and LouAnne.

"What gets you up before noon?" Casey responded.

"Now let me guess," Rosie boomed, "You must be Cinderella. I'm Rosie, and this is my wife, LouAnne." He pushed his large black hand toward Cherie.

Cherie stiffened but didn't back down, reluctantly shaking his hand. "Cherie."

LouAnne fixed Cherie with a haughty half-smile but didn't move forward.

Cherie turned aside to speak with Casey. "*These* are the friends you lived with in Somerville?"

Casey instinctively backed away from the smell of cigarettes and the suggestion of alcohol on Cherie's breath. She made a point of sniffing the air to let Cherie know she smelled like a barroom.

Cherie ignored her. "Worthy's looking for you. He wants you to go to the symphony tonight. The family tickets, you know. I have other plans." Cherie cast a disparaging glance at the contents of the pickup and sashayed back up the steps.

"Well fuck me. More like Cinderella's nasty sister, Drizella," muttered Rosie with a last appreciative glance at Cherie's legs.

But Casey was considering Cherie's message. Symphony? With Worthy? She couldn't. She had way too much to do with moving. Her hair was a mess. She had nothing to wear.

"The black dress," said Lou, watching her face.

In fifteen minutes, they had moved everything in and were sitting around the oak table sipping coffee. Nothing matched, but hey, it was a railroad station.

"Thanks, guys. I really appreciate all your help."

"Gonna miss your saucy little face," replied Rosie with a smile. He cuffed her gently and rose for more coffee. He peered out the window. "It's a great spot. Privacy, convenience, lots of trees, not too big. Everything fresh and painted."

They all started at the ring of the telephone. "My first call," Casey said, reaching for the receiver on the wall. "Hello?" She listened for a moment. "Thank you, I'd love to." She listened for a few moments longer, stared at the telephone for a second, and hung up.

Fifteen minutes later, Rosie nodded toward a couple in a BMW driving past the cutoff to the station. "That your date driving with Drizella?" Rosie turned back from the window. "Waste of great legs," he grumbled into his coffee.

Casey quickly changed the subject. "How about a tour of the White House and then a dip in the pool at the guest house?" On the phone, Worthy had said he and Cherie would be out for a few hours and that he'd collect her around seven o'clock. This was the perfect opportunity to nose about.

Chapter Twenty-One

C asey gave Rosie and LouAnne a tour through the White House, pointing out unique features, paintings of note, and furniture, embellishing her observations with stories Mary had told her. She noticed that the Picasso and another painting had been removed, making her wonder if Mary planned to sell them separately from the estate sale. In the living room, she stopped and glanced at LouAnne who was watching her with a strange expression on her face.

"What's the matter, Lou?"

LouAnne looked away for a moment before answering. "Sure hope you don't get buffaloed by all this." She waved her arms around the room. "Awful easy to let stuff like this take over your life."

Casey bridled and instantly shot back, "You don't think an ex-con piece of white trash like me can appreciate the finer things? Or are you asking if I have enough moral fiber left to withstand the temptations of the rich?" As soon as the words left her lips, Casey was mortified.

"Sorry." She shook her head and continued. "You're too close to the truth. I worry that I like the finer things a bit too much sometimes."

"Easy to get sucked in," said Lou. "We had it all growing up. Everything but a happy family. Ain't that right, Rosie?"

Rosie sat on the piano stool, flipped up the cover, and rested his long fingers on the keys. To Casey's astonishment, his fingers glided over the keys playing the first strains of the "Moonlight Sonata."

"Yep. Ours was a grand, not a baby grand. Didn't sound that much better," he said simply, folding down the cover. "Family shit's best left alone," he added to no one in particular. Turning to Casey, he said, "How 'bout that dip?"

Casey jumped at the chance. "Mary says there's a back way to the guest house." She led her friends down an overgrown path, at times bushwhacking through a tunnel of vegetation.

"I've never been there," she explained. "Mary said I could swim anytime, but somehow I doubt Cherie would appreciate it."

LouAnne chuckled. "So, if a car comes down the drive, we be melting into the jungle, right?"

"Right," said Casey with a sheepish smile.

The path turned suddenly, dumping them into sunlight.

"Holy cow!" exclaimed Casey, gawking at what looked like an A-frame ski chalet.

Rosie looked to Lou with a raised eyebrow.

"She's from Ohio," explained Lou.

To their right was an area big enough for four or five cars to park and a road that led back and intersected with the White House driveway. There were no windows on this side of the A-frame, just steps up to a door. A large pile of carefully stacked wood covered by a tarp stood off to the left.

With a mischievous smile, Casey brandished a key, unlocked the door, and cracked it open. She stepped inside and quickly punched PREZ into the keypad. "Yoooooo hoooo! Anybody home?" she called, just in case there were any other guests or cleaning personnel inside. Silence.

"You gotta key?" said Lou.

"Same key works on all doors on the property."

They filed in. A small foyer dead-ended in a hallway that branched to the left and to the right. Straight in front of them was a rustic wooden door. Casey unlatched the wooden peg and pushed open the door. "What the heck?" she muttered. The small rough-hewn room had no windows. Wooden pallets were built into the walls.

"Sauna," said Rosie behind her.

They followed the hallway at the right into a modern kitchen. At the end of the counter was a long rustic table with eight chairs. Beyond, the whole back portion of the chalet was open to the peak of the A-frame, with windows that spanned the entire A. Behind her, Rosie whistled in appreciation.

"Now, this is my kinda pad." Rosie bounced across the plush carpeting toward a large sunken stone fire pit in the middle of the room. Surrounding the pit, two circular steps of carpet provided cozy seating. A large metal hood suspended over the open fire area connected with a pipe leading up through the roof.

At the opposite side of the room, Casey examined an entertainment center. A plush black leather couch faced the screen with a heavy glass coffee table in front of it. Two large black leather reclining chairs sat at each end of the couch with small tables beside them. On one of the tables, Casey noticed an empty wine glass and an ashtray with telltale butts.

"Get this!" LouAnne exclaimed, looking out the front window at a long oval pool. Casey and Rosie joined her. Surrounding the pool was a wide deck with pool chairs, lounges, and umbrellas. A large propane grill stood off to the left, and a hot tub off to the right.

"Must be forty feet," said Rosie. Concrete stairs led into the shallow water, and there was a diving board at the deep end.

"How the heck do you get there?" Lou asked.

Good question. There was no opening, just glass before them. Casey bet they could see all the way to Boston in the winter after the leaves had fallen. They searched for another door and discovered one between the kitchen and dining area.

Like a small child, Rosie dashed outside, shedding his jeans and shirt as fast as he could. He jumped in and was splashing about like an otter by the time Casey and LouAnne reached the pool. They quickly stripped to their underwear and dove in.

Heavenly, Casey thought when she surfaced. Imagine swimming out here at night under the stars in a heated pool. Skinny dipping even in winter. She giggled and then sighed. Grill a steak, eat before a blazing fire, sip a glass of wine. After dinner, a sauna and a plunge into the pool. She arrested her thoughts before continuing onto an evening of sensual delights. *Get a grip, girl. This is not your life.*

But could it be? A small voice asked. In penance for asking the impossible, Casey challenged herself to do ten laps of the pool. As she was making the turn for the fourth lap, Rosie hoisted his long frame over the side, grabbed a towel, and spread-eagled in a lounge chair with a deep sigh. Moments later, Lou joined him.

Rosie withdrew a joint from his shirt pocket and lit up. After taking a long pull, he passed it to Lou. They smoked, watching Casey swim. Rosie offered her a toke as she lapped by. She shook her head. Had to have her wits about her for the evening at Symphony. When she was finished, Casey joined them, and they basked in the sun in companionable silence.

"The life of Riley—or the Waddingtons. From what you've said about Mary, this doesn't strike me as her kind of pad," said Lou.

"No. This was the first wife, Beth's, playpen. According to Mary, Beth threw fabulous formal galas in the White House that were recorded in *Town and Country* society photo pages. She had this place built for more private parties. She spent every dime Prez earned and then some, and he wasn't even a party animal. Mary really resented how hard she pushed him. She's still bitter about it."

"I'm hungry," Rosie announced, jumping up and heading for the door. "Let's see what they have for munchies."

"We can't raid—" Casey objected, but Rosie was already inside. She ran after him, intent on damage control.

"Nothing but rabbit food and old cheese." Rosie closed the refrigerator door and opened the freezer. "Aha!" He exclaimed as he withdrew a quart of Salted Caramel Chocolate ice cream. "Already opened. Grab some spoons. They'll never miss a little dent."

Casey found three spoons. With great ceremony, Rosie removed the cap. "What the...?" He reached inside.

Casey leaned forward. She blanched at the sight of a sparkling green necklace and earrings wrapped in tissue paper.

"You whiter than normal, girl. Recognize these?" Lou asked. Casey just stared.

"Talk to me," Lou demanded.

"They belong to Mary. She wore them at dinner."

Car doors slammed, and the angry voices announced the return of the younger Waddingtons. Rosie jammed the lid back onto the container and shoved it into the freezer. Lou returned the spoons, and they ran. Casey closed the side door just as the front door opened. They dashed for the path and thrashed their way through the greenery tunnel, speaking only when they reached the entrance below the White House.

"I know you like this toy house, and you relate to Mary, but there's something really strange going on here. How about you come with us for a bit? What's the hurry about moving in?" Lou asked as they approached the station.

Casey was torn. Something was foul in the state of Welton. Was Mary over her head with her new-found stepson and wife? Was she in danger? Could Casey help? How could she tell Mary she'd seen the jewels without letting on that she and her friends had been snooping around the guest house? She'd have to think on it. She also had to admit she was excited about moving into the station. She wanted to rearrange things, put her books on the planks atop old bricks, unpack her boxes, and make the place her own. "Don't worry about me. I'm a big girl," she told her friends.

"Take care, girlfriend," Lou said as they got into Rosie's pickup and drove away.

Casey hesitated before entering the station. She trusted Lou's instincts. Lou sensed what Casey felt in her heart of hearts, that although Casey might be hardened by prison, she was still a small-town girl who was out of her element and vulnerable.

Chapter Twenty-Two

Casey dressed in the same black sheath she'd worn to tea at Mary's with her locket for adornment. She took special care applying her makeup as she contemplated the upcoming evening. When Worthy called earlier, he had explained that "Cherie had other plans" and had rather formally invited her to go to an all-Brahms program at Symphony Hall.

So, was the invitation just a space that needed filling, or a favor for Mary who said Casey should get out more, or what? She had to admit, she was a bit nervous about spending an evening out with the husband of another woman. Worthy was aloof and genteel, with a dry wit and a rather sexy, long and lanky build. She was attracted to the man, but also wondered if she'd be drawn to any frog that jumped her way. Her late, unsuccessful romance with George, another married man, seemed eons ago.

Her thoughts were interrupted by gravel popping in the station driveway. Worthy greeted her with a smile, led her to the shiny BMW, and opened the door for her in an act of gallantry she hadn't experienced in years. Old-fashioned elegance. Maybe it was money manners.

As Worthy navigated the big car toward the Mass Pike, Casey fidgeted in the leather seat and studied the landscape. He glanced over at her and caught her eye. "I'm making you nervous. Let me guess—you're wondering if this is a date, or if you are a placeholder for Cherie?"

Was she that transparent? Heat flooded her face, and she was grateful the overhead light had dimmed.

When she didn't reply, he continued. "I'm a married man, but you need to know that Cherie and I are waiting for our divorce to be finalized while we're visiting Mary. I'd like it to be a date, but it's a little too soon." After his pronouncement, they rode in relative silence, until Worthy interrupted her embarrassment a second time.

"That lovely little gray kitty got your tongue? How'd you like the pool this afternoon?"

Casey froze, mortified, now at a total loss for words.

Seconds later, Worthy chuckled. "Towels."

Of course, they'd dashed off and completely forgotten the wet towels by the chairs.

"You needn't be embarrassed. You're welcome to swim anytime, although I'd advise you to call first. Only because Cherie is fond of throwing some rather kinky parties with her old Welton chums."

Casey looked up at him with raised eyebrows.

He shook his head. "Not my scene," he replied.

He was quiet for a moment before asking if she had had time to get into town much since coming east. Casey guessed that "town" meant Boston proper. "No, only a few times." Once with Lou to go to the Salvation Army store where she'd purchased the black dress, and another time when Rosie and Lou took her for a picnic on Boston Common.

"We're on Soldiers Field Road. That's the Charles River. Across the river is Memorial Drive. The brick buildings with the blue and white cupolas are Harvard. On your right is 'The Business School,' meaning the Harvard Business School."

Casey half-listened to Worthy's voice as he pointed out sights of interest. She was no expert, but it certainly wasn't an eastern or Boston accent. More like the flat Midwest mixed with a taste of the South. It was a pleasing combination. She couldn't think of a way to ask about the jewels in the ice cream container. Did he know about them? Were he and Cherie here to take as much as they could, split it and leave? And if so, was he just toying with her?

A little farther on, traffic slowed to a crawl. Worthy surprised her again by his next observation. "Beth was a lot like Cherie. Beautiful, spoiled, and used to having the very best of everything at her command."

"I find it strange that you call your mother Beth."

"'Mom' or 'Mother' made her appear way too old when I was taller than she. I'm thinking of her because of the A-frame. The White House was her showcase for the society set, gala events to raise money, to see and be seen by who's who in Boston. In private, she had party houses that only her closest buddies saw: the ski chalet in Welton, an apartment in Paris...." His voice trailed off.

Casey didn't want to interrupt his reverie and waited silently for him to continue.

"I'm afraid the long-standing vendetta between Mary and Beth will never end, because no one can win. Els is gone, and he was the prize. They can only injure one another."

"Are they still in contact?"

"Beth called for me but spoke with Mary the other day. Mary told me that she made sure to mention the upcoming estate sale, her way of purging the last of Beth from the White House."

"Why are you here, Worthy?"

"I just turned forty, the magic birthday when I can collect the money Els left in trust for me. Part of the deal with the divorce is that I hand half to Cherie before taking off."

"Where will you go?"

"Don't know yet."

After parking the car in a nearby garage, Worthy offered her his arm and guided her toward the entrance to Symphony Hall, pointing out the Christian Science "mother" church as they crossed against traffic with a crowd of other music goers. Boston seemed to be the same as any other college town, where pedestrians, especially students, viewed cars as a nuisance to challenge with impunity.

Inside, Casey tried not to gawk at the splendor of Symphony Hall while she and Worthy followed an usher down the aisle to a pair of seats in the first row of the second section. The location was perfect for a man with long legs, and for Casey who normally had to weave to the left and right to see beyond taller heads in the row in front of her. She understood why Mary preferred not to use the seats. Mary would look like a gypsy amidst the understated sophistication of the crowd dressed in muted, dark colors. Many people knew one another, hailing friends before the lights blinked, the universal signal to settle down for the program.

Casey was aware that Worthy was watching her with a mildly amused expression, entertained by her reactions as if she were the show. She couldn't help think that tall, elegant Cherie would be much more stunning in her place. Still, heads turned as they passed. "Is there a mark on my forehead?" she muttered under her breath.

"No, Casey. They're staring because you're lovely and fresh, and they're all rusted out."

The lights lowered in final warning, and the audience hushed in anticipation. Casey relaxed a bit. She was at home in the dark where she could observe her surroundings.

Their seats were spectacular, with an excellent view of the first violins practicing arpeggios, tuning, and milling around on stage. Mary had explained that the seats were grandfathered. Beth's family had had a lock on a whole section of seats. Els had continued buying their two seats after Beth ran off, mostly to bother her snooty family, and although Mary had no interest being exposed to cold shoulders after Els died, she continued buying the seats out of spite. Casey glanced over at Worthy, draped in the wooden seat, long legs extending into the aisle. His arm curled protectively around her shoulder, touching her lightly. He was the natural heir to the seats.

The familiar odors of muted perfume, resin, and old wood washed over Casey in a wave of déjà vu and homesickness. Although the concert halls were vastly different, the ambience was much the same as scenes from her childhood attending concerts in Oberlin's Finney Chapel. She remembered how her mother walked her to the Friday night concert series, how the music would lull her to sleep, her head in her mother's lap, and how she would awaken to her mother's gentle caress of her hair and the applause around her. Casey was thankful for the lowered lights.

Worthy's hand patted her shoulder, and he bent his head toward her. "What's the matter, Casey?" he whispered. His warm breath on her ear felt like a caress.

"Homesick," she replied, surprising herself with her honesty.

He removed his arm and took her hand. She jumped at first, surprised by the intimacy, but then relaxed, comforted by the warmth. She sat through the Brahms Double Concerto, hyper-aware of every move and twitch of his fingers. His thumb rubbed the top of her hand lightly, sending messages through her body. Glancing down, she closed her fingers protectively over the scarred stub of his forefinger.

Worthy withdrew his hand to applaud. "Would you care for a little light refreshment, or perhaps a visit to the Ladies' Room?" he asked.

"The latter, please."

"It's over to the left." Worthy nodded slightly toward the far aisle. "If you hurry, you'll avoid a long line." Casey moved quickly, weaving between people who were stretching their legs and rising to hobnob with friends. She waited in a short line for the restroom. As she entered, an attendant greeted her and pointed to an empty stall. Later, the same attendant offered her a hand towel.

At the clink of coins, Casey realized that the woman expected a tip. She fumbled in her handbag. Nothing but pennies and a five-dollar bill. No way she was leaving a fiver. Blocking the view with her body, she palmed a quarter from the dish and tossed it back in with a satisfying clink and escaped.

Her eyes scanned the crowd and found Worthy, elegant, and stunningly handsome in his dark blue jacket and tie, smiling and nodding slightly to a passing woman.

Casey felt her muscles relax during the second half listening to the strains of Brahms' Symphony No. 2. Afterwards, they walked arm in arm to the parking garage. Behind the wheel, Worthy dodged pedestrians and other traffic to get to the highway. "Penny for your thoughts," he asked as the car sailed through the Allston tollbooth.

"I don't want the evening to end," she said simply.

"It hasn't yet," he responded with a slow smile and a long look that sent shivers through her. "Don't worry. I'll be the gentleman."

Casey smiled back, thankful once again for the protection of the darkened car. They talked a bit about the music. Casey couldn't think of a way to mention the emeralds in the ice cream container. All too soon, they exited the highway.

"You're quiet again. What are you thinking about?"

Casey hesitated. She didn't want to believe that he'd be in on stealing Mary's jewelry, but she really didn't know him. What if he was?

Welton had rolled up the sidewalks. They passed the single traffic light between the highway and the center of town and drove up the driveway to the White House garages. Worthy put the car into Park. "What's on your mind?"

Casey stared straight ahead and took a deep breath. "After swimming, we raided the fridge for a snack. In the freezer we found a carton of ice cream." She paused, searching for the right words.

"Out with it," he demanded.

"The carton was packed with an emerald necklace and earrings."

Worthy whooped in laughter, transforming his serious, lawyerly, controlled façade into impish delight.

"You think it's funny?" Casey challenged.

"Yes. No." He laughed again. "You know about the robbery? The theft of pictures and jewelry—specifically the emeralds?"

"No! When did—" Yet again, Casey was without words. She'd spoken with Mary multiple times, but Mary hadn't said a word.

"Mary wants to keep it quiet. No fuss or scandal before her estate sale. I only know about it because I noticed a few empty places on the walls where pictures had been removed. She said she'd report it later for insurance purposes. I asked if anything else was missed. She laughed when she mentioned the emeralds. They're fake. The real ones are tucked away in a safe deposit box."

"You think it's funny that your wife is a thief?"

"She's my wife until the second the trust fund money is transferred to my

121

account. We'll split it—the price I'll pay to be rid of her."

Casey heard the bitterness in his voice but also an underlying sadness behind it.

"She doesn't trust me, worried that I'll take off with everything and dump her. Would if I could. That's why we were together the weekend of the boating accident. It was a charade. Drew knew about the divorce—I told him everything."

"Drew was the friend you lost in the accident."

He nodded.

"What about the paintings?"

"Never see them again. Thankfully, they're insured." He turned and studied her a moment. "You're surprised. Cherie knows where to get drugs. Her friends have all manner of connections. That's how she scores the cocaine."

Casey shuddered at the mention of the substance that had caused her so much pain.

"I know. You were convicted of dealing coke to college students. I also know you were exonerated."

"Seems my life is an open book."

"Hardly. I'm sure there is a lot more to learn about you." He offered an endearing smile, got out, and opened her car door.

Casey heard the loud rhythmic thump of music from the guesthouse. Worthy scowled toward the sound but said nothing as he guided Casey from the garage down the stone steps to the train station.

"Thank you for a lovely evening," she said simply as she unlocked her door.

"The pleasure was mine," he responded in a low voice. He bent quickly and kissed her on the cheek and drew her head against his chest. He caressed her hair, turned, and retraced his steps.

Casey was startled, relieved, and disappointed at his abrupt departure. "Always leave them wanting more," she murmured, closing the door and flicking on the lights. She gasped in surprise. A large vase of asters and mums sat atop a coffee table. The simple linen curtains that she'd ironed that morning now hung on wooden rods on the windows.

She walked into the bathroom and switched on the light. A mirrored cabinet hung over the sink. Mary had been busy, she thought. But, no, Mary couldn't handle anything heavy. Cherie? Couldn't be. Cherie hated her guts and was a lazy cow.

Casey wandered back into the main living area and looked around more carefully. Two pictures hung on the wall. She switched on the overhead light and gazed in wonder at a portrait of herself holding Little Mother in her arms hanging above the church pew she'd brought from Somerville. On the facing wall she recognized a sketch of the kitty she'd made earlier, now nicely matted and framed. Of course, Jackson.

Casey felt a stab of guilt. Jackson had been hard at work making her new home a welcoming place while she'd been out flirting with a married man. She sank into her chair and looked back and forth between the two pictures. His was a much freer interpretation in watercolor. He used colors in ways she would never dream of doing. Hers was tighter with more detail, more of a recording of an image than an artistic painting. Yet he'd liked it enough to have it framed. But not enough to keep, she admitted.

She took down her sketch to examine the framing job. Had he done it himself? It looked very professional. Turning it over, she was surprised to see a handwritten note on the backing sheet. "Dear Casey, This picture is on loan from the collection of Jackson Dempsey and must be returned as soon as he finds an appropriate wall for it." She re-hung the picture and walked to her portrait. She removed it carefully and turned it over. "For lovely Casey, JD."

Casey smiled and ran her fingers across the surface to feel the indentations, pleased with the graceful sweep of his writing, something she wouldn't have guessed from his dark mien.

She re-hung the portrait. Time for a snack. She opened the refrigerator and was greeted by a bottle of white wine, a carton of orange juice, eggs, and bacon. In a bowl on the counter were fresh tomatoes. He'd thought of everything. She knew that he was leaving that night on a trip to California for Mary. He must have spent the evening fixing up the place while she and Worthy were at the Symphony. She gazed out the window toward the White House. Outdoor lights were on, but there had been no light over the garage when they parked the car. Too bad he was her cousin.

The thought snuck up on her, surprising her since she'd just returned from a romantic evening out with another man. Hormones were in overdrive. Why couldn't she meet a single, normal man? She catalogued her recent romantic leanings as she climbed the spiral staircase to the loft: George, her best friend's husband and a womanizer, Worthy, unhappily attached, but still in all, married, and Jackson, her half-crazed first cousin.

Just as she reached the top step, she heard a soft rustling and a metallic clink downstairs. She whirled around and exhaled with relief as Little Mother entered through the cat door with a guttural meow.

Casey frowned at the strange, low voice. She looked closer in the dim light. Little Mother had a mouth full of mouse. Bringing home the bacon for her kittens. "Hello, Little Mother," she called down to the cat. The cat started, dropping the mouse. Should Casey rescue the mouse? It didn't move.

Not wanting to deal with the carnage, Casey climbed the last steps and got into bed for some welcome sleep, but her mind whirled for a long time, feeding on the events of the past few weeks.

Chapter Twenty-Three

Worthy swore softly under his breath as he picked his way in the dark along the path from the garages to the guesthouse, fending off occasional branches that reached out for him. He'd left Casey a lot faster than he had wanted to, but he needed to shut off the jungle beat from the sound system before the police arrived again. Damn, Cherie! The romantic mood driving back from Symphony had shattered the instant he had opened the car door in the garage. The cacophony escalated as he neared the A-frame. He bounded up the stairs. Shit! She'd locked the door. That meant she'd had her sicko "friends" in again. He unlocked the door, punched in the code, and entered silently, dreading what he might find this time.

A cloud of cigarette smoke enveloped him. The lights were off, but he could see the pool lights illuminating the water beyond the large glass window. He walked to the window and looked down. Cherie lounged on a chaise wrapped in a terrycloth robe. Beside her on a small table, light glinted off a wine glass. A small moving red flare told him she was still awake and smoking. He turned away in disgust. The image of Casey's sweet, upturned face, eyes closed, expecting his kiss, flickered quickly through his mind. How the hell had he gotten himself into this awful mess? More important, how could he get out of it?

He groped his way back across the room toward the offending sound system.

Whap! Something hit him against the side of his head. He crashed backwards against the dining table, rolling to the side, arms raised to fend off the next blow.

He ducked instinctively at a motion overhead. Nothing. What the fuck? Squinting upward through the low, smoky light, he spied a noose that had been looped over the central rafter swinging from side to side. He'd run into it crossing the room. He dodged sideways for the wall and flicked on the lights. He was alone in the big room. Below the noose was a stool. Kinky. After casing the rest of the downstairs, he took the side stairs two at a time to check the upstairs bedrooms and bath. No bodies, alive or dead.

Returning to the balcony, his fear changed to anger as he pieced together the scene that must have taken place earlier. Cherie would have watched the action from her favorite recliner up here on the balcony. On the end table next to her chair were a cutting board, razor blade and straw, pink fingernail polish, and an ashtray mounded with stubbed-out Virginia Slims. Underneath the table was a telltale bottle.

Cherie had had kinky parties before, always when he was out. The noose and stool were a classic setup for an autoerotic performance. Cherie didn't like to get all messed up with sweat and semen, preferring to watch others abase themselves before her.

He returned to the first floor and yanked the plug on the sound system. Blissful quiet. He stood still and bathed in the silence.

"I'm out here."

He didn't reply. He locked the front door, opened every window that would open, and turned on the overhead fan.

"Did you hear me?" Cherie's voice was more strident.

Fuck her. He locked the door to his room and flung himself onto the bed. He'd figure out what to do tomorrow. No sense talking with her tonight. She'd be too far gone.

"Come out here!" she howled.

Shit. Woman was a loose cannon. He had to shut her up. He rose and made his way outside. The scene was illuminated by the underwater light from the pool. He sauntered up to the chaise, taking in the long, delicate legs and perfect thighs emerging from her robe. He offered a cynical smile and swiped the bottle of Chardonnay from her side table before she could react. He poured the wine onto the deck and tossed the bottle into the grass where it clinked against another. "Had yourself quite a party tonight."

"So? Did you have a romantic evening with the little tart?" Cherie countered, slurring a little.

"Looks pretty kinky in there."

"What I do is none of your fucking business."

"Listen to me. If you do anything to jeopardize our situation, I'll sign the divorce papers."

Cherie stared at him in stunned silence, fixing him with a malevolent glare that brought a smirk to his face. Then she relaxed. "Nice try, but you haven't received the papers. I would have found them." She smiled sweetly.

He puckered his lips as if sending her a kiss, walked just out of reach, and withdrew the folded Symphony program from his jacket. "Forwarded," he explained.

Cherie lunged to her feet, grabbing for the papers. He backed aside as she swayed, struggling to maintain her balance. She hurled her wine glass at him. He ducked, but some of the wine sloshed over him and soaked the program before the glass fell and shattered on the deck.

Cherie laughed at his surprise. "Looks like you need new papers, and I need a new glass."

"Bitch." As she passed in front of him, he gave her a slight push and watched her fall awkwardly into the pool. He walked toward the door.

Cherie flailed about in the deep end, tangled up in the heavy terry robe. "Help me—" She went under. Bubbling up again, she screamed, "Help!"

"Pity." His voice was calm and controlled. He turned and watched her go under a second time.

"Please!" she wailed, struggling to get free of the robe. She choked on water. Mascara circled her eyes, making her look like a cross between a rabid raccoon and a white rabbit. He rather liked the image.

"Will you listen to me then, my dear?" he asked quietly.

"Yes," she begged and went under for a third time.

Worthy reached for the pool skimmer and poked her with it a few times before she grabbed onto it. He hauled her to the shallow end and then released the pole. It clanged to the deck amidst her wails. The last he saw of her, she was on her knees, heaving into the grass.

He locked his door and got ready for bed, a bitter smile on his face. He'd picked up his mail at the post office box that morning. Indeed, the final divorce decree had been forwarded to him. He'd placed it in a safe deposit box, knowing that Cherie regularly rifled his belongings. Should have left her in the deep end.

Chapter Twenty-Four

Waking alone in the loft Saturday morning, cold and catless, Casey admitted that she'd fallen in love with the little station and exposed herself to hope and a fleeting sensation of happiness, emotions that hadn't served her well in the recent past. Her heart had been captured by the station at first sight, and her imagination had betrayed her, conjuring up unrealistic dreams of domesticity.

She steeled herself for a cold dose of reality. Plans were afoot, plans beyond her control, involving her little gingerbread dream. She'd avoided speaking with Mary about it, not wanting to face the fact that she would have to find a new place to live as well as a job. At the earlier picnic with Worthy and Cherie, there had been a suggestion to use the station to sell goods produced by residents of the White House, but she couldn't remember mention of a timeline or if any decision had been made as to the makeup of the proposed residential population.

She was startled from her thoughts by the ring of the telephone. She hurried down the spiral staircase and answered. It was Mary.

"I'm afraid I'm in a bit of a bind. Agnes was supposed to drive me to West Boylston and help me tag the furniture today, and Cherie was to take care of Vera. Now Agnes has the sniffles, and Cherie is, well, under the weather. I wonder if you would drive us and help with Vera today through Monday morning. I'll pay, of course."

Casey jumped at the proposition; the alternative was looking for a job, so far a depressing and unproductive effort. She dressed quickly and hurried to the White House. After loading Vera into the van using the wheelchair lift, Casey got in the driver's seat, pushed the seat forward, and then adjusted the rear and side mirrors.

She soon discovered that the white whale of a van had the turning radius of a destroyer and took any incline with hiccups, its automatic transmission lurching in and out of gears. She relaxed a little when they got on the highway where she could poop along in the slow lane.

In the back, Mary talked to Vera in comforting tones, but Casey couldn't make out her words over the engine noise. Vera had staged quite a fit about accompanying them, but she appeared subdued now.

She was thankful for the hum of the big engine that discouraged conversation between the front and back seats. It was only Saturday morning. They had the whole weekend to talk about Mary's plans.

Once off the highway, Mary called out the turns from the backseat. Casey drove down a quiet street with well-kept Victorian houses interspersed with a few split levels from the fifties. When Mary directed Casey to turn down a long bumpy gravel driveway, Vera's low-level protests became howls. Glancing in the mirror, she saw Vera struggling in her harness, visibly agitated. Mary had her hands full.

She came to a Y in the road, and Mary directed her left. Before her was a proud Victorian with turrets and spires rising three stories. The house looked as if it had suffered a stroke. The right side was freshly painted and alive with bold turquoise, white and pink colors. In contrast, the left side was the gray of white clothing after it had been through unsorted wash cycles too many times. Scaffolding propped up a sagging section of the porch.

Mary had called the place a "painted lady." Baskets of pink, white, and purple petunias hung from the refreshed side of a wrap-around porch. Rocking chairs and a swing reminded Casey of her Aunt Mae's house, the place she'd called home for the past year. She swallowed hard to deny a stab of homesickness.

"The workmen found some serious rot in the posts and had to halt the painting until it was fixed," Mary explained, following Casey's eyes. "She'll be glorious when she's done," Mary continued, gazing at the old house with affection.

They lowered the chair quickly, and then to Casey's surprise, Mary asked her to wheel Vera around to the backyard. "I have a few things to see to. Why don't you and Vera enjoy the sunshine for a moment."

Although she sat rigidly in the chair, Vera didn't object to this arrangement. Casey pushed the chair across an old slate sidewalk to a patio at the back of the house. She gasped in amazement. From the patio, the walkway led down to a rickety dock overlooking a large, three-acre pond. Nature had reclaimed the flower gardens, leaving only a determined climbing rose bush to bloom. Wood and kindling were stacked next to an open stone fireplace and a rusted grill. Casey smiled at the Queen Anne's lace and the blue cornflowers that crowded an overturned canoe beside the dock. She hauled an old Adirondack chair across the patio and sat next to Vera.

Although they sat quietly basking in the sun listening to the buzz of insects and the occasional call of a bird, Casey was aware of the tension in Vera's posture. What was Mary doing? What was there that she didn't want Casey to see? *None of my business.*

The front door slammed. Casey's curiosity got the better of her, and she rose and wheeled Vera back down the drive. Mary approached the van slowly, carrying a heavy bundle draped in a sheet. Why the mystery? Vera grimaced and waved, calling, "Ai, Ai," as Mary placed the bundle in the front passenger seat of the van.

Casey wasn't certain, but it sounded like Vera was saying "Bye, bye," and she was waving her hand in the air. Was Mary leaving?

No, Mary glanced up quickly, nodded and waved back at Vera, and re-entered the house.

As Casey pushed the chair back to the rear of the house, Vera began to sway from side to side, humming. Casey leaned forward, listening to encourage her. She suspected that the lovely melancholy tune was Irish. Of course, Vera couldn't sing the words, but she surprised Casey with the purity of tone. On the second refrain, Casey ventured in shyly with harmony.

Both of them started at Mary's voice behind them. "That's beautiful." Mary placed her hand on her sister's shoulder. "Vera hasn't sung a note since Jed died. They used to sing together in the evenings. The two of you meld together nicely." Mary draped a shawl that she'd brought from the house across Vera's shoulders. "Will you be okay out here by yourself for a little while?" she asked Vera solicitously. Vera nodded.

Casey followed Mary through a tall front door with elaborate stained-glass panels of roses on both sides. Inside, the air was close and musty from lack of circulation, as if they'd stepped back in time. Sheer nylon curtains grayed with age blocked the direct light, and heavy floor-length drapes sagged at the sides of the windows. Casey admired the high ceilings and carved moldings as they passed into the front parlor. She swiped dust off a chair covered in plastic. Underneath, the lace antimacassar had failed to protect the upholstery from mice. Spiders had enjoyed themselves, weaving intricate webs throughout, but even their delicate strands had a fine coating of dust.

The dining room had been partially cleared. Papers stacked at one end of a heavy round oak table suggested that the area was command central. Built-in china cabinets occupied two corners of the room. On a sideboard, individual pieces of a silver tea service sat wrapped in separate plastic bags.

Mary led Casey through the dining room to the old kitchen at the back of the house. Donning an apron, she made coffee on a nineteen forties' porcelain and chrome range. The short, round-shouldered refrigerator harkened from an even earlier generation. Casey flipped down the sides of an old toaster. Linoleum curled in front of the sink.

Mary donned her bottle-lens glasses and glanced at a list. "The Salvation Army is coming to haul off the downstairs furniture tomorrow morning. We'll have to decide if there's anything worth keeping or putting in the estate sale. Then, we'll do the kitchen. Lots of stuff in here is considered 'collectible' if not antique." Mary must have noted Casey's overwhelmed expression. "Don't worry. We're not going to clean or pack things. We'll just tag what to keep and what to dump. Agnes has already had her pick of things last weekend and will have to live with our decisions.

"I'll take some coffee to Vera, and then we can begin. Help yourself to some stickers from the bag there." Mary nodded to a paper bag on the table and left with Vera's child's cup. Inside the bag, Casey found labeled sheets of colored circles: "Chatham" yellow, "Estate Sale" red, "Home" blue, and "Salvation Army" green.

While she waited for further instructions, Casey explored the other side of the first floor. Walking through the door on the far end of the dining room, Casey entered a darkened room with more covered couches and chairs. She jumped aside, sensing sudden movement on her left, and then whirled back, at a similar movement on her right. She froze, standing stock still, listening, waiting, barely breathing. The front door slammed.

"Casey?"

"Living room," Casey replied stiffly, not moving a muscle. "I think there's something in here," she warned.

"Oh, I'm so sorry. I should have warned you about the mirrors. I hope they didn't frighten you to death. I'll be there in just a sec. I need my fix."

Mirrors? Casey moved her arm and looked to the left, watching a reflected movement at waist level. She turned to the right and repeated the motion with the same result. She walked forward and laughed, seeing her own torso circle the room. A foot-high mirror lined the walls at waist level throughout the room.

A large fireplace provided the focal point, surrounded by heavy couches and a charming antique rocking chair. Framed family pictures stood on a small table beside the rocker. Casey smiled and made a beeline for the chair.

Sitting down, Casey rocked gently back and forth, enjoying the comforting motion of the old chair. Abruptly she stopped when she caught sight of her own smiling face bobbing back and forth wherever she looked. The mirrors were at eye level for a seated person.

In front of her on a small table were three framed pictures, one of a handsome older man, and two of strapping young men who bore a strong resemblance to Mary. Before each picture was a burnt-out votive candle. Behind the frames, withered and dried flowers bent their heads as if in sorrow.

Looking upward to relieve the weirdness of the mirrors and the family shrine, Casey's gaze was drawn to a large rectangular area over the fireplace that was lighter than the rest of the wall. So, Mary had removed a picture. "Oh!"

Casey's head snapped toward the exclamation. Mary's cup shattered on the oak floor. Casey leaped up to catch Mary who looked as if she were about to faint, and led her to a couch. "Mary, what's wrong?"

Chapter Twenty-Five

Mary crossed herself and then held her hand to her chest, at first unable to speak. "'Twas as if I'd seen a ghost. Faith, and you scared me girl, sitting in the rocker, the spitting image of mother..." Mary's voice trailed off as she caught her breath. "Sorry. I'm just a foolish old woman," she said, regaining her composure and her normal manner of speech. She glanced toward the doorway. "Looks like I've made a mess."

She made a move to rise, but Casey quickly assured her that she'd clean up. She raced to the kitchen, returning with paper towels and a bin.

Mary watched her. "Thank you. I owe you an explanation for the mirrors and for Vera's behavior today, but I'll need a little fortification first."

Mary led the way to the kitchen. "As a member of the family, you have a right to know, but I'm warning you, it isn't a pretty story." Mary refilled the saltshaker and shook whole peppercorns into the pepper mill. When Casey didn't respond, Mary sighed and put the kettle on for tea.

Where to begin. How could she explain the world she'd lived in as a child? After a number of false starts, she remembered the Cheshire cat's advice to Alice: "Start at the beginning and go to the end and then stop."

She stared into the distance and told the story as if she were reading it from a book, hearing her voice change to a young woman's Irish lilt as she journeyed back in time.

* * *

I grew up in a small cottage in Northern Ireland with my mother and father, two older brothers, Agnes and Vera, and your father, the afterthought—the baby of the lot. We were poor, as were most families in the village, and Catholic to the bone.

My father was an active member of the IRA, as were his father and grandfather before him. All the males in the family were named Joseph after my father, with place names from family history as middle names: Jud for Joseph Ulster Dempsey, JR for Joseph Roscommon, and Jed for your father, Joseph Enniskillen Dempsey. When the police came asking after Joseph Dempsey, my mother could honestly and safely say where at least one of the Josephs was.

Despite my mother's pleas, my older brothers were sucked into the conflict. My father and two older brothers, plus the males from two other families, became a very effective cell of the IRA, causing no end of murder and mayhem for the British. They were too good. The British deployed troops to the village to eradicate the cell.

Agnes and I were eighteen, friends then, on the threshold of womanhood. Agnes was striking in an ethereal kind of way—soft skin and silky long blonde hair that softened that sharp nose and chin. I looked much as I do today, just twenty pounds lighter.

Vera was two years younger and tailed us everywhere we went. We'd do everything we could to dump her—nothing like being plagued by your little sister when you're trying to meet boys. But it was a small town, and she was hard to shake. She was truly lovely, with hazel eyes and curly brown locks. At fourteen, she was a knock-out and knew it.

When the soldiers came, our men and boys went to ground. Every few nights, they changed location, sending messages with runners so our families could re-provision them with food and arms. We'd carry food under our coats on our way to school and drop it beside the road in designated spots if the coast was clear. Any number of times we'd end up at school laden with food or ammunition because soldiers were on patrol where we were supposed to leave it.

There weren't many eligible bachelors—there weren't that many people in the village—and some of the men and boys had been lost to the Troubles. We couldn't help noticing the strapping young British soldiers, handsome in their uniforms, eager for female company so far from home, soldiers who were even more exciting because they were forbidden fruit.

Agnes and I made a pact: we could talk and flirt with the soldiers, but never be alone with them. They were the enemy, and they were searching for our brothers and father. We justified our actions by saying we were gathering intelligence.

One night after I'd been sick with the diabetes and confined to home for a week, Agnes crept into my room and told me in confidence that she had a crush on a tall English soldier named Nigel. She admitted that they'd met several times alone, against our rules. She described him as a sweet and gentle man who swore he had no issue with the Irish or the IRA and empathized with home rule.

She was smitten by this fellow and began sneaking out at night, returning in the wee hours before Mother would wake. One evening when I was having a particularly bad patch—a hypo, you know—mother stayed up watching over me to make sure my sugar didn't drop too low.

Both of us heard the back door click shut as Agnes snuck out. Mother didn't speak a word. Her face turned to stone. She kept a silent vigil in Agnes' bedroom, waiting in the dark for Agnes' return. I dozed off but was awakened by Mother's fierce whisper, "Whore!" followed by slapping sounds that seemed to go on forever.

"I didn't tell him anything. I swear," Agnes cried out. "I don't even know where they are," she sobbed, "so I couldn't betray them if I wanted, and I never would."

"Hush. You'll wake the house."

Agnes was grounded for the duration while the soldiers remained in town. When I was well enough, I went into the village a few times, but without Agnes, the fun had gone out of it, and I was more frightened than pleased by the soldiers' attentions. Not so Vera. Later she admitted that she had taken up where Agnes had left off with the very same soldier, Nigel. She'd skipped classes to meet him for trysts during the day.

Vera told us she wasn't sure of his empathy for the Irish cause. She asked him to prove himself. One day he warned her that there would be a raid on a family's flat over the drugstore. She passed on the information in an anonymous note slipped under the family's door. There was a raid that night. Of course, the soldiers came up empty-handed because of Vera's forewarning. The next week Nigel informed her of a second raid with the same result.

So, he was a good guy who risked his life to save our loved ones. On the afternoon of the night of the "accident," Nigel came to her in an agitated state. "They've found out where they're hiding. We've got to send a message. You can't go—see that fellow on the corner? He's watching you. Another man is watching your house, and yet another is following little Jed.

"They were mustering when I slipped out. I have to get back. Tell me where they are so that I can persuade the commandant that they're somewhere else. They'll believe me because they know we've been seeing each other."

Vera gave him the information. My father, brothers, and two other men burned to death in a bunker under a barn floor that night. In the last hours before dawn, a shattered Vera admitted to Agnes and me what she'd done.

The next evening, we heard a loud pounding on the door. Agnes, Vera, and Jed dashed to my room. We cracked open the door and watched Mother face four burly men standing on the stoop.

"Give us Vera," the tallest man demanded.

"What has she done?" mother asked.

"She told a British soldier where the bunker was."

"How do you know this?" Mother demanded, not budging from the door.

"He told us." The four parted and roughly shoved a fifth man in a British uniform forward. He fell, his bruised and beaten body sprawling before her on the doorstep.

"Tell her." The leader produced a gun and aimed it at the soldier's head. The soldier moaned but didn't speak. The leader placed the barrel between the soldier's eyes.

"She's just a child. I used her. She had no idea. She didn't—" The man's voice was silenced by a vicious kick to the temple.

Mother stared at the soldier's inert form for a long moment and then nodded and backed up to let the men into the house.

Vera pushed us aside and ran for the back door. She wasn't fast enough. They were upon her in seconds. One tied her wrists, and the other ripped off her nightshirt and tore a strip for a gag.

"No gag. I want to hear it all. Use the shed behind the house." Mother's voice was flat.

The men pushed a struggling Vera to the door.

"Do what you must, but don't kill her. I want her to lead a long life remembering what she did." Mother closed the door.

"Jed," she shouted. "Run to the church to Father Tomas. Tell him to send a doctor. Go!"

Jed ran out the front door.

"Mary. Agnes. Sit with me. Let this be a lesson to ye both." She knelt and clasped her hands to pray as tears streamed down her cheeks.

We listened to Vera's pitiful screams. Mother rose twice to throw a log on the fire. When the screams stopped, an awful silence followed. Finally, we heard footsteps and the dreaded pounding on the door.

"Stay where you are," Mother commanded. She opened the door. The tall man held Vera's limp body in his arms.

"Ye'll have to leave straight away, ma'am," he said. "They'll be coming for you when they realize he's gone missing." He nodded to Nigel's still form. Two of the men started to drag the body away.

"Leave him."

The tall man nodded and carried Vera into the house, and laid her on the sofa.

"She'll not walk to betray us again, nor write, nor speak." He threw a bloody piece of flesh onto Vera's body that he'd been gripping in his hand. It was the end of Vera's tongue. "But she can still look at herself in the mirror and hear what others have to say about her." Just as the men left, another man in rumpled pajamas burst through the door carrying a medical bag. It was our village doctor.

Blood gushed from Vera's mouth and from cuts around her mouth. The doctor took a quick look at Vera and grabbed a poker from the fireplace. "Help me hold her mouth open." Mother and the doctor opened Vera's mouth and tilted her head backwards. The doctor raised the poker and cauterized her tongue where it had been sliced off.

Agnes fainted, and I threw up, adding vomit to the stench of burning flesh.

Mother made us watch as the doctor staunched the flow of blood from Vera's vagina and anus. When he began to attend to Vera's other injuries, broken bones in hands and feet, and blasted kneecaps, Mother turned to us. "Pack one small bag each. We leave before dawn."

The doctor gasped. "She's near dead. She can't travel. She needs to be in the hospital."

"No. Do what you can. Call for a hearse. Now." She left the room to silence further objections.

In the dark of night, the doctor helped carry an unconscious Vera to the hearse and placed her in the back seat. He gave Mother bandages and medicines with instructions and asked where we were going.

"You don't want to know. I thank you for your help." Mother gave the doctor an envelope and walked to the driver's side of the hearse. "I'll be driving. We'll let you know where the hearse is after we're safely away. Give us two days." She took the driver's seat behind the wheel. We stopped at the church to pick up Jed and drove out of town.

I turned at the last moment to see the cottage one more time. At first, I thought the glow was the sun rising. Then the flames licked out the windows, catching on the thatch and exploding. Our youth and a young British soldier disappeared in a ball of flame. There would be no going back.

We came to America to live here with Mother's sisters. Mother and Agnes never forgave Vera and never spoke with her directly again. Mother would wheel Vera in here every evening after dinner and park her in front of the fireplace. In her chair, there was no way that Vera could escape the reflections of her deformities. Mother would light the votive candles to

Father and the boys and rock in that chair for hours, never speaking." Mary was silent for a few moments staring at the chair.

A few months after we arrived, we found out that Vera was pregnant. Mother and I raised the baby, Jackson. Agnes married the first man who asked her out just to get out of the house. He left her for parts unknown a year later.

Mary looked up and saw the tears streaming down Casey's stricken face. She rose and enveloped her in a long hug, wishing she could have protected her from her family's history.

Chapter Twenty-Six

Mary continued to talk, but Casey's mind was stuck on Vera's tragic teenage mistake and the resulting lifelong punishment with constant reminders in cruel mirrors and the shrine to the dead. Yet despite this hideous history, Vera managed to joke and sing and carry on. Mother Dempsey and Agnes never forgave Vera, but Casey could tell that Mary had never ceased to love her little sister.

Casey still couldn't find her voice.

"Our story has taken many turns. There was pain, but there was also love and joy. This house was our home for many years, as no other place can ever be. All the old aunties lived and laughed and loved...and died here. Jed was here with us as a boy and later as an older man, and this is where Jackson grew up. We had many wonderful moments."

Mary rose and pulled aside the drapes. She gazed out the back window toward the patio and the pond beyond. "When you told me about your Aunt Mae's house in Oberlin, and your childhood home, the old inn, you spoke of them with love and not a little longing, but you also told me that dreadful events happened there. Yet, just last week you were thinking you might return."

"I was talking nonsense. They've sold my bed," Casey joked, but then realized she owed Mary more explanation. "My brother has taken my old room. They hired a new children's librarian—my old job, and the fellow has a new flame. Time to move on," she added with a smile that wouldn't fool anyone.

"Well, I certainly am glad that you came," Mary said softly.

When Mary continued, her voice returned to normal, and she was all business. "We'll have to remove the mirrors—they're just screwed in. I'll take away the pictures of Father and the boys. I've already removed Mother's portrait." Mary nodded to the bare spot. "I doubt that Vera will venture in here no matter what I do.

"We'll spend the afternoon downstairs. I brought a cooler of food in the back of the van. We can have an early dinner and then begin first thing tomorrow with the upstairs rooms. How's that sound to you?"

"Fine. Where should I put my bag?"

"I thought you'd like to stay in the attic. It was Jed's room and then Jackson's growing up. Leave the bag in the kitchen for now, otherwise, I'll never get you back downstairs."

What a tease!

Casey and Mary spent the rest of Saturday morning on the first floor tagging items using Mary's sticker system, following a master list Mary had prepared. Despite Mary's pre-planning, four large boxes of miscellaneous items remained in the center of the living room, awaiting final disposition.

As Casey lugged another heavy box toward the front door, she wondered why, if Mary were made of money, she hadn't hired someone to help her with the sorting and hauling. Then it occurred to her. She had. Casey was perfect for the job. Toward the outside world, Mary was private and protective, and Casey was family. So far, it was a fair *quid pro quo*, a few days' labor for a temporary place to stay. But she couldn't help but feel that she was in limbo, operating without any stated agreement.

At lunchtime, Casey wheeled Vera inside and made grilled cheese sandwiches while Mary mixed a shake for Vera. They munched and sipped in companionable silence, enjoying the respite from the morning's work. After draining her cup of tea, Mary pushed back from the table. "You'll have to excuse us for a bit. Vera and I need our afternoon nap."

Casey tried unsuccessfully to hide her surprise.

"Don't worry. I'm okay. I need more rest when I have a low-grade infection to give my system time to regroup, and Vera's tired from this morning's upheaval."

143

In the past, Casey had never spent a full day with Mary, only two or three-hour stretches at most. Mary was very clever about hiding her illness. Often Casey had to remind herself that Mary was only partially sighted, and that she operated within a very narrow window of health, vulnerable to threats a normal body could easily shrug off.

"Before I go, I have a special favor to ask of you." Mary grabbed a couple of paper bags and led Casey into a small room off the living room. Books lined two walls, and a ceiling-high grandfather clock and an antique mahogany desk occupied a third. A comfortable, brass-studded stuffed leather chair and ottoman stood in front of a bay window.

"Mother left the old desk to Jed. He never had the chance to use it. Once it's cleaned out, it's yours if you want it."

Casey stared tongue-tied at her reflection on the polished surface of the desk. She drew her fingers across the deep, rich mahogany wood. "It's lovely. Won't Jackson want it?"

"No. He wants the clock."

"You don't want it?"

"No. Mother used to work at the desk in the evenings with Vera sitting in her chair next to her, listening to the ticking of the clock. Both pieces have to go."

Mary opened the lid with great care, exposing a mountain of papers stuffed inside. A few errant pages wafted to the floor. "You can't tell from all the clutter, but inside there are slots for papers and small drawers. I moved back here for a year or so after Els died and used the desk when Mother's health was failing. That's why it's such a mess.

"It would take me forever to sort through these papers using my magnifier. Almost everything here is tossable, but it's the 'almost' part I worry about. There are pictures and old report cards—family things that I should keep or that you and Jackson might want. None of the bills are important. I have all the financial information and critical papers in a separate file cabinet."

Mary retrieved a key from the front glass partition of the clock and wound it up. "Wake me around three, will you? Otherwise, I'll sleep all day and toss and turn all night."

CHAPTER TWENTY-SIX

"Three o'clock it is. And ... Mary, I don't know how to thank you."

"Don't even think about it. I hated the idea of selling it in the auction. Now it will stay in the family."

After Mary left, Casey pulled up a chair and eased the heavy desk lid onto its pullout rests. Clearly, Mary had planned this. She'd dusted and polished the desk in preparation for her surprise. Under the guise of assigning her a task, Mary had given her a priceless antique. No "quid" or "pro quo" involved. If she accepted the desk, and she knew she wanted it, would she feel beholden to Mary? Was she being sucked farther and farther into a program she didn't understand?

Maybe she'd find a few answers inside the desk. She began picking papers from the top of the pile. Many pages were bills marked "paid" with the date, which she dumped into one of the paper bags Mary had left. Just as Casey was tempted to pitch the lot, she came across a number of personal letters, school photos of Jackson from fifth grade, and a checkbook with a balance and blank checks. No photographs or correspondence from her father. Mary had probably put all the pictures in the scrapbook. Still, she had hoped to uncover other glimpses into his life.

Returning to the task at hand, she created a "save" pile for pictures and personal letters and a "don't-know-what-to-do-with-it" pile for miscellany such as old thimbles, marbles, fountain pens with mother-of-pearl inlays and rings of keys of every make and size. Many of the papers were records and medical notices cataloguing the decline of Mother Dempsey and her sisters.

Under a title to an old Studebaker, she found a letter addressed to Mr. Elsworth Waddington, written in a somewhat childish-looking hand. The letter had been opened, so what was the harm? Casey removed a single sheet and read the handwritten note.

Father,

Don't come to school again. Your visits upset Mother and embarrass me. You made your choices. I'm making mine. I don't wish to see or hear from you again.

Worthy

She lowered the paper. How devastating for Els! According to Mary, he was a proud man who must have been mortified to be told he was an embarrassment to his son. And the boy was injured himself. "You have made your choices" came from a child, rejected when his father left him and his mother for someone he loved more. Mary had commented about the tempestuous and acrimonious relationship between Beth and Els both during and after the divorce. Worthy had to have been scarred by the upheaval and tug of war between parents.

Casey looked at the envelope again. The return address was from the Thatcher School in Ojai, California. Worthy had to be of high school age, given the rough chronology Mary had supplied in their conversations.

Casey returned to the letter, this time for a closer look at the handwriting itself. She'd studied graphology in correspondence courses in prison and later in an adult education course and was fascinated by how much a person's writing revealed about personality. This handwriting certainly wasn't the script she would have expected Worthy to have as a teenager. Since the time of this writing, he must have hardened considerably, becoming a much more self-sufficient and driven individual.

The writing was large, rounded, and forward-slanting, with close spacing between words, suggesting a boy who wanted to be in the center of things, who needed more attention than he received, and who crowded others to get it. The overall gestalt of the writing plus the message painted a picture of a people-oriented pleaser, vulnerable if he felt ignored or unloved. In a word, needy.

She chided herself. Handwritings change as individuals mature. If they didn't, it would signal arrested development. But, even so, this seemed a huge change from the self-sufficient man she'd met as an adult.

Why did she care? Just professional curiosity, she told herself. Sure. But the soft, almost feminine writing disappointed her. She preferred the austere sophistication of the man with a dry wit who had taken her to Symphony earlier in the week.

Casey had watched Worthy take notes while Mary described her plans for the White House. His adult writing was fast and spare, an angular print script with efficient strokes and wide spaces between words. Don't think about him. He had a last-minute spare ticket, that's all. His behavior was consistent with his writing—elegant yet aloof. And the cheek kiss was the obligatory variety, more than required but less than she would have liked.

Casey tucked the letter in its envelope and placed it in the "save" folder, and then attacked the cubbyholes. Each hole was devoted to one of the aunties. Mary claimed responsibility for the chaotic stack of papers, but Casey suspected that the cubbyholes were organized by Mother Dempsey. Casey found nothing more of interest until she reached the right-hand slot, which was crammed full of news clippings. More of Mary's doing.

Most of the articles came from the Welton *Town Crier* and the *Boston Globe* featuring Els receiving different awards or making charitable donations to various causes. In one, the United Way honored him; in another, he donated money to the Welton Council on Aging. A third made no mention of Els but recorded the anonymous donation of two paintings—a Picasso and a Wyeth—to the Museum of Fine Arts. Casey squinted at the pictures. Couldn't be. They sure looked like pictures that she'd seen in the living room of the White House that had been stolen in the burglary.

Casey's mind raced. She re-read the article to make sure that the pictures were a gift and not a loan. What was going on here? Some sort of insurance scam? She couldn't imagine Mary involved in such a thing, but how well did she really know her? No, the fraud would be too easy to uncover. All one would need to do is to call the Museum. Still, it was unnerving. She put the clipping in the "save" pile and moved on to other clippings.

A number of articles came with pictures that had been edited by scissors, revealing Els but not the person beside him, or in others, behind him. She studied the photos with interest. This man was the love of Mary's life. Big, almost beefy, he had dark, piercing eyes, a strong chin, and bushy brows above a straight nose that looked as if it had been broken at least once. He was handsome in a rough-hewn way.

Reading the caption of one of the cut-up photos, Casey identified the decapitated figure as Mrs. Elsworth Waddington. She studied the arms and hands and the height of the figure. Taller than Mary. From an earlier wedding photo, Casey knew that the top of Mary's head only reached Els' chin. This was Beth, the "other" Mrs. W. She placed the clippings and photos in the save pile.

She admired the empty desk interior before closing the lid. She glanced at the clock. The desk had one drawer. Casey eyed it wearily. Suddenly the clock bonged the hour, chiding her into action. Get it over with, there was lots to do and not much time before she needed to awaken Mary.

Opening the drawer, she was surprised to find it devoted to her father's scrapbook, correspondence, a folder of loose newspaper clippings, and the program from his memorial service. She opened the scrapbook and followed his life as a priest through Mother Dempsey's eyes. Under each picture, she'd recorded the date, place, and event in a small, exact script.

Casey smiled. Mary had known that she would find the scrapbook and had timed it so that Casey could become acquainted with her father in a quiet moment alone. She read about her father's years and years of training and then followed his various postings, wishing there were more pictures, but grateful for any information.

In the beginning, he'd stayed in Pennsylvania for twelve years, then was posted to Greece for five years and England for seven. Towards the end of the book, she sensed that he'd moved to new assignments with greater and greater frequency. He'd only stayed at his last three assignments for less than a year. The pattern was counterintuitive, and she fought off the nagging and disloyal worry that he might have been shuffled about in the end in an effort to cover up a problem. She remembered the old priest at the Jesuit center and his suspicion that she was a reporter out to dig up dirt on the Catholic Church.

She closed the book and was about to delve into the folder of correspondence when the clock chimed the half hour. Three-thirty, and she'd promised to wake Mary at three. The letters would have to wait.

She hurried upstairs to the corner turret room and was surprised to see the bed made and no Mary. In Vera's room, the wheelchair sat next to a single bed. A large lump under the covers wheezed and snored lightly. She closed the door quietly and walked down the hall, opening and closing doors until she found Mary sitting on the floor next to an opened bureau drawer. When Casey entered, Mary offered her a smile, but tears streamed down her face. Mutely she handed Casey a shoe box.

Inside, Casey found a cache of U.S. Government-issue checks that had been sent to Daisy from Edward Tarnoff, Colonel, USMC.

In a choked voice, Mary whispered, "Daisy was one of your great aunts. Edward was her betrothed. She saved the checks, a neat little nest egg for them to get started when he returned from the war. He never did. They've expired."

Mary swiped at her cheeks and held out her hand. "Help this old woman up," she said. "I may ask you to sort through these rooms. The only things to keep will be the occasional pieces of jewelry and personal items, like pictures. Everything else can go. There's not much to save in the old servants' quarters on the third floor. We used it for work areas and storage. After dinner, you can check out the attic. You'll find it a fascinating place." She picked up a framed picture of Daisy's young soldier in full dress uniform and put it into her apron pocket.

"But first, food." As they descended the stairs to the kitchen, Mary gave further instructions. "I brought pork chops and veggies in the cooler. You'll find every spice known to man in the pantry, although I can't swear they even have expiration dates."

"I'm not much of a—"

"Nothing fancy, Casey, please," Mary interrupted. "I'd cook myself, but I'm still a bit under the weather. If you're interested, you'll find a wine cellar par excellence in the basement." Mary paused and laughed at herself. "Who am I kidding? I'd like a glass of red wine—preferably a Merlot or a Zinfandel, if you wouldn't mind fetching a bottle from downstairs."

Chapter Twenty-Seven

The chops and roast vegetables had turned out rather well if Casey said so herself and the frozen raspberry turnovers had been impossible to screw up. After helping put Vera to bed, Casey joined Mary at the dining room table. Mary pushed her empty glass toward Casey.

"I thought you didn't drink," said Casey.

"I don't usually, and I shouldn't, but I do love a glass, and this feels like a special occasion."

They were halfway through the Merlot when Casey presented Mary with the "save" folder containing the remnants and personal mementos from the desk.

Mary sighed and smiled, recognizing the pictures and clippings in the folder. She poured herself another glass. "This is it, then?" she said to herself, leafing through the pages.

"That folder, and, of course, the scrapbook and correspondence from … my father, that was in the drawer."

"Of course. You'll want those." Mary hesitated at an article with the head cut out. She offered Casey a wry smile. "Childish, I know, but Beth was such a total bitch. Those pictures were taken before we married and I moved into the White House."

Casey's eyes widened at the sudden epithet, but she sipped quietly, hoping Mary would continue.

"She just wouldn't leave him alone. Even after they'd separated, she'd still pop up at benefits, butting in, getting her picture taken with Els. She probably bribed the photographer…or slept with him.

"Sorry, that's the wine talking. But it used to drive me wild. Els never understood why I'd get so crazy even after we were married and had moved to the White House. He felt sorry for her. She was a 'sad case,' he'd say. I'd call her a drunken slut, and he'd tell me to calm down, that 'jealousy didn't become me.' Of course, that would push me over the edge after all that that woman had done. The evening usually ended with smashed crystal on the back stairs."

"How did you meet him?" Casey asked, hoping to change the mood.

Mary got a faraway look in her eye. "I was his executive secretary. I thought he was a real jerk for the longest time, before I learned that his brusque way of barking orders was a cover for a shy man with few social graces. Sometimes he was downright rude, but I put up with it because it was a good job, and it got me out of the house."

"When did you discover his other side?"

Mary's smile erased the bitter lines that had crept in while she spoke about Beth. "I'd worked for him about six months, long enough to experience a few bouts of his temper. He had a short and sometimes violent fuse, which could be terrifying in such a big man. I told you he was a football star at B.C., didn't I?"

"B.C.?"

"Boston College. A Catholic University. Your father also went there for a year before he transferred to Oberlin.

"Anyway, he was big and strong and a serious force to contend with when he lost it. One morning, I made a careless error, forgetting to remind him of a luncheon appointment, and he chewed me out for that and also for letting one of his partners enter his office unannounced. When he stormed back from lunch, obviously infuriated by something, he stopped at my desk.

"'I don't want any interruptions this afternoon. No partners. No phone calls. No wife. *Especially*, no wife. Not the flippin' president of the US of A. Do you understand?' He slammed the door hard enough to rattle the windows.

"'Yes, sir,' I said to the air.

"Els was not the only person who was upset. Something was happening. The calls started coming in fast and furious, and the callers became more and more demanding and then downright abusive when I refused to connect them. When they began to show up in person, I realized I might not be able to keep them from forcing their way into his office.

"I called Maintenance, and the janitor moved my big metal desk in front of the door with just enough room for me to squeeze into my chair behind it. Earlier that morning, I'd opened a window to air out the offices and had inadvertently let in a few flies, so I sat at the desk swatting away between calls and visitors.

"'Sorry. Strict instructions. No calls. No appointments. No visitors. No exceptions.' You've never seen such behavior among grown adults. The best part was when Beth arrived, all haughty.

"'Tell Els I'm here,' she demanded.

"'Whom may I say—'

"'You know damn well who I am, missy. Tell him his wife is here,' she spat.

"'I'm so sorry, uh…Mrs. Waddington, but he said he was absolutely not to be interrupted.'

"Beth leaned over my desk. 'I'm his *wife*. He'll see me.'

"He specifically mentioned that he would not see 'any partners, his wife, or the flippin' President of the U.S. of A,' I said. 'I'll let him know you were here.' I began to fill out a pink message slip, but she grabbed it and threw it on the floor.

"'Els!' she yelled. 'Els, get out here. Do you hear me?' Her voice escalated with each demand. I had to duck when she began throwing things—a stapler, a pair of scissors, and my coffee cup—against the door. I dialed Security and requested assistance with an unruly visitor. I figured Els could hear her ruckus and wasn't responding, so he couldn't fault me for having her hauled away.

"It was a good thing I hadn't drunk the coffee, because by the time Els showed up, my bladder was ready to explode. I hadn't been willing to abandon my vigil.

"At six on the dot, he came waltzing through the *front* door. He'd ducked out a back door of his office earlier in the afternoon. I'd been protecting an empty room.

"When he saw me behind my metal blockade wielding a vicious fly swatter, he broke up. I'd never heard him laugh or seen the light in his eyes when he smiled, and I fell in love on the spot." Mary drained her glass and pushed back her chair.

Casey reached out and stopped her. "Oh, no you don't. You can't go without telling me what made him so angry."

Mary sighed and looked down. "You're a glutton for sad stories. Beth was the major stockholder in the company, mainly because it was capitalized by her father's money. In a move to gain Els' attention, she and the chief financial officer made a verbal agreement to sell the company. He found out about it at lunch. She was furious because she wanted to be the one to tell him the 'news' and to have him beg her not to sell. While the company buzzed with gossip, he'd removed all of his personal designs, patent applications, and documents from his office and the warehouse.

"The next morning, he asked me to type up his resignation and then asked if I'd like to work for him. I never looked back."

Chapter Twenty-Eight

Saturday evening, Jackson awoke to the drone of jet engines. For a second he was disoriented before remembering he was on an airplane flying to the West Coast. The movie was still playing—some inane drool designed to anesthetize travelers. He raised the window shade. Mary had bought a first-class seat. Strange to be traveling to an earlier time on the same day. Déjà vu from the many trips he'd made back and forth to Stanford. Another life. Then he'd been in coach.

He felt like an imposter, all dressed up like a real person. Well, he would be an imposter soon. Jackson retrieved the envelope Mary had given him from the fancy leather case that still smelled store fresh.

Jackson fingered the business card in the folder. Philip Topham from Peabody and Bishop, a Boston firm Els had retained for years. His mission was to visit Beth Waddington and report back to Mary about her and about Worthy and Cherie's boating accident. What a posturing, self-important prick that guy had turned out to be.

Sure you aren't jealous of all the attention Mary was smothering on Worthy? Resentful of the warm welcome for the prodigal? Who was the real loser in this picture? Still, the guy was a low life with prep school manners and fancy clothes. The jerk had to think he'd just stumbled into a fortune. Maybe he had. And Jackson didn't like the way he looked at Casey.

He wished Mary could let go of her obsession with Beth, but he could certainly understand her need to keep tabs on the woman who had wreaked such havoc in her life. Mary always did her homework or had someone do it for her.

Concentrate, Philip.

* * *

In the airport terminal, he made a few calls to confirm the directions to Canterbury Woods, the new home of Beth Waddington. He rented a car and headed down Route 1 into Pacific Grove. Before the trip, he'd called and arranged for an interview and a tour of the assisted living facility.

He enjoyed Mary's "research" missions because he could pretend he was normal and shed the cloak of guilt that he wore in Massachusetts. He only wished the trips didn't reflect Mary's growing paranoia about any new face that showed up on her doorstep. But in fairness, Casey's imprisonment and Worthy's sudden appearance from out of the past would give anyone pause, especially if that someone was rich.

He limited his cover story to things he knew well in case he was questioned in any depth, saying he lived in Menlo Park not far from Stanford where he'd gone to school, and presenting himself as a lawyer investigating life care places for his mother, Mrs. Topham. She lived in McLean, Virginia and was healthy but lonely, rattling around in the house since her husband died. The story gave Jackson the background he needed to ask the administration and residents of Canterbury Woods all kinds of questions. He parked on a side street off Sinex Avenue, gripped his leather portfolio, and walked into the facility.

An hour and a half later, he ran out of questions. Vicki Somebody—he'd forgotten the administrator's last name— didn't seem to notice. When she placed her hand on his arm and looked up at him with a come-hither smile, he finally realized she was flirting and wasn't about to leave him to snoop on his own. They'd seen three apartment styles, the chapel, meeting rooms, the medical facility, and the library and adjoining great room when her cell phone rang. "Sorry, I have a meeting. How about you eat lunch in the dining hall, and we can meet up again in, say, an hour and a half?"

"Sounds good to me."

"I'll introduce you to a few residents so you have someone to sit with."

"No, no. Go on to your meeting. I'll introduce myself." He watched until she turned the corner to the administrative offices before ducking back into the great room where he'd seen two large notebooks that introduced the residents. He opened the first and was disappointed to see that it was organized by building number rather than alphabetically. Leafing through the pages, he quickly determined that his quarry, Mrs. Waddington wasn't in Building A. He found her in Building B. He was studying the photo with interest when a voice behind him startled him.

"There you are, Mr. Topham. I see you've discovered our version of the college 'wolf' book. I'm Flo, one of the 'inmates' here. Vicki asked me to take you to lunch."

Reluctantly, Jackson closed the book and followed Flo to the corridor where residents hovered in front of double doors. Moments later, he was caught up in the surge to enter the dining room. Flo laughed and led him to a table. "We race to the trough before everything's picked over," she explained. She showed him how they crossed a knife and fork to claim a seat and led him to two long institutional cafeteria-style tables heaped with food. He helped himself to New England clam chowder and two grilled ham and cheese sandwiches.

Flo introduced him all around the table of elderly women. Once one woman ventured a question, they all piled on, peppering him relentlessly while he tried to eat. During a brief lull, he explained that he was scouting life care places for his mother.

"Which ones? What did you think? Why isn't she with you? What do you think of Canterbury Woods so far? Where do you live? Are you married?" They laughed all at once. "We're so nosey. Forgive us," Flo apologized. "Let him eat." Nosey as they were, they were too polite to ask him why he wore a glove on one hand, although he knew from their glances they were dying to do so.

"I plan to visit Santa Rosa, although reports say it's awfully hot, and Mother doesn't do well with heat. Then there's the Manor in Carmel, well …" He paused, "I hear it's on the formal side. I think Mother would prefer the relaxed atmosphere here."

CHAPTER TWENTY-EIGHT

"They're snotty, that's what."

While the other ladies snickered, Jackson shrugged, disappointed that he hadn't spotted Mrs. Waddington. "There seems to be a lot of camaraderie here at Canterbury. Mother's particularly interested in the social atmosphere and how well the residents get to know one another." Out of the corner of his eye, he watched Beth Waddington push her wheelchair through an entrance reserved for disabled residents and pull up to the corner table across the room.

Relieved to see her arrive, he gave the ladies one of his most ingratiating smiles. "Let me ask you a question. How well do you know the residents sitting at..." he looked about as if randomly selecting a table, "the corner table?"

The old ladies glanced sideways at one another, taken aback.

"I'm sorry, I shouldn't ask such a nosey question." Jackson waved his hand as if erasing the slate. But since they'd asked their own nosey questions, he knew he was on safe ground, and his mission was to find out as much as he could about Beth's current situation.

Flo began the recital, and soon the others chimed in. "The fellow on the left was a bigwig at the Monterey Aquarium. He practically built the place himself. The ladies next to him are partners. The taller of the two was an Episcopal priest."

The woman next to Flo continued. "The younger-looking woman with brown hair was a school principal. Her husband's in the medical facility. She sits with him for hours, every day, poor dear."

They worked their way around the table, giving a detailed account of each resident, but stopped when a waiter appeared and asked if they wanted coffee or dessert. Unfortunately, they hadn't reached Beth Waddington.

"Our medical facility is top-notch," Flo commented, picking up on the thread of the poor woman visiting her husband.

"I had a tour earlier," Jackson cut in. He couldn't ask them to revisit the corner table without being obvious. "What happens when a resident needs care that the medical facility can't handle?"

"Oh, they go straight to Monterey Community Hospital. You probably passed it on your way in on Route 1. Matter of fact, the lady in the wheelchair on the far right just returned from Monterey. She had a hip replacement and now gets physical therapy here." The speaker turned to her neighbor. "Her no-account son hasn't visited her once since she got here."

"Now ladies, not too much dirt." Flo steered the conversation back to Jackson and asked him what his mother's hobbies were.

"He wanted to know how well acquainted we all are," the gossip objected. "She doesn't need a wheelchair. She's milking her operation for all it's worth. Next week she'll be blonde again."

Jackson studied Beth while the old ladies quibbled. She held forth telling a story that entertained her companions, waving her hands in exasperation while they laughed. Although her hair showed gray roots, it was clear that she'd been a beauty in her day. Long neck, graceful hands. No jowls or sagging chin. Must've had some cosmetic work done. He realized he was staring and returned his attention to the table.

After lunch, he excused himself and hurried to the great room to revisit the picture book. With his back to the room, he withdrew Beth's photograph and slipped it into his jacket pocket.

He retraced his steps to the medical facility and spoke with two nurses, asking if there were any residents he could speak to about their recent care, especially physical therapy. "Of course, I'd ask you to call them first to ask their permission," he assured them.

The nurses asked him to take a seat while they made a few calls. Ten minutes later he had what he wanted: a nurse's introduction to Mrs. Beth Waddington and directions to her building.

When he found her apartment, the door was partially ajar. "Hello?"

"It's open. Pardon me for not greeting you, but I'm in a wheelchair," called out a well-modulated voice.

Jackson introduced himself as Mr. Topham and gave Mrs. Waddington his spiel.

"Sit," she said, indicating a place on the sofa. "Call me Beth. Does your mother have a particular health problem?"

Jackson was startled by her directness and by the way she fixed him with razor-sharp eyes. The charming storyteller from the dining room had another, much harder side to her. "She's diabetic," he blurted without thinking. He relaxed, remembering that Beth had no reason to know Mary had sent him. "If you don't mind, I'll stand. I woke up with a crick in my back." He made a show of twisting and turning his torso, letting his eyes walk around the apartment.

"The care at the medical facility is more than adequate for what it is, but for anything serious, you've got to go to the Monterey Hospital."

While she told him what he already knew, Jackson made mental notes about the apartment to report to Mary. This Mrs. Waddington was an art connoisseur and a collector of sculpture. There were no family pictures or much of anything personal for that matter, but she had the most up-to-date electronic equipment.

Aware that Beth had stopped her recital, he turned back to her and was surprised to be caught in the crosshairs of her eyes. "Maybe you had better tell me who you *really* are," she said quietly.

Jackson was at a loss for words.

"Doesn't matter. Worthy sent you, didn't he?" Her mouth twisted down to a small, rather bitter smile.

Jackson gave her his most ingenuous smile. Dangerous ground, no matter what he said. "Now, why would he do that?"

"Is he still married to that cow?" In an instant, Beth's face transformed from an aging beauty to a mean-spirited crone.

Jackson stifled the impulse to back away. "The lovely Cherie?" He couldn't help the sarcasm.

"You've met her. Where is Worthy now?"

"Not here, that's for sure. I was expecting at least *one* picture of him on the bureau or the bedside table."

Beth snorted. "And why would I, after he took all my money and parked me in this godforsaken hole? You'd think a boy whose mother gave him everything would at least put her in the Manor." She wheeled herself to a desk, retrieved a folded paper, and handed it to him. Jackson read the announcement for Mary's estate sale, wondering how Beth had received it.

Jackson caught a flicker of concern cross Beth's face before it closed down into a hard mask. "Well, *Jackson*, the last I heard, Worthy was sucking up to his stepmother, your aunt, the *other* Mrs. Waddington, looking for a handout. Tell Mary to leave me alone. If I sound like a bitter old woman, I am. I don't have time for her stupid games, and my son doesn't have time for me. Close the door on the way out." She turned her chair away.

Stunned, Jackson was more than happy to close the door. Evidently, Beth's intelligence gathering was every bit as effective as Mary's. His report to Mary could wait until after he visited Mercer and Franklin, Worthy's law firm. She wasn't expecting him to go there, but he wanted more information about Worthy. He'd stay in San Francisco overnight and prepare for that meeting.

At least Mary could put one of her ghosts to rest. Beth was the two-faced, nasty, bitter woman Mary had described and appeared to be partially disabled. Sure, she'd called the White House to ask about Worthy, but that was understandable, a mother trying to connect with her estranged son. Apparently, Worthy hadn't called her back. It seemed unlikely that Mary would lure her east for the sale. Mary wouldn't want to hear that, but Jackson was relieved. Maybe she'd bury the hatchet now.

Chapter Twenty-Nine

B y Saturday evening, Casey was exhausted. She placed the last dish in the drying rack and listened. No sounds from above. Earlier that afternoon she'd been tempted to sneak a peek at the attic while her aunts took a nap, but had become immersed in the contents of the desk—her new, beautiful piece of antique furniture. She wasn't about to argue with Mary about the gift, but she knew instinctively that it could have commanded a hefty price at the estate auction. When you have money to burn, you can afford such largesse. But the gift was more than that, and she knew it. Mary wanted her to have a family heirloom, a remembrance of her father.

She moved slowly through the darkened rooms of tagged furniture scheduled for disposal, marveling at the amount of stuff in her relatives' lives. How would they have felt knowing it would soon be carted off, dumped, given away, or sold? Mary hadn't had a problem deciding what to do with the larger pieces; it was the little knick-knacks and treasures salted away in cupboards and drawers that had ended up in the "later" boxes stacked in the corner of the living room.

Reluctant to break the quiet spell, Casey navigated by the remaining evening light filtering in through the now-naked windows. She wandered from room to room, ending up in front of the desk. Once again, she stroked the smooth surface. Casey cracked the lid and admired the carving and beveling inside. The desk, plus the remnants from the Somerville apartment and pickings from the dump, were the beginnings of her lifelong collection of stuff. She'd only brought clothing and small items from Ohio, a few family photos, her diploma and college transcript, and the papers that attested to her innocence and wrongful incarceration at Marysville. She had had to go home after prison, she realized that now, but only to learn a bitter lesson—that life goes on relentlessly while you're away, filling in the space you once occupied.

She listened again. The house was tucked in for the night. She returned to the kitchen for her bag. A door inside the pantry opened to stairs that led to the old servants' quarters on the third floor and continued to the attic. She flicked on the overhead light switch, and a bare bulb overhead blinded her momentarily. With one hand on the wall and the other lugging her bag, she crept up steep stairs that had been built for smaller feet. She was thankful for her diminutive size; otherwise, she'd have to crab sideways as she imagined Jackson and Jed must have done.

The stairs dead-ended. Casey balanced her bag on a step and felt around the walls. Nothing. She raised her hand overhead, surprised to feel paper. Who wallpapered a ceiling? She pushed upward, and the ceiling lifted like a trap door on complaining springs while simultaneously lowering a few more steps. Creepy. She loved it.

She mounted the stairs and lowered the trap door behind her. When she rose to her full height, something small brushed against her face. Startled, she ducked and swatted as the object arced back toward her and then laughed at a hairy tarantula attached to a cord for the lights.

She pulled and was rewarded by a series of lights that illuminated the attic. The stairway entered the attic at one end. In a small space to her left were a number of cardboard boxes labeled "JED books," "JED music," and "Jackson." To her right, the room was long and narrow, spanning the full length of the main section of the house. A high peaked ceiling sloped to the edges with storage areas tucked into the eaves. Directly in front of her, facing the stairs, was a single bed with a small table and light.

Yards and yards of extension cords strung the length of the attic attested to the age of the wiring. At the far end of the room, a bookcase crammed with books from top to bottom spanned the entire back wall. Curious. Mary had said there was a bath with a toilet and shower. Casey looked about hopefully, not wanting to make the trek back downstairs if she didn't have to, but there was no sign of a bathroom.

The room was a regular pad and surprisingly neat. She had expected a messy room with clothes strewn about. No jackets, shirts, or jeans. Not even bureaus to house underwear, socks, or sweaters. If the family had cleared the place out, it would be a departure from their habit of just closing the door when someone left or died.

Casey marveled at the furniture they had managed to squeeze up the stairs. On the left, a couch with end tables faced a coffee table. Two armchairs sat opposite it, offering a cozy social area. Chess pieces still poised at attention on the table awaited their masters, engaged in a game long since forgotten. Interesting. No dust. The room had been cleaned for her. Mary had been confident she could lure Casey to West Boylston.

On her right was a desk and a drafting table that must have been Jackson's place to paint. Above a shelf of hockey, lacrosse, and soccer trophies was a miniature community of houses, churches, and other buildings that clung to the slanting wall like ancient Anasazi ruins.

Next to the drafting table, she spotted command central for some sort of school project. Black switching boxes connected by a jumble of wires tempted her idle fingers. She toyed with the closest control switch. With only minor resistance, it flicked from off to on.

Casey jumped at a sudden movement overhead and then laughed aloud. A miniature train engine hauled four cars and a caboose up an incline, chugging along at a good clip on tracks between watering stations, houses, and trees of the small overhead villages. It disappeared into a tunnel. Seconds later, its little light emerged from the far end of the tunnel. Casey watched the train as it made the circuit of the room. Farther on, the train slowed for a crossing, whistling as the barriers lowered, clanged, and flashed.

She turned on another switch. Tiny streetlights lit the little villages scattered about the room. She wondered if the train set was Jed's or Jackson's or if they had both had a hand in the ingenious design of the miniature world.

Casey flipped a third switch activating a larger Lionel model on the far side of the room that chugged along the track in the opposite direction. She was having a ball, playing master of the universe, when she realized that the big train was on a collision course with the smaller train. Before she could figure out which switches to flip, the trains whipped past each other on parallel tracks. The big train gained speed as it went downwards precipitously, hell-bent for the bookcase. Suddenly it disappeared, although she could still hear its muffled progress. She stopped both trains. The bookcase wasn't that deep. There must be a way to get behind the wall.

Casey peered into the space between books where the big train had disappeared. She knocked on the boards behind the bookcase and was rewarded with a hollow sound. If the train went in, it would need to return, either to circle and exit by the same hole or by another. Slowly checking behind books, she followed the bookcase across the room to the eaves on the right side. Nothing. Frustrated, she went back to the left end and renewed her search.

In one place, a larger book was placed on its side. Casey lifted it. With a sudden whir, the wall moved toward her. She jumped aside as a section of the bookcase arced forward, revealing a walk-in closet behind the wall. Peering inside, she spied racks of clothing lining the rear wall. Ice skates and hockey pads, a soccer ball, and other sports equipment were jammed under the eaves to the right. A door on the left opened to a small bathroom with a shower, basin, and toilet.

Casey grinned at each new discovery. What a great place for a kid! Heck, it was a great place for an adult. Delighted not to have to go downstairs, Casey made use of the facilities. Although she knew she was alone, modesty caused her to close the door as she sat on the toilet. The instant the door shut, Casey let out a horrified gasp and then a laugh. She stared into Jackson's teenage eyes, painted in a life-sized portrait on the back of the door. Jackson sat on the throne with a naughty smile, hands folded modestly in his lap, and the words "Holy Shit!" in a word bubble above his head.

Casey examined the hands, trying to remember which hand Jackson covered with a glove. Didn't matter. Both of these hands were normal. Whatever happened to him occurred after he painted this picture.

The train tracks entered the bathroom through a tunnel at waist level, made a loop, and returned the way they came. She smiled at how much fun the boys must have had sending the train through when an unsuspecting friend was in the bathroom.

Casey found towels, soap, and shampoo under the sink. She undressed, turned on the shower, and adjusted the temperature. Glorious hot water rushed over her, washing away the dust and musty smells from the day. She marveled at how much her life had changed in the few months since she'd come East. Her only regret was that her father had died before she could meet him. Thinking back to the discoveries of the day, she realized that Mary had orchestrated the trip as a way to introduce Casey to her family by seeing and touching their world.

She was thankful she'd been able to spend time with LouAnne and Rosie and made a mental note to invite them to dinner to meet Mary and Vera. She'd have to rig a ramp to get the wheelchair into the station, but it was a low threshold and shouldn't be a problem.

Mary had set her up perfectly, with the desk and its contents, and tonight with the attic. She knew Casey would figure out the moving panel. Casey's mind wandered, thinking about Mary. If Mary had such insight, why did she put up with Worthy and Cherie? Worthy wasn't so bad and could be rather charming, but Cherie was a real train wreck. Mary hadn't offered any comments about the couple, but then, she probably wouldn't think it appropriate.

"Appropriate," she said aloud with a smile. Since when did Mary worry about appearing appropriate? She'd been take-it-or-leave-it forthright with Casey. Well, most of the time, Casey amended.

Mary was up to something, and if Casey's hunches were correct, the something wasn't completely above board. From Casey's brief conversation with Jackson, she knew he suspected as much. At least he seemed clueless about Mary's sub rosa schemes, but then, he could be acting the fool himself. After all, he was off on some mysterious research mission at Mary's behest and had made other trips in the past.

Were these suspicious thoughts the rub-off from her prison years that had corrupted her innocent brain? No, Mary's plan was already in full swing by the time Casey visited, so she'd been nursing the dream for a while. Mary planned to give her worldly goods away and was doing so at great speed, citing her failing health as the reason for the foreshortened timetable.

Casey rubbed herself dry in the steamy room. Tomorrow for sure, she needed to ask Mary about her plans for the station. The longer she put it off, the harder it would be if she had to leave. She'd already pictured where her new desk would go, not a good sign for someone who didn't have a guarantee she could stay.

Casey donned a nightgown, scooped up her clothes, and left the bathroom. The button to close the panel was easy to find now that the large tome was removed. She pushed it and padded barefoot toward the bed. From this reverse perspective, Casey noticed new things she'd missed on the first pass through the room.

On a supporting beam close to the drafting table, Jackson had tacked up pictures in various stages of completion. He'd painted the same picture multiple times. Actually, he'd *copied* the same scenes over and over, some attempts clearly more successful than others.

She'd heard of copying the masters as an art school exercise. Jackson had taken it seriously, and he was very, very good. She examined one series with great interest—Jackson's practice runs at reproducing Picasso's *Still Life with Chair Caning*. She took down one sheet and looked at the back. "After Picasso, by Jackson Dempsey." Casey pictured the same image framed and hanging in the living room in the White House before the burglary and smiled.

She studied a cork bulletin board with yellowed newsprint tacked to it, as well as a few photographs. In one picture, a young blonde woman with delicate features and intelligent eyes gazed pensively toward the camera, looking fragile; in another, the same woman was captured with a mischievous flirting expression. Other clippings recorded athletic events, the "big" games, and a few prom shots of Jackson with the blonde woman holding a bouquet of roses. Casey wondered what had become of her. She couldn't help comparing herself to the ephemeral, almost un-worldly beauty in the picture. *Don't go there.* He's your cousin, a talented artist with a history of... *Just don't.*

She could leaf through the books and look at other treasures tomorrow. Before switching off the lamp, she rummaged through the single drawer in the bedside table. She found a pipe, a pouch of sweet-smelling tobacco, and an ashtray and matches. As she replaced the smoking paraphernalia, her fingers touched something that rolled away.

Her fingers explored the back of the drawer, finding two orange medicine vials with labels for Joseph Dempsey. One prescription was for lithium, and the other for Ativan. The dates on the bottles were shortly before his death. He must have returned to West Boylston at the end of his life. She stared at the vials, recognizing the names of the medications, her mind reeling.

One of the inmates in her cellblock at Marysville had been on similar medications. She was bipolar, although the woman had called it manic depression. The woman would get seriously wound up and disappear for a few days, and at other times her eyes would glaze over, and she'd withdraw into herself.

Had her father suffered from mental illness? Was that why he moved around so many times at the end of his career? Casey's mind spun in circles with the possibilities. She replaced the medicine slowly, revisiting what little she knew about her father. Finally, realizing that she didn't have any answers and that she was dead tired, she switched off the light. Another thought haunted her. She'd also read that the illness, like schizophrenia, could be genetic.

Her last thought before drifting into a fitful sleep was that Mary would have removed the medicine if she'd wanted to keep Casey's father's illness a secret.

* * *

Casey lurched awake at a deafening explosion. Disoriented at first by unfamiliar surroundings, she had to convince herself she wasn't in the middle of a dream. She winced at another streak of lightning and explosion directly overhead. A deluge of rain pounded the roof.

She switched on the light and relaxed when she spotted the couch and chess set and the bookcase at the end of the long room. She listened to the storm howl for a few moments before turning off the light and pulling the covers up to her chin. She loved the wild abandon of storms. As a child, she and her mother would huddle together and marvel at nature's temper tantrums.

Suddenly she shot straight up, banging her head on the low overhang of the eaves. Letters, words, swam in the air directly overhead. She scrambled for the light, but when she switched it on, nothing was there. "Casey, girl, you're losin' it," she said, mimicking LouAnne's voice.

But when she turned off the light, the apparition reappeared. Forcing herself to remain calm, Casey read the messages.

"Yea, though I walk through the valley of the shadow of death...."

Casey shuddered.

"Whether or not I shall be the hero of my own life...these pages shall tell."

Farther up, other messages danced before her eyes.

"My feet are fettered, but my fist is free."

They were messages from the past written in ink that glowed in the dark. On one side, printed in bold block letters, *"Paint what you want and die happy."*

She guessed that the smaller writing belonged to Jed and the single, defiant print to Jackson. Many of the familiar lines were incomplete, a reminder to the writer of a passage that held special meaning. She squinted and read the last of Jed's quotations: *"Two roads diverged in a yellow wood...."*

Once again, she snuggled under the covers. *"...and that has made all the difference,"* she murmured to herself, thinking of her mother and Jed and the priesthood. Who was the man really, she wondered, a joyful, loving musician or a mad priest? Or all of the above?

Chapter Thirty

C asey arose at dawn determined to get a head start sorting out her great aunts' rooms on the second floor. She'd reward herself later with time to explore the attic's treasures in more detail.

As she raised the trap door to the stairs, she laughed aloud. Last night she'd felt paper on the ceiling when she pushed up on the trap door. Now she stared into the eyes of a voluptuous nude, although the eyes weren't the focal point of the poster. One of the boys had rigged a hook on the ceiling to keep the door propped open to enhance his viewing pleasure. Fingerprints on the poster where the boys had touched the picture on the way to and from their attic hideaway reminded Casey of old war movies where the hero patted the bottom of a pin-up girl as he ran off to vanquish the enemy. The poster was worn and could have easily served two generations. It must have been strange for Jed and Jackson, growing up in a house full of old women.

She began working at the far end of the second floor, away from Mary's and Vera's rooms. As she'd done before, she made four piles: Dump, Salvation Army, "Don't Know," and Estate Sale. The sisters were all named after flowers: Mother Dempsey was Rose, and then there were her older sisters, Iris, Daisy, Lily, and Petunia. Each room had a bed and bureau, desk and chair, all easy to catalogue. The personal items were the most interesting by far, reflecting the wildly divergent personalities of the sisters.

Iris' spartan room focused on religious tracts, programs, prayers, rosaries, and crosses, praying hands, and prayer-of-the-day calendars. Casey created a new category and labeled it "Church." With a naughty smile, she tucked a set of false teeth in the pocket of one of the tent-like dresses and stuffed them along with lace-up orthopedic shoes into the Salvation Army bag.

Daisy's room was next. Nothing that had crossed the threshold of her room had ever escaped. The closet alone took a half hour with clothes that progressed from tiny to ginormous. Boxes were filled with random collections—shoe polish, a stapler, brass doorknobs, gardening gloves, and a French dictionary. At the back of the closet, she found unopened boxes of alarm clocks, toasters, and a calculator, with passbooks from different banks taped to the outside of each to record the source of the largesse. In the pocket of a moth-eaten wool coat, she found a $100 bill.

Lily decorated her room in hues of mauve, pink, and lavender. Classic evening dresses, heels, and hats from earlier decades would be a fashion bonanza for a drama club prop manager. Lotions and cosmetics on a vanity promised to smooth, soften, gloss, scent, and hide. Casey found pearls and pop-it beads, costume jewelry, and a valuable-looking filigree ring.

Petunia micromanaged her belongings. She lined and labeled drawers and coordinated her clothing with the colors on an artist's palette with matching shoes in boxes below. She'd inserted silverware drawer organizers for her jewelry so that no two pieces touched. Casey shuddered at the regimentation.

Casey couldn't help but wonder what someone would surmise by going through her own digs—clothes in conservative colors: informal, athletic, practical. Sum total: dull. *Quit wool-gathering and get to work.*

She opened the lower drawer of Petunia's bureau and was instantly repelled by the odor of decaying latex. She'd discovered the place where old girdles went to die. Stacked neatly in three parallel piles were the twentieth century's answer to the corset, plus old bras and a pile of grayed nylon underpants that were the recent home of a mouse family. Casey stared in awe at a bra with a three-inch back.

When Casey reached puberty, her mother had come into her room and handed down the wisdom of the ages. "If you can hold a pencil under your breast without it falling, it's time for proper undergarments."

Petunia could have easily pinned a toaster oven under one boob. Casey dumped the underwear and then shook out the other garments before jamming them into a jumbo plastic leaf bag.

Down the hall, a toilet flushed, followed by muffled voices and the creak of Vera's chair on the old wooden floorboards. In addition to the growing list of questions about her father and Mary's plans for the station, Casey wondered if Mary had the energy to renovate this leviathan nineteenth-century house and organize an estate sale. Clearing out these rooms was the easiest part of what lay ahead.

Although she was thankful for the opportunity to "meet" her great aunts through the sorting process, Casey was much more interested in her father's story and in the enigmas of the living: Mary, Jackson, and yes, she had to admit, Worthy. So far, she hadn't learned all that much about her father, but she suspected that Mary was leading her through a discovery process.

All morning she had resisted the temptation to revise the image of her father, telling herself that she didn't have enough information to confirm his illness. She had used the sorting activity to keep her mind occupied, and for the most part, it had worked.

The metallic clunk and hum of the elevator told her that Mary and Vera were beginning their day. Glancing at her watch, she was surprised to find it was time for lunch. She rehearsed a few of her questions while she washed up before joining her living aunts.

She found them outside in the sunshine. Vera sipped her drink from a baby's covered cup, and Mary sat beside her, cradling a mug of steaming coffee.

"Did you sleep well, dear?" Mary asked.

"Yes, until the thunder boomers came through."

"Never heard them, but then, I sleep like the dead. What did you think of the attic?" The question was casual, but Casey could feel Mary's eyes watching her.

"I loved it, as you knew I would. It was a wonderful way to learn more about Jed and Jackson." Casey chose the given name for her father, not knowing how to refer to the man she'd never met. "But I found myself with more questions than answers," she added. She drew up a chair and dusted it off.

Mary smiled and nodded, but didn't take her lead. Instead, she nursed her coffee and withdrew a list from her shirt pocket.

I'll wait her out, thought Casey.

After a period of silence, Mary changed the subject. "We need to talk about the future plans for the little station."

Casey's smile froze as she nodded, dreading Mary's next words. She knew her dreams of living in the little house were unrealistic but hadn't been able to suppress them. She bowed her head, waiting for what surely was to come.

"As you know, I'm thinking of setting up a non-profit organization to serve a residential community. A few possibilities include a halfway house for recovering mental patients or a home for disabled individuals.

"It makes sense to sell the valuable antiques and other items in the White House before such a conversion. I've also researched and submitted applications for grants. However, I realize that I'm not in good health and will need a considerable amount of help no matter which residents we serve. I'd like to know if you have any interest in playing a role."

Stunned by the unexpected question, Casey was silent for a moment. "I should think you have the major bases covered. Jackson could manage the physical plant. You'd need a nurse with experience caring for disabled or psychiatric patients, and, of course, there's Cherie." She looked up for Mary's reaction but received no response. "You have Gilma to manage housekeeping. I'm sure you have lawyers and Worthy for legal and financial counsel. Clearly, you're the boss for strategic decisions."

She looked at Mary with a bitter smile. "I do have experience living in an institutional community and re-entering society, but other than that, I don't know what I could offer."

"Worthy and Cherie are just visiting. I don't expect them to stay. Luckily there are plenty of lawyers and nurses in the area. I need something different. I'm hoping that the person who lives in the little station will direct the residents' activities and possibly sell products we produce in a little store. You'd be perfect."

Casey's mind reeled. The station and a job? Could she?

Mary watched her struggle with a smile.

"I don't know anything about—"

"You're a quick study. No one has the perfect resume for this position. It will be 'learning and labor' for us all, with a touch of love thrown in."

Casey grinned. "Learning and Labor" was the fun-packed motto of her alma mater, Oberlin College. "Yes," she whispered. "I'd need to know more, but I'd be very interested in being part of your project." She jumped to her feet and gave Mary a hug. She turned to Vera, who was beaming and hugged her as well.

When she sat down again, Mary took her hand. "We have tons of things to discuss, and I know you have oodles of questions, but right now we must make a serious dent in the upstairs rooms. I heard you working earlier. How far did you get?"

Casey filled Mary in on her progress.

"Good work! Maybe it won't be such a push after all. Vera, do you want to come in, or stay out here while we scramble up some eggs?"

"Ear, anx," Vera responded. Mary rolled her under the shade of a large oak. "I'll bring you some more juice."

Inside, Casey found eggs and muffins in the cooler and watched Mary refill Vera's baby cup. Mary was moving slowly today. While Mary delivered Vera's drink, Casey whisked the eggs, adding milk, salt, and pepper.

"Casey!" Mary shouted. "Where's Vera? I can't see! What's she doing?"

Casey rushed to the window. Mary stood alone under the tree.

Chapter Thirty-One

Casey ran out the door, scanning the back yard for Vera. Her eyes caught a glint of sunlight on metal on the dock. Vera had pushed her wheelchair to the end of the rickety structure.

Casey tore across the lawn, hollering at the top of her lungs, "Stop! Vera! No!" But she knew she was too late.

With one last mighty shove, Vera propelled the chair into space, arms raised overhead in victory as she and the chair plunged into the water.

Not knowing the depth, Casey made a flat surface dive to the right of the place where the chair had gone down. She couldn't see anything in the murky water. Taking a deep breath, she dove, waving her arms before her to locate the chair. Pond grass curled around her legs, trying to tangle her in its deadly clutches. She surfaced, gasped in air, took her bearings, and dove again. This time her hand connected with metal, and she knew she had the chair. She'd have to release Vera from the harness that strapped her in.

Casey pictured the seat belt apparatus while her hands explored the contour of the wheel. She found the end of a strap and swam with it to the back of the chair. Righting herself, her feet sank into muddy ooze. Still over her head, but shallow. She released the buckle of Vera's harness and tilted the chair to push Vera out of her cradle of death.

The chair rocked forward but stopped and sank backward, settling into the ooze. On top of her foot! Pinned! Her lungs were on fire. She shoved again. Nothing. She gripped a rubber wheel with both hands and forced it forward, releasing her foot. She pushed up off the bottom and broke the surface, coughing in water.

She took in two great breaths and dove again. This time, she tilted the chair by the handles with her legs anchored firmly on the bottom between the wheels. Vera's body fell forward in slow motion. Casey grabbed an arm and hauled her to the surface. Suddenly Vera rolled over, pulling Casey beneath her. One of Vera's thrashing fists connected with Casey's head. Stunned, she released her grip. Vera sank and then bobbed to the surface. Casey swam forward for a new hold. Vera shrieked and struck again, bashing Casey's outstretched arm.

Casey howled and stroked backwards out of reach. Her head reeled in pain and disbelief. Vera went under twice more. Let her?

No. She couldn't do it. She dove and swam underwater so Vera couldn't see her coming. She jerked Vera around and threw her arm over her in a cross-chest carry. Vera rolled over once, taking Casey with her, but when Casey didn't let go, she offered only token resistance as Casey hauled her to shore.

Casey lay flat on her back on the ground, breathing hard, dizzy from the blow to her head. Gingerly she massaged the rising welt above her left eye. Beside her, Vera threw up water and then sobbed quietly. Was she crying because she hadn't succeeded? At the moment, Casey didn't care. She shivered in her wet clothes, closed her eyes and waited for Mary to return with towels and a blanket.

Her struggle with Vera wasn't anything like her Life Saving classes. Sure, their "victims" thrashed and fought, but the rescues had been much simpler in the crystal-clear college pool where you could see the bottom and the person you were trying to save. And, of course, they weren't strapped to a wheelchair sinking into black ooze.

Mary returned and dumped a load of towels and blankets between Casey and Vera. "I called 911." She knelt and began toweling down Vera. Casey blotted her own soggy clothing and wrapped a towel around her head.

They spread the blanket on the lawn next to Vera and rolled her up in it like a cocoon.

Casey was amazed at Vera's size and the dead weight of her inert mass.

Sitting in her chair in one of her tent-like muumuus, Vera's heft was disguised. No wonder Casey was tired.

"Are you okay?" Mary asked, aware of Casey's shivers.

Casey nodded, removed her towel turban, rolled it, and placed it under Vera's neck.

"If you wouldn't mind, dear. Vera will need a change of clothes. You'll find some in the dresser by her door. Once we get her squared away, we'll find you something dry to wear."

Casey stood slowly, weighed down by the water in her jeans. Her sneakers squeaked and sloshed as she walked into the house, leaving wet prints on the hardwood floors.

Vera's room was sparsely furnished with a single bed, a simple pine dresser, and an old commode chair that looked like an antique collector's find. Pictureless, bare walls showed signs of harsh treatment. Casey ran her hand across a deep bash in the plaster, remembering Mary's story about Vera ramming her chair into walls before she installed the bumpers.

In a dresser, Casey found a housedress, panties but no bras. She tried to picture harnessing Vera with a bra and quickly dismissed the image. She selected socks and slippers. Everything Vera wore pulled on and off.

The only signs that the room had been occupied were two ceiling-high bookcases that were chock-a-block with books and a TV. She hadn't thought of Vera as a reader. She pictured her trying to turn the pages with her club-like hands. Doable, but so awkward. Still, if all you could do was read and watch, it was possible.

Closing the door, she imagined the punishing existence that Vera must have led since she was a teenager, realizing that her own prison years may have been richer and more rewarding than Vera's corporal confinement. Once again, she wondered if she had done the right thing, pulling Vera out of the water. Should she have let her go? Too late now.

As she exited the side door, an ambulance rounded the turn into Dempsey Lane, lights flashing but silent. Casey watched it churn up a rooster tail of dust in the dry gravel driveway. Two EMTs jumped out and ran to Mary and Vera.

Casey heard their voices as she approached the group. The lead EMT, a tall, middle-aged woman, spoke calmly and gently to Mary while her hands checked Vera's vital signs.

"Acting up, again, then?" the EMT said conversationally, unrolling Vera to retrieve a wrist for a pulse. "Get my bag and the stretcher, please," she called over her shoulder to her assistant.

"Afraid so. Will she be all right?" Mary asked.

"I'm more worried about you than about her. She's healthy as a horse. How the hell did you get her out?" The EMT glanced at the pier and back at Mary. "Where's her chair?"

"In the pond. My niece pulled her out. Bertie, meet Casey, Jed's girl."

As Bertie turned to greet Casey, her welcoming smile faded, and her jaw dropped.

Casey stepped backward at the woman's visceral reaction. She glanced at Mary who watched Bertie's reaction with undisguised interest.

"Spitting image, isn't she?" prompted Mary.

"That she is." Bertie scratched her head. "But Jed was a priest," she blurted.

"Casey was B.C."

"B.C.?"

"Before the Catholics got him."

Bertie laughed. "I'm so sorry. Pardon my manners." She rose slowly, unbending her long frame like a folding ruler, hand outstretched in greeting.

Casey gave her a tentative, rather self-conscious smile, uncomfortable under the intense scrutiny.

"Mary and I have been best friends for years. Standing joke in these parts. Keep an ambulance parked at the head of Dempsey Lane. What with Mary and her fits, Vera setting herself on fire, the boys and their pranks, and the old girls popping off at random moments, the Dempsey clan needed their own fleet."

Casey was speechless at Bertie's jocular familiarity and matter-of-fact catechism of the family woes. The woman knew Casey's family much more intimately than she ever would.

Bertie glanced at the breathing mound before them. Vera hadn't moved a muscle since she'd last belched up water. "Stirs up a cauldron of trouble better than any able-bodied man could do, then sleeps like a baby."

The assistant returned with the bag and a rolling stretcher. Bertie took him aside and spoke quietly with him for a second. When they returned, they assumed positions on either side of Vera. With the bag shielding her actions, Bertie's deft fingers loaded a syringe with fluid. She placed the syringe on the blanket and wet a ball of cotton with alcohol.

Bertie nodded to the assistant. In one swift motion, he flipped aside the blanket and clamped onto Vera's arms, pinning her. Vera's eyes shot open, looking wildly at them, first in surprise and then rage. With a guttural howl, she lunged forward, her teeth snapping at the assistant. With total concentration and fluid motion, Bertie swabbed and stuck simultaneously, retreating to safety the instant she pulled the needle out of Vera's arm.

"Just a few moments, now," she assured them. She turned to Casey. "Vera plays possum better than anyone I ever met. Pulse betrayed her." They watched Vera's struggles wane and her eyes dull as she succumbed to the medication. Bertie checked her pulse again. "Better," she commented to herself and then gently brushed a lock of wet hair away from Vera's eyes.

"Where's that handsome young Jackson?" Bertie asked as they hefted Vera's body onto the stretcher.

"Not so young anymore. He's in California doing a little research for me." Mary hesitated and then continued. "He seems to be doing much better. Young Casey here actually got him to sketch and paint a bit." Mary smiled over at Casey.

Casey's mind had flooded and stalled. These women were chatting away as if nothing had happened. Didn't Vera just try to kill herself? And Casey, for that matter? She felt the side of her head and considered pinching herself to make sure the scene wasn't one of her wilder dreams. The headache was authentic.

Her mind drifted back to LouAnne's plea for her to stay at the battered women's shelter and her suggestion that it might be a safer haven for Casey than her newly found, dysfunctional family.

How did Mary know that Jackson had painted her a picture? Casey watched them strap Vera onto the stretcher and wheel her to the ambulance. She turned and gazed at the pond to calm herself, willing the feeling to pass.

Suddenly, Bertie's hands clasped Casey's head, turning it to one side. "You're going to have a beaut," she commented. "Vera's work?" she asked Mary.

Mary nodded.

"Watch my finger," Bertie ordered, moving her index finger back and forth and side to side. "One or two?" she demanded.

"One."

"Any dizziness?"

"No."

"Lucky. An inch to the side, and she'd have knocked you out."

"Your turn." Bertie turned on Mary.

"I'm fine," Mary objected, backing away.

"You are *never* fine," Bertie retorted, looking into her eyes and feeling her pulse. "How's it been recently?" she asked, releasing Mary's arm.

Mary shrugged.

"Talk to Bertie," the EMT prompted gently, as if quieting a skittish horse.

Mary sighed. "Sight's deteriorated a bit. I've lost some hearing in my left ear, and I'm working on a kidney infection. Matter of fact, I could use some antibiotics, if you happen to have anything with you."

"You both need to come in with us—"

"You know my rule about hospitals," Mary interrupted.

Casey watched, aware that they'd had this conversation before.

"Mary never enters a hospital unless she's unconscious," Bertie explained. She walked back to the blanket, repacked her bag, and rejoined them.

"Coming? We'll X-ray your noggin to make sure there's no concussion."

"Thanks, I'll stay with Mary."

"Okay, we're off. We'll keep Vera drugged until she's cooled off, poor dear. I'll check in here on my way home."

"Thanks, Bertie." Mary stepped forward and gave Bertie a big hug.

Casey and Mary watched the ambulance turn around and retrace its path down Dempsey Lane, onto the main street, and out of sight.

Casey moved slowly, picking up the blanket and towels, finding new aches with every step. Under the blanket she found two boxes of antibiotic tablets that Bertie must have "dropped" in her haste to pack and leave.

She felt she was in a play where everyone in the cast knew their lines but her.

Chapter Thirty-Two

After Mary retired to her room, Casey returned to the second floor and dragged the heavy bags and boxes to the elevator. Downstairs, she arranged the goods by destination. She fixed herself a cup of hot cocoa and lit a fire in the living room fireplace while she edited the lists cataloguing bag contents. When she finished, she curled up on the couch and fell into a fitful sleep.

She awoke hours later with a headache and an attitude. The headache was easily remedied with two aspirin and a bag of ice. The attitude defied her best efforts and refused to go away. She shivered and threw more logs on the embers and fanned until the fire came alive. The weather was noticeably colder, and the sun was low already. Soon the leaves would turn and fall. *Think positive thoughts.* She could plant daffodil bulbs beside the station before the first frost.

Where would she put her first, very own Christmas tree? The station interior was too small, and besides, she had a cat and kittens. Maybe she could place it out back on the railway platform where the lights would sparkle through the windows. She didn't have ornaments, but outside lights would be just fine, especially under a coating of new snow with a fire in the wood-burning stove.

Mentally she rearranged the furniture in the station's open downstairs area to give her new desk pride of place. She'd need to fix up an office where she could plan resident activities and events. Where did Mary intend to have the little store? Not inside the station, Casey hoped. She didn't relish the idea of strangers milling about amongst her digs. But, of course, Mary hadn't told her that part of the plan. Yet another question.

Rats. Positive thinking was bogus. The little seed of resentment that she discovered while lugging the bags downstairs was growing. She was being pushed forward like a pawn, one square at a time, ignorant of the larger game plan, not knowing if, or when, she'd be sacrificed. She didn't aspire to bishop or castle status. Powerful, but too predictable. But she could easily be a knight that could move in quirky patterns, two straight and one to the side, partnering with the queen. That is, if the queen were willing to share information with her.

She knew her malaise stemmed from Mary's manipulation. It was done with grace, but manipulation nonetheless. Casey's basic authority resistance had finally kicked in after Vera had been taken to the hospital, and Mary had put off her questions yet again with, "Later, dear. Do you mind awfully moving the bags downstairs?"

Had she signed up for the job, whatever it was, too fast? Mary's timing was impeccable. Casey was homeless, out of work, and far from friends and family. On cue, Casey had agreed to a role in Mary's play. But so far, she only got the plot on the installment plan, scene to scene. If she were to play a role, she'd have to give Mary notice that she wasn't interested in games.

She shook her head and winced at the lightning bolt of pain that shot through her temple. She hadn't asked about salary, rent, vacation, health benefits—anything. She didn't even have a job description. Time to write her questions down.

She had questions, but did Mary have answers? It was entirely possible that Mary didn't have a detailed plan, that she was improvising day to day, trying to hold it together, in delicate health with a disabled sister and multiple properties to manage.

Casey was casting about for a clean sheet of paper when Mary walked in carrying two cups of tea. She joined Casey by the fire and wrapped herself in an afghan. Casey had noticed that Mary was often bundled up.

"You've been busy," Mary said, looking at all the bags filling the room. "I couldn't have done it without you. Thank you, Casey."

"You're welcome." Casey handed Mary her accounting lists of articles in the bags. While Mary scanned the lists, Casey dragged in the "Church" box and the "Don't Know" boxes and set them beside Mary's chair.

Mary glanced at the "Church" box. "Write 'St. Julia's' on the outside, will you dear? We can drop it off at the church anytime."

Who's 'we'? thought Casey, feeling a touch of resentment boil to the surface.

Mary made equally quick work delving into the "Don't Know" boxes. She tested the pearls for authenticity by rubbing them against her teeth. Only Lily had sprung for the genuine articles. She set aside the good pearls and the filigree ring. She slipped another ring with a sapphire between two diamonds onto her little finger. "It's an old friendship ring. Lily's beau gave it to her when they were courting. He died in the war."

Casey was about to ask which war but thought better of it. Had to be the Great War. Another family tragedy.

Mary pushed the pearls and the two rings across the coffee table to Casey. "See if the sapphire ring fits. If it doesn't, we can have it sized, but it's a little dicey with a worn band."

Stunned, Casey just stared at Mary with a question in her eyes.

"Go on. It won't fit over my knuckles, and it's a sure thing Vera and Jackson won't wear it."

Of course, the ring fit Casey's finger perfectly. She held up her hand and admired the way the facets glinted in the firelight. So tempting. She wanted the ring, but she didn't want to be indebted. Someday, she'd buy her own jewelry. "It's beautiful, but I really don't want to accept any more gifts." She removed the ring and pushed the jewelry back toward Mary.

"Maybe you'll reconsider after I answer your questions. I know you're frustrated with me and feeling out of the loop on the plans and that you also have oodles of questions about your father and the family. I apologize and hope you'll understand that I only have so much energy these days. I spoke out of turn yesterday when I asked you to join the team."

In the pause that followed, Casey's attitude took flight, and her dreams bottomed out. *Too good to be true. No team. No job. No station.*

Mary took a sip of tea and continued. "I should have waited until the grant money came through before getting your hopes up—and mine as well. We'll hear about the money tomorrow or Tuesday, and we can talk specifics. Then you'll have the information you need to see if you're really interested." She hesitated. "Now. Your questions."

It was a demand, not a query. Whiplash. Where to begin? Casey sought the words but came up empty. Instead, she pulled the two medicine vials out of her pocket and pushed them toward Mary.

"Right, then. By now, you've guessed that your father suffered from manic-depressive disorder."

Casey nodded at the confirmation.

"Your father was a proud man, and, according to him, his sin of pride was his undoing. He got all the talent genes in the family. He was a brilliant intellectual and a fierce debater, a chess champion and a child prodigy on the piano." Mary rose, lifted a thin volume from a bookcase next to the fireplace, and handed it to Casey.

"Mother published his poems at a vanity press to encourage him to write more, but after he took orders, he said that he'd repressed that muse and that the old gods didn't visit him anymore."

"But he still played the piano, didn't he?"

"Oh, yes. Matter of fact, his last assignment was playing the organ at St. Patrick's Cathedral in New York. Unfortunately, he began practicing at unscheduled times, disturbing the faithful and the clergy. The last time he was removed in the wee hours of the night. He came home for good after that."

"The other day, you said he was sick." Casey couldn't keep a touch of earlier resentment from her voice.

"Well, he was. He had a chemical disorder that incapacitated him as completely as any other disease. It was very sad. No, tragic. He could light up a room with his very presence and captivate an audience completely with his fantastic stories. But when he crashed, the spirit left his body.

"His illness got progressively worse over the years and harder and harder to control. Lithium made him feel flat and stupid. He moved slower, and his hands shook with tremors.

"He so enjoyed his highs, I suspect he'd 'forget' to take his medicine just to experience the rush and the exhilaration he felt on the way up. 'I can do anything. Think anything. Play anything,' he explained once. 'It's a physical force inside compelling me, urging me higher and higher. The temptation overwhelms me.'

"After the debacle at St. Patrick's, he never allowed himself another high, his heaven on earth, saying he'd have to wait his turn like the rest of us and hope heaven would still take him. When he was stable enough, he came home to live with us. He stayed in the attic for days on end, doing penance by fasting and by drowning his desire in the bottle. The combination killed his spirit and finally betrayed his body."

Mary paused. "Could I ask you to warm up our tea? I'm cold. I promise that I'll continue with your questions."

Casey did her bidding in a daze, her mind reeling with images of her father, the crazy priest, whisked away from St. Patrick's to his attic where he killed himself slowly through neglect. She took her time with the tea and then stoked the fire, unsure if she was ready for more revelations.

"I see I've upset you. I debated long and hard about telling you this sad story. But there is a chance you've inherited the gene, so I felt you should know. He was the only one of our generation, but I think his grandfather was afflicted. It is difficult to know because they pushed mental illness under the rug out of fear and embarrassment."

Mary looked up and engaged Casey's eyes. "I know his life sounds tragic, but although he suffered, he also achieved heights of inspiration and accomplishment, even bliss, that few mortals ever experience. In the good times—and they far outnumbered the bad in his younger years—he was truly blessed."

Casey hadn't uttered a word throughout Mary's recital. She'd sought information about her father. Now, despite Mary's belief to the contrary, she couldn't help but feel his illness was a curse he couldn't escape, try mightily as he would. "Did my mother know?"

"I'm sorry, Casey. I have no idea. I doubt it, though, because the first time he was hospitalized, he was teaching in Greece after he'd entered the

Church."

Thank whatever Gods that be for small favors, Casey thought bitterly. She hoped that her mother hadn't known the last chapter. "Thank you, Mary. I know that wasn't easy. You knew him and loved him. It must be painful to talk about."

"Just the sad parts," Mary admitted. "But I get along day to day remembering the good times—with Mother, with Jed, with Vera, and with Els. I mostly succeed."

"Mostly?" Casey prompted.

"Yoo-hoo! Anybody home?" They both jumped at the slam of the back door.

"We're in the living room, Bertie," Mary called back.

Seconds later, Bertie walked in and flopped her long frame in an armchair. "Now don't you two look comfy by the fire," she said in greeting.

"We were just talking about Jed," Mary explained.

Bertie sat up. "I can come back later, no problem."

"No, no. Sit. Stay. How's our patient doing?" Mary's mouth was set as if she were bracing herself for bad news.

Loud laughter and shattering glass interrupted the quiet evening.

"Anyone we know?" asked Mary.

"They've been having problems with town kids drinking and partying at closed cottages. Some vandalism." As she spoke, Bertie bundled into her jacket and grabbed her keys. "Back in a sec."

"Where do you think you're going?" Mary asked, but Bertie was already halfway out the door.

Casey rushed to the window and watched Bertie drive the Ambulance down the drive to the Y in the road that branched off to Agnes' little house. Moments later, the wail of a siren split the air, and strobes flashed. Casey squinted at what looked like dark figures darting away from the back of the house and melting into the trees.

Bertie returned and flopped into the chair. "Bunch of kids. Now, where were we?" She glanced at Mary. "Vera's no worse for wear from her dip in the pond." She paused. "We won't get the results of her other tests until

186

CHAPTER THIRTY-TWO

Monday or Tuesday at the latest."

Casey watched Bertie and Mary's eyes lock for a moment. Whatever silent message passed between them wouldn't be shared with Casey.

"What tests?" Casey asked, determined not to be cut out.

"Sorry, Casey," Mary responded. "Vera hates hospitals even more than I do. We have to sedate her to get her in for her annual physicals. We're waiting for the doctor's reports."

But once again, Casey sensed a well-meaning half-truth. None of her business, she chided herself. There's no reason for her to be privy to intimate details of these women's lives.

They sat for a moment in silence. A log shifted in the fire. Bertie was the first to move. "Lots to think about. Mary, have you had anything to eat today?"

"Don't start—"

"You have to eat, especially with an infection."

"Yes, Sister Bertie," Mary quipped, but her voice cracked. "Just give me a moment, will you?"

Bertie hugged Mary. "Of course. I'll run a hot bath to warm you up while Casey scrounges in the kitchen for victuals."

On the way to the kitchen, Casey heard low voices and then Mary's sobs.

Chapter Thirty-Three

While Mary warmed up in the tub, Casey pounded, seasoned, and sautéed the chicken under Bertie's direction, glad to have something to do to distract her from thoughts about her father and Vera. Once they had the chicken in the oven and the vegetables ready, they retired to the living room.

"I'm glad that we have a few moments to talk," Bertie began.

Oh Lord, what now? Casey sat back in her armchair, awaiting the newest unwelcome revelations.

"I'm worried about Mary. She's weak and actually admitted that she has a kidney infection. Not good. She's in danger of having a hypo. I think you know...but that's when her blood sugar drops suddenly. I hate to put this on you, but she won't admit herself to the hospital, and I'm on duty tonight. I told her the only way she could stay here was if you would check on her during the night. She agreed but made me promise not to pressure you in any way." Bertie glanced at Casey.

But you will. "Why won't she go into the hospital?"

"We can't force her, and frankly, she's better off treating herself. She knows her body. The hospital staff operates strictly by the book, holding blood sugar levels within a lower, prescribed range that doesn't work for Mary. Her system is too volatile to run low. It's ironic, but when she's in a hospital, she's in greater danger of serious fluctuations than if she monitors her levels at home. That said, she's extremely vulnerable when she's got an infection that can send her system into a tailspin. Stress is also a major debilitating factor."

Casey took a deep breath. "What do I need to know?"

"A number of things. They're simple, but important, and could be lifesaving. As I said, Mary's sugar levels can drop precipitously, so she needs to run a bit high on sugar while she's here."

Like an engine on high test, thought Casey.

"First of all, you should know how to take and read a blood sample." Casey listened attentively while Bertie described the fine art of finger pricking and reading the results on a diabetic blood monitor.

"Have you ever given a shot? Are you afraid of needles?" Bertie stared into Casey's eyes. "You *must* be honest with me."

"No, and no."

"Do you think you could give Mary an injection?"

Casey frowned. "Why wouldn't I just call 911?"

"Good question. Because you can't hover over her twenty-four hours a day. If you find her unconscious, you won't know how long she's been out—a minute, or an hour or more. Time is the critical factor. If she goes into a coma, we have big trouble. If she's unresponsive, don't hesitate. Give her a shot."

Coma? Unresponsive? "Oh, no." She shook her head. "You need a nurse, not a history major."

"I've already called around. Unfortunately, it's dinner time on Saturday night, and I haven't been able to locate either another available EMT or a nurse. I'm sorry. I didn't mean to frighten you. There's very little chance she'll have a hypo tonight."

Bertie waved the air as if she were erasing her earlier words. "You've seen her drinking Glucozade when her sugar levels are dropping and she needs a quick fix. She also takes tea with lots of sugar and a biscuit. Tonight, we'll eat dinner late in order to give her plenty of fuel to get through the night. Her most vulnerable time is around 2:30 am, when her metabolism is at its lowest. I'm just asking you to sleep in Vera's room tonight and set the alarm to check on her then."

Against her better judgment, Casey nodded. Mary had welcomed her as family, given her a place to live, and offered her a job. She could sleep in

Vera's room for a night. Give Mary a shot if she had to, and call 911. She'd hoped to escape to the attic, but Mary's health took precedence. "Show me what to do."

Bertie led Casey to the kitchen and retrieved what looked like a bright orange eyeglass case from the old refrigerator. She opened it. "This is a glucagon." She took out a syringe and a small vial. She showed Casey how to shake, load, and tap it to remove air bubbles.

"Place the syringe against the fleshy part of her hip and give her the full dose. If she's just going out, you have a half hour before calling Emergency. She should start coming to within a few minutes. Keep her warm."

"How can I recognize the beginning of a hypo?"

"Her speech will slow and lose coherence. She may smile at you as if she knows what you're saying, but watch her eyes. They glaze over, and her pupils become pinpricks. What she wants is to sleep. Don't let her! Walk her. Sit her up. Use cold water. Sing. Ply her with Glucozade and sugar. If she tells you to 'Fuck off,' don't take it personally. At that point, her overriding desire is to be left alone. Give her the shot and call us.

"Another thing, don't be surprised if she gets sick. It's a normal reaction to the shock of the medication. Rule of thumb: a shot needs a bowl by the bed."

"Why would it make her sick? Isn't it what her system needs?"

"The medicine tells the liver to release all the stored sugar it's been hoarding. Like a fight or flight mechanism: all or nothing. There's no halfway measure, at least not yet. So, we're fighting an underdose with an overdose, and that causes a massive reaction." Bertie hesitated and looked Casey in the eye. "Diabetes is a dreadful, unrelenting, merciless disease." She put her hand on Casey's shoulder. "Can you do it?"

"Yes."

"Good girl. I'll leave the Glucozade and the loaded syringe in the fridge. When she's at the White House, that's where she keeps it."

"Is the tutorial about over?" Mary asked, entering the kitchen in a heavy terrycloth robe.

"Perfect timing. Casey's a fast study. You'll be in good hands if you need

190

it," said Bertie.

Casey sure hoped so.

Chapter Thirty-Four

Casey washed up after what had turned out to be a very successful dinner. She could hear Mary and Bertie talking quietly in the dining room but couldn't make out the words over the sound of the water.

Despite Bertie's stern order to Casey not to blame herself for foiling Vera's suicide attempt, Casey wondered if she had done the right thing. If Vera really wanted to die, shouldn't she be able to make that decision? Who was Casey to decide? Casey stared out the window toward the pond. What would she do now, this instant, if Vera tried to roll off the dock? Could she let her sink?

"Casey, dear, could you join us for a minute?" Mary called out.

Casey dried her hands on a towel and joined Mary and Bertie in the living room. She took a chair across from the best friends, noting their somber expressions.

"Now, all of what I'm going to say depends upon the grant coming through. If it does, and we're a go, Bertie has agreed to take on the medical responsibilities for our White House project."

Bertie looked up and smiled, clearly pleased with her decision.

"I've been after her for months, but she just now threw her hat into the ring. Bertie has all the qualifications we need. She's both a psychiatric and a medical nurse. She headed up the training program at the University of Massachusetts teaching hospital for years and has impeccable nursing credentials and experience. The young EMT you met this afternoon is ready to take on full-time responsibility, and she's confident she's leaving that program in good hands."

Casey grinned at Bertie. Bertie offered her hand for a high five, and Casey met her halfway. She turned to Mary. "What's the grant you're talking about?"

Mary offered a non-answer. "One rule of the rich: never touch principal." She then continued. "There's another matter you should know. Bertie has convinced me of what Jackson has been saying for some time; there's no way that I can manage the White House and continue to care for Vera. Bertie, Vera, and I will take up residence in the gatehouse. It's the perfect size. Vera will stay on the first floor, so there's no need for an elevator." She smiled at Bertie. "Frankly, Bertie blackmailed me into this, saying it was a condition of her decision to join us. I'm stubborn, but I'm not stupid, and her arguments make sense.

"Bertie suggested calling the converted White House 'The Dempsey House' or some such thing. If we want to go the dual route, we can have the east wing be the Vera Dempsey Wing for our disabled residents, and the west wing, the Jed Dempsey Wing, for psychiatric outpatients. Nothing has been decided on that score yet, though."

"Don't you need to decide these things in order to write a grant proposal?" Casey was still confused about why Mary needed a grant.

The phone rang, startling them all. Bertie answered and handed the receiver to Mary.

"Hello?" Mary's expression bloomed at the response. "How are you?" *It's Jackson!* she mouthed to Casey. She listened for a moment.

"How did the visit with Beth go?"

Jackson was visiting Beth? Casey forced her jaw to close. Why in the world would Mary send Jackson across country to visit Beth? She looked at Bertie with a question in her eyes. Bertie raised her eyebrows and shrugged.

Mary responded to Jackson's comments with "uhms" and "ahs," and asked an occasional question. "Did you get any pictures?"

Casey heard Jackson's low tones, but couldn't make out the words.

"No. No. It's just hard for me to imagine her in a wheelchair. Are you sure she's not faking it?" Mary listened and then laughed. "I warned you about her." She paused. "Everything okay with you so far?"

Moments later she responded to a question of Jackson's. "One or two incidents, but I'm taking my meds, don't worry. One thing—Vera rode her chair off the dock into the pond this afternoon. She's none the worse for it—Casey fished her out—but Vera's overnighting at the hospital. She's okay, but Casey has quite a shiner from the struggle."

Casey waited with growing impatience, while Jackson reacted to the news. Mary's tone shifted to metallic. "You *what?*" She turned away from Bertie and Casey and spoke through her teeth. "That was *not* part of—" Jackson must have interrupted her. She shook her head at what he was saying and then stared into the distance for a long moment. "Let's keep that between you and me for now. I'll fill you in when you return." Mary paused. "Yes, I knew." She took a long breath and turned back to the table.

In a brighter tone, she announced, "There's someone here who'd like to speak with you who has something special to tell you." She smiled at Bertie and Casey. Casey felt the heat rising in her face and was disappointed when Mary handed the phone to Bertie.

"Hi, Babycakes." Bertie and Jackson joked for a minute before Bertie told him she'd decided to join the project and about the plan to move into the gatehouse. She beamed at his response and then shifted topics. "Casey took a few mean hits, but she's a little powerhouse. Other than bruises and a stunning black eye, she seems all right. Let me put her on."

"Hello?" Casey was aware of two pairs of eyes watching her as she talked with Jackson.

"I'm amazed you could haul her out," Jackson said. "She's a big woman."

"Lifesaving class," Casey said simply, rubbing the welt on her head.

"Listen, Mary won't show it, but stress can put her system into a tailspin. She'll bear watching. She won't ask for help, and she'll refuse to go to the hospital—"

"Bertie gave me a crash course in diabetes care this afternoon," Casey interrupted.

"Good. I'll be back soon to give you a little relief. This isn't an easy family, as I'm sure you've discovered."

Understatement! She quickly changed the subject. "Thanks for all the work you did in the station. I love the picture," Casey said, grateful that he couldn't see the color in her cheeks.

"You're welcome." After a short silence, Jackson surprised her. "How was your date with the heir apparent?"

None of your business. Casey made her voice light and carefree. "Fun. All Brahms. It's a gorgeous concert hall, but you know that." *Quit blithering!* She paused. "When will you be back? Little Mother misses you."

"And you?"

"Well, maybe a little."

"Aren't *you* going to ask me how I'm doing?"

Casey detected a trace of petulance in his voice. "No. You're a big boy."

He hesitated. "Wouldn't mind another temple rub."

Casey was speechless. Was he flirting, or did he have a headache? Better safe than mortified. After all, he was a close relation. "Well, cousin, that might be arranged."

"Right. Take care of Mary." Jackson was off before Casey could hand the phone to Mary who was signaling that she'd like to speak with him again.

"Sorry, he hung up." Casey rose and escaped to the kitchen to avoid the questions brewing in their expectant faces. Ears on high alert, this time she rattled dishes but didn't turn on the water.

"Doesn't she know?" asked Bertie.

"Apparently, not," Mary responded.

"Not fair," Bertie scolded, but there was humor in her voice.

"All in good time."

Dammit! More games. Casey banged around the kitchen putting away dinner dishes and pans.

Chapter Thirty-Five

Casey rattled around a bit longer to get her growing frustration under control. She waited for Bertie to leave before taking Mary a cup of tea. "So, Jackson, the bearded man who doesn't live under the bridge, collects cans and feeds a stray kitten, suddenly jets cross country to visit Worthy's mother. What's the story?" she demanded as she placed the tea before Mary.

Mary waited until Casey settled in a chair before evading her question. "First of all, you needn't worry about me. I've lived a long life with this disease, and I know how to regulate my system. Jackson is protective, and Bertie is a mother hen." Mary clucked to lighten up her severe scolding attitude.

"Fair enough," Casey agreed, wondering if Bertie had replaced the glucagon in the refrigerator after her tutorial. "Jackson."

"Okay, Jackson's research. I sent him to confirm that Beth was incapacitated and living in a residential care facility. I had hoped ..." Mary offered a wan smile that quickly faded. Well, let's just say, I never thought Beth would end up that way. Sometimes I forget that she's a bit older. It's hard to picture her creaking around in a wheelchair like Vera. Too bad."

"Too bad?"

"I hate the bitch, may she roast in hell," Mary spat with venom, revealing lines around her mouth that Casey hadn't noticed before. "Do I surprise you? Beth was a monster. Still is, I'm sure. She turned everyone around her into monsters, including me. Jealousy and money. They eat you from the inside." She paused and refreshed her face with a kindly expression. "How I do go on, harping on my pet peeves."

"It doesn't sound as if you had an easy go of it," Casey probed, sensing a lot more to the story.

Mary's whole body shivered. She pulled an afghan around her shoulders. "I guess I should redeem myself so that you won't think I'm completely hateful."

"You're not—"

"Beth. Where to begin. I've already told you about our first encounter. It was far from the last. She never accepted the fact that Els chose a 'shanty Irish slut' over her own precious blue blood."

Casey frowned. "But, didn't *she* divorce *him?*"

"Just another move in her game plan. She drained all his assets and took off for the West Coast. He stayed in the White House, which she knew he couldn't afford. She assumed he'd have to come crawling back to her. She got custody of Worthy, her most valuable piece, demanded outrageous support payments, and then slapped a restraining order on Els. You've seen Worthy's hand. Beth slammed his fingers in the car door in one of her drunken rages."

Casey winced as if the door had crushed her own fingers.

"In court, Beth swore that Els did it."

"They believed her?" Casey's voice was incredulous.

"Evidently. Worthy was so traumatized he stopped speaking. She sent him to stay with grandma."

Mary twisted the napkin in her lap.

"Right before the court appearance, they had a bloody row. She threw most of the dinnerware and a few lamps at him and then called the police to report a domestic disturbance. After the police left, she fell down a flight of stairs. Should have killed her, but drunks fall differently, and she came away with a few mean bruises. She told the judge that Els hit her."

Mary's busy fingers jerked the napkin into a knot. "But that's not all, by far. Els went to Worthy's private school to talk to him and tell him that he hadn't hurt Beth, that she'd fallen. Worthy was off campus at a soccer match. The police hauled Els off in handcuffs. I had to bail him out.

"That's when Worthy wrote the hurtful note to his father. Beth must have been furious when she found out, because the letter eliminated Worthy as a pawn in her game."

"I'm surprised Worthy would tell her about the letter," said Casey.

Mary smiled to herself, but it was a bitter smile. "I couldn't be sure he would, so I sent her a copy."

"Did she give up then?"

"Oh, no. After Els and I married, she began making late-night drunken phone calls. Her next stunt was to break in—well, walk in; we hadn't changed the codes on the locks. She took every picture of Worthy in the house and then defaced our wedding picture. God, I felt so violated! Els and I sighed with relief a few months later when she married a fund manager and stayed in San Francisco." As if to demonstrate, Mary released a long sigh and settled back in her chair. "That marriage lasted less than a year, and then she was right back on the telephone with her late-night drunken phone calls."

"Why not get an unlisted phone?"

"Believe me, I suggested it, but Els resisted. He always hoped Worthy would have a change of heart and call one day. That hope practically destroyed our marriage." Mary hesitated, as if deciding whether or not to continue. She picked up her teacup, acted surprised that it was empty, and looked at Casey expectantly.

Casey wasn't about to fall for the empty teacup ploy. She fixed Mary with an expectant look of her own.

Mary hunkered further into her chair and released a real sigh of resignation.

She's a master. Casey waited her out.

After a last-ditch glance at her cup, Mary spoke. "You might as well know the worst of it. Beth called sober a few days before Worthy's prep school graduation. She was in town to see her parents, and Worthy was flying in from the West Coast to collect his reward check from the grandparents.

"I guess I need to explain. Worthy was carefully trained to respect money. Every birthday, Christmas and significant event such as graduation, he got a sizeable check from Beth's parents, but only if he showed up in person to collect it. Otherwise, Grandma had her personal assistant sign and send an empty 'Thinking of You...' card. Els said the cards were identical except for the handwritten note 'on your birthday' or 'this holiday season.'"

Casey shook her head in disgust. More manipulation.

"Oh, yes, little Worthy was carefully taught. Beth paraded her little prize before her parents as their living legacy, a 'worthy' recipient of their fortune. Of course, that enraged Els. He set up a trust for Worthy. So competitive. After her parents died, Beth inherited and then managed to fritter it all away, investing in the wrong husbands and corporations.

"Anyway, Beth said Worthy had decided it was time to reconcile with his father. After all, by then Els had made a second fortune. Els agreed to meet them in Chatham, knowing I'd never let Beth inside the White House. They were to arrive separately: Beth from a pampering at some spa in Nevada, and Worthy from Los Angeles.

"Beth arrived first and ordered in a special catered dinner for the occasion. They had a few drinks waiting for Worthy to arrive from Logan Airport. Finally, Beth called the airport and reported that Worthy's flight had mechanical problems and was delayed. Later I discovered that the flight from L.A. had arrived on time, just that Worthy was never on it.

"You must understand that Els was never a drinker. You can see where this is going."

Casey nodded. She wasn't sure she wanted Mary to continue but didn't know how to interrupt gracefully.

"Drinks before dinner, wine with dinner, and then the graduation bottle of champagne, waiting for the prodigal who would never arrive.

"I sat by the phone at the White House for hours, hoping to get a call from Els. Later and later. Nothing. Finally, I scolded myself, told myself he loved me, and went to bed. I couldn't sleep, imagining one horrible scene after another.

"By morning, I couldn't stand it any longer. I called. Beth answered. I asked to speak with Els.

Mary mimicked Beth's voice. "Els, it's for you."

"I heard murmuring in the background and Els' sleepy protests to leave him alone."

"Els, wake up, honey. It's your secretary," Beth said for my benefit.

"Ruth, what's up?" Els growled into the telephone.

"This is your *other* secretary," I said and hung up. The phone rang and rang and rang while I threw a few things into a bag. Before leaving the White House for West Boylston, I grabbed the punch bowl and smashed it on the back step." Mary shivered, her face contorted in remembrance of pain past. She took a moment to regain her composure.

"Mother let me stay two weeks before she threw me out."

Casey gasped. "How could she—"

"No, no. She was right, even though it seemed hard at the time. She asked if I loved Els. I said I hated him. 'But, do you *love* him?' she persisted. When I said I did, she asked if I was going to let that whore have him, and if I had any backbone left. I said, 'It can never be the same.'

"Probably not. Move over. You're bleeding on me," she said. "Mother wasn't the huggy type.

"I was right. It never was the same." Mary's eyes seemed focused on a distant memory. "But it was always worth it."

Mary looked down at her cup again. "Now, could I have another cup of tea? Maybe a few extra teaspoons of sugar and a biscuit."

Casey took her time in the kitchen. She didn't want to hear more about Beth and the ongoing melodrama of Mary's life. When she returned to the living room, she asked about the little blow-up with Jackson. "You sounded rather angry with Jackson earlier on the telephone."

Mary cast her eyes about the room and then waved her hand as if warding off an insect. "I was disappointed and took it out on Jackson. I didn't want to believe Beth had thrown in the towel after so many chapters—there are countless stories that I haven't told you. Just a week or so ago, I was so hopeful. I thought Beth had taken the bait when we had the burglary.

"By the way," Mary interrupted herself, "just so you don't think I'm into insurance fraud, I still have the insurance papers for the pictures that were stolen tucked under my mattress in the White House."

Casey cocked her head to the side in stunned silence at Mary's abrupt change of subject.

Mary's voice rose, and her energy increased as she sidestepped into the new topic. "You've seen Jackson's practice pictures in the attic, so you've probably figured out that the burglar got bogus artwork. Jackson copied the pictures of the masters in an advanced art class. Students were supposed to work from reprints, but Jackson had the real thing right here in the White House. He painted the first copy while Els was overseas buying some villa. When Els returned, I'd replaced the real picture with Jackson's. Els couldn't tell the difference."

Mary's eyes sparkled as she told the story. "Over the years, many guests and a number of significant dealers admired the pictures. When I finally came clean. Els was furious that he'd been duped until I reminded him that others with trained eyes had also been fooled. It was his idea to give the originals to the Museum. He loved the idea of conning the sycophants who paraded through our house, business execs and pols who pandered to his wealth.

"The emeralds are fake. She did get a few hundred dollars in cash, and Els' jade chess set and a few silver pieces, but they were going into the sale anyway."

"She? How do you know—"

"Jackson saw a woman carrying things from the White House. I had hoped the woman was Beth, but apparently not. Probably Cherie."

"The estate sale was a trap for Beth?" Casey's mind reeled as Mary peeled back yet another layer of the story.

"Sorry, I guess I left a few things out. When Worthy and Cherie showed up at the White House, I wrote a note to Beth to make sure she knew they were here."

"How nice," Casey muttered.

"May she roast. I wanted her to know that her darling boy was betraying her. From Worthy's own mouth, I knew that he and his mother were on the outs, so I suspected that he hadn't told her his whereabouts."

"How did you know her address?"

"Easy. I called the Welton *Town Crier.* Beth always renewed her subscription to the paper to keep tabs on Els, and, after he died, on me. I said I was Beth Waddington and asked if my assistant had renewed my subscription. When the woman said yes, I asked her to confirm the address because I hadn't received the last month's issue." Mary smiled at her own cleverness. "That's how I knew to send Jackson to Pacific Grove.

"The evening you met Worthy and Cherie, Beth called and demanded to speak with Worthy. I gave her the phone number at the guest house."

"Why all the games?" Casey asked, trying to keep the growing resentment out of her voice.

Mary drew the afghan closer around her. "Beth loved the White House as much as I hate it. I knew it would kill her to see it made into a home for the disadvantaged. The house was a symbol of what she had lost and was determined to regain. Ironic, because she had given the house to Els in the divorce, believing that he'd never be able to pay the taxes and upkeep.

"Els and I lived in three rooms of that mausoleum for years while we struggled with his new company. As I told you, Beth had destroyed the first company, running off with the CFO and cashing in her controlling stocks. Long story short, Els made another fortune. The only weapon left in Beth's arsenal was Worthy who so kindly played into my hand. With both Worthy and the White House as lures, I knew she couldn't stay away. I wanted her to see her boy working for me and her beloved White House dismantled.

"But now my last hope for revenge has been defeated by age and infirmity."

Casey watched the wind go out of Mary's sails as she finished speaking. *Serves you right.*

"You're very thoughtful," Mary ventured.

Casey clasped her hands together and looked down, speaking softly, almost to herself. "I've been a fool." She turned aside to hide the emotion on her face, but she couldn't contain the resentment welling up inside. Mary was playing with everyone. The newly built foundations of Casey's dreams shook and cracked and crumbled. The plan was all about revenge.

"Too good to believe," she whispered. "I wanted a place to belong so badly, I opened myself up to hope."

CHAPTER THIRTY-FIVE

"Casey, let me—"

Casey stood, opened her arms, and regained her voice. "And here it was—a ready-made home, a family, and a job. Mine for the taking. Handed to me on a silver platter. Throw in an antique desk, a few valuable rings, a dump sticker. Adorable kittens. Two handsome young men.

"All for revenge. Your bright, shining, philanthropic venture was just the end game in a thirty-year civil war. A spite war neither you nor Beth will ever win because the prize died. And Jackson. He's no homeless troll under a bridge, but your nephew, doing your bidding. Another pawn in your game." She glared at Mary. "Time for bed."

She carried Mary's cup and saucer to the kitchen and smashed them in the sink.

Chapter Thirty-Six

Casey's hands trembled as she picked up the pieces of china from the sink. Where the hell had that outburst come from? Why such anger? And why take it out on Mary? Mary didn't owe her one thing. Nothing. Yet she'd been more than generous.

Casey dumped the broken pieces of china into the trash and wiped down the sink. Mary had no obligation to tell Casey about her vendetta with Beth, or for that matter, about anything. Okay, she'd dangled the idea of a position for Casey, but clearly, everyone understood that plans were up in the air.

So, what was Casey's problem? She avoided introspection whenever possible—too much pain and loss. But maybe it was time to admit that she was barely holding it together. That she was afraid. Afraid that she wanted too much, was too needy, too vulnerable after the wreckage of her past dreams.

Okay, she hated feeling used, manipulated, and out of control. But how had she been used? One weekend of work, in exchange for a place to stay and the opportunity to "meet" her father and his family. Manipulated? How? Because she didn't know everything about Mary's plans? Even Mary didn't know the details. Lots of things were undecided.

Out of control? Absolutely. Casey wiped down the counters and then sat with her head in her hands. She was homeless, unemployed, and thrown into a melodrama with a whole cast of dysfunctional players. Even with her shiny new BA in History, she hadn't gotten one nibble on recent job applications. Tonight's temper tantrum with Mary could ruin the best prospects she could possibly imagine.

Consider things from Mary's point of view. Casey was clearly damaged goods: the out-of-wedlock daughter of a priest who'd spent ten years behind bars, who showed up on Mary's doorstep less than a month ago. And Mary, single and diabetic, responsible for a suicidal, disabled sister, had only one card to play: money. Of course, she'd be cautious.

Do something useful. Move the van over to Agnes' driveway so it would be out of the way so that when the trucks come to haul goods away in the morning, they'd have easy access to the front door. Casey put on her jacket and checked in the pocket to make sure she had the keys to the van and grabbed the flashlight by the door. Outside, a few early evening stars peeked through the light clouds. No moon. The cool evening air washed over Casey. She raised her arms to the heavens to stretch and release the kinks in her muscles and the images from her conversation with Mary. The kinks left, but the images wouldn't budge.

So, slow down. Apologize. See what happens. Be open but be careful. She walked slowly toward the van, mulling over Mary's revelations. Why hadn't the battle ended with Els' death? Mary was the one married to Els, so Beth had lost. But she'd done such damage in the battles that Mary still wanted to cause her pain, to pay a price for the years of turmoil and grief.

But they lived on different coasts and had their own lives. Maybe that was the problem: they didn't have new lives. They were stuck in the past, unable or unwilling to move forward.

Casey started the van and drove down to the intersection with Agnes' driveway. She turned and continued to the little house. Before she stopped completely, she jammed the van into Park, smiling at the grinding sound as the behemoth lurched forward. Great. Now she was punishing a stupid van for her own dark mood. Lighten up.

Fuck it! She slammed the door hard. A dim light shone from an upstairs window at the back. Agnes had probably left a light on to dissuade potential thieves but hadn't bothered with a timer.

Darkness was descending quickly. Casey turned on the flashlight to walk back to Mary's house. Her sneakers crunched on the gravel.

What was that? Casey jumped to the side of the drive and crouched, dousing the light. Angry voices. A shot. Casey's heart beat so loudly she didn't hear the music at first.

Music? Yes, Casey recognized the unmistakable theme from *Murder, She Wrote* from endless nights of mind-numbing television in prison. She laughed, but her hands shook when she switched the flashlight back on.

"Afraid of your shadow, Casey girl?" she chided aloud. She walked back toward the house, mostly to prove to herself she wasn't chicken. Besides, she admitted, she was curious. Mary had called it a bungalow, but it was a full-sized Cape with two stories. Curtains blocked the downstairs windows. At the back of the house, she almost stepped on a piece of broken glass. The music was replaced by wailing sirens. Casey winced, but refused to be frightened.

She cast the beam about. Storm shutters were stacked against the shingles of the house beside a back stoop. One of the shutters was bashed in as if someone had kicked it. The arc of the flashlight beam glinted off broken glass covering the stoop and the ground around it. Someone had thrown a bottle through the back door window.

Carefully she dodged the broken glass and raised the flashlight to peer inside. The kitchen was empty. Cabinet doors were open showing bare shelves, and the refrigerator door was ajar. Agnes had packed up and gone. Whatever she hadn't taken with her was probably now the property of the kids who broke the window. But why hadn't they taken the TV?

Not her problem. She turned to leave, careful to follow the beam of her flashlight and avoid the glass. As she walked, Casey's thoughts returned to Mary and her lifetime obsession with Beth. It had poisoned everything, even Mary's "philanthropic" project. Mary had already planned the project before Casey had arrived and Worthy and Cherie showed up. Mary had incorporated them into her schemes as an added bonus. She'd probably used Jackson all along, although that might not be fair.

What about Worthy? Casey hadn't seen him that many times, but he definitely was aware of her, and been very attentive the evening they went to symphony. But then, he had a history of inappropriate choices: according to a comment Mary had made on the ride to West Boylston, he'd married Cherie to spite his mother. Was he attracted to misfits? Casey would fit right in. Not everyone would find her prison time a positive trait, or be fascinated by her scar.

George, her first love, who knew her full story, had shied away after toying with her. His voice, overheard a year earlier, came back to her. "Casey knows as well as I do that I could never marry an ex-con."

"Stop it! Stop it! Stop it!" she ordered, trying to re-bury her shame. But she couldn't stem the tide of psychic scars he'd left, scars far uglier than the knife wound on her forearm. What respectable man would think twice about her?

As she trudged along, Casey forced herself to repeat the mantra of her life. *I didn't do anything wrong.* But I sure have been in the wrong places at the wrong time, no question, definitely mortgaging her future. Wrong. She was too high risk for a mortgage. She thought about Jackson. She'd felt a natural bond with him. Oh, come clean, it was more than that. But he's my first cousin.

So what? The unbidden thought popped into her mind. She'd already been punished for breaking laws when she was innocent. Casey smiled as she pictured Jackson with Little Mother and felt guilty relief when she reached Mary's house and had other things to do to occupy her mind. She locked up and turned off the lights before retiring to Vera's room.

After her conversation with Bertie, Casey had retrieved an old wind-up alarm clock from one of the Salvation Army boxes. Now she set it for 2:30 am when she would check on Mary. Casey reviewed the lesson Bertie had given her earlier and hoped that she wouldn't be tested on her new knowledge in the middle of the night. She drifted into a fitful sleep.

Chapter Thirty-Seven

C asey raised her arms and breathed in great gulps of air. Her body lifted upward with the motion. She was off the ground, rising like a balloon. Unbelievable! Higher and higher. She lowered her arms to her shoulders and slowed her ascent. When she looked down, her whole body shifted horizontally. She moved her arms right and then left, banking and turning. When she raised her head, she gained altitude; when she lowered her head, she dove toward the earth. Soaring! Flying!

Below her someone with a sense of humor had mowed the lawn, dissecting it into checkerboard squares by cutting alternate rows horizontally and then vertically. Two figures stood at the edge of the lawn.

Casey lowered her head and dove down for a better view. On the strange patchwork lawn, Mary and Jackson struggled with a rope. Mary looked positively regal draped in a long white robe like a Roman statue. A tiara of emeralds atop her piled-up curls glinted in the sunshine. Jackson tugged mightily on the rope with one hand, holding his scarred hand behind his back. Smoke wafted over them, momentarily clouding them from view.

Before Jackson, a deep chasm had opened in the ground, belching fire and smoke. On the far side of the pit, pulling with equal force, were Worthy and…could it be? …Queen Beth, elegant in a black evening dress with a dazzling crown of diamonds. Worthy laughed as he pulled on the rope, but he, too, only used his good hand. The sides were equally handicapped.

Casey circled the pit.

"Help us, Casey," Mary called as Casey passed overhead.

Casey landed and rushed to join the line between Jackson and Mary, adding her strength to their side. Beth and Worthy dug in their heels but couldn't hold. They lurched forward, losing valuable ground. As they edged inexorably closer to the abyss, Casey let go. *What was she doing?* This game was deadly. She disliked Beth, but she wasn't willing to kill her. This wasn't her battle. She'd already been to prison. Mary could let go if she wanted.

"C'mon, Casey! We need you," shouted Mary.

Casey ignored Mary's pleas and looked to the heavens. She raised her arms and was aloft again. Above the trees, she surveyed the scene below and saw Cherie and Vera beyond the pit. Cherie smoked and sipped wine from a lounge chair apparently unmoved by the life-and-death drama playing out before her, while Vera hollered incomprehensible words of encouragement from her wheelchair.

Off to the side of the human checkerboard at Mary's end, Casey spied a toppled bishop and a king. She swooped down for a closer look. The bishop looked like a priest, and the king—could it be Els? Oops! Too fast! She raised her head to slow her momentum.

From above, the game looked ridiculous. Why bother? Everyone could avoid the pit if they simply let go. She shouted down to Mary, "Stop! It's not worth it!" but Mary either couldn't hear her, or ignored her, intent on revenge.

Time for a bit of sport. Casey dove directly at Cherie making rat-a-tat strafing noises. Cherie screamed and threw up her arms in the air, spilling wine all over herself, and then was covered by a cloud of cigarette ashes caused by Casey's wake.

Vera aimed her new electric wheelchair at Cherie, powering forward to mow her down. Cherie jumped aside at the last moment. Vera howled with glee and returned to the sidelines to cheer on the home team.

Aloft again, Casey gasped as Mary slumped forward. Beth laughed and pulled harder. As Jackson neared the pit, a geyser of fire leapt up in front of him. He howled, perilously close to the edge.

Worthy released the rope, leapt nimbly over the pit, and took Mary's side. Beth screamed at him and pulled valiantly, but she weakened with the strain. Her body withered, shrinking and aging as Casey watched in horror from above. Jackson and Worthy hauled on the rope in unison, drawing her to the brink.

"Not fair!" yelled Casey from above, as if she could affect the outcome.

At the very last moment, Worthy changed sides again, evening up the forces.

The pit widened, belching huge clouds of steam and smoke and releasing flames that licked upward. The hotter the fire, the faster Casey flew, fueled by thermals from Middle Earth. She screamed through the air, completely removed from the earthly scene below, spinning, arcing skyward, diving toward the ground, and pulling up at the last moment. What a way to go!

Too fast! Slow down! But her arms were tired from the strain. She arched her back and threw back her head. Instantly, her speed slowed as she became vertical. She stalled! Like a rocket without a booster, she dropped straight down, faster and faster, plummeting toward the ground. With a super effort, she dipped her head and leaned forward, only to spiral out of control, arms glued to her sides. No way to stop. She turned her head to the side to protect her face. "No!" she screamed as she crashed.

Moments later she moved her head. Her face and arm hurt from the impact, but she was alive. Or was she? A sudden white light blinded her. Was she dying? Was this the tunnel? *I love you, Mom, LouAnne, Rosie—who was she leaving out? Mary—*

"Casey!"

Someone grabbed her arm. "Casey, wake up!"

Casey's eyes flew open. She raised her hand to shield her eyes from the overhead light. Mary was at the foot of the bed, holding her arm, shaking her gently. Casey lay on the floor in Vera's room, tangled in sheets.

"Calm down, honey. You're safe. You were dreaming."

Casey looked up at Mary and offered a wan smile. It took a few moments to ward off the horrors of the dream and to regain her wits. Slowly, she untangled herself from the sheets feeling foolish.

Suddenly she sat up straight. "What time is it?" She grabbed the clock from the bureau. Five o'clock in the morning. "I never heard the alarm. A lot of good I've been." She rose and gathered up the sheets and bedding.

"I turned it off earlier while you were sleeping." Mary helped her remake the bed. "I knew you were exhausted with all of the work, with Vera, and my stories of woe. I was worried that it was too much, too soon, and I was right. I'm sorry I upset you so."

"It wasn't you. It was a dream. I was flying and...then I crashed." But the dream *was* about Mary and Beth and their never-ending vendetta. All the players were ensnared in the deadly battle except Casey. For a few blissful moments, she was above the fray, free of earthly concerns.

"Looks like you need to practice your landings." Mary looked at her with a sad expression.

"The soaring was so wonderful. I could bank and turn, dive, and climb. Higher and higher. But the crash was terrifying."

"You're sounding a bit like Jed describing his mania. You've had way too much trauma for a young woman. Maybe you could use some time away from all of our craziness. Go home for a bit and think about whether or not you want to be part of this damaged family."

Oh no! She's telling me to go.

"There's nothing I'd like more than for you to stay. It's just that things are becoming so ... well, complicated. I couldn't bear it if anything happened to you. You're like the daughter I never had."

"What do you mean, 'if anything happened to me'? Other than a bad dream, I'm perfectly okay. I'm not going to go mental on you. Jackson's the one to worry about, not me." The second the words left her mouth, Casey wanted to take them back.

"Believe me, I've thought about that, too. After the sale, I'll ask him to take time away as well. He may need some distance from me, so he's not saddled by the past." Mary gave Casey a hug and a kiss on the cheek before switching off the light. "Try to get a few hours' rest. We still have lots to do tomorrow."

"No," Casey called to the darkness.

A few seconds passed before Mary returned and turned the light back on. "No, *what?*"

"No, I won't budge an inch before the sale is over and you're feeling better.

I need to know *you're* okay. You see, I've become quite fond of you as well."

Chapter Thirty-Eight

C asey smelled smoke. She shook her head. *Wake up!* She had to get out of these stupid nightmares. *Wake up!* she demanded.

But she was awake. And there was smoke wafting in through Vera's open window. She threw off the covers and ran to see. Hungry flames licked up the sides of Agnes' house next door. As she watched in disbelief, a deafening *whoosh* and an enormous fireball consumed the house. She slammed the window shut and dashed to Mary's room and shook her awake. "Fire! Agnes' house is on fire!" She handed Mary a robe from the bottom of the bed and herded her downstairs.

She rushed to the phone and dialed 911. "There's a fire next door to Mary Waddington's house on Dempsey Drive." She paused. "What's the address here?" she asked Mary.

"Two twenty-one."

Casey repeated the number. "No one's home, but there's a van with a full tank of gas parked in front of the garage. At least there was." She paused again. "Casey Cavendish. I'm Mary Waddington's niece. We're okay. Thank you." She listened a minute before hanging up and turning to Mary. "We need to go outside in case the wind picks up."

The police and fire department arrived within minutes.

"Douse that van before it blows," the Fire Chief hollered. Despite the quick response, the firefighters never had a chance. The place was reduced to a heap of soggy ashes and a brick chimney.

As the firemen drenched the smoldering remains, the Chief joined Casey and Mary on the lawn. "Tell me what happened. How did you discover the fire?" he asked Casey.

"I thought I was dreaming—I'd had a nightmare earlier. When I smelled smoke, I knew I was awake. I rushed to the window and heard a loud *whoosh*." Casey stared at the wreckage in disbelief. "It burned so fast."

"Too fast," muttered the fireman. "You said you heard a sound. Try to make the noise."

Casey made her best imitation of the sound. "It was like an enormous gust of wind," she added lamely.

The fireman left abruptly and spoke to two policemen in a cruiser before barking new orders to his men.

One of the policemen approached them. "Hello, Mary. Long time since I've seen you in these parts." The man's protruding belly, ruddy skin, and popping eyes made him look like a bratwurst about to explode.

"Hi, Vaughn," Mary responded weakly. "Not since Mother's funeral. Meet my niece, Casey Cavendish."

"Hello, Ms. Cavendish. Call me Vaughn."

Casey offered her hand and started to reply, but her voice was drowned out by another order from the Fire Chief.

"Get those assholes out of here!" he shouted to the policeman in the cruiser, pointing to a mobile TV unit that had pulled into the driveway.

On command, the officer hit the siren. The cruiser spit gravel backing up and slammed to a skidding-halt inches from the press wagon. The officer jumped out of the cruiser, shouting and waving the newscasters out of the drive back into the street.

To Casey's surprise, Officer Vaughn was still holding her outstretched hand. "Oh, Boy!" he exclaimed, but his eyes weren't on her bruises. They were fixed on Casey's nipples clearly profiled through her nightie. "Let's go inside," he said. "Mary's shivering, and you won't want to be captured on film...this way," he suggested with a sly smile.

Casey wrenched her hand away and stalked toward the door with as much pride as she could muster.

"Shame about Agnes' house. Good thing she wasn't home," Vaughn said to Mary. "I'm afraid I'll have to ask you ladies a number of questions."

"Will you join us for coffee? Casey, would you mind making some?" suggested Mary. "I need to sit down."

Casey bounded up the stairs and threw on her clothes before doing Mary's bidding. *Slime bucket!* Protect and leer. In the kitchen, she waited for the very last shudders of the coffee maker's gurgling death rattle, before making up a tray and grabbing the pot.

"Heard about the excitement Saturday," Vaughn said. "I assume Vera spent the night at the hospital."

"No secrets from you," Mary replied.

"Not a good time for secrets." Vaughn looked expectantly at Casey as she placed the pot before him.

"Help yourself."

Vaughn scowled and poured himself a cup in silence.

Mary frowned at Casey's rudeness, but Casey ignored her.

"Whose van is it?" Vaughn asked.

"Mine," Mary replied. "Of course, I don't drive." She turned to Casey. Her voice shook, and all the color had drained from her cheeks. "I had no idea you were going to drive the van over there last night. You could have been killed!"

Casey placed a comforting hand on Mary's arm and explained. "I moved the van to Agnes' place to get it out of the way because the movers and Salvation Army trucks are coming today."

"You're selling the place?" Vaughn asked Mary.

"We haven't decided yet," Mary demurred.

Casey raised her eyebrows but didn't speak.

Vaughn suddenly turned to Casey. "What time did you move the van?"

Casey glowered at him but answered his direct question. "About eleven."

"No sign of anything at that time? Nothing unusual?"

Mary interrupted and told Vaughn about the rowdies and the crashing glass earlier in the evening and how Bertie had scared off the partiers.

"Good old Bert. Anything else?"

"There were shutters stacked against the back of the house. One was bashed in. A light and a television were on in a bedroom upstairs." Casey hesitated. "I was surprised. The back door window was broken, and there was glass on the back stoop. I knocked and called, but no one answered."

"Did you go inside? You *sure* no one was in there?" Vaughn's voice sharpened.

"Agnes is in Chatham," Mary explained. "I spoke to her yesterday. She was too sick with the flu to help us with the packing."

"Sounds like Agnes," Vaughn commented dryly.

Casey added, "I figured Agnes had left the light and TV on to ward off potential vandals."

Officer Vaughn relaxed at their assurances. "You figured right. Light and TV have been on solid this week. You'd think Agnes would be bright enough to put 'em on a timer." He shook his head and sipped his coffee.

He turned quickly to Casey. "Do you smoke?"

"No." *Why was he asking ...*

"Good. Filthy habit. Mind?" The last was directed to Mary. He lit a Marlboro, blowing smoke toward Casey, before Mary could object. "Where's Jackson?"

Mary's face hardened and her eyes turned to ice. "California. Why?"

"California?" Vaughn ignored her attitude.

"Casey, Bertie, and I all spoke with him on the telephone last night. He was in his hotel room in San Francisco."

"Had to ask. Fire Chief thinks the house was torched." Vaughn took another drag on his cigarette and balanced it on the saucer as if it were an ashtray. "Strange to think kids would break in and not steal the TV."

Mary stood and glared down at Vaughn. She spoke slowly in a sub-zero voice. "Jackson didn't set the fire, if that's what you're implying."

"Doing my job, Mary. Don't get yourself into a snit."

"Knock, knock."

Mary turned her back on Vaughn and opened the door for the Fire Chief. He entered, talking. "We'll need to watch for a while longer, but the fire's pretty well run its course. Not much we could do. I'm afraid the house is a total loss. We saved the van, but the paint's blistered. It was close." He wiped his brow and then reached inside his outer protective gear, producing a plastic bag containing a glove with cutout fingers. "Anyone recognize this?" he asked, handing the bag to Casey.

Casey swallowed hard. Had to be Jackson's. "Where'd you find it?" she asked, avoiding both his direct question and his eyes. She glanced at Mary who was staring at the glove.

"Beside the garage. Look familiar?" he probed.

Casey made a show of examining the glove, giving Mary a second or two to recover. "Looks like an old work glove that's seen better days." She shrugged and handed the bag back. "Officer Vaughn just had a cup of coffee. Would you like one?" As she spoke, she grabbed Vaughn's unfinished cup of coffee with his smoldering cigarette balanced on the saucer, turned, and started for the kitchen.

"I wasn't finished," Vaughn objected.

"Oh. Sorry," Casey flipped the cigarette into the cup, turned, offered Vaughn her sweetest smile, and replaced the cup before beating a hasty retreat into the kitchen.

"You know," Mary said quietly, "That looks like one of Jackson's gloves. I asked him to put up the storm shutters on Agnes' house last week. He didn't have time to finish the job, because I needed him to go to California for me. As I just told Vaughn, Jackson's on the West Coast."

Mary reached for the plastic bag, but the fireman withdrew it. "I didn't see any shutters," he commented in a neutral voice.

"They were leaning up against the back of the house last night," Casey called from the safety of the kitchen.

"Sheeeeit!" Vaughn slammed back from the table and spat on the floor.

Casey returned with a fresh cup for the fireman and an expression of surprise for Vaughn. Fortunately, he'd taken only a small swig before he saw the floating cigarette, or she'd have a larger mess to clean later.

"Whaddja do that for?" he demanded, wiping his mouth on his sleeve.

"I wasn't thinking. My brother smoked. Filthy habit." Casey ignored Vaughn's fury and placed the cup she was carrying in front of the fireman. "Cream? Sugar?" she asked.

"No, black's fine." He turned his face away from Vaughn, struggling not to laugh.

"*Ms. Cavendish* parked the van at Agnes' house last night," Vaughn explained to the fireman, spitting out the "Ms. Cavendish" part. "She mentioned the shutters before you came in, saying one looked kicked in."

"Nothing left of any shutters now," muttered the fireman, regaining his composure and returning to the seriousness of the fire.

"The kids probably snuck back and lit the house to get back at Bertie for shooing them off," suggested Vaughn.

"Could be, but I'd be really surprised they'd torch a house," said the fireman.

"Hey, they're not stupid. They'd know no one was home. They're bad actors, but they're not killers," said Vaughn.

"Not this time," replied the fireman.

Chapter Thirty-Nine

L ater Sunday morning Casey helped move the last miscellaneous items into the van. Everything hurt. Her head and arm ached, and her foot had ballooned so much she had to leave her sneaker untied. Vera had meant business. Casey's eye was swollen half shut and the side of her face was blackened with bruises.

Bertie and Mary were sequestered behind closed doors in the dining room deep in conversation, "keeping out of the way," as Mary put it. Although Casey knew she had no reason to be privy to their conversation, once again, she felt excluded.

The plan was for Bertie and Mary to spring Vera from the hospital in the van and bring her to Welton later in the morning. Casey would ride with the movers to show them where to put the pieces depending upon the colored stickers affixed to each—the "keepers" to the White House and the "spoils" to the garages for the estate sale and Goodwill.

When it was time to leave, she hiked painfully up into the cab of the truck where she was squished between two mammoth men. They drove in silence for a few miles before the driver's curiosity finally got the better of him. "You been run over by a truck or what?"

Casey's mind was so numb that she resorted to the truth. "My aunt slugged me and ran over me in a wheelchair."

The driver shrugged, but the guy riding shotgun asked, "I'da thought a bitty thing like you could get outta the way."

"We were underwater."

No more questions. The men talked about the fire for a few miles. She listened, half awake, mesmerized by the sound of the engine and the motion of the truck.

"Think it was Irish lightning?" the mover in the shotgun seat asked his partner.

"Sure saves knockin' it down. Place's worth more today than it was yesterday."

Casey was suddenly awake and attentive. *Irish lightning?*

"'Specially if you got insurance."

"Don't think they pay if it's arson."

"Still worth a lot more." The driver opened his side window to smoke, drowning out further conversation.

Would Agnes torch her own house or have someone else set a match to it? Wouldn't make sense if she couldn't collect insurance. Casey was too exhausted to think more about it and dozed until they woke her in the White House driveway.

After explaining the color-coding scheme and showing the men around, Casey limped back to the station and sank into the lone chair in the living room. Although it was bare, Casey felt welcomed by her little house with its new paint smell and light streaming through the windows. She mentally placed the desk in different locations, deciding on the far wall under Jackson's portrait of her. She'd have to make curtains for the bathroom, but she couldn't remember what they'd decided to do with the sewing machine.

Casey found a paper and pencil and struggled to make a to-do list, but her head kept bobbing forward. Just as she was nodding off for the second time, the movers delivered her desk along with a bunch of boxes she hadn't expected. The last item they brought in was Mother Dempsey's rocker!

After they left, Casey stroked the polished surface of the desk, drew up a straight chair, and examined her treasure, opening and closing the bottom drawers, and exploring the cubbies and smaller drawers. One little drawer didn't slide open easily. Casey tugged gently on the brass fixture, and it opened, but to her surprise, the carved housing of the inner drawers also moved. She poked and pulled at it for a second. It wiggled like a loose tooth. She'd have to glue it. Unless ...

220

She grasped the housing by its ornamental carving and pulled the piece straight toward her. The housing was hollow. She smiled. She loved hidey places. Inside, she found a plain sealed envelope. Mary knew she'd find it.

Casey opened the envelope, and a picture fell out. Her mother must have been in her twenties when the picture was taken. On the back, she'd written, "For Jed, All my love, Em." The edges were tattered as if it had been touched many times. He'd kept it all those years. It was the saddest and most wonderful gift she'd ever received.

She should shower, but her arms and legs were lead weights. She settled in the rocker. Little Mother mewed through the cat door and jumped in her lap, circled and curled into a ball, giving her an excuse not to move. She looked around the room with a smile on her face, glad to be away from the weirdness of the West Boylston house and the scene of the fire and yet grateful for the gifts of the desk and the chair that were part of the strange story.

* * *

She was awakened at dusk by a telephone call from Mary letting her know that she and Bertie had arrived at the gatehouse.

"Give me five minutes, and I'll be up to help you." She splashed her face with water, threw on a sweater, and hiked up to the gatehouse as quickly as her tired muscles would allow. As she approached the smaller house, Mary finished giving instructions to Bertie who was unloading boxes onto a dolly and ferrying them inside.

"Hi. I thought you were coming back straight away." Casey peered into the van. "Where's Vera? Is everything okay?"

"As fine as we're going to be, I guess." Mary sounded tired. "As you know, Bertie and I decided we'd be much happier living here with Vera than in the White House." Mary talked a blue streak, telling Casey things she already knew. "It's for the better. I've always loved the gatehouse. I wanted to move into it with Els, but his pride made us stay in the big house. Anyway, Bertie and her boy helped me pack up things. That's why it took us so long."

"But, how about Vera?"

Mary's blithering came to a halt, and she leaned against the blistered van. She looked down and swallowed hard. Casey was surprised to see tears welling up in her eyes and even more surprised when she found herself reaching out to touch Mary's arm to comfort her.

"I'm sorry, but there's just no easy way or good time to tell you. Vera has ovarian cancer. We've had a series of tests and consultations with oncologists in the past few months. The prognosis is grim."

"Oh no. No." She took Mary into her arms and rocked her until she quieted. "She knew, didn't she? That's why she..."

"Yes. But she's wanted to die since she was a girl."

"I should have let her—"

"No. Don't. You had no idea she had cancer, and even if you did, you couldn't have let her die that way."

Casey wasn't so sure. It would have been easy to let go of the chair. And probably much less painful in the long run—or was it the short run, now—to let her die quickly.

Mary wiped her eyes. "Now, I'll be a total blubbering mess if I don't keep moving. Come inside and see our new home. It's dusty and stuffy, but I'm sure you will be able to see why I've always wanted to live here." Mary proceeded to give Casey a brief tour of the cottage.

Casey nodded attentively, although she knew she wouldn't be able to remember a word later. The image of Vera propelling herself off the dock in her chair flashed on and off throughout Mary's recital. Vera wanted to die so very badly. And she, Casey, had decided that she should live on, suffering in pain after a lifetime of misery.

"What do you think of it?"

It took a moment for Casey to realize she'd been asked a direct question. She cast around quickly. "It's light and airy," she bluffed with a sad smile. "So different from the White House." She rubbed the side of her head where Vera had slugged her. She hadn't wanted to be rescued.

Mary's face became wistful. "I fixed it up between fortunes. I think I told you, Els would make a fortune, lose it, and then go on to make another. At one point, must have been fifteen years or so ago, he was off in England for a few months chasing down some money-making scheme. We had moved into the four rooms in the White House where Vera and I live..." she paused, "lived, closing off the rest because it was too expensive to heat."

Vera had wanted to die so much that she'd almost taken Casey with her.

"I thought it would make sense to move down here and decided to surprise him by fixing it up whilst he was gone. It was hard work, but so rewarding."

"You did it yourself?" Casey asked, finally turning her attention to Mary.

"All for naught. Els would have none of it. Wouldn't even set foot inside the place. He was furious. He said if I wanted to play dollhouse, it was dandy with him, but only 'over his dead body' would he leave the White House. I finally understood that moving out of the White House into this lovely little house would mean failure. Loss of face."

"Sounds like he enjoyed a challenge," Casey commented lamely. Vera would love this house.

"He hated to lose at *anything*. Hated it. Even a game of cards or a set of tennis. 'Fierce competitor' were words often used to describe him in articles. 'Relentless,' 'ruthless,' 'driven.' When we first fell in love, we did lots of fun things together, but as the challenges and the barriers mounted, he had less and less time for leisure. When he did play, he was dead serious about it." Mary sighed, exhausted from trying to keep up the story.

"What would he think of your plan for the White House?"

"Oh, he approved."

Slow on the draw at first, it took Casey a moment to catch Mary's tense. "Approved? I'm sorry, I'm not following..."

"Forgive me, dear. Els and I were such soul mates. After he died, I'd often pose questions, and just *know* what his answer would be, as if he'd spoken right into my ear. Must be my Irish soul, thinking I can communicate beyond the pale. I still conjure his response to most any question, although, as the years pass, I find myself asking him less often." Mary paused. "You must find this very strange. Enough. I'm knackered, and you must be as well. Vera and I won't move until after the estate sale. Bertie's assistant will pick her up shortly and take her back to West Boylston. Walk with me to the White House, and let's call it a night."

After seeing Mary to her door, Casey limped down the stone stairs toward the station in the dark. She wasn't afraid of the night shadows. Never had been. It was the daylight hours that posed the most problems. Her mind wobbled back and forth in a kaleidoscope of images of Vera intermixed with new, troubling questions from the weekend.

Why was Mary angry with Jackson? And why did the policeman ask where Jackson was? Mary and Bertie had known that Vera had cancer and were waiting for tests. That's what Mary had been weeping and whispering about. Irish lightning sure sounded like arson. Casey's mind spun in circles. Considering the motley crew of players, did any project have a snowball's chance of getting off the ground? How sick was Mary? Why would she apply for a grant? And back to the beginning. Should she have let Vera go? Why was Mary angry with Jackson? Was there any reason to hope that any good would come of all of this?

So tired. She'd sleep a dreamless sleep tonight. Too bad. At least in her nightmares, she could fly.

Chapter Forty

On Monday morning Worthy knocked on the screen door of the White House. Mary waved him in and motioned toward the kitchen table behind her.

"Why on God's earth would I do you a favor?" Mary spoke into the telephone. She listened and offered up a few absent "Ums" and "Ohs" at appropriate moments, before interrupting. "Maybe I will. Maybe I won't. You'll just have to come see."

She hung up and joined Worthy at the table. By the look on his face, he had heard the shrill protests of the woman on the other end of the line as Mary had replaced the phone in its cradle. "Beth."

"I wouldn't have thought you two would be in touch. What does she want?"

"She wants you to call. She asked me to hold off on your trust check until she arrives."

"Arrives?"

"Next weekend. She'd like first dibs on a few items in the estate sale. She also mentioned that there are matters to settle with you and Cherie." Mary gave Worthy a quizzical look. He squared his shoulders, but didn't respond. Instead, he pushed her mail across the table.

Mary feigned interest in the letters, setting bills aside and tossing the junk mail into the trash.

"I had to sign for this one." Worthy handed her a larger envelope.

Mary read the return address and pounced. She opened the envelope and held the cover letter close to her eyes. "YES!" She grabbed the telephone, squinted, and dialed a number that she'd written in large numbers on a scrap of paper and posted on the bulletin board next to the table.

"The grant?" asked Worthy.

Mary nodded. "We got it!" she exclaimed when Casey answered. "We got the grant!" Casey whooped. "I'm too tired to meet with you today. Come over tomorrow, say mid-afternoon, and we can discuss what it all means, and then go out for a celebration dinner." Mary listened to Casey's excited chatter on the other end of the line.

"Oh. Yes. I understand." She tried to keep the disappointment out of her voice, but knew she wasn't successful. Casey had invited her friends LouAnne and Rosie over to see her new home. Mary listened for a moment longer. "Are you sure?" She didn't give Casey time to reconsider. "That would be wonderful, dear. I'd love to meet them. You're positive it won't be too much work? You've had a pretty rough weekend."

Worthy's head tilted at her last remark.

"Good. Then it's settled. I'll bring the wine." She hung up before Casey could object.

"Now, back to our agenda." Mary handed two checks to Worthy. "Here's the check for the balance of the trust that Els set up for you, and a separate check for your legal services. Thanks to your legal advice, we're all set to go. Too bad you're not licensed in the state and couldn't be the lawyer of record. That would have been a delicious touch."

"Thank you." Worthy examined the checks. "Frankly, I'm surprised you'd bother to write a check for the trust money."

"I thought you might like to deposit it before you left." She let a silence hang between them before making her next comment. "It takes three business days for a check to clear."

Worthy looked up to the right, calculating. "So, if I deposit it tomorrow, that'd be Friday. Perfect."

Mary offered a sly smile. "Beth won't be pleased to see Cherie."

Worthy pushed back from the table. "Will you mention the impending visit to her?"

Mary shook her head. "Hadn't planned to. I'd hate to spoil the surprise."

"Thank you, Mary. I'll clean up a few loose ends and be on my way."

"Where will you go?"

"I'll send a card."

Mary laughed at the improbability and shook his hand in farewell. As she watched the back of him, she was surprised that she cared where he went or what happened to him. He was a cad, but such a charming one.

Chapter Forty-One

On Tuesday morning unpacking the boxes the movers had left at the station had been like the Christmas of Casey's wildest dreams. Mary and Bertie had thought of everything: china, towels, bedding, silverware, pots and pans, a vacuum cleaner, and mops. The added bonus: Casey didn't have to iron and fold the wrapping paper for her Aunt Mae to use the following Christmas. The biggest prizes, of course, were Jed's desk and Mother Dempsey's rocker.

By mid-afternoon, she'd emptied all the boxes, found temporary homes for most of the treasures, and stacked the boxes and packing materials outside on the station platform. She'd take the lot to the dump tomorrow. Casey smiled at the thought. She was now an official resident of Welton with her very own dump sticker on the Muttmobile. Soon she'd learn more about the role Mary had in mind for her for the White House project. A line from her favorite children's story, *Solomon the Antique Cat*, crept into her mind. "If only the cats in fish town could see me now."

It was getting cold. She made a fire in the stove with wood Jackson had left stacked outside on the platform. She wrapped herself in one of her great aunt's afghans and curled up on her new couch in front of the flames, bone tired. So much had happened in such a short period. She needed time to sort through her thoughts and dreams to make sure that she was in charge of her own life. She felt like a little girl playing "Mother May I," except now it was "Mary May I." Mary had just awarded her ten giant steps. Casey wasn't sure her legs were up to it, and even if they were, where the steps would lead.

* * *

Casey shivered and pulled the afghan around her shoulders. Must be a draft. She should go to bed and snuggle under the covers.

A floorboard creaked across the room. Casey sat bolt upright, momentarily disoriented. She looked about the room and then gasped, hugging the afghan to her chest.

Worthy rocked back and forth in Mother Dempsey's chair, watching her with a small smile on his face. "You should lock your door. This isn't small-town Ohio. For sure, you shouldn't leave the keys in the lock outside." He held up her key ring and jangled the keys.

"And you should knock, instead of scaring a body half to death! How dare you just—"

"Actually, I did knock. When there was no answer, and the keys were in the door, I got concerned. But there you were, so blissful in front of the fire. I didn't have the heart to wake you."

Embarrassed at her immediate reaction to cover her chest and her Ohio-sounding retort, Casey put her feet on the floor and straightened her shirt.

"What the hell?" Worthy jumped up from the rocker and made it to her side in two strides. "What happened?" he asked, studying the shiner he hadn't been able to see until she sat up.

"It's a long story." Casey turned her head away, wishing she could dive down a rabbit hole.

Worthy gently turned her face back to him. "That's a beaut. Any other wounds?"

"None you can see."

"Here." Worthy returned to the rocker and picked up a bottle of wine next to it.

Taken aback, Casey accepted the bottle, noting that it was already cooled. She opened a number of cabinets before she found the crystal glasses she'd unpacked earlier, aware of Worthy's eyes tracking her every move. She rooted around in the silverware and utensil drawers. "I'm afraid—"

Worthy produced a corkscrew from his pocket. "Let me." She watched him deftly uncork the wine and pour two glasses. "Here's to you," he said, meeting her eyes in a toast.

Nothing she could do but clink his glass and try to hide her cracked and dirty nails and the blush that was creeping up her neck. Damn him. He looked so elegant in his slacks, cashmere sweater, and loafers.

"To what do I owe the honor of this visit?" Casey said to deflect attention from her bruises. She knew she sounded peevish, but he should have given her fair warning before waltzing in on her.

"Okay. I'll go first, but you're not off the hook. First of all, as I told you before, Cherie and I have decided to part ways."

"It's really none of my business."

"I had hoped it would be. I didn't want you to think I was just leading you on."

"Why would I think that?"

"Things aren't always what they seem. I met you as a married man. Why should you trust me?"

Why indeed?

"After the dust settles, I'd like to see you again."

Worthy's straightforward expression of interest caught Casey off guard. "What do you mean, 'after the dust settles'?"

"Mary told me this morning that Beth plans a surprise visit later this week. I have no desire to see her. Time for me to move on. I have a few errands but should be gone by the end of the day. Let's just say, Cherie will be less than pleased."

Casey frowned. "Doesn't she know—"

"No, and I'd appreciate it if you didn't mention either my going or Beth's impending visit."

"You're going to leave her holding the bag?"

Worthy threw his head back and laughed.

"I didn't mean—"

"I know. Just an interesting image."

Casey didn't pursue the topic. Clearly, he didn't want her nosing into his failed marriage or his relationship with his mother. Fair enough. There were plenty of things she'd rather not talk about, too. "Where will you go?"

Worthy was quiet for a moment and his expression turned serious. "The last few years with the firm made me very jaded about justice. Now, when I'm leaving the law, I've encountered a situation where all the players will get what they deserve." Worthy took a sip of wine. "That's a long answer to a straightforward question. "I have no idea." He shifted his weight. "Now, tell me about the shiner."

He pulled the rocker closer as Casey gave him an annotated version of Vera's dip in the pond and her stay in the hospital.

"So much for a quiet weekend in the country."

"Actually, it was pretty quiet. Except for Vera's incident and the fire."

"Fire?" Worthy leaned forward, almost spilling his wine.

"No one was hurt," Casey reassured him. "But the house next door burned to the ground. The Fire Chief suspects arson, and one of the movers made a comment about Irish lightning." Casey stole a look at Worthy. "You know, an insurance fire."

"Where were the occupants?"

"Mary's sister lived there, but she was in Chatham last week, so the house was empty."

"Convenient." Worthy unscrewed the cork from the opener and toyed with it. "Who owned the house?"

"I assume that her sister owned it, but I don't know that for a fact." Casey sipped her wine and waited for his reactions, but Worthy didn't comment further or ask more questions. He seemed preoccupied.

After Casey had been quiet for a few moments, Worthy pulled himself together. He took her hand. "I'm glad you're safe, but now I should let you get some rest. I'm sorry I frightened you."

Casey walked him to the door.

"Promise you'll lock your doors. Take care of yourself. I wouldn't want anything to happen to you."

Casey nodded. He leaned toward her with a sad smile, drew his fingers across her unbruised cheek, and was out the door before she could say fare-thee-well.

Chapter Forty-Two

"Too fancy," Mary muttered to her image in the mirror, reminding herself that the dinner was for Casey's cellmate from Marysville. She changed clothes for the third time, settling on black slacks and a cashmere sweater, and a jacket. The sweater was a little rich, but she loved the way it felt. She swapped the gold jewelry for a silk scarf. Better. Luckily, she was running her blood sugar levels high and had color in her cheeks to offset the darkening circles under her eyes.

She sat down on the bed with a sigh. Even dressing took too much energy. One thing at a time. The first order of business was to get the kidney infection under control. The doctors wouldn't flush her kidneys to get rid of the damned ketones poisoning her until the infection cleared up. It was good that she was just going next door to dinner.

Mary added a flashlight and her insulin kit to a tote bag full of wine. What was she forgetting? A corkscrew. She threw one in the bag and walked out the front door, across the drive, and down the steps to the station.

Casey had turned on the outside light for her. Mary lifted the brass knocker from the West Boylston house that was now mounted on the station door. Before she could knock, Casey opened the door and gave her a hug. Stepping inside, she was further greeted by the aroma of fried onions mingled with the scent of a wood-burning stove.

Mary looked around, speechless. Casey had transformed the place from a bare, businesslike station into a cozy, if eclectic, home. Mary noted Mother Dempsey's rocker by the stove and Jed's desk against the far wall. She squinted but couldn't make out who was in the little picture above the desk, but it looked as if it belonged there. Turning full circle, she noticed the breakfast table from West Boylston beautifully laid with china, crystal, and a vase of flowers.

Mary felt Casey's expectant eyes. "It's gorgeous, dear! You've done a wonderful job." Mary took a seat beside the fire to warm her hands and feet. So cold. Cold from inside out because of lack of circulation.

"I don't know how to begin to thank you. Most people acquire things over time. The boxes you and Bertie prepared created an instant home. You thought of everything."

Mary held up a hand. "It's temporary." She noticed Casey shrink back a little. "You'll want to make the place your own. Keep what you need or really like and take the rest to the swap shed at the dump." She smiled as Casey visibly relaxed. "How are your aches and pains?"

"They'll pass, although I look a fright. How are you feeling tonight? And how is Vera?"

Mary dodged the first question with a partial truth. "Much better than I felt this afternoon, thank you. Sorry to cancel our meeting, but I needed the rest. Besides, I figured I'd give you time to arrange things. I spoke with Vera this afternoon, although she was difficult to understand when I couldn't read her face for clues. She sounded … peaceful and strangely happy.

"When the oncologist spoke with Vera, Bertie, and me yesterday morning, Vera didn't react one way or the other to the prognosis. She just nodded. But later, Bertie said Vera became the perfect patient. Nurses joked with her and laughed at her outrageous antics. She can be quite the clown when she wants to be. I can understand it. She's so cooped up most days, it must be good to be the center of attention and see new faces. Bertie will bring her back to the White House sometime this evening."

Casey poured two glasses of white wine from a bottle that was already opened and handed one to Mary. "Still, I wonder if I…."

Mary waived off the glass and looked at the bottle. "None for me. This looks nice. What is it?"

"Beats me." Casey handed her the bottle. "Worthy brought it over yesterday afternoon."

"Making his round of goodbyes," murmured Mary. She heard a car door slam and peered through the window to catch a glimpse of Casey's friends. All she could make out was the side of a van with printing she couldn't read.

"Delivery!" a man called out, banging the new brass knocker.

Casey opened the door to a tall Black man.

"Oh, dear. I'm expecting laundry. He must've turned down the wrong driveway," Mary apologized, standing to correct the error.

The man produced a large bouquet of carnations from behind his back and gave Casey a hug and a kiss on the cheek. Mary's jaw dropped. Another door slammed. Seconds later a tall Black woman engulfed Casey in her arms, swinging her off her feet.

"How you be, girlfren'?" They laughed and hugged.

"Lookin' good, least on one side," said the man with a wolfish grin. "I swear you always meant to be Black."

"All you get's dinner, Rosie—" The woman stopped in mid-rebuff, seeing Mary standing off to the side.

"LouAnne, Rosie, meet Mary Waddington," said Casey.

"So pleased to meet you," LouAnne said in her best Wellesley manner, extending her hand to Mary.

"Ma'am," nodded Rosie, following suit.

Mary took her hand and then Rosie's, so stunned she was speechless. Then she broke up laughing.

"What I say?" Rosie asked, smiling down at Mary.

"Nothing," Mary said, "Nothing at all. Pardon me, but ... but Casey never said you were Black," she blurted.

Casey raised her eyebrows in a question mark.

Mary shook her head.

Rosie shook his big forefinger at Casey. "Devil's in the details, sister."

Mary regrouped. "What's it say on the side of your van?" Mary asked.

"Rosie's Farm," said LouAnne. "We run a shelter for battered women. We don't advertise our location for the protection of the women who stay with us. 'Rosie's Farm' had a nice ring to it."

LouAnne's expression turned serious. "Casey *did* tell you that she and I

234

were cellmates in Marysville?"

"Yes, but I just assumed from everything I've read that the inmates were segregated."

"You're absolutely right, Mrs. Waddington. We had white, Hispanic, and African American cell blocks. Casey was thrown in with us for punishment because she refused to identify the inmates who'd attacked her. I'm sure you've seen her scar."

Mary returned to her chair beside the stove, and LouAnne took a seat on the couch. Rosie draped his long body along the church pew rescued from the Somerville apartment. Casey served wine in her new crystal glasses along with a platter of cheese and crackers and then returned to the kitchen area to fuss over dinner.

"Mighty fancy, girlfren'," LouAnne called out to Casey, fingering the cut glass crystal of her wine glass. "And the desk is a lovely antique," she said to Mary.

Mary wondered at how easily LouAnne switched from proper English to street patois.

They discussed the White House project and the grant for a while and then moved on to LouAnne and Rosie's work at the Farm and their current funding emergency.

Mary watched Casey return with a new bottle of wine and assume pride of place in her new old rocking chair. The resemblance between Casey and Mother Dempsey was uncanny.

Rosie stood up to stretch his limbs from the hard church pew and circled the room. He stopped in front of Casey's picture of Little Mother. "Nice work." He moved on to Jackson's portrait of Casey. "This one's good, too, but different. It shows you to proper advantage," he said, mimicking LouAnne's Wellesley speak. Then he switched back to street talk. "It the picture you tole us about, done by the troll with the burnt-up hand lives under the bridge?"

Mary tilted her head at Casey in silent scolding.

Casey turned sheet white and seemed to shrink two sizes. "Forgive me, Mary. The first time I met him, I didn't know who he was, and he scared the daylights out of me." Casey turned back to Rosie. "The troll is my cousin, Mary's nephew, Jackson Dempsey. He did most of the work fixing up this place. Actually, he's quite handsome these days. He's out on the West Coast this week, doing some work for Mary."

It was the second time Mary had heard Casey refer to Jackson as her cousin. Casey knew Jackson was Vera's son. Time to clear up any confusion about blood relations. "Well, he's Casey's step-cousin. The artist is the son of my adopted sister, Vera."

Casey turned to her with a look of surprise. "You never told me—"

"Oh, surely I must have told you about Vera and Agnes," Mary babbled, knowing that she hadn't. "My parents adopted the girls after their parents died in an accident. My mother and their mother were best friends in school. You must've noticed how different Vera and Agnes look from the Dempseys."

Mary watched her niece process the information. Casey offered a nod and a small smile. Color returned to her face as she turned away and busied herself refreshing the cheese platter.

Casey walked to the kitchen window. "Looks like Vera's home. Too bad we don't have the ramp built yet, or she could join us."

"Maybe we can help," LouAnne said as she joined Casey in the kitchen area. They whispered a few words that Mary couldn't hear.

"Dinner's served in fifteen minutes," Casey announced.

Casey was giving her fair warning, time to take a shot of insulin before the meal. What she really needed was another nap. Mary excused herself, retrieved her insulin bag, and retired to the bathroom. Inside, she could barely turn around. Originally built for passengers awaiting the trains, the skimpy room had been halved by the addition of a shower. She felt up and down on the wall for the light switch. Must be on the outside wall. She had to sit on the toilet to juggle her equipment. She knew she should check her levels again but didn't have the energy. Besides, the light from the little overhead window wasn't strong enough to read the results.

No problem with the insulin. She listened carefully to the clicks as she adjusted the dial of the Nova pen. She pulled down her slacks, aimed the needle, and plunged it into her hip.

She almost dropped the pen. A woman's high-pitched shrieks pierced the air.

Chapter Forty-Three

C asey put two fingers to her mouth and whistled. Rosie ran downhill full stride behind Vera's wheelchair, as if he were in a marathon. Vera howled in delight. Rosie pulled back and slowed as they approached the station stairs.

"Okay, lady. Reach for the sky," Rosie ordered.

Vera obeyed, and he scooped her bulk into his arms. She giggled and squeaked as he carried her up the stairs and through the door. LouAnne grabbed the wheelchair as if it were a bag of potatoes and hauled it inside. Within seconds, Vera was sitting before the fire. Mary greeted her with a kiss.

When Vera caught sight of Casey, the glee melted from her face. "Owwww. I orry. Oh orry. Or-ive eee."

Casey gave her a big hug before she could say any more. "I'm sorry, too. And you don't need to be forgiven. I understand. Still friends?" she asked.

Vera nodded, but she had tears in her eyes.

"You and Rosie have apparently met. This is my friend, LouAnne."

LouAnne stepped forward and automatically offered Vera her hand. Vera didn't flinch, offering LouAnne her club.

"Oh, I'm sorry, forgive me…" LouAnne exclaimed.

"My ails are a right," said Vera, offering a crooked smile.

LouAnne gave Mary a quizzical look, but Rosie interpreted. "Her nails are a fright."

LouAnne guffawed.

"How do you know what she said?" Mary asked, astounded.

"Soul mates, ain't that right, Vera?" Rosie winked at Vera.

"Rosie's always been able to communicate with people, no matter what the problem. It's a gift." LouAnne looked over at Rosie with obvious pride.

Casey filled a juice glass with white wine, stuck a straw in it and placed it in the holder on Vera's chair, and then made the rounds filling other glasses. She moved to top off Rosie's glass, but he covered it in refusal.

"Wife says I'm the designated driver. At least tonight. They may repo the wheels in the morning."

"We have a long day tomorrow. A board meeting," LouAnne added, taking Rosie's hand.

"While you're up, dear, would you mind making me a tea with a touch of milk and two sugars?" Mary asked.

"Coming up," Casey replied, a little surprised at Mary's request. "Are you feeling okay?" she asked quietly as she passed Mary's chair.

"Fine. Please don't worry about me."

Casey retired the empty bottle of wine, put water on for tea, and returned to the party.

"I'm confused, orry. Oops, sorry," Mary babbled. She looked at Rosie's left hand and then at LouAnne's.

Casey had followed Mary's eyes from hand to hand and picked up on the source of her confusion. "I told Mary you were brother and sister," Casey explained.

"Well, we are. Sort of," said LouAnne.

"Sort of?" Mary asked.

"I'm sure you've noticed the different ways I speak. My mother and I are from the projects in Columbia Point, the streets, basically. She was a hooker who got caught out with me, and decided to keep me. Rosie's father is a judge. They met during criminal proceedings in one of my mother's court appearances."

Rosie continued the saga in perfect English. "My mother died when I was in prep school. Father shocked everyone when he brought home his new bride and her daughter. LouAnne showed me the streets. I taught her etiquette."

Mary shook her head from side to side, and then nodded. "Sure, and it makes sense now. Rosie, Roosevelt...you're Judge Washington's boy, and you must be—" Mary looked from Rosie to LouAnne and stopped short.

"I see you remember the case," LouAnne said. "I killed my husband when I caught him abusing my little girl."

Conversation stopped. All eyes turned to the kitchen area at the sound of hissing and popping from the stove.

"Yikes!" Casey rushed to the stove and turned off the heat under the pot of water that was boiling over. She got out a cup and saucer and then realized that she had neither tea nor sugar.

"Be right back," she called over her shoulder, heading for the door.

"It's all right, Casey. Don't make a special trip," Mary called back. "Anything sweet will do."

"Are you sure?" Casey asked. She looked in her cupboard. "Oreos?"

"Perfect."

Casey listened to the murmur of voices while she added another place at the table, put a few cookies on a plate beside Mary's seat. She was relieved and delighted at how well they seemed to get along. She stared at the table for a moment and then added a bowl of Parmesan cheese and salt and pepper shakers. Finally, she tossed the salad, making sure to include Rosie's black olives.

"Dinner's ready," she called. She ushered her very first guests to the table. She'd prepared lasagna, salad, and Italian bread and had LouAnne's favorite coffee, frozen yogurt, and Hershey's chocolate sauce for dessert.

"Last time we had Italian bread, you used it for a bat." Rosie regaled them with the tale of their Last Supper food fight in Somerville.

Casey was pleased when LouAnne and Rosie heaped their plates with seconds. She noticed that Mary seemed a bit withdrawn but didn't want to embarrass her by asking her how she felt a second time. She was surprised when Mary abruptly changed the subject.

"Sounds like you're having funding problems. How many women stay in your shelter?"

"It varies, but we're small. Our max is ten to twelve comfortably, sixteen

240

in a pinch. Why?" LouAnne asked.

"Have you seen the guest house, the one where my stepson and his wife are staying?"

LouAnne and Rosie looked down at the same time.

"I, uh, showed them around when they helped me move stuff from Somerville," Casey admitted.

Mary smiled. "Shortly, that house should be vacant. If you doubled up in the guest rooms, we could take in some of them for the short term. Maybe longer, but that would take an addendum to the grant."

"Miz Waddington, we didn't come here to aks no—" LouAnne stopped and corrected herself mid-sentence. "... ask for your assistance."

Mary waved her down. "Faith, and I know that. I had to wangle an invite out of Casey at the last minute."

"They all Black ladies, ma'am," cautioned Rosie.

Mary cocked her head to the side. "Do you think they'd feel uncomfortable here?"

"Heated pool. Sauna. Green grass underfoot. Biggest problem be gettin' 'em to leave." A small smile crept up the sides of Rosie's mouth.

"What?" asked Mary.

"Nothin'," demurred Rosie.

"Spit it out," Mary demanded.

"I was just thinking on writing the biographical addendum to your grant," he admitted.

"Trust me," Mary smiled. "We just got money with a widowed, legally blind, shanty Irish diabetic director, a half-burnt troll who collects cans for general manager, a nine-fingered attorney with partial memory loss, and—"

"I ave annerr," interrupted Vera.

Rosie's laugh died on his face as he looked at Mary. She nodded. "Cancer."

"O aye. I aaa ie."

"Okay? You're happy?" Rosie repeated, looking again to Mary for confirmation.

"It's a sad story. Vera has wanted to die since she was a girl. Now she knows she won't have to live to a grand old age. Sad for us, but she's really happy about it."

Rosie looked to the side for a long moment digesting the information. Then he smiled at Vera. "Okay, sister. Gimme a high club!" He raised his fist, and they batted each other. "But we're not done with the resume. I married my sister."

"I did hard time for manslaughter," said LouAnne.

"And I'm an ex-con, illegitimate daughter of a Jesuit priest," concluded Casey.

Mary stood slowly. "Delightful as the evening has been, I'm afraid you'll have to excuse us. We old ladies have to retire."

Casey led the unlikely parade back to the White House where Rosie and LouAnne said their goodbyes.

"It's been a delight to meet you two. Please call me when you know about your funding," said Mary.

Chapter Forty-Four

C asey helped Vera prepare for bed and then put on the kettle for tea. Until Mary and Vera moved to the gatehouse, they'd still eat and sleep at the White House. When the kettle whistled, Casey fixed a weak cup of tea with light milk and three teaspoons of sugar for Mary and a regular cup for herself. "I think it went rather well tonight, if I do say so myself." She placed a few shortbread biscuits beside the cup on Mary's saucer.

"Uh huh." Mary muttered. Casey carried the tea to the table where Mary sat before an open folder of papers.

Vera rolled into the room in her nightgown.

Casey smiled at Vera. "You and Rosie sure hit it off."

"Uuut."

"Yes, he is cute," Casey agreed. "Would you like anything, Vera?"

Vera didn't answer. She stared hard at Mary and pushed her chair up to the table. "Ary?"

"Umm."

"Ary!"

No answer.

"ARY!" Vera pushed on Mary's arm with her club.

Oh no! Casey bent over and looked into Mary's glazed eyes. Hypo! Casey ran to the refrigerator, grabbed a bottle of Glucozade, and rushed back to the table. She unscrewed the cap, gently cradled Mary's head in one arm, and raised the bottle to her lips.

Mary sipped, but most of the liquid dribbled down her chin.

"More," coaxed Casey. She raised the bottle higher to force more liquid into Mary's mouth. Two gulps. Casey waited a moment and tried again. Only one swallow. "C'mon, Mary. Help me out here." Casey repeated the motion two or three times, daubing the liquid off Mary's face with a napkin.

"A little more." Mary turned her head aside like a petulant child. Casey righted her head, but Mary's teeth were clenched shut.

"Looks like you've got a problem."

Casey almost dropped the bottle.

Cherie emerged from the cellar, each hand gripping a bottle of wine. "We're out of wine," she explained as if anyone had asked. "Didn't expect Mary back so soon."

"She's having a hypo. Give me a hand!"

Cherie put down the bottles and joined Casey. She gripped Mary's jaw with one hand and waved her other in front of Mary's vacant eyes. They didn't flinch or track the motion.

"On her way out," said Cherie. She released her hold. Mary slumped forward onto her arms, knocking over her cup and spilling the tea.

Cherie tugged at an open folder on the table under Mary's arm.

"We've got to give her a shot," said Casey.

"Wrong." Cherie yanked to release the folder but couldn't move Mary. "I don't give shots without wearing latex gloves."

Casey put her hands under Mary's arms and tried unsuccessfully to lift her inert body. "Help me move her, will you?" Casey turned to Cherie.

Cherie shook her head. "Too heavy. Dead weight."

"At least bring her medicine." Casey realized she wouldn't be able to get to Mary's hip for the shot. Instead, she rolled up her sleeve of her sweater to get to the shoulder muscle.

Cherie returned and handed her the syringe. "Don't be squeamish now. It's just a little needle," she taunted.

Casey took a deep breath and aimed.

Suddenly Vera lunged forward and batted the syringe from Casey's hand, sending it flying across the room.

"What the hell?" Casey yelled. She shoved back from the table and dove to the floor, searching for the syringe. Had to be down here somewhere. There! Casey crawled under the table, reached under a chair, and retrieved the syringe. She rose and carefully wiped it off before returning to Mary.

Vera pushed her chair to the refrigerator. She pounded on the door with both clubs. "Oh! OH!"

Casey raised Mary's sleeve.

Vera howled, "OOOOOOH!"

Seconds from the injection, Casey froze. "No?" She looked at the Nova pen in her hand and almost fainted. The dosage was cranked to the maximum. Wrong medication! She needed the orange case syringe not the insulin pen.

Casey raced to the refrigerator and grabbed the orange case. Her mind replayed Bertie's instructions, and her shaking hands obeyed. Shake the vial. Insert the needle. Empty the syringe into the fluid in the vial. Pull back the plunger to re-load the syringe. Tap the needle for air bubbles. Casey inserted the needle and gave the shot. Then her knees buckled, and she sank into the chair beside Mary.

"Close. You almost killed the golden goose."

Casey had forgotten Cherie. She turned but had a hard time speaking. "Why did you—"

Cherie slammed out the door.

Vera pushed up close to Casey and looked into her eyes. "Oh ay?"

Casey closed her eyes and took a few deep breaths to calm her heart. "God, I almost killed Mary."

Vera pointed to the clock.

"Right. Twenty minutes." Bertie said to wait twenty to thirty minutes after the injection to give Mary a chance to come around before calling 911.

The three of them sat in limbo for the next ten minutes: Mary slouched forward on the table, Vera in a wheelchair, and Casey in shock. Casey played and replayed the earlier scene. She told herself to stop, but the images kept rolling. Less than a week earlier, she had saved the life of one aunt who dearly wanted to die. Tonight, she almost killed her other aunt who'd struggled all her life to live.

245

Cherie gave her the wrong syringe! Casey had been a split second away from injecting Mary with an overdose of insulin.

She forced herself to move. She found paper towels and mopped up the tea from the table. Liquid had seeped onto the folder that Mary had been reading. Casey kept one eye on the clock while she retrieved and wiped off the wet and damaged pages. At the back of the folder, she came upon an article with a picture of a young boy holding up his bandaged hand for the camera. She looked closer and then read the tab on the folder, "Worthy." No time for it now. She closed the file. Mary must have been reading it before dinner, but why would Cherie want it? Five more minutes and she'd call an ambulance.

* * *

Within seven minutes of Casey's call, a Fire Department emergency vehicle rolled up the drive, lights flashing. Two men rushed to the back door before Casey could call out to them to tell them which door to use. They had been here before. Casey gestured toward Mary's slumped figure at the table.

The first EMT identified himself as Eddie. He took Mary's pulse and looked into her eyes. The second man snapped on plastic gloves and retrieved a small vial from a bag. "I'm Vince. How long's she been out?" he asked as he squeezed a gel onto his fingers.

Casey glanced at the clock. "Twenty-seven minutes. I gave her a shot of—" Casey couldn't remember the name of the medicine. She pointed to the orange case and the syringe. The man glanced at the case and nodded. He pushed up Mary's lips and rubbed the gel on her gums.

"She's taking antibiotics for a kidney infection. We just finished dinner. Lasagna. She gave herself a shot of insulin right beforehand. A few Oreos." Casey searched her brain for any other pertinent information.

"She won't like it, but we gotta take her in," said Eddie. He ran out the back and returned moments later with a stretcher. Vince continued talking while they gently lifted Mary and strapped her down. "How you been, Vera?"

"Oh ay," Vera replied. She watched the men's every move like a protective hen.

"And who might you be?"

It took Casey a second to realize he was speaking to her. "I'm Mary's niece. Where will you take her?"

"Newton-Wellesley Hospital."

"Is that far?"

"Five minutes, the way Eddie drives. You're not from here, then."

"Ohio," Casey answered, as if it would explain her ignorance.

Vince turned to her and gave her a long look. "You've got quite a shiner there yourself."

"How long will it take for her to come around?"

"Depends on how bad her infection is. You did good with the shot." Vince and Eddie rolled the stretcher toward the door. Eddie reached into his pocket and retrieved a card and pen. He wrote a phone number on the card. "They'll keep her in intensive care until she's stabilized. Give 'em a few hours before you call. Don't worry, she's been there before. Take care of Vera and get some rest."

They were out the door before Casey could thank them. She watched them slide the stretcher onto a lift. Seconds later, the doors closed, the siren wailed, lights flashed, and Mary was gone.

Chapter Forty-Five

I t all happened so fast. Casey sank into the chair next to where Mary had been sitting only moments before. She'd almost killed her aunt. She shook her head. Cherie had handed her the wrong syringe. Cherie was a nurse. She knew better. But Casey had come within seconds of giving the wrong injection.

Vera motored her chair next to Casey and placed her disfigured hand on her arm.

"Thanks," Casey said. She placed her hand over Vera's. "You okay?" she asked.

Vera nodded.

Casey stared at the table before her. Something niggled at her mind, not making sense. What had Cherie said? "We're out. I was just getting more wine." But Worthy had said they were separated. So why would "they" need more wine? Casey stared at the folder in front of her as if it could offer a clue.

Mary always put things away in their correct places. She kept her surfaces bare. She said she wasn't naturally tidy, she was sight-impaired, and it was the only way she could function. Would she leave a folder on the table? When Vera, Mary, and Casey returned earlier that evening, Mary went directly to the table, distracted. Why? By the folder? What was she reading?

Casey scanned the table. Mary hadn't been reading. Her magnifying glass wasn't on the table. She couldn't read a thing without it. Casey rose and found Mary's magnifier in its place in the basket on the counter.

Casey returned to the table. There was another possibility. Cherie had come in while Mary was out and removed the folder from the filing cabinet. They'd surprised her when they came back early, and Cherie had ducked into the cellar. Mary noticed the folder on the table and went to investigate before succumbing to the hypo.

Casey returned to the "Worthy" file and held the article with a picture of Worthy up to the light. A little boy with one hand in a large bandage and the other in a baseball glove stared at the camera. Casey winced. It must have been so traumatic. His mother had hurt him—the first person a little boy would look to for safety and love.

Mary said that Beth had been drinking heavily. She shouldn't have been driving in her condition, especially with a small boy in the car. As Casey remembered the story, Beth had slammed the car door on Worthy's fingers. Worthy had run off with his mangled hand and hidden for hours, his fear greater than his pain. No wonder that the adult Worthy seemed aloof after such trauma. But why would Cherie want to read about this? Surely, she knew the story.

Earlier that afternoon, Casey'd been embarrassed when Worthy had found her sleeping and disheveled. He looked immaculate when he'd come to say goodbye. He said he and Cherie had agreed to part ways. Casey closed her eyes and felt his fingers caress her cheek, and heard his voice, "I'd like to see you again." She'd hoped for a kiss, but he stroked her cheek instead.

Casey sat bolt upright. She stared at the picture and drew her fingers across her cheek. He'd been facing her. He reached out with his right hand and—could she be mistaken? Hadn't she felt the stub of his forefinger? Maybe. Maybe not.

Think! Casey watched Worthy uncork the wine. That image was clear. She hadn't been expecting a kiss then. His left hand held the bottle while his damaged right hand uncorked the bottle. But ... in the picture, the bandage was on the left hand. She thought back to the evening at Symphony. She'd held his damaged right hand. Could the poor little boy have had two dreadful accidents? Casey pushed the picture of young Worthy toward Vera. "I thought Worthy injured his *right* hand."

Vera shook her head no. She raised her own deformed left hand.

Casey stared aghast at the article. The Worthy she'd met wasn't the Worthy in the picture.

Snap.

Casey wheeled at the sound. Cherie stood at the kitchen sink with her back to them.

"What are you doing?" Casey demanded.

"Tidying up," Cherie replied.

"You gave me the wrong syringe. I almost killed Mary. You're a nurse, for God's sake! You know better."

Cherie turned and pulled on a second surgical glove with another snap. She glanced at the open folder on the table.

Casey gulped and pushed back from the table.

Cherie walked toward her, a small smile on her face. In her right hand, she held Mary's Novapen.

Casey's eyes fixed on the syringe of insulin.

Cherie chuckled. "Don't be coy. You've seen the picture and figured out our little charade. But she can't talk. You can." She advanced a few more steps.

"So, who are you?" Casey asked.

"Oh, I'm the real Cherie Waddington."

"Why not leave now, before you do something you'll regret?" Casey jockeyed to the right.

"I'm not leaving until the check clears."

"Check? What check?" Casey snatched the folder from the table and threw it at Cherie.

Cherie rounded the table laughing as the papers fluttered to the floor. In a swift motion, she dipped down, grabbed the article with the photo of Worthy, and crumpled it.

"Surprised? Surely, you're not dumb enough to think I'd spend my vacation with a dried-up widow and her freak sister. This week is Worthy's fortieth birthday. I was trying to figure out how much the trust will be worth in today's dollars."

Keep her talking. "What happened to the real Worthy?"

Cherie lunged.

Casey dodged, toppling a chair in Cherie's path before slipping into the dining room.

All was dark. The long table was stacked high with boxes. Casey hefted one of the smaller boxes to her shoulder. Quickly she pulled a chair next to the door and stood on it, the box cradled overhead. She'd have to hit Cherie's syringe hand to have a fighting chance.

A shadow came through the doorway. Casey heaved the box with all her might. It smashed onto the floor.

Cherie entered and kicked it aside, facing Casey. "Nice try."

Casey jumped off the chair and backed up. "Mary'll be out of the hospital tonight or tomorrow. She'll stop payment."

"Fool. She doesn't know. She may have noticed the folder on the table, but she can't see without her magnifier."

Casey didn't dare turn her back on Cherie. "How do you expect to get away with this?"

"Easy. When I checked up on my patient, Vera, I heard a suspicious noise. Oh no! There was a burglar in the house!" Cherie enjoyed her re-enactment of the faux drama as she inched forward. "I grabbed the first thing I could find to defend myself." She advanced another step, protecting the pen so it wouldn't be an easy target. "And then I was attacked by the greedy ex-con."

Only three more feet. Kick the pen with the left foot and barrel into her? Or take out her knees?

An earsplitting scream pierced the air. Cherie whipped around. With a mighty push, Vera launched herself from her chair, hitting Cherie full force, sending them both crashing to the floor.

Casey rushed forward. "Vera!"

"Get her offa me," shrieked Cherie. Vera's bulk pinned her to the floor.

"Vera!" Casey knelt beside the tangle of arms and legs. She grabbed Vera's arm and leg and slowly rolled her off Cherie. Cherie jumped up and dashed away.

Casey turned Vera's head toward her.

"Aaank ooo." Vera smiled. "Aaank ooo. Ov ooo."

251

Thank you? Love you?

"Nooooo!" Casey cried. In the dim light she saw the Novapen stuck in Vera's midriff. Gently she removed the needle. "No, no, no ..." The cartridge was empty. She kissed Vera's forehead. "Love you, too."

Casey needed help fast. *Move!* Get to the phone in the kitchen. "Hold on, I'll get help!" She dropped the pen and ran.

Chapter Forty-Six

C asey yelped and skidded to a halt, staring into the amused eyes of Cherie who blocked her way holding another syringe.

"That was a wasted cartridge, but, lucky me, Mary keeps a backup with her testing kit." Cherie cranked the new pen to the maximum dosage and withdrew the protective nib from the needle. She held the syringe up to the light and tapped it. "Silly. Who cares about air bubbles?"

Casey backed over Vera's inert body into the dining room.

Cherie hummed as she stalked her.

The only door left led to the conservatory. Casey edged toward it, her eyes fixed on the lethal needle. Too close. Cherie smiled and lowered her head to attack.

Casey charged, waving her arms, screaming at the top of her lungs. Cherie jumped backwards to protect the pen, giving Casey the split second she needed to turn and dodge into the conservatory.

The room was pitch black. Casey felt her way along the wall. She bumped into a chair and toppled a lamp giving away her position.

Cherie entered and switched on the overhead light.

Casey ducked behind the piano, gauging the distance to the front hallway and the stairs. Her foot grazed the piano stool. It rolled forward. Perfect. She edged around the piano, guiding the stool before her. She stood up straight, raising her hands overhead in surrender to distract Cherie.

Cherie cocked her head to one side, watching Casey advance. Their eyes locked.

"You've got me. How 'bout I leave and save you an extra body to clean up?" Casey offered.

Cherie shook her head.

Casey kicked the stool hard into Cherie's legs and dashed for the front hall.

Cherie crashed backwards. "Fuck!"

Casey hit the hallway light switch. In the foyer, movers had left piles of boxes. A couch, and heavy chairs blocked the doors to the east wing. Close behind her, Cherie swore as she cut off access to the front door. Only way to go was up.

Casey grabbed Mary's prized African violet from the hallway table and flicked off the light. She climbed the stairs, holding the railing with one hand and gripping the plant in the other.

Cherie hit the light switch and followed.

Casey looked over her shoulder. Cherie mounted the stairs, syringe raised on the ready. Throw the plant to slow her down? Cherie could fend it off like she had the box. Go for the light. Casey hurled the plant as hard as she could at the overhead light. The plant and glass exploded with a loud pop, plunging them into darkness.

At the top of the stairs, the hallway branched to the left and right. Which way? No time to think. Casey turned to the right, guiding herself by hand along the wall. Her fingers found a doorjamb and a knob. Locked. Farther along a second door opened. She walked forward and bumped into soft cloth. Linen closet.

"Casey, I'm coming," Cherie taunted in a singsong voice.

Another sound. Outside, the dogs barked as an automatic garage door opened. Casey moved forward again, reaching the end of the hall. Turning around, she found two more doors off the far side, both locked. Where was Cherie?

A car door slammed. Mary's room had to be on the other side of the stairs. It would be open, but now she'd have to get past Cherie. Casey crept forward, listening. Heavy breathing. Click. A flicker of light.

What's she doing? Casey inched closer. She smelled perfume. Cherie was directly in front of her. Casey held her breath and slid sideways to pass her.

Click. Cherie's lighter lit the scene.

Casey stared directly into Cherie's eyes.

Cherie lunged, lighter in one hand, syringe in the other. Casey jumped to the side and bashed the hand that held the lighter.

"Shit!" Cherie shouted.

Darkness as the lighter skittered across the floor and dropped down a step. Cherie patted the floor, scrabbling to locate it. Casey groped blindly down the hall, testing doors until she found Mary's room at the end.

Inside, she turned on a light and slammed the door. Damn! The door was so old, she'd need a skeleton key to lock it.

The garage door closed. Casey ran to the window. A man walked toward the house. Jackson? She pushed the window but could only force it up a few inches. She stared at the figure in the dim evening light. Too tall. Had to be Worthy. Or whoever Worthy was. Casey had a fighting chance against Cherie, but not the pair of them. Whose side would he be on? Don't be stupid! He was a con artist working with Cherie. He was here for money, not for her.

How could she block the door? The only pieces of furniture large enough were a bureau and an easy chair by the window. The bureau wouldn't budge.

Cherie rattled doors as she advanced down the hall.

Casey heaved the big chair left and right, walking it slowly forward across the carpet.

"Where are you?" Cherie sang.

Casey jammed the chair against the door. She thought of Vera downstairs on the floor. She had to escape.

Below, the kitchen door slammed. "Cherie? Cherie! Where are you?"

Cherie pushed and opened the door about five inches. Casey grabbed a clock from the bedside table. When Cherie's pushed again and poked her face through the doorway, Casey cocked her arm and threw. The clock smashed into the door inches from Cherie's eyes.

"God damn you!" Cherie spat.

"Jesus! Cherie? What's going on?" Worthy called from below.

"Get up here, Drew. I need your help."

Footsteps pounded up the stairs.

Drew? Was that his real name? Whoever he was, he'd have no problem forcing the door open. She cast about for anything she could use as a weapon.

She froze for a second before a picture of herself on the far wall. "Mother Dempsey," Casey whispered at the portrait that Mary had transported from West Boylston. No wonder Mary recognized her. She should have made the connection. Her name was Cassandra *Rose* Cavendish.

Muffled voices at the top of the stairs grew louder as Cherie and Worthy argued. "Put that damn thing away. Leave it to you to fuck everything up. Go downstairs. I'll talk to her."

No time for family history! Casey tore her eyes from the picture and turned to the window. What were the chances she could jump and not break every bone in her body? Better than facing the two outside the door. How long would it take for an overdose of insulin to kill? She had no idea, but if there were any chance Vera was still alive, Casey had to get help.

She peered out the window. Yes! The huge beech tree that she'd sat under at the picnic abutted the house and Mary's window.

Behind her, the doorknob turned, and the door pushed the armchair backwards.

Break the window! Casey cast about and grabbed a straight chair, and hauled it to the window.

"Casey, it's Worthy. I won't hurt you. Cherie's crazy. You and I have to get out of here."

You and I? Yeah, sure. Casey swung the chair against the window like a bat, splintering the wood and smashing the glass. She punched out the sharp edges with one of Mary's shoes.

"Stop! Listen to me, Casey. I know you're confused and scared."

Casey gripped the window frame, put one foot on the windowsill, and hiked herself up, catching her balance at the last moment to keep from falling forward.

"Casey!"

She cried out in pain as a shard of glass sliced her palm. She leaned forward. The tree was only a few feet away, but if she missed...Casey looked down and shuddered.

The door behind her yielded as Drew shouldered into the room. "Casey, don't!"

She launched, grabbing onto the nearest branch. It bowed and bent under her weight, lower and lower. With a sickening crack, it snapped, and she fell. Her head smashed against a lower limb before she hit the ground. Stunned, Casey struggled to right herself. The dogs howled. Searing pain shot through her temple, muting the pain in her hand.

The backdoor slammed. Floodlights lit the scene, blinding her. Through blurred vision, two Cheries ran toward the tree, both gripping syringes.

Casey rose to her knees and stumbled toward the garage. The backdoor slammed a second time, and over her shoulder two Drews appeared. Casey wove toward the garage and the dogs. Her slippery fingers fumbled with the latch and opened the door to the dog pen. Guinness and IRA barked and jumped and nudged her in greeting.

"She's in with the dogs." Cherie shouted.

Casey flung open the gate. "Watchem!" she commanded pointing toward the blurry figures, praying that the dogs would understand what she wanted. Suddenly alert, the dogs turned and bounded forward, snarling and barking.

"Halt!" The huge dogs stopped just short of the couple, growling, jaws flecked with foam. Cherie and Drew backed toward the house. The dogs followed, heads low, eyes fixed on their quarry, one command from attack. The couple ducked into the back door.

Casey leaned against the garage struggling for balance. Her joints were putty. Had to get help for Vera. But first. She whistled for the dogs. Couldn't leave them outside. If they attacked humans, they'd be put down. They bounded back to her. "Good dog. Good dog." She closed them in their pen and staggered down the drive.

She felt the growing lump on the side of her head. Swollen and tender. Her fingers came away sticky. From her hand or her head? Her body was bruised all over, but as far as she could tell nothing was broken except possibly her head. She shook it to clear her vision and nearly passed out from the pain.

She made slow progress past the side of the house and then aimed herself toward the stone stairway between the White House and the station. When she found the railing, she gripped it for balance, descending the uneven steps in the dark. She wobbled side to side like a drunk, fighting for equilibrium. If only she could sit for a moment. So tired. Her head hurt.

No! Get help! Telephone. Call an ambulance. How long had it been?

A glint of light off the station's new brass doorknocker shone like a beacon. At the base of the stairs, she stumbled on a rough patch and fell to her knees. She wanted to lie down. *No, Vera needed help.* She crawled forward. *C'mon!* She forced herself to her feet and stood, weaving. She set her jaw, fixed her eyes on the knocker, and lurched forward.

The door was unlocked. She didn't dare turn on a light. She felt her way to the kitchen counter and then along it to the wall. She patted until she located the phone. She lifted the receiver.

"Casey," Drew's voice called softly from outside.

Casey's knees buckled. She dropped the phone and grabbed the counter to keep from falling. She cracked open the back door and eased her way onto the station platform, feeling her way along the side. How high was the platform? At least three feet, maybe more.

Lights came on inside the station, sending a swath of light through the back window onto the wooden platform. No choice. She dropped down, landing in the brush, and crouched against the side just as the back door opened.

"I know you're here, Casey. You left the phone off the hook. Looks like you're injured. There's blood on the counter. Let me help. I promise I won't hurt you." Drew's voice was soft and persuasive.

Could she trust him? Her head throbbed with every heartbeat. *"Leave it to you to fuck everything up,"* he'd said to Cherie.

Footsteps approached the side of the platform. The beam of a flashlight played across wooden slats.

The footsteps stopped.

"Hello, there," Drew said in a soothing voice.

Chapter Forty-Seven

"**P**retty little girl."

What? Pretty little...?

"Come. I won't hurt you."

Little Mother responded with a coy mew. Casey exhaled and closed her eyes. He sounded so gentle. What did he want with her?

The front door of the station slammed. "Looking for your new honey?" Cherie's voice pierced the air. The back door of the station creaked open.

Casey heard lighter footsteps on the platform. "You better hope you find her before I do," Cherie continued. "Take her with you. I'm going back to the guest house to call the police."

"What the hell happened?"

"I was nosing about in Mary's file cabinet to find out how much money the trust was worth. I had to leave a folder on the kitchen table when Casey, Vera, and Mary came back early after a dinner down here. Mary had a bad hypo. While they waited for the EMTs to arrive, Casey read an article about Worthy's accident that showed him with a bandaged hand. A bandaged *right* hand. She figured it out."

"So, you best leave as well."

"Oh no. Just you. Mary's in a coma in the hospital. She never read the article. Vera can't talk, so it's my word against Casey. I'll tell them I surprised Casey upstairs stealing from Mary's safe. She came after me with a syringe. Vera lunged for her and saved my life, poor old dear."

Click. Cherie's lighter. The smell of tobacco.

No, don't believe her!

259

"You're lying."

"What makes you so sure?"

"Casey wouldn't hurt Vera. And, m'dear, you're still wearing surgical gloves."

Silence. "Not anymore." *Snap. Snap.* "As the police will soon discover, Casey kindly withdrew the syringe from Vera, leaving her fingerprints on it. I have no idea where she is, but I'll tell them that she probably took off with my no-good, philandering husband. *Worthy's* reputation precedes you, Drew. And I'll finally get what's due to me for all those wasted years. All of it. I've decided not to share. Plus some lovely jewels and some mad money."

"Ah, but what happens if Mary recovers and discovers the truth?"

"Easy. I'll confess. I'll say you threatened to kill me after the accident if I didn't cooperate. That you're a retired Navy Seal with a violent temper who beat his wife. I feared for my life. You're not Worthy, but I'm still Cherie. Looks like you're the fool."

The door slammed.

"Bitch!" Silence.

Oh, God. This can't be happening. I'm screwed.

Drew's voice came from the back door of the station. "Casey, if you're out there, listen to me. I may have deceived, but outside of the military, I've never hurt anyone. I have to leave. Come with me. I really like you. We can make a fresh start."

Casey held her breath. Every inch of her body hurt.

"Cherie's crazy. She'll kill you if she can. Even if she can't find you, it's your word against hers. Who do you think they'll believe?"

He's right. I won't have a prayer. I'll look like the impersonator, the ex-con who claims she's Mary's niece. But how could she trust Drew? If he was impersonating Worthy, what had happened to Worthy? Casey shuddered.

Drew paced across the platform.

"Cherie took my keys, so I'll have to take your little dog car. You'll have to hide in case she comes looking for you."

One day, she had nothing: the next, she had it all. Now, she could lose it all over again, but dammit, she wasn't going back to prison.

Leave Mary. Vera. Jackson. Little Mother. Her little station. Her job. These people could be her family; the station, her home. She'd found the best possible situation. Leave? No. Forsake her dreams? No!

"Last call, Casey."

After a long silence, Drew spoke again. "I'm sorry." He walked back inside. Moments later, the front door closed, and the Muttmobile growled alive, stalled twice, and then crawled up the hill to Church Street.

Chapter Forty-Eight

Within moments of Drew's departure, the heavens opened. Pouring rain drenched Casey as she huddled beside the platform. Shivering, she struggled to her feet in the dark and took a step. Lightheaded and dizzy, she crashed against the side wall of the station and slid to the ground. She pushed her head between her knees. She wasn't going anywhere fast, but she had to move. For sure, Cherie would return to the station. She closed her eyes and forced herself to breathe in and out slowly, calming her pounding heart as the emergency vehicles arrived.

Sirens and then silence as floodlights and strobes from a fire truck and ambulance lit the front of White House. She watched the scene with a curious sense of detachment, mesmerized by the intermittent bursts of light. Figures rushed about, at first quickly, then slowly, entering and leaving the White House. Rain soaked through her clothes. For some reason, she was holding her breath. Waiting.

Finally, two men emerged from the front door of the White House, rolling a stretcher between them. They loaded it into the ambulance. The strobes turned off, and the vehicles wound slowly down the driveway. No sirens. No lights. No reason to hurry.

Vera. Casey buried her face in her hands and sobbed.

When she looked up again, she could focus, no longer seeing double. The pounding rain had lightened to a drizzle.

In the darkness, a beam flickered at the top of the stone steps leading down from the White House to the station. Casey watched the beam lower step by step. At the foot of the stairs, a hooded figure walked toward the station.

Had to be Cherie. Casey groaned. Even if she could get inside to the telephone, Cherie would be on her in seconds. The arches of the Church Street underpass towered thirty feet away. If she could reach the tangle of shrubs choking the stairs leading up to the street, she'd have cover. Not too far to run, or even walk. But she'd have to crawl. She couldn't risk passing out.

She moved forward on hands and knees like an unsteady toddler, tilting and swaying and crashing sideways when she lost her balance. Her sodden jeans protected her knees but weighed her down. Twenty feet more. Casey looked over her shoulder. The figure approached the station's front door. Faster. Gravel ground into the cut in Casey's injured hand. She stifled cries of pain. Cherie was close enough to hear.

The outside station light flooded the scene. Casey flattened to the ground. After a few minutes, she inched her head to the side and dared to look backwards. Inside the station, dry, unhurt Cherie walked past the window.

Nothing Casey could do except go for it and hope Cherie didn't glance outside. Casey dragged herself to the brush on her belly.

The station lights went out. The beam of the flashlight arced about and shone on the front door while Cherie locked it. The light made slow circuits around the outskirts of the station like a searchlight beacon sweeping prison grounds. Casey ducked and froze as the light passed over her. Instead of returning to the White House, the light advanced toward the underpass. Had Cherie seen something?

Casey had to move. There wasn't enough tall cover in the brush, but the far side of the underpass was overgrown. No time for crawling. Slowly Casey rose, steadying herself before lurching five steps forward. She froze, gasping from the effort, clinging to the damp stones of the arch.

Behind her, the light stopped and lowered.

Click. Click. "Damn."

Cherie was trying to light a cigarette in the rain. *Click.* The lighter flared, showing Cherie drawing on a cigarette. When the flame disappeared, Casey propelled herself the remaining distance to the far side of the arch, feeling her way along the stones.

When her hand hit air instead of stone, she lost her balance, fell forward, and sank to the ground behind the arch. Had she made any noise? The flashlight beam illuminated the archway. Casey shrank back into the brush. Her hand touched heavy plastic fabric. The hollow chamber under the arch magnified Cherie's approaching footsteps.

The fabric felt like a tarp. She raised it and felt dry ground underneath. Cherie was closing in. Casey crawled under. Pitch black. Seconds later, footsteps stopped beside her.

Silence. Casey smelled the cigarette. She drew in a slow breath, held it, and waited, motionless. After what seemed like an eternity, Cherie's footsteps retreated through the archway. The ground vibrated as a vehicle crossed the bridge overhead. Casey waited a few moments before she exhaled and peered out from under the tarp. The flashlight beam and red cigarette ember climbed the stairs to the White House and were gone.

Chapter Forty-Nine

A deep rumbling awakened Casey. When the ground trembled, she sat bolt upright and pushed the tarp aside. Pain pierced her temple as if she'd been stabbed with an ice pick. She lowered her head to keep from fainting.

Light filtered through nearby trees, warming the dark tarp cover. Blue sky and warm sun greeted her. The ground tremors continued regularly. Not an earthquake, just cars passing overhead on the Church Street bridge. A leaf blower droned nearby.

As a child, Casey loved raking huge piles of leaves and burning them in the driveway, throwing buckeyes into the pile and waiting for them to explode. If she closed her eyes, she could smell the fallen leaves and hear them crinkle underfoot. Nothing like the smell of burning leaves.

As reality sank in, a sickening sense of *déjà vu* took her breath away. For the second time in her life, she was certain to be accused of a crime she didn't commit. The unfairness of the situation flattened her. It just should not, could not, happen twice in one lifetime.

She glanced at her watch and gasped. She checked the direction of the sun. Afternoon! She'd been out for over twelve hours. Had to be Tuesday afternoon. Slowly, she crawled under a bush for cover and peed. Every motion was painful, but the worst part was her lack of balance.

Cherie knew she was hurt and that there was a chance she hadn't left with Drew. Cherie couldn't have seen Jackson's tarp in the dark and rain last night, but it would be easy to spot in the light of day. Much as she wanted to sleep another twelve hours, Casey had to move. She couldn't even be a troll under the bridge.

Casey explored Jackson's orderly collection under the tarp: bicycle pump, bottled water, canned cat food and an opener, a bowl, and a box of dried cat food. Not much here. But Casey didn't want to hide under a bridge. She'd come East to find and be found, to discover her father. To make a new life in the world of others.

She sighed. She'd always be different. The only thing she could control was how she configured her "outsiderness." But, dammit, she'd found family, friends, a home, and a job. Until yesterday. The more Casey thought about the unfairness of it, the angrier she got.

Where could she go? Not far, in her condition. No identification. No car. No money. Locked out of the station. No telephone.

Cherie. Why hadn't Cherie come back and found her by now? Too hung over? Casey took long gulps from Jackson's water bottle. She tried to open a tin of cat food, but couldn't make her swollen and bruised fingers twist the opener. She threw the can against the wall. *Sure, that'll help.* She hurled the opener after it.

She grabbed a box of dry Friskies. Good, it was already open. She shook pellets into her mouth. Gag! She read the label. Ocean whitefish. She forced more into her mouth and washed it down with water.

No way to contact LouAnne and Rosie. Her only hope was to reach Mary or Jackson. Where was he? Still on the West Coast or had he returned? She had to hold on and stick close by, poised for the chance to get to one of them before either Cherie or the police found her. Cherie didn't want her to be found, at least not alive, and the police ... Why weren't they looking for her?

Wait a minute! Maybe her best bet was to go directly to the police. They'd have to at least investigate her claim that Drew was an imposter and that he and Cherie were here to rip off Mary. Vera's death would still be Casey's word as an ex-con versus Cherie's, but at least Cherie would be challenged.

But how could she prove it? Casey almost smacked her forehead; the answer was so obvious. Surely someone had a picture of the two men. Both Mary and Jackson had met the phony Worthy/Drew and could identify him. But it was even easier than that. The real Worthy's mother, Beth, was coming. She could identify the players. That's why Drew took off.

How to reach Mary or Jackson. She wouldn't be able to get past the electronic fence that surrounded the rear of the White House. She'd have to go to the exposed front. It was her only chance.

Casey rose slowly and staggered forward. She wobbled back and forth and side to side, struggling to keep her balance. Lightheaded, she leaned against the inside of the arch and sank to the ground before she fell. She wasn't going anywhere. She pounded the ground in frustration.

When she looked up, she saw her newly painted little station basking in the sunshine. Until she had first set eyes on it, she hadn't realized how much she'd yearned for a place of her own. The derelict little building with boarded windows and ratty roof had spoken to her. Like her, it didn't belong in the rich setting next to the white mansion. Like her, it was secretive, dark, small, dowdy, and abandoned.

But they'd both changed. Yesterday, she'd given a lovely dinner party in the newly renovated station with friends and family to celebrate the grant and the promise of good times to come. Today…

A pickup truck wound up the drive to the White House. Casey watched while a man got out and helped a woman out of the passenger's seat. Jackson and Mary? Would the hospital release Mary so soon? Mary hated being in the hospital. She'd come home at the first opportunity.

"Jackson! Mary! Over here," she shouted at the top of her lungs. Neither figure turned. They were too far away to hear her. How could she get to them when she had the balance of a drunk?

Another wave of *déjà vu* rolled over her. In her mind's eye, she pictured an old friend of hers walking her bicycle down the street, too drunk to ride but able to navigate with the support of a bike.

Jackson's bicycle leaned against the side of the station next to the water spigot. It would make a strange walker, but it could give her stability. She'd have to crawl to get to it. Crawling would be safer anyway. She rolled onto her hands and knees and began the slow journey toward the station.

Chapter Fifty

Mary walked through the back kitchen door, followed by Jackson. The house was quiet. No Vera to greet her for the first time in...how many years? Mary was too tired to calculate. Her eye was drawn to Vera's new electronic chair, righted and wheeled against the kitchen wall. She refused to look at the doorway where Jackson had told her they'd found Vera's body.

Vera was the reason Mary got up in the morning. So many years together. They'd developed their own language of nods and gestures. Two or three words and a raised eyebrow could send them into a fit of giggles.

Mary glanced at Jackson. Unshaven and rumpled after taking the red eye from San Francisco, he'd gone directly to the White House, and had been greeted by an officer who questioned him and then informed him of the events of the night before. In their brief interchange, the officer had informed him that Casey left with Worthy. Jackson hadn't wanted to believe him and had walked the property but found no trace of Casey. The door to the station was locked, and the Muttmobile was gone.

He'd given Mary the news of Vera's death and the events as far as they were known when he'd arrived at the hospital that morning.

The place looked like a war zone. Behind the kitchen table, papers were strewn across the floor. Walking from room to room, Mary saw the place in a new light with scars on the moldings where Vera's chair had crashed into the woodwork and the peeling edges of wallpaper.

Although they had removed Vera's body, evidence of a fierce battle remained. It had been a mess before with boxes and furniture from

West Boylston, but this was destruction. Boxes and lamps were toppled. Potshards and pieces of glass littered the hallway leading to the stairs, and her shoes ground into dirt and leaves from her African violet. Upstairs the destruction was limited to her room. Her chair was moved, and the window smashed. Her clock was in pieces by the door.

Mary worried about Jackson. He looked stoic, but Mary knew that his expression—or rather, lack of one—was protective coloration. He was withdrawing, clearly distraught about the death of his mother and the absence and the disappearance of Casey.

"Join me downstairs for a spot of tea," said Mary, more as a command than an invitation. Give him something important to do. Keep him busy.

In the kitchen, Mary put the kettle on and made two cups of tea.

"I'm going to need your help in the next few days," Mary said, glancing up at the morose expression on Jackson's face. "Vera wanted to be cremated, but I have no idea how to arrange it. I'm also thinking we could have a real Irish wake with close friends and family: no funeral."

Jackson nodded but didn't speak. They sat in silence for a few moments.

"I'd also like your help moving me into the gatehouse. Not tonight. I'll stay here."

Again, Jackson nodded.

"There's a lot to do with all the boxes and furniture from West Boylston." No reply.

"And, I'm afraid there's one last thing. Someone will have to fetch Agnes sooner than later. She needs to know what's happened to her sister and to be present for the wake. Will you drive to Chatham and bring her back?"

Jackson gave Mary a dour look. "Making busy work for me is good, Mary. But you'll owe me one for Agnes." Jackson crossed himself and intoned, "Dearly departed sister, beloved mother of...."

Mary gave a bitter laugh at the truth of Jackson's mimicry. She walked Jackson to the door. "Go, and God be with you."

Once the door closed, Mary sank into a chair. Her life, and her project were in tatters. Casey was gone. Casey had questioned her decision to save Vera after Vera threw herself into the pond, but Mary found it hard to

269

believe Casey would harm her.

But how much did she know about the girl, really?

Mary had just started to nod off when the doorbell rang. Who could that possibly be? Slowly she made her way to the front door. Officer Durkee of the Massachusetts State Police introduced himself and asked for a word.

"You'll have to come to the back where I'm comfortable."

After a few preliminary comments, Officer Durkee sat at the kitchen table and posed a similar question. "How long have you known Ms. Cavendish?"

"A few months. But I've seen a lot of her during that time," Mary responded.

"Moved right in, didn't she?"

"Well, I'd meant to fix up the station for some time now—"

"I understand Ms. Cavendish represented herself as the daughter of your brother, Joseph Dempsey. What proof did she offer of her parentage?"

Where was he getting his information? Not Jackson, so had to be Cherie. "She didn't need proof. She's the spitting image of her grandmother, Rose Dempsey. What are you suggesting?"

"Was Ms. Cavendish with you when the house next door to your family home in West Boylston burned?"

"Yes."

"Did you know that less than a year ago, Ms. Cavendish was the only one who escaped from a fire in Ohio where four others died?"

Mary sat back in her chair. "Yes, but—"

"There's a lot of death and fire and crime following this young woman. This morning I spoke with a librarian in her last job before she moved to Welton. She hinted at an affair between Ms. Cavendish and a married man, a professor at the college. From what we can determine, Ms. Cavendish has now taken off with another woman's husband."

"How do you know that?

"We have a witness saying Mr. Waddington drove off in Ms. Cavendish's car with a passenger in the front seat. The car was found this evening at Logan Airport in Central Parking. It doesn't look good. We're checking flights, but an ex-con knows how to get other identification. We don't know if they flew out or took a bus, rented a car—or whatever."

Mary slumped in her chair.

"And..." the officer leaned forward, "...Cherie Waddington says her husband took the claim check and picked up her jewelry from a store in Wellesley yesterday afternoon. He told the clerk the jewelry was a gift for their wedding anniversary."

Mary looked down, but not in time to conceal a small smile.

"What do you find amusing, Mrs. Waddington?"

"I have no problem believing he took the jewelry. There was no love lost between the two."

"The wife says everything was fine until Ms. Cavendish weaseled her way into her husband's affections."

"Your choice of words suggests you have already made up your mind on the matter."

"Ma'am, I'd appreciate it if you would take inventory of your valuables and report anything that's missing."

"Today, all I want to do is to take a long bath and sleep. It's all such a shock. Yesterday my dear sister was alive. Casey and I had a wonderful celebration party with Vera and friends. Today, Vera's dead, and Casey's gone." Mary's voice trailed off.

"Party? Who was at this party?"

Mary didn't respond.

"Tell me more about the party."

She'd only add fuel to the flames if the police learned that LouAnne and Rosie were at the station the night before. "I'm sorry, officer, we'll have to continue this later. I'm just home from the hospital this morning and feeling weak." Mary pointed the officer toward the door.

Chapter Fifty-One

Mary awoke from a fitful nap to the sound of voices downstairs. She thought about the detective's earlier words while she dressed. The Worthy/Casey thing worried her. Could she have been so blind? Well, she was legally blind, but she had always been able to trust her instincts about people. There had been a spark between the two, but was there more? Had there even been time for more? Don't be dull. You fell in love with Els the instant he laughed.

She descended the steps holding the rail, avoiding potting soil and the leaves of her ruined plant. Tears threatened when she remembered how Vera had loved the violets. When she reached the kitchen, Cherie and Detective Durkee were sitting at the table talking and sipping coffee. He had a notepad and pen beside his cup.

"I didn't want to wake you, Mrs. Waddington, so I decided to talk with your daughter-in-law while you were taking a nap. She agreed to meet me here. Although I spoke with Ms. Waddington briefly earlier, we need to record the exact details for a formal statement. I'll speak with you later."

Mary poured herself a cup and walked to the table to join them. "I'd like to hear the details of what happened. Don't mind me. I'll just be a fly on the wall," Mary said with a smile for Durkee and a grimace for Cherie.

"Sorry, Mrs. Waddington. I'll need to speak with each of you separately."

"Hmmmph. I don't understand all the secrecy."

"Standard protocol, ma'am."

"Later, then. I'll just gather my things." Mary walked back to the counter and emptied her cup into the sink, and then, with her back to them shielding her movements, pressed the intercom button so that she could listen to their conversation upstairs in her room. She made slow, deliberate progress back upstairs. She pressed the intercom button next to her bed.

"Go on, please." Durkee's voice came through loud and clear.

"I had come back to check on Vera and help her to bed. That's when I discovered Casey upstairs. I'm not sure what she was doing up there, but when she came downstairs, she had one of Mary's Nova pens in her hand. She chased me and threatened me with it."

Mary shook her head. She didn't believe that for a second.

"Vera rolled forward and lunged to intercept Casey. Casey turned quickly. Vera wasn't strapped in. She fell forward onto the syringe. I'm sure it was an accident. I tried to help Vera, but had to fend for myself when Casey came at me again with Mary's backup Nova pen."

"What happened then?" Durkee asked.

"Casey chased me into the dining room and then the conservatory. I threw a lamp and pushed a piano stool in front of her, but she kept coming. She blocked the front door, and boxes for the estate sale filled the doorways to the east wing. The only place I could go was up. But Casey was right behind me. So, I grabbed a plant from the table and threw it at the overhead light."

Mary frowned. The trail of destruction she'd seen fit with Cherie's story, but she still found it hard to believe.

"I dashed upstairs, looking for a place to hide. I tried all the doors on the east wing, but they were locked. So, I crept back and surprised Casey when she reached the top of the stairs. In a scuffle, she dropped the syringe. I got it, and she realized the tables were turned. She ran. I cornered her in Mary's room."

"That's when I heard Worthy come home. I was foolish enough to think I could talk with her and get her to come out, but she'd shoved something against the door, and I couldn't reach her. I knew she hadn't meant to hurt Vera. She panicked. When I heard glass shattering, I dashed downstairs and outside to see what was happening.

"Casey jumped for the tree outside Mary's window, but the branch broke, and she fell to the ground. Worthy and I rushed to help her. When Casey saw me, she ran to the side of the garage and opened the door to the dog pen. The next thing I knew, she set the dogs on us. All I remember is backing away from snarling jaws until we reached the house. "

"Casey must have told the dogs to halt," said Officer Durkee.

"Now that you mention it, I think she whistled them back. After all, Worthy was beside me, and she wouldn't want those dogs to shred her new love."

Cherie's voice paused. "Once Worthy closed the door behind us, I ran to Vera, but she had stopped breathing."

Mary let out a sob.

"What was that?" asked Officer Durkee.

Mary held her breath, tears streaming down her cheeks.

"I don't know. It's an old house. Anyway, I heard Worthy in the front room. When the door closed, I went to investigate. He was gone. I called after him, but he didn't respond.

"When he didn't come back, I knew something was up. Casey was crazed and dangerous. Who knows what kind of weapons she might have at the station? He could be hurt, even killed."

"You said she was injured," Durkee said.

"Which would make her even more desperate. What I saw next ... When I got to the steps leading down to the station, I saw Worthy in the driver's seat of Casey's car. It looked like someone—"

"Where were you exactly?" Durkee interrupted.

"Halfway down the stone stairs."

"In the dark," Durkee said.

"Yes. That's why I said it *looked like* Casey in the passenger seat, but I couldn't swear to it. I collapsed right there on the steps when I realized what had happened. He'd taken off with another woman."

"*Another* woman?"

"Yes."

There was a moment of silence. When Cherie spoke again, her voice cracked. "He'd had a number of affairs before. Ours was a rather volatile marriage. Before, he'd be gone for a night or a weekend, but he always came back with his tail between his legs."

"And you took him in."

"I loved him." Cherie sobbed.

This actually sounded believable, thought Mary.

"Loved?" Durkee's question echoed Mary's thoughts.

"I don't think he's coming back this time. At first, I couldn't believe he'd leave with her, but then, he did have a penchant for trash. You do know Casey spent ten years in prison, don't you?"

"Are you sure he's gone?"

"Later this morning, when he didn't come home, I went to the bank. He cleaned out our checking account. He took his passport from the safe deposit box."

Mary smiled. She noted that Cherie hadn't mentioned the trust check. Cherie knew it wouldn't have cleared and planned to collect the money later.

"When I returned to the guest house, I started to catalogue what was left. Worthy had given me a gorgeous collection of diamonds—they were a guilt gift after I caught him with his secretary. I was having the gems set by a jeweler in Wellesley. I couldn't find the claim slip. I looked everywhere. Turned the place upside down, but I remember clearly where I'd put it. When I called the jewelers, the woman who answered asked if I liked the new settings. Worthy told the clerk it was an anniversary present and even had her wrap up the boxes."

Once again, Mary smiled at the thought of Worthy outsmarting Cherie. But even though Cherie's sobs sounded genuine, Mary couldn't take it anymore. She marched downstairs, through the dining room, and into the kitchen.

All conversation ceased as she walked to the counter and made a show of turning off the intercom. She turned and glared at Cherie who dabbed at her eyes with a tissue. "Good show, but I don't believe you for a moment. You're a consummate actress. Your marriage was on the rocks. The only reason you're here is to collect Worthy's inheritance. None of your problems have anything to do with Casey. I don't believe that she would chase you about the house with one of my syringes. She has no reason to hurt you, and she would never harm Vera."

"So, if she's innocent, where is she?" asked Detective Durkee.

Mary studied her hands. "I don't know if she left or not. If she did, I certainly can understand. She already suffered from one wrongful conviction. Vera's death would be her word against Cherie's." Mary stared hard at Durkee. "Do you believe this woman?"

Durkee shifted his weight. "Until I speak with Miss Cavendish, Ms. Waddington's description of events and the physical evidence is all I have to go on. We're checking for fingerprints on the syringe. We'll also be looking for Mr. Waddington for questioning. Contact me immediately if you hear anything from either one of them. The worst thing Cavendish can do is run. No one on a jury will believe her if we have to catch her. And we will."

Chapter Fifty-Two

After the officer and Cherie left, Mary headed to her room. In the hallway she stopped at the ruins of her African violet. She should at least try to root a leaf or two. She collected a few unbroken specimens and scooped up some of the dirt.

Back in the kitchen, she filled a teacup with the dirt, gently tamped in the leaves, and watered carefully, making sure not to get the leaves wet. Who was she planting the violets for? Not Vera. Or Casey. Where could she be? How badly was she hurt? The officer mentioned blood on the telephone at the station. Although Mary was a lapsed Catholic, she crossed herself and said a prayer for the girl.

She almost dropped the cup when the doorbell rang again. She wasn't expecting anyone. She walked to the living room and drew aside a curtain. "Jesus, Mary, and Joseph!" she whispered. A tall blonde woman pressed the doorbell a second time. Mary waited a few moments before peeking out again. Beth Waddington stared directly at her and punched the bell hard.

Mary took her time walking to the door. She opened it and grimaced at her old *bete noire*. "Worthy's not here." She watched Beth's facelift for a reaction and was disappointed when there was none.

"I know." As Beth breezed through the door, she shrugged out of a sleek leather jacket and handed it to Mary.

Mary looked at the coat for a second before dropping it into the dirt on the floor. "Cherie's just returned to the guest house, if you'd like to see her," she offered, using the annoyingly helpful receptionist's voice she had perfected years ago.

277

"Exactly the one I've come for." Beth examined the wreckage in the hallway and then gave Mary the once-over. "A little the worse for wear, are we? You look positively dreadful. And the house ... what the hell happened here?"

"Thank you." Mary ignored Beth's question. "Worthy left when I told him you were coming. By the way, there's a wheelchair in the kitchen should you feel a bit faint, although you seem to have miraculously recovered from your hip replacement." Mary led Beth through the labyrinth of boxes and toppled furniture into the kitchen.

Beth followed. "You really should change the code to the gate."

Mary nodded. "'Twould keep some of the riffraff out. Care for tea?" Mary studied Beth's flawless face, coiffed blond hair, and gravity-defying figure and estimated the cost of vanity in the tens of thousands. Although doctors had worked miracles, they hadn't been able to remove the bitterness that aged Beth's otherwise perfect façade.

"How civil of you. I prefer Chardonnay."

"There's an open bottle in the fridge. Glasses in the cupboard." Mary pulled up the cowl of her sweater to cover her sagging chin.

Beth poured herself a glass of wine. "Did you write him a big fat check?

"None of your business, but, yes. Actually, I wrote two checks. One for legal services—he was doing some work for me—and the other from the trust account Els set up for him."

"Excellent!" Beth raised her glass to Mary as if in a toast, drank half the wine, and refilled the glass.

Confused by Beth's reaction, Mary asked, "How did you know Worthy wasn't here?"

"Easy. He's dead."

Mary's insincere smile faded. She lowered herself carefully into a chair at the kitchen table, giving herself time to decide how to play her cards. "Dead? But I saw him just yesterday...."

"You never were too bright. I said Worthy is dead. Dead. You've been played for a complete fool. You wrote a check to an imposter." Beth gave a hollow laugh and sipped her wine before continuing. "Worthy and Nan

Cunningham died in a boating accident. Cherie and Drew Cunningham, Worthy's partner at the law firm, survived."

"But—"

"You fell for the chopped-off finger. That's how they met. Worthy sat next to Drew on a cross-country flight. After a few drinks, they discovered that they both had missing digits on their forefingers and that they were both lawyers."

Mary assumed a stunned expression as if the information were new. Even with her flawed eyesight, she'd known the man who called himself Worthy was an imposter the moment he walked in the door. She'd followed Beth and Worthy from afar for years.

Beth sipped her wine and continued. "Drew was from Virginia. He'd met Nan as a hooker. He didn't have the Ivy degree or the pedigree to work at Mercer and Franklin, Worthy's law firm, but he did have a drop-dead gorgeous wife. Worthy used his clout as the 'comer' at the firm and took Drew under his wing, and evidently," Beth smiled and took another sip, "Nan, to bed."

As Beth spoke, Mary replayed earlier scenes of the Worthy/Cherie charade. They had been good, but not perfect. Worthy didn't know the name of his dog. He recognized a picture that wasn't there in his childhood. There was a touch of the South in his speech and manners. Cherie would jump in when he was confused, making excuses for both mood and memory. Mary made herself frown. "I don't understand," she prompted.

"Worthy paid Cherie off for a divorce with a pile of my money. Cherie kept the money, but also thought she could get him back. He'd crawled back many times before, mostly to spite me. But not this time. Cherie found out that he had consulted a divorce lawyer and that he and Nan planned to visit you to collect Els' inheritance money."

Mary nodded to keep the conversation going. She hadn't known that Worthy cuckolded his best friend and partner before the accident. Cherie was a woman scorned and about to be divorced. And Drew wouldn't have any compunction about taking Worthy's money after Worthy helped himself to Drew's wife. The pile of money Beth paid Worthy to dump Cherie could account for the diamonds that Cherie had had set at the jewelers.

"So, apparently, your son was an untrust-*worthy* prick..." Mary paused to let her bad pun sink in, "...who married his mother, only to discover what a shallow, greedy bitch she was." Mary shook her head again. "It all fits, but how can you be sure about the accident?

"Oh, it was no accident."

Chapter Fifty-Three

C asey gripped the handlebars to keep her balance as she pushed Jackson's bicycle uphill. When she'd begun her walk, the bicycle had seemed lightweight. Halfway up the hill, it had cement tires. As she struggled along, she thought about the disastrous sequence of events. The boating accident had happened while the two couples were on vacation together in Maine, far from the legal firm and mother dearest in California. Maybe Drew really did have a concussion when he was thrown from the boat. Cherie identified, or rather, misidentified, the body of her husband.

Casey stopped to catch her breath. Drew left because Beth was coming. Cherie knew Casey had figured things out and was dead set on stopping her from telling anyone and blowing their scheme wide open. But something still didn't make sense. If the real Worthy died in an accident before the divorce had gone through, why couldn't Cherie claim the inheritance money? Why the elaborate charade?

Casey pushed the bike forward. Now the cement tires were mired in molasses.

Mary was home from the hospital. Was she in danger? Think! Casey plugged doggedly uphill. Even if Cherie couldn't find Casey, it wouldn't matter if Cherie could silence Mary. Then it would be Casey's word as an ex-con versus a respected nurse. Casey could be charged with manslaughter for the death of Vera and be sent away for a long, long time.

When she reached the intersection where the White House drive and station drive met, she stood still to gather her energy, resting leaden arms one at a time by her side. At the gate, she entered the code and turned the bicycle toward the White House for the final push. Mary's drive was paved, making it easier to navigate. After she passed the gatehouse and the driveway to the guest house, she came to the circular drive in front of the White House. A car she didn't recognize was parked in front. She pointed the bike down the side walkway leading to the back door.

As she neared the kitchen, Mary walked past the window. Thank goodness! Casey swallowed hard and pushed with renewed energy, surprised at how much it meant to see a woman she hadn't even known existed a month before. If she could talk with Mary, she could warn her, and they could go to the police. Closer, it looked like Mary was speaking with someone, but the window was closed, and Casey couldn't hear the words.

She released the bicycle and staggered to the window. She grabbed onto the frame for balance and peered inside, forcing her weary eyes to focus. Mary sat facing her at the kitchen table. Dark circles ringed her eyes, and she used both hands to guide the teacup to her lips. Casey waved, but Mary couldn't see her.

Casey glanced at the empty doorway where she had last seen Vera. "Thank you," Vera had said. "Love you." Now, her new wheelchair was propped against the far wall.

Cherie sat across the table from Mary with her back to Casey. What lies was she feeding Mary? Mary nodded and occasionally replied. They seemed to be having a civilized conversation. Seeing healthy, beautiful Cherie enjoying a glass of wine at Mary's table was almost more than Casey could bear. The woman was a killer! But what could Casey do? In her condition, Cherie could easily overpower her.

Chapter Fifty-Four

Beth studied her manicure. "I watched a movie of the boat race and crash that was taken by a young boy. The boy's father discovered it and took it to the police." She sipped her wine. "Cherie and Drew were in a boat—one of those cigar-shaped speedboats—that chased and overtook Worthy and Nan in a similar boat. Cherie was at the wheel. As they came alongside, Cherie hauled down on the wheel and bashed into Worthy's boat, forcing it onto the rocks."

Mary winced, imagining the boat splintering and exploding in a fireball. But what was even more terrifying was the lack of affect in Beth's voice as she described the death of her only child. She could have been giving Mary a recipe for chicken fricassee.

"How did you see the movie?"

"A nice detective brought it to me for identification."

"That must have been horrible for you."

"Spare me your sympathy. You sent the estate sale flier to hurt me."

Mary nodded. "True enough, but hurt is one thing. I wouldn't wish the death of a son on anyone."

"How noble."

"So, the movie shows Cherie intentionally smashing into the other boat. What was Drew doing?"

"Waving and pointing at the rocks. He was shouting, but you couldn't hear anything above the scream of the engines. The impact threw him overboard."

"You said you were here to confront Cherie. I don't understand why the police didn't arrest her after viewing the film."

"Cherie is a very clever liar and a good actress. She told the officers investigating the accident that it was the first time she'd been at the wheel of the boat. She said she and Worthy were having a friendly race with Drew and his wife. In all the excitement, when Worthy yelled at her and pointed, she thought he wanted her to turn right. She cried. The police believed her."

"Why don't you tell the police the truth and let them do their job?" Mary asked.

"Two reasons. First, I wanted Cherie and Drew to make a fool out of you and bleed you dry. Evidently, they succeeded admirably, although I hate to think the little cunt will profit from it."

Spoken without inflection, Beth's crude words sounded more sinister to Mary than if she'd said them in anger. "Believe me, she won't get a dime. The check will bounce."

Beth raised an eyebrow.

Mary laughed. "I may be a fool, but I'm not a complete idiot. That money was spent long ago. You can't squeeze a dry sponge. You don't honestly think I'd go to all the trouble for an estate sale if I had money? I'm flat out broke."

"I don't believe you."

"Believe what you want. Els' last big gamble failed. When he died, there was nothing left but properties scattered around the globe. I sold one every year or so to pay taxes on the others. Just this week, I signed over your precious White House to a charitable foundation."

Beth gestured toward the empty wheelchair. "Where's your sister?"

"She's dead. Murdered by an overdose of insulin." Saying the words aloud brought on a sudden wave of sadness and a lump in her throat. "Ironic, isn't it? You show up looking like a million dollars, and you rot away in an old folk's dorm, eating cafeteria mush and playing bridge on Tuesdays. We, or rather I, can live in style at the gatehouse for the duration, looking and feeling like a burnt-out shell."

"Glad you find some humor in it."

"You said there were two reasons you didn't go to the police. What's the

284

second?"

Beth offered a twisted smile. "They don't have the death penalty in Maine. Besides, I have a better plan."

Mary looked into the ice-blue eyes of Beth Waddington and shuddered.

"Mind if I look around?" Beth rose from the table.

Mary kept her voice neutral. "Knock yourself out. We've postponed the sale, so if there's anything you want, let me know."

"So I can buy back my own stuff?"

Mary sighed. "Why not bury the hatchet? I'm too sick and tired to fight these old battles."

Beth whirled about and came nose-to-nose with Mary. Her eyes blazed, fueled by raw hate, although a smile still curled her lips. She whispered through clenched teeth, "You sit there with a stupid smirk on your face and tell me a sob story about living off Els' fortune. You took it all—Els, my home, my life." Her voice rose as she spat out the words. "The only way I'll bury the hatchet is in your head. We were a beautiful, successful family before you wrecked everything!"

Mary held her ground, refusing to shrink from the invasion of her space. "Right. You were a drunken whore who slammed your little boy's hand in a car door."

Beth slapped Mary hard in the face.

Chapter Fifty-Five

"**N**o!" Casey banged on the window. When Cherie turned toward her and screamed, Casey realized her mistake. The woman was blonde and beautiful, but no longer young, and definitely not Cherie. Casey lurched toward the kitchen door. She yanked it open and aimed herself toward the woman who had attacked Mary. The woman backed away as Casey lost her balance and fell to her knees.

"Casey, you're hurt!" Mary cried. Mary turned to the other woman. "Take her other arm," she ordered, and to Casey's surprise, the woman obeyed. Together they led her to Vera's wheelchair. Casey glared at the blonde woman but was too dizzy to offer any resistance.

Mary wet a dishtowel and daubed at Casey's face. "All this blood. We've got to get you to a doctor. Where does it hurt?" Mary asked.

Casey offered Mary a wan smile. "Bruises and a concussion. I don't think anything's broken. I look much worse than I am."

"Oh, my dear, I'm so glad to see you. I've been worried to death. Cherie said you'd taken off with Worthy. I didn't want to believe her."

"My son is dead," the blonde woman said in a flat voice. She studied Casey from a safe distance.

After a moment, Casey recognized the woman from Mary's clippings. "Beth Waddington."

"Ms. Cavendish," Beth replied. "I'm surprised you know who I am."

"I could say the same."

Beth scowled first at Mary and then Casey. "I hire only the finest detectives. And, you share an unfortunate family resemblance. What the hell happened to you?"

Casey took Mary's hand. "She's right. Worthy's dead. And Cherie killed Vera. I swear it."

"Tell me what happened," said Beth.

"When Vera and I figured out Worthy was an imposter, Cherie came after me with Mary's Nova pen. Vera surprised her and fell on the pen." She turned to Mary, "I'm so sorry." She paused a moment before continuing. "A long story. Cherie chased me, but I escaped to the underpass by the station. Worthy—or Drew—left in my car."

"Very interesting. So, Cherie's looking for you." Beth rose and stalked from the room.

Casey leaned forward. "Mary, you could be in danger. Call the police."

"First, a doctor," Mary responded.

Beth reappeared with a roll of packing tape. She smiled sweetly at Mary. "No, first I'll help you down to Casey's new home, the station. You'll call Cherie and tell her you've found Casey, that she's hurt, and you need her help."

Mary cocked her head toward Beth but didn't respond.

"But I'm afraid your niece will have to stay here," Beth continued. She placed the roll of tape on the table in front of Mary. "Tape her wrists to the chair."

Mary didn't move. The two women glared at one another. Casey shrank from the current of hate arcing between them.

Beth raised her other hand and pointed a small revolver at Casey. "Better leave her here alive than shoot her, don't you think?" She could have just asked Mary to pass the salt and pepper. She thrust the tape into Mary's hand. "Tape her hands, then her feet. Move!" she snapped.

Mary picked up the tape and fingered it. "You know I can't see well. How can I find the start of the tape?"

"You'll do wonders if you care for your niece."

Mary found an edge and unwound a strip of tape. "How did you carry a gun on the airplane?" she asked.

"I didn't have to." Beth waved the gun in front of Mary. "Look at the handle. Recognize the pearl inlays? It's Els' old gun. He kept it in the piano bench."

Casey watched Mary gently tape her hands to the sides of the wheelchair. "Why did they concoct such an elaborate charade?" she asked. "Why couldn't Cherie collect Worthy's inheritance as a widow?"

"Now, her feet."

Casey felt the soft touch of Mary's hands as she wound tape around her ankles.

"Apparently, you're no brighter than your aunt. Worthy had her sign a prenup. She wouldn't get a penny in a divorce and none of his inheritance upon his death." Beth smirked. "Cherie couldn't let him divorce her and run off with Drew's wife, so she killed him. But she couldn't collect if he were dead, so...."

"So, now what?" Mary asked.

For the first time, Casey heard a suggestion of fear in Mary's voice. Casey fixed her eyes on Beth.

"A slightly modified plan. I'll get two birds with Els' gun ..." She turned and smiled at Casey. "...and pin it on the obvious suspect, the gold-digging niece ex-con."

Casey leaned forward. "I have an easier suggestion. If you really, *really* want to punish Cherie, send her to prison. With her looks, she'd be a prime target—worse than anything you can imagine. No muss, no fuss, and no need for further violence." She studied Beth's face for a reaction but saw no change in expression.

"I'm sure you speak from experience, and I appreciate the image." Beth checked Mary's taping. "But some pleasures cannot be shared." Beth pronounced Cherie's sentence as if she were reading from Ecclesiastes. She turned to Mary. "And, I have absolutely no reason to spare you."

"How do you expect to get away with it?" Mary asked.

"Easy. I was never here." She put down the gun and wiped off the bottle and glass. "No one named Waddington flew this weekend. I have multiple IDs from my marriages. And, a nice old lady is staying with me in my apartment in Canterbury Woods, accepting trays for me from the dining room. We're not supposed to go to meals if we're sick or incapacitated."

"So, why leave me here?" Casey asked.

"Simple. I need someone left standing who could have committed such crimes."

Such crimes? "Taped to a chair? Who'd believe I taped myself to a chair?"

"No one. But you won't be taped for long." Beth smiled. Casey saw the blow coming but couldn't move. The gun grazed her temple. She felt a searing pain before all went dark.

Chapter Fifty-Six

Mary was exhausted after the long walk from the White House down the steep steps to the train station below. She sat in the rocking chair in the station with her hands clasped and taped in front of her. "You don't have to go through with this. Casey and I can expose Cherie easily. She'll go to prison. As you said earlier, no one has any inkling that you've been here. Go back to California, and let us clean up this mess."

"I think this will work nicely." Beth examined Mary's new Nova pen. "Let's see. One must be the smallest dose." The pen clicked as she twisted the cylinder up to the maximum. She removed the protective nib from the needle and squirted a tiny amount of the liquid into the sink. "Now, for the phone call."

"I won't do it." Much as she hated Cherie, Mary wouldn't be a party to murder.

"Oh, but I think you will. Cherie's a killer. My son. Your sister. She'll kill your niece, too, if we don't stop her. Miss Cavendish didn't look like she could put up much of a fight."

Mary pictured Casey, unconscious, injured, taped to Vera's chair. "Still, you don't have to—"

"Worthy was my only child!" Beth's face twisted into a hideous mask. "He was the only part of Els I still had, and *she*—" Beth stopped mid-sentence. She pulled back her shoulders and composed her features. After a few long breaths, she looked down at Mary, smiled, and spoke in a calm, slow voice, like an irritated parent reasoning with a recalcitrant child. "Just call Cherie

290

and say, 'I'm at the station, and I need your help.' Easy."

Keep calm. Take another tack. "Cherie won't come. She doesn't care if I'm in trouble."

Beth tilted her head to the side as if thinking. "Tell her you've found Casey and that she's injured."

Mary lowered her eyes and pretended to consider the suggestion. She took her time before responding. "Okay," she agreed. She stood and walked slowly toward the counter and reached for the telephone.

Beth snatched the receiver off the wall. "Nice try, but we don't need the police quite yet."

Mary sank back into the chair. "Please. Casey's hurt. She hasn't done anything to you. She needs help."

Beth modulated her voice to a sincere register. "Cherie first. Then we'll get help for Casey." Beth put the syringe on the counter and withdrew a scrap of paper from her jacket pocket. Els' revolver bulged slightly in her other pocket, and a roll of packing tape circled her wrist like a bracelet.

She may be mad, but she's very efficient, Mary thought. Beth had not only washed and wiped off the wine bottle and glass she'd touched at the White House, she'd retrieved her soiled jacket and collected Mary's insulin kit before "helping" Mary down to the station.

"I don't believe for a moment that you'll let us live."

"Don't take this personally, but I don't care enough about you or your niece to kill you. If you'll make this call, I'll give you the telephone when I leave so you can get help." She dialed the number on the paper in her hand, listened for a second, and then held the telephone to Mary's ear.

What choice did she have? One ring. Two. Three. Maybe Cherie wasn't—

"Hello? *Hello?*" Cherie's husky, cigarette voice sounded expectant.

"Cherie. It's Mary."

"Oh." Cherie's voice flattened.

"I need your help."

"Sorry, I'm just on the way out."

"Good. I'm down at the station. I found Casey hiding under the platform. She's hurt and needs attention."

Silence. Mary imagined the gears churning in Cherie's head.

"Okay. I'll be there in a few minutes." Cherie hung up.

"Good girl," Beth said as she wiped down the telephone with a dishtowel. Her eyes scanned the room. "Kind of cramped in here." She looked out the window. "It's such a nice day. Let's get some fresh air." Beth picked up the syringe and opened the door. "You first."

Outside, Beth looked around. "Sit and bask in the sun for a few minutes." She pushed Mary down onto the top step. From behind, she unwound more tape. "Just so you don't try to do anything stupid," she said, covering Mary's mouth. Beth examined her handiwork and then ducked out of sight behind the bushes at the side of the station.

Chapter Fifty-Seven

Disjointed images and sensations crowded Casey's mind like pieces in a complex jigsaw puzzle. Her temple throbbed, and she couldn't move her arms or legs. Gradually her eyes opened, and the pieces began to fall into place: the bloody dishtowel in the sink, the teacup on the table, the scent of expensive perfume.

It would be so easy to drift off again. But when she closed her eyes, other, more sinister images appeared. Pushing the bicycle up the hill. Beth's icy eyes. Mary taping Casey's hands and feet to the wheelchair. The little revolver with the pretty handle that she had seen too late to duck. And then, Beth's words. "I need to have someone left standing who could have committed such crimes."

Casey's eyes popped open. *Such crimes? What crimes?*

With each new image, the fog lifted, and her mind cleared and focused. She was all alone. Mary and Beth were gone. Beth was after Cherie. Well and good. But there was more. "Two birds with Els' gun," Beth had said. Mary was the second bird.

How much time had passed? Was Mary still alive? Casey had to get help. She tried to move, but her hands and feet were taped securely to the chair. She wiggled her fingers. The fingers of her right hand touched something, and the chair jolted. Casey froze. Slowly she inched her fingers forward again. There! She'd found the joystick on Vera's new electric wheelchair.

Casey nursed the stick forward. The chair advanced. She pushed to the left. The chair obeyed. When she withdrew pressure, the chair stopped. She curled her forefinger around the joystick and pulled backwards. Too much pressure! The chair jolted and crashed into the wall, sending pain ricocheting through her brain.

When the pain subsided, she aimed the chair toward the back door, lurching forward in fits and starts as she learned to drive. If she could get out to Church Street, she could get help.

Casey stared at the closed door. She couldn't reach the doorknob, much less turn it. Couldn't even kick it. She was well and truly fucked. She threw back her head and howled like Vera.

Slow down. Use what's left of your head. Vera opened that door. Her hands weren't taped, but she couldn't grip the doorknob with her damaged fingers. Think!

Casey pictured Vera wheeling herself toward the door. She had punched something. A square metal plate with the symbol of a wheelchair on it was at chair height to the right of the door. Of course, she'd seen that stupid plate every time she'd walked through the door. Vera hit it to trigger the automatic door. A lot of good the plate would do her, trussed up like a turkey. Unless ...

She jockeyed the chair back and forth until she was parallel to the plate. Stretching her body to the right as far as she could, Casey head-butted the plate. She almost passed out with the new offense to her head, but the door rumbled open.

She pushed the joystick forward, and the chair bumped over the threshold and through the door. She roller-coastered down the access ramp, pulling back on the control and edging sideways to stay on the walkway. The chair slowed as it rolled uphill. She pushed forward full throttle. Zero to four in sixty seconds. The chair was a pig. But when she turned onto the driveway, it would be downhill. After the gate, it wasn't far to Church Street.

Jeez! The gate. She couldn't punch in the code. Casey rounded a curve, and the gate came into view. It was wide open. Of course, she'd opened it herself when she walked the bike through earlier. She urged the slow-moving chair forward. Maybe she could still get help for Mary.

Casey pulled back on the joystick. She sat stock-still, holding her breath. In front of her, a black BMW turned left out of the guest house drive and approached the gate. Cherie!

The car stopped. Had Cherie seen her? Cherie drove through, but she didn't close the gate. Casey released her breath. Good thing Cherie was careless about security. Casey watched the Beemer's tail lights. Instead of continuing straight out to Church Street, the car turned down the lane leading to the station.

The last pieces of Casey's mental jigsaw puzzle fitted into place. Beth and Mary were at the station. Beth was after Cherie. But Cherie wouldn't respond to a call from Beth. That's the reason Beth took Mary with her—so that Mary would make the call to entice Cherie. Casey had figured out earlier that if Cherie took out Mary, Vera's death would just be Casey's word versus Cherie's. If Cherie found Casey first and could silence her, Cherie would be the only witness.

If Casey could get down the driveway and then to the street, surely someone would stop for her. Or run her over. Nothing to lose. Except her life. And Mary's. Two out of the three Mrs. Waddingtons were pure evil. She jammed the joystick forward.

The chair picked up speed on the downhill slope. Faster and faster, the hard wheels jounced the chair side to side. Casey struggled to keep it straight. She was flying on the ground, barely in control, when she realized that there was no way that she could operate the brakes. She didn't even know where they were. She aimed the speeding chair at the mid-point between the gate's stone pillars and prayed.

Chapter Fifty-Eight

D amn Beth! The tape hurt. Insult to injury. Mary considered her options given the planned ambush. Was there any chance that Beth would let them live? Slim to none. Should she try to warn Cherie—give her a fighting chance? Why? Cherie was worse than Beth. Still. Mary groaned at the irony: Beth was her only hope.

Els' BMW pulled up beside the station. Cherie got out, flicked her cigarette to the ground, and strode toward Mary.

The bushes behind Cherie parted.

Mary's reaction was pure instinct. "Look out!" she cried, but her words were muffled and too late.

Cherie screamed as Beth stabbed her in the back with the syringe. Cherie's hand reached behind her and came forward, clasping an empty syringe. She turned and lunged for Beth, but Beth quickly sidestepped and tripped her.

Mary watched the scene with a mixed sense of detachment and horror. Cherie got up slowly, weaving a little. There was nothing Mary could do. Nothing she wanted to do. This was how Cherie had killed Vera.

Beth backed toward the station. Cherie followed, head down, and lunged again and again, closer. The insulin was kicking in.

Pop.

The gun! Beth still had Els' little gun.

Cherie cried out, stumbled, and grabbed her knee. She limped forward a few steps and fell. She dragged herself toward Beth, who stayed just out of reach. Cherie crawled. Beth retreated. Cherie's unanswered cries turned to pitiful whimpers and then stopped. As she reached the stairs to the station, she slumped forward.

Beth stood watch over her for a few moments. Then she walked to Cherie's side and kicked her. Cherie didn't respond.

Mary's muted cry of protest amused Beth. She kicked Cherie again.

After a few minutes, Beth picked up the syringe and wiped it off on Cherie's shirt.

Beth rotated toward Mary.

"Nothing personal, Mary. You're such a cipher, but it's not tidy to leave witnesses."

Mary looked down the barrel of the gun. She closed her eyes, tilted her body to the side, and shoved herself off the stair.

Chapter Fifty-Nine

C asey whipped through the gate and then, to her relief, slowed on the uphill grade leading to Church Street.

A spine-chilling scream pierced the air. The sound came from the direction of the station. Mary? Was she too late? Casey jammed the joystick forward, but progress was slow uphill. After a loud popping sound, the scream weakened to a wail and then to pitiful cries.

Had Beth just shot Mary? Casey turned the chair at the juncture of the drive and the lane leading down to the station and motored forward as fast as the chair would go. The cries stopped. In the scene below, Beth stood over a figure lying on the ground. Then, she walked toward the station and bent over. She hauled Mary to a sitting position, pushed her against the clapboards, and then slapped her hard in the face. She backed up and aimed the gun.

"No!" Casey screamed. She launched the chair down the steep hill. Leaning forward, she played the control. The right wheel hit a rut. The chair lurched sideways, riding on one wheel. Casey threw her weight backwards and jammed the control to the left. The chair jounced back onto two wheels and rocketed downhill.

Beth rotated and aimed the gun at Casey.

Eyes focused on the gun, Casey never saw the curb. The wheels rammed into the stone, catapulting Casey and chair. For a split second, Casey stared into Beth's startled eyes before the gun exploded and the chair crashed.

Chapter Sixty

Two weeks later, Casey watched the strange collection of family and friends that had gathered around the fireplace pit in the center of the guest house to pay respects to Vera. They were holed up in the "Waddington Compound," as members of the press were calling it, because it was the only building on the property that was out of sight of prying eyes and flashing bulbs. Reporters roamed the perimeter of the property, and press vans lined Church Street. A policeman had been deployed to keep the rubbernecking traffic moving.

Her hands were enclosed in gauze to protect the raw skin and cuts. She had a concussion, a broken nose, and a broken arm. Her skin was a rainbow of colors, yellow from old bruises inflicted by Vera, khaki green from bashing into the tree, and eggplant blue-black from the wheelchair crash.

Outside, the dogs howled. Jackson had just let them out in case an over-zealous reporter decided to breach the electric fence. "We can expect to see pictures of snarling lurchers on the news tonight," he said. He sat on a recessed step next to Casey. He put his arm around her, and she leaned against him for support. "That's better. You look like hell," he said, his eyes taking in the damage. "Are you in pain?"

Casey shook her head very slowly. "Drugs." She looked Jackson up and down in return. "You look great," Casey gave a little smile that hurt her split lip. The fire felt wonderful. To her left, Bertie sat next to Mary, holding her hand. Agnes huddled across from them in an afghan, sniffling. Casey sat still and listened while Mary regaled them with childhood memories of Vera in Ireland.

In the spirit of an Irish wake, Mary's eyes danced as she described how Vera had tortured the nuns with her inventive pranks. Then Bertie recounted her friendship with Mary and Vera after they came to America and how, despite the wheelchair and her injuries, Vera had been an integral part of their young lives. Jackson spoke of his mother's love and beautiful voice and how she would hum him to sleep. Casey kept it simple. "She saved my life."

Mary turned to Agnes waiting for her to speak.

"Mind you, I loved her. She was my sister. But she was our cross to bear." She looked up and met her stepsister's eyes. "You know it's true," Agnes' eyes blazed. "Mother wouldn't even say her name!"

When she spoke, Mary's voice was low and measured. "Mother made a promise to God. If He would let Vera live, she would punish her. She wouldn't speak to Vera, but she loved her. She fed her, bathed her, brushed her hair—"

"Oh, stop!" Agnes couldn't let it go. "Vera sapped the life out of our house. She wanted to die, and I, for one, am glad she did."

"Enough!" Mary commanded. "If you can't be civil, your room is upstairs to the right."

"All I did was speak the truth." Agnes sniffed and dabbed at her nose before turning on Mary. "Why did you burn down my house?"

Without blinking, Mary responded. "After the remains of that little eyesore were bulldozed away, the value of the West Boylston property increased substantially." She turned to Casey. "It never occurred to me that you'd move the van to Agnes' house. And Agnes, the house never belonged to you. Els and I bought it to get you out of the big house."

"You gave me the house in Chatham because you can't afford it anymore. You felt guilty that Mother left the big house and her money to you," whined Agnes.

"That's enough," Mary commanded.

Turning to the others, Mary asked them all to join hands in a circle. "We're here to celebrate the life of Vera Dempsey." Agnes balked until Bertie took her hand and drew her into the group. There was nothing she could do but take Jackson's hand to close the circle.

Good move, thought Casey. It's hard to stay angry at someone while you are holding hands.

Mary looked over at Casey before she spoke. "We need to remember that Vera greeted her death as a blessing, not a tragedy. She had enough love in her heart for us all. We will miss her dearly." Mary led them in a moment of silence.

"Yoo-hoo!" Rosie and LouAnne barged through the door just as the circle broke up.

Mary smiled when she saw who it was. "Come on in," she called.

"Time for food," said LouAnne. They put the bags on the kitchen counter and then went back outside, returning with more bags and a cooler.

"How did you get through the police barricade?" Mary asked.

"We met the chief earlier when Casey moved in. Somehow he recognized us." Rosie chuckled.

Mary made the introductions while they unloaded several large casseroles, Italian bread, salad fixings, and ice cream. The cooler had soft drinks, beer, and wine. Rosie tossed Jackson a bag of chips to open and gave him the job of filling drink orders. LouAnne and Bertie started chopping up vegetables and lettuce for the salad.

Casey listened to the kitchen banter and stared into the fire. Her eyelids were so heavy. She would slip away and crawl under the covers as soon as she had the answers to a few questions.

They ate dinner around the fire. Jackson cleaned his plate and went back for seconds. Casey thought back to when she had first met him at the station. He'd made a remarkable recovery from the man who'd bashed his head against the stone wall underpass. Casey remembered how hopeless she'd felt hiding under the tarp, eating cat food.

Mary filled the others in on the events after Beth arrived. Casey tuned in when Mary got to the part where the wheelchair bashed into Beth. She had no memory of anything after the crash until she awoke in a hospital room.

Mary had been unable to free herself. Bertie had found them an hour later when she brought some of Mary's belongings from West Boylston. All four women were rushed to the hospital in two ambulances. Beth had a broken collarbone and ribs from the impact of the chair. Cherie was in an insulin coma.

"Cherie never recovered. When treated right away, you can bring the person out of it." Mary explained. She looked hard at Casey. "There was nothing you could have done to save Vera," she said, reading Casey's thoughts. "Beth is under arrest."

Casey was also under house arrest, at least until the authorities could sort out the details of what had happened, but she had been released in Mary's custody.

"What do you think will happen to Drew if they find him?" asked Casey.

"The Maine police may want to question him about the boat accident, although Beth made it clear, Cherie was the one who drove the other boat onto the rocks. As for me, I have no interest in pressing charges." She glanced at Casey. "No point. He lost his wife, his house, and his job. He has enough money to begin again, but he'll need a new name."

"How about Beth?" Jackson asked.

"Murder, attempted murder, and battery."

In the lull that followed, LouAnne and Rosie collected plates, and Bertie began loading the dishwasher and cleaning up. Jackson excused himself, saying he'd be back in a few minutes. Agnes called it a night and went upstairs to bed. Casey found herself alone in the circle next to Mary.

"I still have questions."

"I'll bet. I'm so sorry for all that's happened. Go ahead."

"After your hypo, when I studied the picture and figured out that Worthy was an imposter, I checked with Vera for confirmation. She nodded in agreement but didn't seem surprised. I figured then that you and Vera had known the man wasn't Worthy all along. But later, when Beth said, 'Worthy is dead,' you looked genuinely shocked."

Mary smiled. "I was only surprised that Beth knew her son was dead. It was the first I'd heard about the boy with the camera."

"But you hadn't seen Worthy since he was six or seven years old. How—"

"I told you about how Beth lured Els to Chatham. But it wasn't the last time they were in contact. He told me that he had to keep in touch with her because she was the mother of his child.

"But when Worthy reached his majority, and Els still kept up with Beth, I was consumed with jealousy. I tracked every move Beth and Worthy made. Private detectives, newspaper stories, telephone messages...

"I had focused on Beth, but also received reports about Worthy. I knew about his graduations, his honors, when he took the job at the law firm. I'd even seen a photo of the firm's two boy wonders giving each other a high five, showing that both had missing forefingers. So, I knew Drew was an imposter."

"Why didn't you expose them right then?"

"When Drew and Cherie showed up, the picture changed dramatically. I confronted Drew, and he told me the truth about the 'accident.' He said there was no way to prove what he said. I'd needed to file a few documents for the foundation, so I promised not to expose him if he would do some legal work for me. But I couldn't resist scribbling a note on an estate sale announcement telling Beth that Worthy had come for a visit. I wish I had just let the sleeping bitch lie."

"Drew explained that Beth had given Worthy a big sum of money to pay off Cherie for a divorce. Beth hated Cherie. Cherie was barren, and Beth wanted grandchildren."

Casey was trying to keep up. "So, you knew that Cherie had caused Worthy and Nan's deaths?"

"Yes. But it was a crime of passion. I doubt she could have planned it. I understood her jealous rage. I've had some of the same feelings myself." Mary glanced up at Casey and then continued in a lower voice, "I misjudged Cherie, though. I had no idea she would kill in cold blood. I'm responsible for your injuries and mental anguish. I hope you can understand, even if you can't forgive what I've done."

Casey's mind reeled. She hadn't known the extent of the games Mary had played with Beth.

"Last Wednesday, I wrote a few checks to Drew—one for legal services and another for Worthy's inheritance. He kept the first and deposited the second. Then he stopped at the jewelers and picked up the diamonds Cherie had purchased with Beth's divorce money, said goodbye to you, and took off, leaving Cherie to wait for the inheritance check to clear."

"Did he know it would bounce?"

Mary smiled and nodded. "He was no fool."

The others joined them, carrying bowls of ice cream.

Casey looked around. "Where's Jackson?"

"He said he'd be back in a few minutes," Bertie assured her. Then she turned back to Mary and asked, "What happened to Worthy's inheritance, anyway?"

"Well, you know that Els' last big money-making scheme failed. He never did anything halfway, so we lost our shirts. After he died, I cashed in everything I could, including Worthy's account, before selling the properties one at a time. Now all the houses are sold except the station, the Chatham house, and the gatehouse. We even have an offer on the West Boylston house. Finally, I had to admit that I was broke."

Jackson interrupted her reverie, entering the guesthouse carrying a large cardboard box. When he put it down next to Casey, it yowled. Jackson laughed and raised the lid. Little Mother and her kittens lay snuggled in a blanket inside. Watching the tiny kittens was the perfect antidote for the earlier tension.

Casey had one more question. "Why all the secrecy about money?"

Mary took a moment before answering. "There are a number of reasons. First of all, I think I told you before, I don't trust anyone when it comes to money. Especially family. Look at how Worthy ripped off his mother.

"And, I didn't want to worry you, Jackson. You were still struggling and vulnerable. Vera knew, of course. She knew everything." Mary's voice quavered. She stopped for a moment. "And then there are the public reasons. I didn't want to be hounded by real estate sharks. It's bad enough when they think you're rich. Floundering calls in the bloodsuckers.

"Probably the biggest reason is pride. Townsfolk had always wished Els and I would fail. He'd left one of theirs for an Irish tramp. It's one thing to be a filthy rich, sick old widow, and another thing entirely to be a poor, sick

304

old shanty-Irish widow.

"I've kept the foundation plan under wraps for as long as I can. When the town discovers what I have in mind for the White House, there will be an enormous hue and cry."

"Do you think they can stop the plan?"

"I hope not, but time will tell. Any change will be challenged, but—" Mary started to elaborate but looked up. "You're exhausted, Casey."

Casey didn't object when Jackson scooped her up in his arms and carried her to the downstairs bedroom. He covered her with a comforter.

"Thank you. I could sleep forever, or at least for a week."

"I'll be here when you wake up." He left and returned a minute later with the box full of cats and placed it next to the bed. Jackson stroked Little Mother and her kittens before walking to the door. "Were you really interested in that guy Drew?"

Casey shrugged and smiled at him as he closed the door.

Instead of sheep, and to ignore her aches and pains, Casey counted her blessings. She'd found a place where she could grow roots, where she belonged. She'd joined a strange and tragically decimated and dysfunctional family and rekindled old friendships with LouAnne and Rosie. She'd made a new friend in Bertie, and Jackson was...well, who knows where that would go. Maybe Worthy or Drew or whoever he was now would come back for a kiss. She had the promise of gainful employment, as yet undefined, that came with a home of her own in the little Church Street station. She even had a cat.

Acknowledgements

Thank you, dear readers. You make my world go round.

Endless gratitude to members of my writers' group: Mark Ammons, Cheryl Marceau, Frances McNamara, and Leslie Wheeler, for valuable critiques and edits, without which there would be no story. Thanks also to beta readers Ron Kelly, Ellen Richstone, and Susie Woodworth, who offered useful comments and critiques along the way. Special appreciation for Robert Carlock and fellow writers Bruce Robert Coffin, Gerald Elias, and Barbara Ross, who read and provided comments for the back cover.

Thanks to Level Best Books, especially Verena Rose and Shawn Reilly Simmons, as well as fellow Level Besties who constitute a vigorous and vibrant community of authors. I'm also grateful to the members of Sisters in Crime/New England (too numerous to name!) who have been so very supportive over the years and members of Mystery Writers of America/New England.

Most of all, bless you, dear husband Jeffrey, for your continued encouragement and love throughout the writing process. You're the best.

About the Author

Katherine Fast is an award-winning author of over twenty-five short and flash fiction stories. She was a former contributing editor and compositor for six anthologies of Best New England Crime Stories. *The Drinking Gourd* was her debut novel. *Church Street Under* is the second novel in the Casey Cavendish series.

In her prior corporate career, she worked with M.I.T. spin-off consulting companies, with an international training firm, and as a professional handwriting analyst.

She and her husband live in Massachusetts with their German Shepherd and three cats.

SOCIAL MEDIA HANDLES:
Katherine Fast: Facebook and Linkedin

AUTHOR WEBSITE:
Katfast.com

Also by Katherine Fast

Casey Cavendish Mystery 1: *The Drinking Gourd* as well as over 25 short and flash fiction crime stories.

Printed in the USA
CPSIA information can be obtained
at www.ICGtesting.com
LVHW041447311223
767834LV00046B/389